FRAGMENT

E.V. LEE

For more information about E.V LEE visit

www.evlee.yolasite.com

Cover Artwork by Ken Dawson www.ccovers.co.uk

Editing by Nicholas Wilson

For my wonderful wife and my two amazing daughters.

I love you all so much.

A special thanks to my good friend Steve.

Part 1

They've promised that dreams can come true –

but forgot to mention

that nightmares are dreams, too.

Oscar Wilde

Prologue

"Where the hell am I?"

I'm lying flat on my back, staring into the blackness above. I have no idea who or where I am, how I got here. I don't even know where here is. I sit up and pull my knees to my chest.

The ceiling, the floor, the walls, all are made of glass. Beyond the glass is an impenetrable darkness. There are no doors, no windows. I crouch against the wall and look about my enclosure like a frightened animal. The blackness waits beyond with an air of uncertainty, yet the box is illuminated with a soft yellow glow. There's no light source, no bulb, no electrical panel. The light emanates from the air itself, a persistent glow that comes from nowhere.

That's when it hits me: I'm in a glass box! No doors, no windows, no ventilation. I take a deep breath to fill my lungs. What if I suffocate in this glass prison? But I'm not struggling to breathe. I'm not dizzy. I exhale slowly, try to settle my panic. It doesn't appear I'm going to suffocate. At least, not yet.

I get to my feet, feeling vulnerable in my nakedness. I cover myself, forearm over my breasts and hand between my legs. Then I walk to the edge of my enclosure and peer out. There's nothing. It's black as night. I can't even see my reflection in the glass, not even the hint of an outline.

I rest my forehead on the wall, feeling like a goldfish in some psychopath's bowl. I'm neither warm nor cold, just helplessly captive. I'm suddenly afraid, and the fear wrenches my insides. Silent screams echo in my head like the drone of a thousand hushed bees. Then I'm getting heavy, weighed as though I'm pushing through treacle. My glass-prison shrinks, the darkness ready to enshroud me. I slide down the wall and let my arms fall to the floor beside me, revealing my nudity. There's a small spec of light flickering in the distance beyond the glass, somewhere out there in the blackness. Its flicker gives me a distant sense of hope. It's the last thing I remember.

Chapter 1

Jessa hit the off button on her alarm clock. It was 7am and time for her run.

Sitting up, she peeled off her sleeping shirt, soaked in sweat from the horrible dream she had just woken from. She tossed her slimy shirt onto the floor, then cowered at the sting of the cold, lifted her covers to her chin and shivered. The gloom of the early morning had her room bleached in grey. She sat there trying to remember the dream. It had left a lingering sensation of unease, vague images flickering and then gone. She was left with a void where the dream had been, disoriented and confused.

This wasn't Jessa's only bad dream recently. She often woke in a cold sweat, her subconscious leaving an imprint of something strange in her mind as she slowly seeped into wakefulness. Most of her bad dreams were about the last murder case she had been working on before going on compassionate leave.

Jessa had been a Detective Chief Inspector for a little over a year when two young women were murdered in the city. An eighteen-year-old female had been brutally raped and murdered while walking home from a nightclub; another student the month after. These had been Jessa's first murder enquiries and the images of the mutilated bodies were engrained in her mind. They were like Polaroids stapled to the insides of her eyelids. She saw them every night when she lay down to sleep.

Other dreams haunted her as well ever since her dad's fatal heart attack three weeks before. He had been a builder his entire life, in top physical shape. His death had been sudden and unexpected. Mick, her father's labourer, had called the ambulance from the job site as soon as her dad collapsed, but he had died before the ambulance arrived.

The dreams were always the same. Jessa would sink through black, murky water, arms and legs flapping as her lungs burned for air. No matter how hard she tried, she could never reach the water's surface. She would be pulled deeper into the murk. Then, just when her lungs were about to give out, her dad's strong arms would plunge into the water to save her. But he was always too late. Fetid water filled Jessa's lungs and she slipped deeper into the depths of darkness.

In the last week, Jessa's different, more violent dreams had left her with an overpowering awareness of being trapped; a yearning for something or someone she didn't understand. She thought maybe it was a mixture of the grief she felt after her father's death and the horror of the murder case. Or maybe it was something altogether different, something she would never comprehend.

Jess slipped out of bed and scampered to the bedroom door, grabbed her dressing gown off its hook and wrapped it around her, then flicked on the light switch. It was time for her run. It was time to shrug off the strange feeling left over from her dream.

Ever since going on compassionate leave, Jessa had been immersing herself in exercise. She woke up early every morning to run the same eleven-mile loop of the River Exe. It wasn't that she needed the exercise. Jessa was exceptionally fit, legs lean and firm. It was more about coping with the loss of her father, finding a distraction to keep busy, and filling her days with activity to avoid crashing headfirst into a depression she might never drag herself out of. Soon, Jessa would need to deal with her dad's affairs, sort through his personal belongings, arrange for the house to be cleared and ready to sell. But not yet. Not today. Maybe tomorrow or the day after, but not today.

February never had been Jessa's favourite month. It had no redeeming qualities. Everything from the naked trees to the bruised sky looked lifeless and miserable. Today, the grim February morning only worsened Jessa's dark mood.

An early morning fog lay over the River Exe like a blanket of candyfloss, two swans floating through the haze like ghost ships. The sky rumbled, threatening rain, and an icy chill nipped at Jessa's face as she jogged along the quay area of the river, running past the craft boutiques, chic pubs, and posh restaurants.

Then an unexpected vision exploded in Jessa's mind. The vision was so powerful the world around her evaporated and contorted into another reality. It lasted only a second, then vanished without a trace, leaving her utterly bewildered. She bent and gasped for air, huffing as the rain began to fall. She rested her hands on her knees, nausea washing over her, the light from her headtorch bobbing along with her breath.

What the hell was that? She thought. Her heart pounded in her chest. The clouds darkened and Jessa fell to her knees in tears. Turmoil crashed against her like a tsunami.

Chapter 2

The fog over the river had almost vanished, small wisps lingering out there in the distance like lost souls in a graveyard. The rain was coming down hard, Jessa cold and soaked to the bone. All she wanted was to get home and take a warm shower and wash away her emotional anguish. She was so miserable that when she walked over Cricklepit Suspension Bridge, Jessa barely noticed the homeless man sitting under his tarp, leering at her from his nest of filth.

Jessa's end terrace three-bedroom house overlooked the River Exe, its shabby Edwardian frontage an eyesore next to the modern apartments crowding it. The quay area was slowly becoming an affluent part of the city. Professional couples were buying every apartment they could get their grubby hands on, often worth more than Jessa's degraded abode with its rotten windowsills and broken gutters. Jessa's front garden was even uglier than the rest of the house. Enclosed by a low brick wall with a corroded iron railing, the garden itself overgrown with wild brambles and weeds. But Jessa had no time or patience to fix it—to fix any of it. She employed Mary to clean the interior once a week, only so she didn't have to. Mary was old and well past retirement, but she did a good job.

Jessa's father had promised to do the repairs, replace the windows and gutters, spruce up the garden, maybe even replace the roofing shingles. But he was dead now. He wouldn't be painting the front of the house red, white, and black, the colours of the football team he had supported his whole life. He wouldn't be cleaning the gutters, trimming the weeds, replacing the kitchen. He wouldn't be doing anything. Not anymore.

Now the shoddy exterior and neglected paint was a reminder to Jessa she would never again see her dad. She walked up the concrete path with her eyes on her shoes, not wanting to look directly at the house, not wanting to think about him. Overgrown brambles scratched her legs as she hurried through the garden and onto her front porch. "Really should do something about that fucking garden," she said to herself. Then she turned the key and went inside.

The inside of the house was tastefully decorated, a job an ex-girlfriend had done a few years back. Jessa preferred a minimalist style, sparse and simple. She despised clutter and unnecessary things. In Jessa's world, everything needed meaning and use. Anything else was pointless.

Entering the hallway, Jessa heard movement coming from the kitchen. Pots tinkering, drawers opening and closing. She thought Mary had come to clean the house. But no, it was Friday. Mary only came on Wednesdays.

Now Jessa was nervous. She held her breath, eyes fixed on the kitchen door as she crept down the hall. She very carefully placed her head torch on the small oak table in the hallway, then took out her keys and positioned the biggest of them between her fingers ready to stab someone in the eyeball. The front door was still wide open, Jessa dripping rainwater onto the laminate as she slinked silently through her own house. She was almost at the kitchen door when something clattered to the floor and someone said, "Shit." Then the ping of metal as something was thrown into the sink.

Jessa grabbed the door handle, heart beating so fast it sounded like blood gushing into her ears. Rain droplets trickled down her face and splashed onto the floor. She gently pushed open the door and peered inside.

The woman in Jessa's kitchen had made herself quite at home, bobbing her head to the music from her Beats headphones while buttering toast at the worktop. She didn't notice Jessa in the doorway with her key in her fist like some poor man's gauntlet. And Jessa, for a few seconds, didn't realize who it was dancing and buttering toast in her kitchen. Her black hair was shorter. She had lost a few pounds and her skin had a darker, radiant sheen to it.

Realizing who it was, Jessa immediately felt self-conscious. She was soaked and probably looked like a drowned cat that had just crawled out of the gutter, but Vee looked more beautiful than ever. Jessa hadn't seen Vee for almost a year, and now here she was, in her fucking kitchen unannounced. No warning, no contact for months. Was Vee expecting to walk straight back into Jessa's life, no questions asked?

Vanessa finished buttering her toast and turned around, saw Jessa standing in the doorway and smiled. She took off her headphones. The fuzzy bass of her music filled the silence between them. "Hi, babe," Vanessa said, so damn casual as she took a piece of toast from her plate and chomped down on it. Still, there was apprehension in her eyes.

"Hi, babe?" Jessa said. "You scared the shit out of me, Vanessa. What the fuck are you doing here?"

Chapter 3

The weather had turned worse by mid-morning. Rain lashed against the windows while the wind beat at the loose boarding of the house, making a racket as Vee and Jessa sat on the sofa in the lounge. They hadn't seen each other in a year and the tension between them was thick, almost tangible in the eerie stillness of the house. Scented candles burned on the pine coffee table, their little flames dancing violently.

"Why have you come back?" Jessa said, twisting a coffee mug in her hands.

"I heard about your dad," Vanessa said, slowly caressing Jessa's knee. "I'm so sorry for your loss, Jessa. I'm sorry for everything."

Jessa stared vacantly across the room, the smashing of the wind against the house threatening to give her a nervous tick. Otherwise, it was silent. She was thinking how much she had loved Vanessa before violent words tore them apart. And now Vanessa was back, rubbing Jessa's leg on the old weathered sofa in the middle of a rainstorm. Part of her was glad. Part of her couldn't forget Vanessa's fury as she packed her bags and walked out on her a year ago.

"I missed you every single day," Vanessa said. "I wish I had been here for you when your dad—"

"Then why weren't you?" Jessa spat. "I needed you more than ever. I almost lost my fucking mind trying to solve that case." She turned to the rain-streaked window, struggling to fight back tears. "I needed you. I needed you so bad."

"I know," Vanessa said. She was still rubbing Jessa's knee, sending shockwaves of hot electricity through Jessa's body. She didn't know what to do about it; slap Vanessa's hand away or relax and give in to the warmth of her fingers. Did she really want Vanessa back in her life? Vanessa had bailed on her when she needed her the most. How could someone forgive something so cruel? How could Jessa open herself up to be hurt again? And yet… Vanessa's touch was electric and Jessa realized just how much she had missed her. God knows, she had missed her!

Jessa took a sip of coffee, watching the logs crackle and pop in the wood furnace, listening to the storm batter the house. "I hate it, you know. I hated you not being here when I needed you."

"I know," Vanessa said again. She took hold of Jessa's hand. "It was hard for both of us. I needed you too and it was like I didn't exist. I ran and I'm sorry. I took the easy way out and I know it was cowardly. All the same, if we stayed together we would have hated each other in the end."

Jessa pulled her hand away, placed her coffee mug on the table and then hoisted her legs onto the sofa. Somewhere outside, a siren wailed.

"I'm glad your back, Vee. Because I... I..." Jessa began to weep. "Because I really need you now."

Morning turned into afternoon, then faded into early evening, Jessa and Vee still sitting on the couch talking while rain pelted the windows and the world outside drowned.

They never spoke about Jessa's father. It would have been too much too soon. Instead, Vanessa went on about her travels through South East Asia, snuggled beside Jessa as she showed her pictures of elephants and tigers, her motorbike expedition across Northern Thailand. And then it got late. They traded coffee for red wine, drinking from plastic cups. Vanessa was saying, "I half expected the locks to be changed when I got here."

Jessa shrugged. "Never got around to it. After so long, I just forgot. I never thought you'd come back."

"Here." Vanessa took a key out of her purse and offered it to Jessa. "I guess it's about time I gave this back to you. I should probably get going anyway. Mum said I can stay with her until I get myself sorted. Another cup of wine and I'll be too drunk to go anywhere."

Jessa eyed the key, hesitant to take it. "Are you planning to stick around, Vee?"

"Yeah." Vanessa smiled. "I'm not going anywhere."

Jessa paused, biting her lip. Only now did she realize how much she had truly missed Vanessa, smiling at her on the couch with those warm brown eyes she had first fallen in love with. "You know what," Jessa said, closing Vanessa's fingers over the key, "keep it. I want you to stay."

Vanessa's smile took over her face, showing the cute little gap between her front teeth. "You mean it?"

"I do."

Vanessa squealed, "I'm so happy," and placed her cup of wine on the table. "Get over here. Give me a hug." She wrapped her arms around Jessa, kissing her passionately on the lips. "I'm here for you now, babe. I'm not going anywhere."

Chapter 4

I've been sitting here for an eternity, staring at the flickering ball of light in the distance. I think it might have gotten bigger, or maybe it's my mind playing tricks on me. Either way, the light fascinates me.

I woke up with a start, opening my eyes to the darkness flowing over me like a blanket of silk. I am still in the glass box. I still have no recollection of myself or why I'm here. The whole situation is alien to me, especially this feeling of nihility. I'm not hungry. I'm neither hot nor cold. I have no sense of hearing. I already screamed at the top of my lungs and didn't hear a thing. When I pounded on the glass I felt no pain. It's as though I'm dead, without feeling, completely numb.

Oh, and totally helpless in a glass case.

Now I'm sitting with my legs stretched out and my back against the glass, staring at the flicker of light. Hours have passed, maybe minutes. It's impossible to tell the time in here, if time even exists wherever I am. All I have to focus on is the spot of light.

Something changes. There's an aura circling just to the left of the light. I lean forward and squint, try to decipher the distance or a shape but it's impossible. I get up without taking my eyes of the swirling mass of colour that's appeared and walk to the other side of the box. I've come to terms with my nakedness and am unbothered by it.

As I peer into the nothing, the aura suddenly explodes in a show of dazzling light. The shock of it rocks me onto my heels. The blackness vanishes as if someone just pulled away a covering hiding my enclosure revealing a light so pure it almost blinds me.

And then it's gone.

I look around in a daze. My glass walls are gone. I'm in a place vaguely familiar, surroundings hard to distinguish. It's like I'm in an old faded Polaroid and all the details have been bleached by the sun. Yet I feel like I know this place. I'm overwhelmed by the smell of butter and honey; the smells are coming from the trees in bloom that line the road I'm standing on.

There are buildings in the distance, but I can't make them out. Closer to my left is a blurry structure above the trees. It looks like a large barrel on stilts. A water tower, maybe?

Another burst of light erupts, blinding me again. When I open my eyes, I'm in the trunk of a moving car.

My heart's having a fit. I'm scratching at the fabric of the trunk, kicking at the panels. It's hot and I'm sweating like a pig. I fumble along the floor for a weapon, for a crowbar, for a screwdriver—anything that might help, but there's nothing. It's dark and I can't see. It's nearly impossible to move and I feel claustrophobic.

My head hurts, and when I touch my right temple it's warm and sticky. I realize there's blood running down my face. Now I'm scared. I fear that I'm in serious danger. The car swerves, my head bounces off the panel, then the car skids to a halt. The door clunks open, gravel crunching as someone walks around the car towards the trunk. I'm nervous, waiting for the trunk to open, no idea who's out there, legs tensed and ready to kick.

The lock disengages with a click and the lid pops open, a warm breeze washing across my skin. By the cold light of the moon I see my captor, his face set against the black sky. I feel like I recognise the man standing over me, and I gape upwards in surprise.

My surprise turns to fear as his gloved fist punches me in the cheekbone.

Chapter 5

"Jessa. Jessa, babe, are you alright?"

Jessa was covered in sweat as she squirmed in her sleep, murmuring words Vanessa couldn't make sense of. She looked like she was having some kind of fit in the sombre glow of the bed lamp, tangled in the sheets and muttering to herself.

"Jessa, babe, wake up." Vanessa gave her a little shake, trying to wake her. She kept moaning and flailing. "Babe, come on, you're having a bad dream."

Jessa's eyes snapped open and she gasped violently for air. She bolted upright so fast Vanessa couldn't get out of the way, and Jessa's cheekbone smacked into Vanessa's forehead.

Vanessa reeled backwards. "Ow!" She rubbed her head, checked her fingers for blood. "What the hell, babe?"

Jessa sat on the bed panting, bewildered. Sweat trickled down her back, free flowing like condensation on a windowpane, beading on her forehead and dripping from her chin. "Babe..." Vanessa went over and put her hand on Jessa's shoulder, her hand almost slipping off her wet skin.

Jessa turned slowly, eyes glazed, expression vapid. For a moment, Jessa didn't feel the bruise forming on her cheek. She didn't know where she was. She didn't recognise Vanessa, her girlfriend, the woman she had fucked only hours ago, sitting concerned beside her on the bed.

"I remember," Jessa said, eyes coming into focus. "There were trees, a tower, and..." She stopped, replaying the dream in her head and blinking rapidly. "I was trapped in the trunk of a car. Then a man attacked me." She grabbed Vanessa by the wrist. "It felt so real. He punched me in the..." Jessa reached for her cheek, feeling the throb from the impact with Vanessa. "... in the cheek."

Jessa was honestly disturbed. She stared at Vanessa in horror, trying to make sense of the fragmented dream. She thought the pain had followed her into the real world.

"It was only a dream," Vanessa said, caressing Jessa's back even though it was slimy and gross. "You're okay. Everything is okay."

Vanessa's soothing words did nothing to calm Jessa. "You don't understand," she snapped. "These dreams… I've been having these dreams for weeks but could never remember them. I always know when I have one, but then it drifts off before I can recall what happened. I wake up with these intense feelings of…" Jessa trailed off, trembling. The dreams had haunted her for so long. She held her breath and the rain outside seemed to stop. The whole world stopped.

"But I remember now. This one was different."

Vanessa said nothing. She had no idea what Jessa was talking about. Dreams were dreams, weren't they? Dreams were always confusing. Or maybe Jessa had been alone too long. Maybe sleep deprivation, jetlag, a bottle of wine, and hours of passionate sex had left Vanessa too dumb to understand.

Either way, Vanessa had to tread carefully. Her relationship with Jessa had only been rekindled a few hours ago. She couldn't go calling the girl loony or dramatic. It was surprising enough that Jessa had allowed Vanessa back into her life so quickly, and after so much time without contact; no letters, no emails; no phone calls. Vanessa would do anything to stay by Jessa's side, and that included tolerating whatever oddness was going on in her sleep. Vanessa was sure Jessa's bad dreams were somehow related to her father's death. They'd go away with time.

A light pitter-patter of rain fell against the window, the night outside dark but for the faint glow of a streetlamp. Looking at the alarm clock, Vanessa saw it was 4am. She had only gotten three hours of sleep and desperately needed more rest.

"Let's go back to bed," she said, seeing Jessa less agitated.

But instead of inviting Vanessa back to bed, Jessa threw off the covers and stood up. "I'm going for a run," she said bluntly. She crossed the room, picked up a pair of socks from the floor and began to pull them on. "I need to clear my head."

Vanessa was in shock. "You're serious? It's four o' clock in the morning, babe." Vanessa had already figured Jessa was in a fragile state of mind, trying to reconcile the death of her father. But this was extreme.

"I'll be back," she said, wiping herself off with a towel. "Go back to bed, Vanessa. I won't be long." She was putting on the rest of her running gear, Vanessa yawning on the edge of the bed, a little turned on by Jessa's pale breasts as she stretched on her running tights.

"Are you sure you're okay?"

"Fine." But her expression was blank. She was thinking about the dream, rolling the bizarre scenes over in her head.

Vanessa used to have a bad habit of upsetting people (especially Jessa), but after her trips through Asia she felt more mature, less selfish and more tolerant of people's behaviour. The old Vanessa would have said something vulgar to Jessa for acting strange, something incidentally cruel. Instead, she accepted Jessa's 4am run. She knew Jessa was having a rough time. Jessa needed love, not insults. The new Vanessa was ready to give her girlfriend all the compassion she could handle.

"Be safe," Vanessa said, "and watch out. Okay, babe?"

Jessa didn't respond. She was ready, moving towards the door with a vacant look.

"Jessa!"

"Huh?" She stopped mid-step, turning on Vanessa as if she had been caught sleepwalking.

"I said be safe. It's 4am, babe. Be careful. That's all."

The vacancy washed from Jessa's face and she smiled. "Sorry, Vee." She crossed the room and jumped onto the bed, gave Vanessa a kiss, running her hand across her cheek. "I won't be long." Then she put her hand between Vanessa's legs, rubbing her gently through her soft cotton panties. "Get some rest and don't go anywhere. Okay? I'll be back soon."

"Where would I go?"

But Jessa was already off the bed and walking out the door, leaving Vanessa alone with an agonizing heat in her loins and the incessant rain beating against the window.

Vanessa woke up around one in the afternoon to find the bed half empty. The sky was grey outside and it was still drizzling. Water sloshed onto the roadside as a passing car drove through a puddle. Vanessa got out of bed and went for a shower.

Jessa was sitting at the small table in the kitchen, writing in a notebook when Vanessa strolled into the room. "Good sleep?" she asked, smiling warmly.

"Kinda," Vanessa said with a cheeky grin. "Someone woke me up in the middle of the night for a little hanky-panky."

Jessa's smile was devilish. "Wonder who that could have been. I might have to install a security system." The bruise on her cheek wasn't quite as black as it had been; it appeared to already be healed. Still, she looked beautiful to Vanessa. She always had.

"What are you up to?" Vanessa asked.

"Nothing. I was waiting for you to get up, you lazy mare." Jessa closed her notebook, not wanting to share whatever it was she had been writing.

Vanessa took the hint, turning away and asking if Jessa wanted coffee.

"Actually," Jessa said, "I thought we could go for lunch. I know the weather's shit, but we could try the new Italian place over on the quay."

"Sounds good," Vanessa said. "I'm so hungry I could eat an Italian stallion."

She used to love going out to eat with Jessa. It was fun for the two of them. They were both attractive women, Jessa tall and blonde, Vanessa shorter and much darker. When they walked into a pub or restaurant together, men and women would stare at them like they were supermodels. Vanessa loved the attention. Jessa didn't. But that was why they had so much fun together. They were so different.

Jessa's mood had clearly lightened since the early morning, and it had certainly improved from the broodiness of yesterday afternoon. Vanessa hoped coming back into Jessa's life was going to help her in some way. She still felt guilty for leaving. The case Jessa had been working on when Vanessa left had been high-profile, brutal enough to make the national papers. Jessa had wanted to prove herself as a new detective, and the workload had put pressure on an already tense situation in their relationship. It had not ended well.

While off traveling, Vanessa had tried to follow the case, but getting her hands on an English newspaper or stable Wi-Fi had been challenging. There was no British newspaper outlet in the dusty village of Banlung, Cambodia. It had been on her way to Vietnam, in the city of Bavet, that Vanessa managed to track down a dodgy internet café, strung-out Cambodian kids playing online games on computer consoles from the 90's, ants on the keyboards and centipedes crawling along the floorboards, electric cables run along the walls like spiders' webs and trailed across the floor as if someone had spilled a big bowl of electric spaghetti. The U.K's Health and Safety Board would have had a field day! After a quick internet search, Vanessa managed to find the local Exeter Echo pages and the headline:

Killer Caught After a Year on the Run.

Turned out, Jessa had tracked the murderer to Poland after a string of similar attacks on young women in France and Poland. Kozlowski, a Polish lorry driver, had been arrested three weeks after Vanessa turned her back on Jessa and left the country.

Jessa stood up from the table as Vanessa was pulling a carton of orange juice from the fridge. "We really need to do some shopping," Vanessa said, frowning into the empty refrigerator.

Jessa snuck up behind Vanessa, put her arms around her waist and rested her chin on her shoulder. "You smell good," Jessa said. She backed up, turning Vanessa to face her. "You know, I've been thinking. It's time for me to move on. I've been putting it off, trying not to think about it."

Jessa's voice cracked as she struggled to spit out the words. "I need to sort out my dad's affairs. I need to go to his house..." Her eyes were getting moist. She had to suck in a deep breath to keep her composure. How could words be so difficult? The rush of emotion was overwhelming. "And I can't do it on my own. I fucking can't, Vee." A single tear fell to her cheek, Jessa's bottom lip trembling.

Vanessa smothered her in a warm embrace, tears now falling from both their eyes. Yet somehow, Vanessa felt relief. She had been worried Jessa would wake up and come to her senses and ask her to leave. She thought Jessa would say she didn't need a deserter back in her life.

"Of course I'll help you, babe." Vanessa squeezed her harder. "When do you want to go?"

"Soon. I want to go soon, Vee."

They parted, looking into each other's eyes. Both their cheeks were wet. "Can we get some lunch first?" Vanessa asked, half laughing, half crying. "I'm starved. I need that Italian stallion."

It felt like an enormous weight had been lifted off Jessa's shoulders. "Of course we can eat!" Saying those words aloud— admitting to herself that she needed to sort out her dad's affairs and that she couldn't do it alone—it was the first step to taking back control. She had put it off for too long, refusing to even think about the funeral arrangements. But now Vanessa was back. With Vanessa's help, Jessa could do it, no matter how hard it may be.

"Get your coat," Jessa said, wiping away tears. "I'm starved too."

Chapter 6

It was three days since Vanessa's return, three days since Jessa had told herself she needed to move on and sort out her dad's affairs. In those three days she had busied herself with exercise and spent most of her time with Vanessa, simultaneously avoiding her dad's house and the affairs she was supposed to be sorting. Three days of dodging her duties and now Jessa sat behind the steering wheel of her car, staring at the brightly painted front door of her father's house while rain trickled down the windscreen. The engine purred softly. She hadn't moved in ten minutes. Some part of her expected her dad to open the door with a big smile and wave her in. But he never came out. The house glared back at her like a concrete monster waiting to swallow her whole.

She had always loved this house. It had been home for most of her life. Her parents bought the property twenty-five years ago as a detached bungalow with a loft. Over the years, her dad added rooms and extensions, sprucing it into the four-bedroom house with a double garage and built-in office that now loomed so ugly before her. When had it gotten so ugly? She used to feel love and warmth when in this house. Now all she felt was sadness. It was the house she had grown up in; the house where her father had organized garden parties on the massive three acres of land for her sixteenth birthday, for her graduation; the house in which her mother had slowly withered and died from cancer.

A few years back, Jessa's father had told her there was no mortgage left to pay and that the house would be hers once he died. Now he *was* dead. She hadn't wanted to believe in a time when her dad wouldn't be around, but that time had come. He was gone and the house was hers. Not that she wanted it. She would have traded the house and all the money in her bank account for another hour with her father, with her mother who had died so young. But this was the real world. All Jessa could hope for was an easy sale, preferably to a family with young children who could enjoy the place as much as she had.

"Jessa, babe," Vanessa said. The rain was torrential and was beating on the bonnet of the car like a succession of tribal drums.

"We've been sitting here in silence for ten minutes. Are you ready?"

Jessa turned to her girlfriend, eyes heavy, the burden of what she must do clear in the lines of her face. "Yeah. Let's go."

She turned off the ignition, opened the car door and got out. Rain soaked her immediately, splashing onto the driver's seat and the inside of the door panel. Then she was running to the front porch, Vanessa scurrying behind her while fighting with the broken zipper on her jacket; it would only go up halfway. They stood on the porch, hair dripping, the rain driven from the dark sky, hard and merciless. Jessa stared at the door handle. She didn't want to go in. She took the key from her pocket, nearly dropping it because her hand shook so violently.

"I don't think I can do this," she said, hesitating with the key in the lock. All she had to do was turn the handle and go in.

Vanessa gently put her hand over Jessa's. "We'll do it together."

Jessa nodded, staring in terror at the key in the door.

"On the count of three," Vanessa said. "One, two, three."

Jessa felt as if she was entering the house for the first time. It took her a moment to orientate herself, standing in the hallway, feeling sickened by the familiarity of the house and its memories. It was mustier than it should have been, the smell of age and abandonment thick in the air. She had to take a seat on the padded storage bench and put her hands between her knees, trying to shake off nausea, trying to compose herself. A pair of her dad's slippers sat on the floor next to the front door like an obedient dog waiting for its master to return home. The house was eerily quiet. The grey light from outside cast murkiness along the hall, rain pelting the giant windows above the doorway. Vanessa turned on the lights and banished the gloom.

The hall was painted pale yellow, the floor a clean oak laminate. There were three doors on Jessa's left: the cloakroom, the study, the en-suite. A guest room on the right and the door leading to the family room. Jessa got up and moved across the hall, family photos lining the wall with pictures of childhood memories and family holidays. A few photos of her mum and dad hung in the centre. Jessa had never really studied these photos before, not with so much interest. There was a photo of her mum and dad standing on a beach, Mum looking beautiful with her natural blonde hair and tanned skin. Her dad, slightly shorter than her mum, was wearing a ridiculous fedora and the tightest speedos money could buy. They looked happy. They watched the little girl playing in the sand by their feet. Jessa must have been two or three years old. The picture must have been taken on one of their many trips to Greece, before her mum got sick.

God, she missed her parents so much.

"Where would you like to start, babe?"

Jessa looked at the top of the stairs, face as pale as porcelain. Something insisted she look in the master bedroom. "The bedroom." She said hesitantly.

Vanessa nodded. She took Jessa's hand and began to lead her towards the staircase, but Jessa pulled back. "No, Vee. I need to do this on my own."

"I'm not leaving you, babe. I said I will do this with you and I meant it."

"Please," Jessa said, voice so weak she seemed to be begging. "I need to do this on my own. Go see what you can find in the office. The keys are in the cabinet in the utility room."

Jessa was still staring at the top of the staircase. She wouldn't even look at her girlfriend. Vanessa reluctantly let go of Jessa's hand and went to the kitchen to find the keys.

The door was ajar as Jessa approached the bedroom. She paused for a moment, taking deep breaths, trying to compose herself before slowly pushing open the door.

The bedroom faced south and on a sunny day light would fill the room through the large floor-to-ceiling windows. Today, the room was grey and cold like Jessa's mood. It hadn't changed since her mother decorated it a few years before she had gotten ill. The décor was tasteful if not outdated, a by-product of her mother's affinity for interior design. Laura Ashley floral wallpaper behind the bed, the rest of the walls painted pale shades of Farrow and Ball.

Her mother used to spend hours resting on the Chaise lounge under the windows, looking out over the Tors of Dartmoor in the far distance.

Jessa came to stand in front of her mother's giant wardrobe, looking at herself in the reflection of the dusty mirror. She felt completely disassociated from the person staring back at her, as if the reflection wasn't hers, as if it was some other woman who had invaded her body. Jessa hadn't changed much physically. She had lost a bit of weight. But she looked irrevocably different. She felt different, too. She didn't know what she was looking for in the mirror, but she felt strange, as if something was waiting for her. The feeling had started when she first entered the house. Maybe she just needed to feel close to her dad. Maybe holding one of his shirts would bring her comfort. Or maybe it would make her cry.

Jessa went to open the wardrobe's door, but her reflection didn't move. Her hand was raised, but her reflection still stood slack and depressed in the mirror. It gave her such a warped feeling of displacement that she shrieked, "What the fuck!" and spun around, half expecting to find her real self lurking sinisterly behind her—but the room was empty.

"You're fucking losing it, Jessa." Her heart rate skyrocketed, eyes gone fuzzy with tears. When she looked back at the wardrobe, her reflection was distorted like a blurry photograph, though the rest of the room was perfectly normal. She was a smudge on the mirror. Her hairs tingled and stood on end, an abrupt sense of claustrophobia crippling her. She wiped away fresh tears and tried to focus, and that was when her blurry reflection tried to leap out of the mirror and attack her.

"Dear god!" Jessa screamed as she fell backwards onto the bed.

"Help me! Help me!" A deafening cry filled her head, Jessa clasping her hands over her ears.

"Help me! Help me!"

She couldn't tell if the pleas were in her own head or if they were coming from the blurred image in the mirror. But there was no mistaking it was her voice.

22

"Leave me alone," Jessa shouted, rolling on the bed with her hands over her ears. She fell off and hit the floor. "Leave me the fuck alone!"

The cries got louder and louder, Jessa sure her head was going to explode. *"Help me! Help me!"* She looked up at the mirror, the blurry image thumping and pounding on the glass, screaming for help. *"Help me! Help me!"*

Jessa curled herself into a ball on the bedroom floor and screamed hysterically, "Leave me the fuck alone!"

The thing in the mirror kept calling out for help. *"Help me! Help me!"*

Then it stopped, silence rushing into the room like an icy wind. The distorted image in the mirror was gone and the only sound left was the loud rumble of thunder overtop Jessa Summers' desperate screams.

Chapter 7

Now I'm positive the ball of light is getting bigger. I don't know what it is or why it's there, but it's definitely getting bigger and brighter.

I tried screaming again, mostly out of boredom. I called for help and pounded on the glass. Nothing happened. Now I'm thinking about the visions. The fragmented images replay in my mind like choppy video clips and they make no sense. Where was I? The smell of trees, the water tower, all so familiar yet so distant. The trunk of the car. Who was the man in the night with the gloved fist? I thought I recognised him, but maybe not. Maybe I'm dead. Maybe this is Hell.

Looking at the flickering ball of light, the aura again makes an appearance, the colours more vivid than last time. It's like watching the northern lights bloom in the vacuum of space, but more beautiful. I sit cross-legged and wait for the explosion I know will come; absent fear, absent worry. I've come to accept this place. I am eager for more visions. I need answers. I need to know why I'm here. If this is the afterlife, what's the worst that could happen? The swirling colours pulse and I shut my eyes just as they erupt into pure whiteness.

I'm standing in a field of green grass, under a beautiful blue sky. In front of me is an easel, and a short distance beyond is the most magnificent white tree in bloom, giving off the scent of honey butter. The sun's hot on my face. I breathe deeply to absorb the intoxicating aroma. The painting on the easel is of the tree, vivid oil colours making it lifelike. I'm not sure which is more beautiful, the tree or the oil painting of the tree. Another burst of light blinds me and now I'm in the front seat of a car.

I'm dazed, vision blurry. It's almost impossible to move my arms. My chin bobs against my breastbone as my head wobbles with the movement of the car. My seatbelt is tight against my breasts, digging painfully into my neck. I lift my head feebly, squinting my eyes, warmth running down my forehead. I touch it, look at my fingers and see blood. I wonder if I've been in a car accident. I wonder who else is in the car.

But there's no one. I look left and right, the small movements making me want to vomit. There's nobody with me. I'm in the driver's seat and the car is creeping forward, crunching loudly over gravel. I try to open the door, but the car jerks. My body shouts in agony as though every inch of me has been beaten. I grab the steering wheel, and with what little strength I have I try to stomp on the brake. It's jammed. I give it a few more panicked stomps but it doesn't budge. I look in the rear-view mirror and see the moon heavy and bright in the night sky.

The car's picked up speed. I'm coasting fast down an embankment. In the rear-view mirror is a silhouette, I'm sure, of a man on the roadside behind me; a sinister shadow in the empty night. Then I'm looking out the windshield. I want to scream but there's no time. I'm wobbling out of control as the car jolts downward into a dark oblivion.

Chapter 8

Vanessa had never heard screams like that. She had never thought a human being could make such unnatural sounds, such desperate shrieks of terror. They tore through Vanessa like shards of glass, had her racing through the house and up the stairs, shouting, "Jessa? Jessa, are you alright?"

She found Jessa curled on the floor by the wardrobe, shaking, holding her head, still screaming bloody murder. Vanessa had to coo to the poor girl, stroke her hair and tell her everything was going to be alright. It took a full two minutes before Jessa stopped screaming and started to whimper, then another five minutes before her sobs quieted and she lay shell-shocked in Vanessa's lap, moaning incoherently about ghosts and mirrors.

"Did you hear it?" Jessa asked, sniffling. "Did you hear its calls for help? You must have. Please tell me you heard it."

"All I heard was you," Vanessa said, stroking Jessa's hair. "I heard you screaming and thought someone was murdering you. I sprinted up the stairs to find you on the floor. That's all, babe. I didn't hear anyone calling for help."

"You must have heard it…" Jessa's expression was twisted— fear, confusion, upset because of Vanessa's blatant disbelief. Jessa was looking at the mirror, wondering what the fuck had happened. She looked like a whimpering wreck. Maybe she *was* going insane.

"I believe you,' Vanessa said. And she did, in part. She believed Jessa had heard the calls, believed she had seen something begging for help in the mirror. She also believed it had been Jessa's imagination, a delusion brought on by grief. It looked like Jessa's new fragility ran deeper than Vanessa first thought.

A few minutes later and they were still on the bedroom floor, that endless pitter-patter of rain falling against the window. Vanessa had missed England during her travels, but not the goddamn rain. She managed to calm Jessa down, get her onto her feet and lead her from the bedroom and down the stairs, Jessa looking like an abused child being guided out of a traumatic household, and into the passenger seat of the car. Jessa was in no shape to drive. She stared vacantly out the window as Vanessa started the engine and drove away from the house, driving them cautiously along the dismal county roads back to Exeter.

When they got back to the house, Jessa went straight to her bedroom and crawled under the blankets fully clothed. "I'm tired," was all she said before closing her eyes.

Now it was almost midnight and Jessa was still fast asleep. Vanessa lay awake beside her, thoughts and doubts rampaging through her mind. The bedroom was lit bleakly from the streetlamp outside. The fucking rain was relentless. Vanessa watched Jessa take deep, rhythmic breaths. She looked angelic now, her features soft and adorable, a far cry from the demonic banshee who had been screeching on the floor a few hours ago.

This was not the first time Jessa had exhibited borderline psychotic behaviour, and Vanessa would have been lying if she said she wasn't worried. Before their relationship ended a year ago, Jessa had been on the verge of a complete mental breakdown. Mood-swings, low self-esteem, episodes of frantic crying, the whole nutty package. Vanessa had pleaded for Jessa to get professional help, but Jessa was too bloody stubborn to acknowledge she had a problem. The stress of her job became too much. She got erratic, withdrawing more and more from Vanessa. And Vanessa couldn't handle it. She lost a piece of her own mind, bailed on Jessa and bought a ticket to Thailand.

Still, Vanessa carried her guilt through her travels. She regretted not being there for Jessa when she needed a friend. She loved her girlfriend deeply and wanted to be strong for her, wanted to understand what was going on in her damaged mind. But it was hard. And now that she was back, Jessa's behaviour was alarming in a whole new way, even more unpredictable than before. Vanessa felt it was more than just grief that tormented Jessa. Visions, dreams—none of it made any sense. They had been together only a few days and already Jessa was beginning to withdraw. Surely she was in need of professional help. Maybe Vanessa could contact Jessa's doctor, even her sergeant. The police must offer bereavement counselling for their staff. And now the compassionate leave was making sense... Jessa was clearly not fit for duty.

Jessa began to stir beneath the covers, murmuring softly, eyes moving rapidly behind her eyelids. Vanessa pushed herself onto her elbows, watching in horror as Jessa groaned and began to thrash about like an epileptic, arms flailing as if to defend herself from an invisible rapist.

"Jesus..." Vanessa turned on the lamp, kicked the covers off and watched Jessa grunt and fight with an invisible assailant. "You've gotta cut this shit out, babe." Vanessa snatched hold of Jessa's wrists like a snake wrangler grabbing two ornery pythons. "Wake up!" She shook Jessa, trying to control her raw strength. "Wake up, babe. Come on!"

Jessa was too strong, bucking Vanessa about on the bed. Vanessa lost control and got a fist to the temple. "Ow!" she cried, dizzy from Jessa's wild punch.

She managed to grab hold of her wrists again, this time screaming loud enough to wake the neighbours. "Jessa, wake up! Damn you, girl, wake up!"

As abruptly as it began, Jessa stopped flailing. Her arms flopped onto the mattress and her body went limp as if the life had been sucked right out of her. A sudden eerie silence filled the room.

Jessa lay there sweating, her breath laboured, her eyes dull with confusion. Vanessa was the first to speak. "You okay, babe?"

"Car crash!" Jessa said. "I was in a car and it went over a bank. I couldn't get out. I tried but I couldn't."

"It was just a dream," Vanessa said. "Just a dream. You're okay now. I think maybe—"

"I was in a field. It was a perfectly sunny day. I was painting a tree, a beautiful tree. I could smell its scent. It was like honey butter. It felt so real, so vivid." Jessa's eyes were distant as she struggled to recall the visions in her dream. "It felt so real."

The room had gotten very cold. Goosebumps peppered Vanessa's dark skin and she shivered, half from the bitter chill and half from Jessa's mystified rant. And now she was silent. Vanessa had no idea how to respond to Jessa's ravings. How did she lend comfort at a time like this? Vanessa got off the bed and took Jessa's gown off the back of the door. "I'll make us some tea," she said, putting on the gown and hugging herself against the bitter cold.

Minutes later, Vanessa returned to the bedroom with two cups of earl grey to find Jessa sound asleep and snoring softly, wrapped in the duvet. Setting the cups gently on the bedside table, Vanessa noticed Jessa's small black leather notebook sitting beside the alarm clock. Assured Jessa was out cold, Vanessa picked up the notebook and rubbed its cover with her thumb, the peeling leather like small flaps of rough skin. She knew it would be wrong to open the book, like snooping on someone's personal diary. All the same, something was wrong with Jessa and she needed to find out what. Maybe the notebook contained some pertinent secret about Jessa's dreams.

"If you want my help, I need to know what's going on."

She opened the book, reading the words scrawled messily in the glow of the lamp. It was random words and sketches, chaos written across the pages, some of it totally illegible and some of the doodles complete nonsense. Some words were repeated over several pages in thick capital letters:

HELP ME!
TRAPPED!
WATER TOWER?
CAR CRASH!
ACCIDENT??
TREES?
ALMOND /HONEY?

The words glared at Vanessa from the white pages as she tried to make sense of them. There was something quite disturbing about the lettering and drawings, not so much in the meaning of the words or the images themselves but the way they had been written. It was as if Jessa had been possessed when she wrote in the notebook. There was one repeated phrase that alarmed Vanessa the most:

SOMEONE WANTS TO HURT ME!

Chapter 9

The sound of the vacuum woke Vanessa, its angry buzz echoing throughout the house. Every inch of her ached from fatigue. She hadn't had a good night's sleep since returning to the U.K. Jet lag was a bitch.

The bed was empty. Vanessa rolled over, glanced at the alarm clock and saw it was 8:27AM. The bruise on her head throbbed from where Jessa had hit her last night. "We've really got to do something about these nightmares, babe," she muttered, climbing out of bed. She slipped into one of Jessa's gowns, enjoying the faint scent of Jessa on the fabric. She noticed the notebook was gone from the table. Sunlight peered through the window, streaked with condensation. Vanessa hoped today would be better than the last.

After using the bathroom, Vanessa walked through the house, following the buzz of the vacuum towards the kitchen. As she sauntered wearily down the hallway, the vacuum glided out of the lounge, followed by a shrill scream.

"Shit," Vanessa said, stumbling against the wall.

Mary turned off the vacuum. "You gave me an awful start, dear," she said, hand to her breast. "I didn't realise anyone was home."

"You nearly scared me to death, Mary!"

Mary had aged since Vanessa saw her last. She was still spritely, but her hands had started to gnarl with arthritis and the skin around her face and neck sagged like it might slide off and fall into a soggy mess on the floor.

"Have you seen Jessa?" Vanessa asked.

"She was driving off when I arrived," Mary said, oddly focused on the vacuum cleaner.

"Did she say where she was going?"

"No, dear. She was driving off. She was already in her car."

Vanessa hesitated, then asked in a quieter voice, "Did she look okay?"

"She looked fine. Is everything okay, dear?"

"Yeah," Vanessa said, trying to sound convincing, "everything is fine. Cup of tea, Mary? I'm going to put the kettle on."

"That'd be lovely, dear." Mary said as she turned the vacuum back on, the burring noise doing nothing to improve Vanessa's sore head.

Vanessa was calling. Her name flashed on the display of Jessa's phone as it buzzed on the passenger seat of her car. The call went to voicemail while she sat staring numbly at her dad's house again. She had a sense of déjà vu, still half expecting her dad to open the bright red door and step onto the porch with open arms. The sky was clearing, patches of blue breaking apart the grey swells of rainclouds, casting shadows over the house. It was still chilly, but at least it wasn't raining.

Jessa wasn't sure if it was a good idea to be back at the house, especially on her own after her nasty meltdown yesterday. But it needed to be done. This chapter of her life needed to be closed. She needed to move on.

She had the same feeling from yesterday, the odd sense of something waiting for her in the house. She wondered if it was something her dad wanted her to discover. It felt like an instinctual pull guiding her to a great secret. She was uncertain what correlation this feeling had to her visions. Her detective brain worked overtime to mull over all these jumbled, incoherent thoughts.

Two pigeons swooped onto the lawn, their bug-eyed heads bobbing in search of food. Her dad had fucking hated pigeons, always calling them *dirty germ-ridden creatures*. Jessa had wanted to take her father to the new restaurant overlooking Exeter's impressive cathedral, but the place was perpetually overrun with pigeons. He'd never go with her. "I'm not eating my food anywhere near those plague-carrying sewer rats!" he would say.

Jessa sighed, watching the fat pigeons hop around her father's lawn, picturing him scowling from the window and cursing under his breath. Then her phone buzzed again. She didn't need to look to know who was calling. She left it vibrating on the seat and got out of her car.

When Jessa slammed the door shut, the pigeons flapped their wings hysterically and took flight, and Jessa smiled to herself. Her dad would have laughed at the stupid birds being scared into the sky. It was the tiny victory Jessa needed to affirm her confidence. She strutted across the garden and walked back into her dad's house.

*

Vanessa was getting agitated. Voicemail again!

She tossed her phone onto the sofa and began to pace, worried, frantic, a thousand terrible scenarios swirling around in her head. She needed to know where Jessa was. The girl was unstable! She might hurt herself!

The clock on the mantel ticked away the seconds in a torturous tick-tock, tick-tock. With every second that passed, Vanessa got a little more stressed. She felt helpless, psychotic for overreacting, and incredibly concerned. Where was Jessa? What was she doing? Did she even need Vanessa's concern? Jessa was a big girl. She was a police detective for fuck sakes! She could look after herself... right? But then again, what would have happened if Vanessa hadn't been there yesterday when Jessa threw herself into a fit of hysteria?

Vanessa picked up her phone and rang her girlfriend. Voicemail again. She left a message: "Answer your phone, babe. I need to know you're okay. Where are you? I'm worried sick."

She tossed her phone on the couch and sat down. What could she do? She sat there listening to the incessant tick-tock, tick-tock of the clock on the mantel. It sounded like a goddamned time bomb about to explode.

The bedroom was brighter than it had been yesterday. Jessa stood in the same spot staring at the mirror, her reflection framed by a glistening white flame as the sun's rays reflected off the glass. The strange sensation was back. There was something waiting for her here.

Nervously, she grabbed the wardrobe's door handle, eyeing her reflection in case it attacked her again. It didn't. Her reflection moved as it should have. With a slow breath, she slid open the door. The mirror vanished and a burning ball of anxiety escaped her lungs as she exhaled. No monster. Not today. But as her anxiety fled, it was replaced by an ocean of grief. Her dad's striped shirts hung neatly on the rail, a devastating reminder of who her father was.

He had lived a modest life, spending little on himself, but had always been a sucker for good quality shirts. He never threw any of them away, no matter how worn they got. The smell of him on those shirts was overpowering as Jessa glided her fingers across them. Tears spilled down her face, looking at her dad's favourite blue and white checked shirt. She took its sleeve and wiped her tears with it, feeling the softness, remembering her father. It felt like her dad's character was stitched into the seams of the garment. He would never wear it again. The abrupt realization of this hit Jessa like a train and she slipped to her knees, weeping feebly, grasping at her father's clothes.

It was a mistake coming to the house alone. Jessa had thought she was strong enough to tackle her fears head-on, but she was weak and pathetic. She lay half in the wardrobe, her father's clothes against her face, tugging at her hair, feeling completely unhinged. Grief, remorse, guilt, and anger consumed her. She sobbed into the rack of shirts, pulling on her hair, trying to calm down. It felt like she was going to pass out. The room spun, Jessa gasped, began to hyperventilate, and quickly put her head between her knees. "Just breathe. Come on, Jessa, breathe."

Jessa closed her eyes and breathed deeply through her nose, held her breath until her lungs burned, then exhaled. The taste of bile lingered in her mouth as she repeated—inhale, exhale. Inhale, exhale. And the nausea and dizziness subsided. She sat up, throat dry, desperate for a drink. She used the sleeve of her jumper to wipe her face, eyes red and sore. It took her a few seconds to focus. She was on the floor and could see along the bottom of the wardrobe, neatly organised shoes, empty sports bags, a stack of old building magazines, and a shoe box.

Jessa recognised the shoe box immediately. It seemed out of place nestled between her dad's belongings, like a splash of colour in a black and white film. The shoe box had been used as a keepsake after her mother died. Jessa had decorated it with her father, using colourful tissue paper, sequins, and buttons to bedazzle the red cardboard. There was a photograph stuck to the centre of the lid, the corners curling where the glue had dissolved. The word 'Mummy' in bright green sequins and a heart made of red ones spanned the length of the lid. The photograph, now pale and discoloured, had been taken days before her mum passed. Even ravaged by cancer she looked striking, elegant. Jessa felt paralyzed seeing her mother like that, smiling back at her from the picture.

She was certain this was the thing that had drawn her to the master bedroom and the wardrobe. This box was what she had been meant to find. She stared at it, unable to muster the courage to touch it. She was uncertain of its significance. She knew there were photographs inside, pictures she had drawn as a kid, some of her mum's jewellery and the head scarf she had worn until the day the cancer finally claimed her. With great apprehensiveness, Jessa retrieved the box. She held it as if an ancient artefact, hands shaking, fearful the box might crack and crumble to dust in her fingers, all those memories lost.

Its edges were worn and split, and the tissue paper decorations were faded with age. She set the box in her lap and ran her finger across the sequins gently, touching the letters around the edges of the photograph. It took all her willpower to open the lid. A ray of sunlight crawled up her back, warming her spine, giving her a gentle push of encouragement. With a deep breath, she looked inside the box.

Two hours and still no contact from Jessa. Vanessa was going stir-crazy, but she didn't dare leave the house in case Jessa returned. It had been wet and miserable for the last three days and now the sun had returned, doing its best to brighten the sky. She thought about taking a leisurely walk along the quay to check out the artisan workshops, maybe grab a coffee in one of the cafes. Maybe it would be a good distraction. But she couldn't bring herself to leave the house. Jessa was out there somewhere, fragile and unstable, and Vanessa was worried sick.

She had contemplated asking Mary if she would drive her to Jessa's dad's house. She didn't think Jessa would have gone there after yesterday, but who was to say. Anyway, it didn't matter. Vanessa had asked Mary, "Do you still drive that old green and white mini?" And Mary had replied, "No, dear. I sold it six months ago for a pretty penny. Now I catch the bus everywhere."

There was no bus route to Jessa's dad's house, situated in a rural hamlet twenty-five minutes from Exeter. Vanessa had no way to get there unless she wanted to walk for three and a half hours. "She'll be back soon," Vanessa said to herself, sitting on the sofa and staring at her mobile phone. "She probably just went to get groceries. It's not like she would go back to her dad's house. Not after yesterday."

Vanessa got up and went into the kitchen, opened the fridge and stared at the empty shelves. Jessa's minimalist lifestyle was barebones, not a speck of edible food in the house. "Yeah, probably went to get groceries."

She sat at the table, spun her phone in a circle, then picked it up and called Jessa. Voicemail again. She didn't leave a message this time. Now she was hungry and frustrated. The shop was only a ten-minute walk from the house, and she decided to go get something to eat. She needed food and distraction and a walk would work well to empty her head. She went downstairs and laced up her Converse. If Jessa wasn't home by the time Vanessa got back, she would call the police.

Jessa didn't feel the same love for her mum that she felt for her dad. Her mum died when Jessa was only young. She hadn't really known her. Her mother was a collection of photographs and keepsakes, like the silk headscarf neatly folded inside the shoe box. It was black with a yellow paisley print, looking like flossy gold treasure in a tiny treasure chest. Jessa picked it up, surprised to find a padded envelope wrapped inside the smooth silk scarf. Unfolding it, a white enveloped dropped into her hands. 'Jessa' was written on the envelope in her dad's handwriting.

She stared at her name as if it were written in Chinese. It didn't fully register. Slowly, Jessa turned the envelope over. She wondered when her father had written it. What kind of horrible secrets were contained inside? Jessa was unsure she had the energy to open it, to embark upon another emotional rollercoaster when she already felt so deflated.

Jessa placed the scarf neatly back in the box, opening the envelope and removing a thin bundle of papers from it. She could feel the importance of the notes bleeding onto her fingertips. Whatever was written here was something her dad wanted her to know.

She unfolded the pages to find a short letter with official documents clipped to it. She set the documents aside and started on the letter. It was dated exactly one year after her mum had passed. She scanned the paragraphs with feverish intrigue, franticly trying to absorb the information. The more she read, the more it felt like a noose was tightening around her throat. The noose got tighter with each confounding sentence. The words began to blur. Sentences morphed and letters scrambled. The words melted off the page, leaked onto the floor, stretched to the ceiling in a web of black ink, splotching the walls, making the room dark, Jessa trembling as a tide of blackness swallowed her.

Chapter 10

I've given up caring about the length of time I have been in this strange place, trapped in the middle of god knows where. I am starting to believe I am dead and my soul is suspended in some transient dimension. I can see my hands, my body, my feet—I'm still naked—but it's almost like my physical self is just a memory, like I'm only recalling a form I used to have, caught in the realm between life and death where all that remains is my fragmented memory. I'm waiting for the lights to come back and teleport me to somewhere new.

Finally, they come.

I'm standing on the same backroad as before, only this time I can see the environment more clearly. I'm surrounded by a gentle windstorm of pink and white leaves, the trees along the roadsides shedding them by the thousands, the colourful leaves swirling around me like a kaleidoscope of butterflies. The air is thick with honey butter, a powerful and overtly significant aroma. On my left is the water tower jutting over the treetops, standing on its spindly metal legs like a makeshift space capsule about to launch. There is thick blue lettering painted on its hull, maybe a town name, but it's fuzzy and I can't read it. I stand on my toes and squint through the hurricane of leaves, and that's when I'm struck by another immense flash of white light.

In front of a mirror, leaning on a wash basin. I'm trembling; tears flood my eyes, a feeling of betrayal. The furnishings are luxurious, an expensive white sofa in the corner, grey tiles in the rainforest shower, stylish mirrors and marble surfaces, silver automatic faucets. A hotel room, complimentary toiletries, soaps, shampoos—free toothbrushes, handtowels. Everything has the hotel's name stickered to it with a fancy label, but the writing blurs when I look at it. It's the same with the mirror. My reflection is a pastel haze.

Someone's saying something outside the washroom door but the sound's muffled like I'm underwater. I open the door and step into an elegant hotel room, the furnishings emblazoned with gold flakes to make the patrons feel like royalty. On the bed is a man. He's mostly naked, his features fogged like my reflection was in the mirror. There's a painting of two blue peacocks above the bed, the two birds facing each other, their tail feathers entwined between them to make a heart shape. Their tails are mesmerizing shades of blue, red, green, and dozens of dark eyespots. Outside the window is a white Victorian lake house, not far off in the distance. It's strange how my memory recalls detail of some things and not others.

A white flash blinds me and I'm lying on the bed naked with my back arched and a man knelt between my legs. My wrists are tied to the bedposts, one with a pair of handcuffs and the other with a zip tie. I'm trying to struggle free. I can feel the thickness of his cock as he thrusts it into me. Something about this is confusing. The man moans and pushes himself deeper inside, wraps his hands around my throat and fucks me harder. He's roaring, choking me, dribbling spit into my face. Now I'm dizzy. I can't breathe. White spots grow in my vision as a dozen black eyes spy down on me from the painting.

Chapter 11

Jessa shuddered awake with a sharp gasp, jerked upright and gawked around her room.

No, not her room. This place reeked of disinfectant. Jessa sat in a hospital room no bigger than a broom closet. There was a cabinet and a trolley with a blank monitor on it beside her bed, an armchair in the corner for someone to watch Jessa while she slept. The walls were the dull yellow of vomit, the flimsy curtains parted, granting a view of the swaying trees outside, the roofs of office buildings and Haldon Hills covered in mist even farther in the distance. The waning sunlight cast ugly shadows across the small room. People were talking outside the closed door, their voices muffled.

Jessa lifted her wrists in front of her face, looking for ligature marks of any kind, but there were none. Just a dream. Just another terrifying nightmare. More fragmented images, more confusion. The last thing she remembered before passing out was opening her father's letter.

That damn letter. It came to her in an abrupt flash of memory. Her dad's letter was a revelation she didn't need. It ruptured her already damaged heart as she heaved forward in the hospital bed. Jessa knew she was on the edge of a mental collapse and was trying desperately to maintain control over her sanity. The visions and dreams were bad enough without her dad's letter to jumble her feelings even more. And now she had the sickening remembrance of a man ramming his filthy cock into her. She knew it wasn't a real memory, just another strange and horrifying dream, but it still thoroughly disturbed her. It had felt like being raped in some perverted snuff movie. It made her sick to her stomach. If it was some kind of premonition, the sex wasn't consensual. The one and only time Jessa had sex with a man had been traumatic enough, back in university when she was confused about her orientation. Sex with a man had straightened her out damn quick. She'd yet to do it again.

Sitting in that hospital bed, Jessa had never felt so alone. She thought her head would explode, felt that something deep within her soul was trying to claw its way out. Again, a feeling of displacement scared the shit out of her. She desperately wanted to go for a run, to feel her muscles burn, to feel the release of endorphins and the stabbing pain of a cramp. She felt claustrophobic in the tiny hospital room and just wanted to run away. An abrupt panic had her shaking, full of pressure and ready to burst if she didn't get out of the bed and out of the room quick.

But she couldn't see her clothes anywhere, and she couldn't very well dash out into the hall in her flimsy white hospital gown. She looked for the call bell, ready to tell a nurse she would be voluntarily discharging herself immediately. Then the door opened. Vanessa poked her head inside.

"You're awake," she said with a smile, her warm brown eyes instantly cooling Jessa's panic.

"How long have I been out?"

Vanessa approached the bed, placed her holdall on the floor and gave Jessa a kiss. "A good few hours. How are you feeling?"

"Fine."

Vanessa wrung her hands, looking out the window at the swaying trees. "You had me worried sick, babe."

Great, now Jessa felt guilty on top of crazy. She hadn't meant to upset Vanessa. But she had been so obstinate to finish with her dad's house she had been a total bitch. She had gone on her own, ignoring Vanessa out of some stubborn need to face her fears alone. She should have known better. Vanessa genuinely cared and wanted to help her through her hard times. And besides, she was the only person Jessa had left. It was about time she started treating her better.

"I'm sorry," Jessa said, squeezing Vanessa's hand. "I was selfish. But I'm glad you're here."

"I brought you some stuff," Vanessa said, gesturing to the holdall. "A change of clothes and some other basic things. Nothing special. No alcohol. No nude mags."

Jessa chuckled. "Thanks, Vee. I appreciate it, especially after I was such an asshole. I didn't mean to worry you. I should have told you where I was going."

41

"Yes," Vanessa said firmly, "you should have. I'm here for you. You know that, right? Whatever is going on in that head of yours—" She tapped Jessa playfully on the forehead. "I'm here to help. I love you, babe. You need to let me in. I want to understand what you're going through."

Tears welled in Jessa's eyes. The genuine warmth and compassion Vanessa showed her at that moment was benevolent and it took what little strength she had left to stop herself from breaking down right there and then.

"I really appreciate your concern", she said, biting her lip to keep the tears at bay. "I'm so lucky you came back. It's just…" She looked out the window, gazing at the distant patchwork of hills. "I don't know how you can help me right now. I don't even understand what's going on with me, Vee. I'm a stranger in my own mind."

Vanessa got them coffee from the vending machine down the hall, then the two girls sat on the edge of the tiny hospital bed drinking from paper cups.

"What happened?" Jessa asked. "How did I end up here?"

Vanessa leaned back, took a sip of coffee and sighed. "When you didn't answer your phone, I got worried. I thought I was being stupid at first, overreacting like an idiot. But then hours went by and you still didn't answer. Something didn't feel right, babe. I didn't think you would have gone back to your dad's house after what happened, but I had no idea where else you would have gone. I had no way to get to you. I would have asked Mary for a lift, but she told me she sold her mini six months ago."

"So, what did you—"

The door opened. A small Filipino woman in a green nurse's uniform poked her head into the room and said, "The doctor will see you soon."

"Okay," Jessa said, smiling back at her.

"Anyway," Vanessa said once the door was closed, "I called the police."

Jessa gasped. "You called the police? Seriously?"

Vanessa shrugged. "I didn't know who else to call." Droplets of rain peppered the window, the late afternoon already fading to night. "I spoke to DI Radisson. I told him about your little breakdown yesterday, saying I was probably just being silly, that I didn't want to waste police time. Still, I asked if he could send someone to your dad's house."

Jessa took a sip of coffee. Her expression was unreadable as she watched Vanessa talk.

"Anyway, the police found you on the floor of your dad's bedroom. They called an ambulance and brought you here."

"Rads is a good guy," Jessa said. "We worked on the Kozlowski case together. We became good friends over the last year." She watched the light fade beyond the window, a little ashamed of herself for being found by her colleagues in such a vulnerable state. She wasn't angry at Vanessa for calling DI Radisson. She was angrier with herself for allowing the situation to happen.

"I don't remember anything," Jessa said, placing her empty coffee cup on the cabinet. "Did they say how long I was unconscious for?"

An announcement echoed through the hallway from the PA system. Some doctor with a long and unusual name was to report to the ER immediately.

"Well," Vanessa said hesitantly. She shifted on the bed, unsure how to phrase it. "Shortly after the police found you, when you did wake up, you rambled about some pretty strange stuff. Peacocks, a man in a hotel room. You said you were on a bed, tied to the posts, getting strangled..."

Jessa inhaled sharply and pursed her lips, recalling the faceless man as he thrusted into her, the pain of the bonds around her wrists.

It was just a dream.

"You kept falling in and out of consciousness, repeating the same things over and over. You got hysterical and screamed about a letter from your dad. They had to sedate you, babe, to calm you down. These dreams are starting to creep me out. They might be more dangerous than you think, Jessa."

"The letter." Jessa stared at Vanessa, a sudden sharpness in her voice. "Where is it?"

Vanessa bent down, unzipped the holdall and took out the letter, passing it to Jessa. "Babe, what—"

"Did you read it?"

"No." Vanessa sighed. "I didn't read your letter. Radisson gave it to me when I arrived at the hospital. He said you were clinging to it and wouldn't let it go. What's in the letter, Jessa? Tell me? Let me help you."

Without looking, Jessa handed the envelope over to Vanessa. "Open it," she said. She was getting teary again, watching from the corner of her vision as Vanessa tentatively opened the envelope and took out the letter, unfolded the pages and began to read.

Soon, Vanessa also had tears in her eyes. "Oh Jessa," she said, looking up from the papers. "I'm so sorry." She put down the handwritten letter from Jessa's dad and the crinkled adoption certificate, then gave Jessa a fierce hug. "Everything is going to be alright, babe. I'm here. Everything is going to be fine."

Chapter 12

My dearest Jessa:

You reading this letter probably means your old dad is no longer around. Please don't be sad, my love. I'm with your mum now and we are both admiring you from above. Writing these words is the hardest thing I have ever done, and I want you to know before you read on that your mum and I loved you with all our hearts. You are so wonderful and special, and we are very proud of you.

All your mum and I ever wanted was a child, a little cherub we could love unconditionally and devote our lives to making happy. After years of trying to conceive, we were finally gifted a beautiful baby girl with big blue eyes and a heart-melting smile. It was one of the best days of my life when I held you in my arms for the first time. You were our little miracle and we were so blessed and so thankful that you came into our lives. You were eleven months old when we finally took you home and we became a family. See, your mum and I were unable to conceive a child naturally. Your mum had a condition called Primary Ovary Insufficiency, which meant it was very unlikely she would ever get pregnant. After years of failed fertility treatments, we decided to adopt.

The adoption process took a few years to complete, and when we finally saw you we were instantly smitten. You were a bundle of absolute joy. We were not offered much information about your birth parents. All we knew was that your father was unknown and your mother died a few months after you were born.

I can't imagine how you are feeling right now, but please believe me, Jessa. Your mum and I wanted to tell you this earlier. There were so many occasions when I tried to pluck up the courage to tell you, but I could never do it. I was scared that if you knew the truth, it would somehow change what we had, that maybe you would be disappointed, angry, or even resentful. Before your mum passed away, you were too young to understand. After, well, it was difficult for the both of us. We dealt with our grief in different ways. I kept mine locked away inside of me, focusing on your well-being, while you expressed your grief through confusion and anxiety, anger and isolation. After her passing, I devoted all my time to making you happy, to making life as easy for you as possible, and to being the best dad I could be. I hope I didn't disappoint you.

You may think I was being selfish for not telling you about the adoption, and I would understand if you do. But please believe me when I say I only ever had your interests at heart. It may not be possible for you to understand how I could have kept something like this from you until after my death. You may even think I am a coward for not telling you in person and waiting until I was in the ground. All I can say is that I am sorry, Jessa. I promise that I have always loved you more than anything in this world. I dedicated my existence to making you happy.

Dad xx

The wood burner crackled and flames licked at the logs, Jessa seated on her sofa in a thick hoodie and jogging pants, wool socks up to her knees. She was trying to keep warm, but it was her own numbness that insulated her the most from the cold. Her dad's letter lay unfolded on her lap, the words striking her heart a little deeper each time she read them. The day was dismal, a torrent of fucking rain splashing against the window as if someone stood outside spraying the glass with a hose. It was unusually cold for March, the temperature hovering just above zero. The bitter wind rattled the sash window frames.

DI Paul Radisson sat opposite the sofa, his handsome features crinkled as rain dripped off his hair and into his coffee mug. An awkward silence hung between them as they sat quietly and listened to the crackle of wood and the rattle of the windows.

He had promised to check in on Jessa after her return from the hospital. Upon hearing about Jessa's recent episodes from

Vanessa, Radisson's concern for his colleague's mental health had been renewed. He had worked closely with Jessa on the Kozlowski case, experiencing first-hand Jessa's low moods and depressive states, which had worsened near the end of the case. Jessa took a damn beating that year. The case chewed her up and spat her out. The media pressure was torturous, and the pressure from her colleagues almost broke her. It was Jessa's resilience and damn good detective skills that finally helped solve the Kozlowski murders, and Radisson admired her for sticking it through to the end. She was young, beautiful, good at her job, and powerfully determined. And mentally fragile. It was also unfortunate (for Radisson) that she had no interest in men. Radisson fancied her like crazy. He had flirted with her for weeks after they first met and had fantasized constantly about shagging the pants of her.

DI Radisson was thinking about how Jessa had changed after the investigation. Before the case was solved, Jessa had been stressed but reasonable, working nonstop. Once Kozlowski was behind bars, things changed. Jessa's vulnerabilities floated to the surface. Cracks in her mind became visible. She grew withdrawn and distant, her behaviour erratic. Now with the loss of her dad, whom she had adored so fervently, and his confession of having adopted Jessa, Radisson feared her already broken mind would fissure even more.

"Don't torture yourself," he said, unable to suffer the silence any longer.

Jessa stared out the window, absently handling the letter in her lap. She was absorbed in her own dark thoughts.

"Jessa?"

"My whole life has been a lie," she muttered. "Why would my parents keep this secret?" She waved the letter in the air, then discarded it next to her. "How fucking selfish could my father be? Not only do I have to cope with him dying, but now I find out he was never my real father in the first place. I find out in a fucking letter!"

Jessa took a deep breath, fighting away tears. She didn't want to cry in front of Radisson. "How could I not have known? I've been so naïve. I'm a detective and I had no fucking idea."

"You couldn't have known," Radisson said. "From the photos I've seen, your mum looks just like you. You're practically twins: long blonde hair, blue eyes, pale skin. The similarities are shocking. Try to focus on the relationship you had with him," he said, shuffling awkwardly in his chair. "Focus on how much they loved you, how much your dad loved you. There's no use getting mad at the dead. You're a grown woman, Jessa. It doesn't matter if you were adopted or not. What matters is your parents loved you."

A gust of wind hammered the window, shaking the frame violently, the glass sounding like it was about to shatter. The noise somehow angered Jessa even more. "It's not about love," she said, finally looking DI Radisson in the eyes. "It's the fact that he didn't think he could tell me when he was alive. We were so close. I thought we trusted each other, yet he waited until after his death to give me such brutal news. Why even tell me at all?"

DI Radisson grimaced, thinking about his own parents and how he might feel if he were adopted. He didn't think he would care. He was mindful Jessa's thinking was not completely rational or totally lucid.

"I know it's hard to understand, Jessa. I don't know how I would feel in your shoes, but I'm sure I would focus on the good stuff. They both loved you. That much is clear. He was probably scared after losing your mum. He didn't want to lose you too. He feared the truth would chase you away from him."

Jessa scooched off the couch and stuffed another log into the burner. "I don't know, Rads, I'm not sure what to think." Flames licked the edge of the wood burner, the glow from the fire colouring Jessa's face a ghoulish sort of orange.

"Who knows why people do the things they do," Radisson said with a shrug of indifference. "I've been at this job long enough to know grief affects people in different ways. Nothing really surprises me anymore." He stroked his short beard, watching Jessa crouched by the fire. "You know, most people never stop grieving. They carry it with them forever."

DI Radisson was speaking from personal experience, of course. His wife had come home to find him in bed with one of the PCSO women from the station a few years back. Spurned, his wife raced out of the house and drove off into the stormy night. The roads were icy and dark. His wife lost control of the car and never survived the crash. She had lain dying in the snow while Radisson continued to fuck his whore. He'd never forgiven himself. The grief would follow him to Hell.

Now Radisson wanted to change the subject. "Tell me about your visions," he said. "Are they the same ones as before?"

Jessa's cheeks went red. "What's Vee been telling you?"

"She's worried about you, Jessa. We all are."

She shook her head. "I'm fine, Rads."

He could feel her angst. "Don't get mad at me, Jessa. I just want to help. Talk to me."

"I said I'm fine," she snapped. "Fuck." Jessa hung her head, feeling guilty for her continual outbursts. "Sorry, Rads. I do appreciate you looking out for me. But honestly, I'm fine. I just need a little more time. A few more weeks and I'll be back to work. Everything will be normal again."

But Jessa knew she was far from fine. She gave DI Radisson a half-hearted smile, hoping she could deceive one of the sharpest inspectors in the Force. Because it was not only grief that troubled Jessa. It wasn't only her father's death that fragmented her sanity. It was the visons, the dreams, the otherworldly vividness of her nightmares. They meant something but she didn't know what, and the unknowing was part of what made her feel so insane. It felt like she was staring at an unsolvable puzzle that only she could somehow piece together. It was maddening.

She flicked her eyes up to meet Radisson, looking serious. "There is one thing you can do for me."

"Sure," he said, shifting in his chair. His arse had gone numb. "Anything you need, Jessa."

"Can you find out if Kozlowski—" She shuddered at hearing the sick fucker's name. "Can you find out if he has any associates in prison. I need to know if any of the bastard's friends have been released recently or are pending release. I want to know about any outside friends, visitors, writers, infatuated fans—anyone at all in contact with him."

DI Radisson gave her a bemused look, stroking his beard. "Kozlowski... making friends? He was a loner, Jessa. You know that. We scrutinized every aspect of the sicko's life. He had no friends, no associates. He worked alone and no one in their right mind would partner up with that fucking nutcase."

"Probably not," Jessa said, "but I need to know. You asked me about my visions. I know it doesn't make sense and I must sound crazy, but I think someone wants to kill me. I think my visions are somehow linked to Kozlowski. I think he wants me killed as revenge for putting him away."

"That does sound crazy," Rads said. "Completely fucking crazy. If I didn't know you better, I'd think you were pulling my chain..." He trailed off, wondering if Jessa's disturbed brain was making her paranoid.

"Please, Rads." Jessa looked desperate.

"You're serious... You know what, I'll see what I can do."

As DI Radisson drove through the heavy rain and congested traffic, passing over the Exe bridges, he thought about Jessa's theory. There was no way that Kozlowski could hatch an elaborate revenge plot against her, especially not from behind bars. And besides, Kozlowski was a mindless killer. His MO wasn't revenge. It was cold-blooded murder. Not to mention there were dozens of other officers involved in the psycho's arrest: French police, other investigators from the U.K, dozens of Polish Border Police, a handful of Interpol agents. Jessa had helped catch him, but she was only one cog in the machine. Her picture had been splashed across a few U.K tabloid papers, hailed for finally thwarting Kozlowski's killing spree, but the two had no personal interaction. Even if they had, Rads was sure Kozlowski would get no satisfaction from Jessa's death. Not unless he did it himself.

DI Radisson turned onto Rydon Lane heading towards the station, wipers slashing madly across the windscreen. He had promised Jessa he would contact Detective Novak from the Polish Police Headquarters and inquire about Kozlowski's possible acquaintances. He doubted the bastard had any, but it was a favour to Jessa. She was obviously paranoid. Hopefully, if Radisson could deliver Jessa hard evidence that there was no assassination plot being planned against her, she would relax a bit. God knew she deserved a bit of peace.

Chapter 13

Vanessa used DI Radisson's visit as an opportunity to hop across town and see her mother. She had been holding off due to Jessa's erratic behaviour, not wanting to leave her alone for too long. It was the perfect chance to pack up a few more clothes and enjoy a short break from the drama.

Now she was walking back to Jessa's house from the bus stop, getting soaked by the damned rain. The miserable weather seemed endless. She stood in the hallway of Jessa's place and slung her rucksack onto the floor, unlaced her shoes and muttered to herself, "This rain can just go and fuck itself. Damn British weather."

Her socks were soaked through, jeans wet, skin slimy and cold. It didn't help that the house was freezing, maybe half a degree warmer than outside. She could see the mist of her breath as she hugged herself and shivered, listening for any hint of a sound in the house. There was no noise at all. It was dreadfully quiet.

She made her way to the lounge, feet leaving wet, silvery footprints on the laminate floor. She pushed the door open and smiled at the warmth of the room; it was cosy and hot. Heat radiated from the wood burner and Jessa was relaxing on the sofa in the light of the fire, legs curled beneath her as she tinkered with her laptop.

"It's freezing outside," Vanessa said, moving swiftly to the wood burner and rubbing her hands.

Jessa didn't look from her computer screen.

"How was your visit with Radisson?"

Jessa looked up, blinking dumbly at Vanessa as though she hadn't heard her enter the room. "Oh. Sorry, Vee." She closed her laptop and put it on the sofa beside her. "The visit was fine. Rads is good. I'm good. Really, there's nothing to worry about." She gave a smile that wasn't very assuring. "But look at you, Vee. You're soaked. You've got to get out of those wet clothes before you catch hypothermia."

Vanessa was still shaking, lips dark purple from the cold. A puddle had formed by her feet. "Yeah," she said, teeth chattering, "I think I'll take a hot shower."

Jessa sprang to her feet, all smiles and giggles. She wrapped her arm around Vanessa's cold wet body and began to shove her towards the door. "I'll take one with you." Jessa gave her a fun smack on the bottom. "Let's go, Vee. Let's get you warmed up"

Vanessa woke up in the late afternoon to find Jessa snoring adorably beside her, face half buried in a pillow. Vanessa wanted to close her eyes and go back to sleep, enjoy Jessa's warm skin against her and drift off—she was still relaxed and tired from all the sex and hot orgasms in and out of the shower—but she knew if she went back to sleep, she wouldn't wake up until morning. And that would be a bad idea. She still needed to reset her body clock to British time.

And besides, she was hungry.

She padded her way downstairs, cursing under her breath at the merciless cold. "You've got to get central heating installed, babe. This is unbearable. I'm going to freeze my fucking tits off."

In the kitchen, Vanessa opened the fridge and was pleased to see it stocked to the brim with a variety of edible, healthy food. She picked a pre-packed sushi platter and left the kitchen, sneering at the ice slowly forming on the inside of the window. On the inside! If it got any colder, it was going to snow. Vanessa hated the bloody snow. England came to an annoying halt at the first hint of a snowflake.

She made her way into the lounge, which was still warm thanks to the wood burner. A stray log still burned softly in a nest of orange embers. But Vanessa wanted real warmth. She missed the sweaty heat of the Vietnamese night. It took her a minute to load the iron furnace with a few logs, then she plunked down on the sofa and began to chomp away at her sushi.

Jessa's computer sat on the cushion beside her. She eyed it warily, then looked away, concentrated on her sushi, took a bite… drifted back to the computer. She wanted to know what Jessa had been looking at. The white light blinked slowly, indicating sleep mode. That meant whatever Jessa had been browsing could still be on the screen. All Vanessa had to do was open the laptop and take a look. Just one little look. Where was the harm in that?

A crack from the wood burner made Vanessa jump, her heart startled into a panic. She dropped her last piece of sushi. She felt like a naughty little kid, nervous to be caught stealing candy from the sweet jar. She felt disloyal, but opened up the laptop anyway. Vanessa picked up the computer and ran her finger along the pad, surprised when the screen flicked to life without a password. She shook her head and then glanced at the lounge door expecting Jessa to burst through it and catch her red-handed.

Moving her finger across the pad, Vanessa clicked on the internet browser. The window opened to an image search, a picture of a big brown water tower taking up half the screen.

"What the fuck were you searching for, babe?"

The words were still in the search bar: 'water towers in Poland.'

There were almost a dozen tabs compressed along the top bar. Vanessa clicked on the next one. It was a list of search results for, 'Polish trees in bloom.' Pictures of blooming trees crowded the bottom of the screen.

"Oh, babe…" Vanessa figured it out immediately. Jessa had been searching for the images from her dreams.

The next tab showed paintings of peacocks. There were various oil paintings of peacocks, none that made any sense to Vanessa. Some were just cartoon pictures. Clicking on the next tab, Vanessa just about shrieked and dropped the laptop on the floor. Staring back at her from the computer screen was a monster. It was a monster with dark, soulless eyes and thick-rimmed glasses. Even in a photo the man was menacing. His murderous stare made Vanessa uneasy and sick to her stomach. She felt a shiver run down her spine as the man's unnatural, deathlike stare pierced the screen. She quickly slammed shut the laptop. But it was too late. Kozlowski's hideous face had been already seared onto her retinas. The face of the serial killer would come to haunt her at night.

Chapter 14

The light in the blackness has not only increased in size, but has also changed its shape. It's become oval, about the size of a vanity mirror. And now that I sit here staring at it, I find it difficult to discern whether it has truly gotten bigger or if I'm getting closer, my glass prison gradually floating towards it—or it towards me. Its density is also different. Before, the light was pure without a blemish, but now I sometimes catch glimpses of grey floating through it like wisps of smoke before they evaporate. I've heard whispers, too. More than once I have heard muffled voices, a soft murmuring that could have come from the blackness or within my own mind. It's hard to say.

I sit here waiting for the eruption of light, replaying the only memories I have over and over on a loop. It doesn't help. They're void of meaning. The trunk, the water tower, the trees, the man and the hotel room—none of it completes a picture or forms a coherent memory. I assume once more that I am dead. Perhaps I am here to solve the apparently violent circumstances of my death.

Ah, here comes the aurora, the blinding light.

I'm back in the hotel room, the painting of the peacocks with their heart-shaped feathers like some sick joke above the bed. I feel angry, wrestling with the man as he tries to restrain my arms. He's all but naked in his briefs. He's shouting at me. His voice is muffled and I can't understand it. His words are lost on a non-existent wind. I still can't comprehend his face. I push him back, fighting hard to get away. I rip one of my hands from his grip and slash him across the face with my nails; my claws sink into the soft flesh of his cheek and draw blood. I want so much to scratch his eyes out. He slaps me hard across the face and I fall to the floor.

The man disintegrates as the burst of light erases the room in whiteness.

I'm now driving down a remote stretch of road, familiar trees on one side and nothingness on the other. The night is warm and the breeze is cool against my face, gushing in through the windows. It feels like I've been crying. The left side of my face is sore. The road is desolate and in my rear-view mirror hangs a lonely white moon.

Through my windscreen is a lightshow of constellations, a billion twinkling stars speckled across the black night sky. I marvel at them for a moment before headlights glare in my mirror. Someone's coming up on me fast. My heart hiccups. I brace for impact, but the car doesn't crash into me. It tailgates me instead, flashing me with its bright lights and revving its engine.

Now we're coming to a bend in the road. The car—it's an SUV—pulls up beside me and honks its horn, speeding in the wrong lane. He's screaming at me through the passenger window, furious, shaking his fist, spitting on his steering wheel. He wants me to pull over, but instead I accelerate out of the turn and race down the straightaway.

I try to outrun the man, but he's too fast. The SUV overtakes me, swerves in front of me and hits the brakes hard. I gnash my teeth and rip the wheel to avoid a collision. My tyres screech as I fishtail into the oncoming lane. High pitched screams pierce my ears. All I can smell is burning rubber. I hit a ditch at the side of the road, skid off the loose dirt, snake across both lanes, and finally come to a gut-retching stop. I'm breathing in ragged gasps, fingers gripping the steering wheel. I want to swear and scream and pull out my hair, but I don't make a move. I'm in shock. Just up the road is the SUV, its brake lights glowing like the red eyes of a demon. The driver opens his door and gets out.

He's walking towards me. I'm trying to restart the ignition, but my goddamn hands won't work. They feel glued to the wheel. I'm frozen. He's getting closer. I want to recognise him. Is he the man from the hotel? Before he can reach my window, the man and my surroundings are erased by a bright light.

Cool rain falls from the night sky, splashing off my raincoat. I'm on a lawn, freshly mowed, looking at the rear of a house. I'm hidden in the bushes.

There's a TV set on in one of the ground-floor rooms. The dim glow of the porch light illuminates the back door. I can't discern the finer details of the house. I only see that it is large and well-maintained. I have something cold and heavy in my right hand.

My surroundings suddenly start to shift and break apart. I'm on my knees in the wet grass below the bushes, digging with my bare hands like a frenzied dog digging for a bone in the rain. My hands are bloody and caked with dirt. I finish digging the hole, take a plastic bag from my jacket pocket and put a handgun inside it. Then I toss the gun into the hole and hurriedly cover it with soil.

Chapter 15

Vanessa wrenched into wakefulness, sat up in bed and looked around the room in a panic. She was certain the breaking of glass had woken her. She held her breath and stayed perfectly still, listening for any movement. The clock read 3:47am. The wind whistled outside and rain splattered the glass. Jessa's side of the bed was empty. She was gone.

A deep sinking sensation punched Vanessa in the stomach as she switched on the lamp and climbed out of bed. "Where the hell have you gone this time, girl?"

A loud bang from downstairs startled Vanessa and she quickly threw on a dressing gown, crept into the hallway and to the top of the stairs. She was on full alert, straining hard to hear and staring down into the darkness. There was nothing to see except outlines of the furniture downstairs in the hallway. The house creaked as the wind blew, and sinister shadows danced in the shade at the bottom of the stairs. For an ephemeral moment, Vanessa thought she was in a horror movie. She was the protagonist who was supposed to creep down the stairs in the dark without turning on the lights to be attacked by some evil fiend lurking below in the gloom.

"Fuck that," she whispered, and turned on the light for the landing.

Brightness instantly dispelled the murk. She descended the staircase, halfway down hearing another bang from the kitchen. Vanessa wasn't an easily spooked girl, but she felt her knees go weak and her heart gallop out of control. She was scared—for herself and Jessa. There was another, louder bang as she approached the kitchen. Vanessa felt her skin chill as a bizarre cold strangled the air. She pushed open the kitchen door and fumbled for the light switch, shocked to find the back door open and a cold wind wiping through the room. It was the source of the banging. The wind was slamming the back door against the kitchen cabinet. There were shards of glass on the floor, broken cups and plates that had fallen from the cabinet. There was no sign of Jessa.

The door banged against the cabinet as another squall of wind blew in from outside, making Vanessa shiver and clench her teeth. She scampered across the kitchen, meaning to close the door before it snapped in half, but she slipped on the wet floor tiles. "Fuck!" she screamed as her legs went out from under her. Vanessa's knees smacked the floor and she winced, the pain erupting like a volcano and making her want to puke. She took a few deep breaths, muttering profanities, then managed to get to her feet and look out across the stormy garden. There was something in the far corner of the garden, small and twisted near the ground like a stray dog.

No, not a dog. Vanessa squinted hard through the dark, letting her eyes adjust to the night, and after a moment saw that it was Jessa crouched in the dirt. She was frantically clawing at the ground. She wore nothing but white panties and a white top, both soaked and see-through from the rain.

"What the fuck is she doing?" Vanessa asked herself.

She limped across the garden, her bad knee crippling her movement. "Jessa, babe, what the fuck are you doing out here?"

Either the wind blew away Vanessa's words or Jessa ignored her. She was digging in the dirt with her bare hands, hair whipping around her face, oblivious as Vanessa loomed over her. She put her hands on Jessa's shoulders. "Babe, get up. What are you doing? Have you gone fucking mad?"

Jessa was in her usual loopy dream state, easily guided to her feet, acting like she was under a hypnotic spell. Her skin was as cold as an ice statue.

"You're going to freeze out here," Vanessa said. "What the hell were you doing?"

Jessa stared emotionlessly at the hole she had dug in the ground. She said nothing.

"Come back inside," Vanessa said. She hugged Jessa and lead her towards the house. "We've got to get you warmed up. It's going to be alright, Jessa. Everything's going to be fine. It was just another bad dream."

Standing in the hot shower, unanswered questions raced through Jessa's mind. Her visions were becoming more vivid, more memorable, pushing her to mimic them in the real world without any memory of doing so. She had no recollection of going downstairs into the rain and digging in the garden. And it scared her. It really scared her.

What were the dreams about? What the fuck were they trying to tell her? For now, she had no idea about any of it. The man in the hotel. The man in the car. The gun and the house in the night. Had she killed someone? Had she been planning to kill someone? If the dreams were somehow premonitions, Jessa figured something seriously fucked-up was waiting for her around the corner. She wasn't authorised to carry a firearm. She didn't even own a gun. This meant the gun from her dream had probably been illegal. She had been hunkered in the bushes of someone's garden with an illegal gun. She had been about to commit a murder.

Chapter 16

It was 8am when Jessa finally woke up and slithered out of bed, only to be greeted by another dismal day of rain and wind. She was climbing into her running gear when Vanessa scowled at her from beneath the blankets. "Do you really think you should be going out on your own, Jessa? I mean, after what happened earlier, I think you should stay here. Something is obviously wrong. Come back to bed and keep me warm."

"I need to run," Jessa said plainly. "I won't be long. Cook me one of your amazing omelettes and we can have breakfast when I get back."

"I don't think you should go," Vanessa said, harsher this time as she got onto her elbows. "What if something happens?"

Jessa snapped. "Vee, I'm fucking fine. I don't need you to worry about me, okay? I'm a grown woman."

"How can you say that?" Vanessa said. "How can you possibly believe that you're fine? You woke up in the middle of the night and went digging on her hands and knees in the garden like a crazy person. You're far from fucking fine, Jessa."

Jessa opened her mouth to retort, to say something nasty, but she could see Vanessa on the verge of tears.

"I'm worried sick over you, Jessa," she said. "You need help. I'm fucking scared. These episodes you're having are getting worse. What's next, you kill me in your sleep?"

Jessa tied her hair into a ponytail and put on her sweatband, then sat on the edge of the bed and took Vanessa's hand. "Don't be ridiculous, Vee. I would never do that. Honestly, I'm just tired and stressed. I need a bit of time to get my mind back." She gave Vanessa a kiss and a smile. "I'm a big girl, Vee. I'm going for my run. When I get back, we can talk about it some more, okay?"

"Alright," Vanessa said, defeated.

Jessa got up to leave, saying, "Don't forget that omelette," as she jogged out the door.

Vanessa was fuzzy from fatigue. Her knee hurt from last night. Her anxious heart wouldn't stop palpitating. And the third cup of coffee wasn't fucking helping.

Jessa had returned from her "short" two hour run and was now seated on the floor in front of the wood burner, cradling a cup of earl grey, her slender fingers a little purple from last night's excavation. Vanessa was on the couch, wrapped in an oriental throw. "So," she asked, "where do we start?"

"I'm not sure," Jessa said. "It's all very confusing, Vee. All I know is I'm not going crazy. I might be acting weird. I might not be thinking straight. But I know I'm not going crazy."

"Then what's going on, babe? I want to understand. I want to help. I know you've had a tough time losing your dad, and now there's this whole adoption mess, which obviously you will need to come to terms with, in your own time. But you don't have to bottle it all up. I'm here and you can talk to me. You don't have to deal with this on your own."

Vanessa paused, licking her bottom lip. She wanted to make a suggestion, but she didn't want Jessa to snap at her. "And," she said, "if you don't feel you can talk to me, at least talk to someone. A counsellor maybe, or even DI Radisson. Just talk to someone."

"I did speak to Rads," Jessa said. "When he came around to see me, I asked him to do me a favour."

"What kind of favour?"

Jessa sighed. "It's going to sound mad, Vee, but I promise I'm not going crazy."

Vanessa looked at her earnestly. "Just tell me, babe. Whatever it is, just tell me."

"The visions, the dreams—I don't think they're anything to do with grief or with the adoption. Of course, those things have been traumatizing and I'm not sure how I feel about the adoption. I haven't had time to process it yet. But the dreams, Vee—I think they're trying to tell me something. I think they're premonitions."

Vanessa recalled the words in Jessa's notebook: **Someone wants to hurt me.** She narrowed her eyes at Jessa. "What exactly do you think these dreams are telling you?"

"I'm not sure. Most of the dreams are unclear and make no sense. However, I think they're linked to the Kozlowski case. I asked Rads to find out what the sick fucker's been doing since he was put away."

"Kozlowski?" The image of the psychopathic monster on Jessa's computer flashed in Vanessa's head, making her queasy.

Jessa said, "I think he's made connections on the inside. I think he wants me killed."

"Excuse me?"

"I'm not crazy, Vee!" Jessa said. "You must believe me. Please, Vee, I'm not nuts."

"I know you're not, babe. It's just…" Vanessa shuddered. "…hard to comprehend. Do you see Kozlowski in these dreams? Does he do things to you?"

Jessa shook her head. "No, not Kozlowski himself. I think he wants me killed, but it's not him I see in my dreams. The man in the hotel room, the one chasing me in the SUV, is not Kozlowski."

"So, who is it?"

"I don't know," Jessa said with a shrug. "I haven't seen him clearly enough to recognise him. I'm hoping Rads can help me find out."

"What did he make of all this?" Vanessa asked, wondering if DI Radisson thought Jessa's theory was as far-fetched as she did. Jessa did speak with enough conviction to be believable. But premonitions about a locked up serial killer wanting revenge was just ridiculous.

"He promised he would make some enquiries, but I don't think he believed a word I said, Vee."

*

It was late afternoon when DI Radisson paid the girls a visit. He rang the doorbell and Vanessa came to greet him. When she opened the door, Rads was busy trying to pull the brambles off his coat.

"You really ought to get that garden seen to," he said, stepping out of the rain and into the foyer. "It's a bleeding jungle out there."

"Yeah, maybe if it ever stops raining," Vanessa said. She took Radisson's wet coat and hung it on a peg.

"Just don't leave it too long," he warned. "If it grows any more, you won't be able to leave the bloody house."

Di Radisson followed Vanessa through the hallway, staring eagerly at her tight arse. She had her big ol' bottom stuffed into a pair of light grey jogging pants, and Rads was fantasising about ripping them off and giving her an enthusiastic spanking. Vanessa was fit and damn sexy. And now he was thinking about how much money he'd pay to see Vanessa and Jessa going at it in the bedroom. Just thinking about it started to get him hard and he felt himself fluster. The last thing he wanted was the women seeing him standing in front of them with a fucking hard-on. He started to blush and immediately thought about Shelia, one of the admin support assistants at headquarters who looked a lot like Shrek, only a whole lot uglier. Even her teeth were green. He thought about Shelia licking his face with her slimy tongue and that did a good job of squashing his libido. By the time they walked into the lounge, DI Radisson's cock was as limp as a dead fish.

Jessa sat on the sofa, computer on her lap as she scribbled in her notebook. She smiled when she saw Radisson enter, closed her laptop and gestured for him to sit in the uncomfortable bucket chair. The inspectors' arse was still sore from the last time.

"I spoke with Novak this morning," Radisson said.

Jessa nodded, waiting for more.

"Well, he said Kozlowski is in intensive care. He's been there for some time. The doctors don't think he's going to make it."

Vanessa asked, "What happened?"

"He was attacked by some other inmates. I'm sure you're familiar with how rapists are treated in jail. And well, Kozlowski is the worst of 'em. They wanted to teach him a lesson. They slashed his eyes with a razor blade. Then they tried to slice off his cock."

Vanessa's eyes damn near popped out of her skull. "You're serious?"

"Serious. They nearly cut it clean off. He lost a hell of a lot of blood in the process."

"What about his contacts?" Jessa said. She didn't care about Kozlowski's rapist cock being cut off. She just kept thinking, *there must be a link.* "Before he was attacked, did he have contact with anyone, inside or out?"

DI Radisson cleared his throat, shifting uncomfortably on his sore arse. "Novak confirmed what I already thought. Kozlowski's kept to himself ever since being incarcerated. He never spoke to anyone; no one ever spoke to him. There were no letters, no visitors. Jack fucking squat."

The room fell silent. Vanessa squeezed Jessa's hand, understanding the gravity of Radisson's words. Then the brash bastard spat them into the room. "Your theory is wrong, Jessa. Your dreams can't be a warning about Kozlowski. The fucker has no friends and now he has no cock. I'm pretty sure he'll be dead soon. If someone wants to hurt you—if you've turned into a fortune teller and are having premonitions of a murderer in your dreams, it's not Kozlowski."

Jessa lurched forward. "If it's not Kozlowski, then who the fuck wants me dead!"

Chapter 17

The flash of light came instantly this time, and now I feel the warmth of the sun on my face and a warm breeze ruffling my hair. The scent of honey butter drifts off the blossoming trees, invigorating my senses. I feel safe. The smell give me a sense of peace and serenity. I'm standing in front of the oil painting, the colours so sharp and vibrant that the tree appears to be growing out of the canvas. I scan the environment; it's like I am looking at a 3D puzzle. Most of the pieces are in place but there are still areas showing spaces of blankness.

The blooming tree sways in front of me, and far beyond the field is a mountain range. Spinning slowly, I see the field is enclosed by trees that look the same as the one I'm standing in front of, only smaller and less magnificent. The water tower is on my left, tall like a bulging sentinel above the treetops. The letters on the cylinder are painted blue. The name of a town, surely. It's becoming clear. The letters are coming into focus… W…I…N…

And then everything is gone.

I'm slumped on the floor of the hotel room. My face stings from where he slapped me. The man's pacing the room, hands on his head as he mutters words I cannot hear. I'm dazed, defeated. I want to lift myself up but I'm too weak. My will to fight has been robbed from me.

Now the man towers above me, looking disappointed. I can see his face, his square jaw, high cheek bones, silvery grey hair and receding hairline. He's almost handsome. I still can't recognise him, even though his face is clear to me. He comes closer and I notice tattoos on his arms—his arms are stretching to pick me up.

No, not to pick me up. He's reaching for my throat.

Chapter 18

Jessa woke with a gasp. Her hands went instinctively to her throat. She could still feel the man's hands wrapped around her neck, and it took a second for her to relax, realising she was home, safely in the darkness of her room.

She turned on the bedside lamp and slipped the notebook from under her pillow. Vanessa stirred, turned over, then came to rest. She was still deep in sleep. It was 2:14 in the morning and the room was so cold it hurt to breathe. Jessa's breath exhaled as vapor. She ignored the icy chill against her skin and scribbled into her book:

--Man in hotel room – who is he? High cheek bones. Grey, receding hairline. Muscular with tattoos. Tanned. What is connection?
--The trees have significance – what species? Scent= honey butter.
--The word on the water tower. Win???

Jessa leafed through the other pages, playing back each scene she could remember. Each note corresponded with a segment in one of her dreams. Maybe—just maybe, if she stitched them together, she could come up with some answers.

--The SUV. Trapped in the boot of a car? The accident. Same location? Same incident?
--The man in the hotel room – was he driving the SUV?
--Why was I in possession of a gun? Whose house?
--Where is all this happening?

She didn't understand. If the visions were in no way associated with Kozlowski, then who were they linked to and what the hell were they trying to tell her? Too many unanswered questions crowded her thoughts, her detective brain trying to analyse every bit of information. It would have been a relief to discover Kozlowski was the missing link. At least then she would have known. At least then she would have had something to work with.

Someone wants to hurt me.

But if it wasn't Kozlowski, then who was it? This was the question that haunted Jessa the most.

A shroud of depression lurked in the shadows of Jessa's mind, waiting to steal what little spark remained in her eyes. She was sinking into her own dark chasm of despair and a crushing pain inside her skull felt like her head was full of cement. Her mind was empty like a blank slab of concrete. It was just past ten in the morning and she had been searching the internet since dawn. Despite what Rads had told her, the Kozlowski connection still lapped the edges of her thoughts. She was not going to dismiss the possibility altogether, not until she found something to replace it with. But there was no one else she could think of. Kozlowski was her only lead.

She sat on the rug in the lounge cross-legged, basking in the heat of the wood burner as she stared at her laptop. Printed pages and handwritten notes were scattered over the rug. None of it was doing any good. None of it was helping. The words and images became a mess of jumbled data and Jessa's brain had stopped processing it. She needed to clear her mind before she had another meltdown. She needed to regain her strength and start thinking like a detective. Looking out the window, she decided a long hard run would do her good. The sky was dark and full of menace, ready to unleash an unrelenting rage, and Jessa wanted to bathe in it.

"But maybe a quick nap first," she said, closing her laptop. "Just a quick nap and then I'll clear my head."

A great rumble of thunder woke Jessa from sleep. She had dozed off on the sofa. When she opened her eyes, Vanessa was sitting on the floor in front of her. She had Jessa's laptop open and Jessa's notebook in her lap, all the loose papers stacked in a neat pile.

"What the fuck are you doing?" Jessa asked, sitting up.

Vanessa startled, looked back at Jessa like a dog caught rummaging through the rubbish. "I'm trying to make sense of this, babe." She picked up the notebook. "You still believe the dreams are about Kozlowski, even after what Radisson said?"

"I don't care what Rads said, Vee." Jessa snatched the notebook out of Vanessa's hands. "He hasn't delved deep enough. He's taken Novak's word and dismissed the whole thing. But there's a connection. I can feel it." Jessa took the laptop from Vanessa and put it on the couch with her notebook. "Anyway, you shouldn't be snooping through my fucking things, Vee."

"I'm just trying to help, Jessa. I want to understand, but I'm finding it really hard to make any sense of this. Maybe your dreams are just dreams, babe. Dreams are weird. There doesn't have to be significance to them. They're just dreams. You're going through a very emotional time and I think your mind has created a kind of coping mechanism. Babe..." Vanessa bit her lip, looking shyly at the floor. "I think you need professional help."

Another growl of thunder rumbled through the house, the two girls divided by a tense silence. Jessa stood up, clutching her notebook against her hip. "I'm not fucking crazy, Vanessa. And I don't need help. Not from you and not from anybody!"

Jessa marched out of the room, slamming the door behind her like a stroppy teenager.

Chapter 19

I'm beginning to think I've been murdered. For what reason, I have yet to determine. All I know for certain, if my visions are any indication, is that I did not die of natural causes. I have yet to fit the visions into chronological order; they come sporadically and it's impossible to say which event came before the other. Yet I sense what I'm seeing is about to take a more sinister twist.

I'm gazing now at the screen of light in the distance, smoky silhouettes flitting in and out of focus. Some of these shadows are thicker than others. Some linger suspended in the whiteness for a long time, while others appear and vanish almost instantly. They have no visible profiles or contours, and no pattern to their movements. They are a rogue band of dancing shadows. Then the aurora comes to their left, that awe-inspiring blast of white.

Someone's got me by my hair, forcing my face hard into a pillow while they straddle me from behind. It feels like I'm going to suffocate. They push me deeper into the pillow and I can't breathe. Fearing I'm about to be killed, I panic and try to struggle free, gasping for air while my assailant rams my face into the pillow with all their might. My lungs burn, I try to scream. Then my head is yanked back and I suck in a gasp of air, my neck feeling like it's about to snap. No faster do I catch my breath than I'm shoved back into the pillow. Now the son of a bitch is punching me in the kidneys. It must be a man. He's got a heavy right hook.

I go to my happy place. The beating goes on and I close my eyes and whimper, picturing myself in the one place I've always felt safe and liberated from the torments of the wicked world; a place where lush grass stretches like soft green silk under my feet; where the air is saturated with the intoxicating aroma of butter and honey; where the almond trees bloom.

Chapter 20

Vanessa was stunned by Jessa's outburst. How fucking dare she! Vanessa wanted to follow her into the kitchen and tell her how bloody selfish she was being. She wanted to tell Jessa to stop being so fucking despondent. All Vanessa had been trying to do was help, and yet Jessa had lost her temper and flipped out. It was like Vanessa's love was making things worse.

Maybe she would go stay with her mum for a few days, give Jessa some space to breathe, to think things over on her own and to realize how damn lucky she was to have Vanessa around. She didn't want to leave Jessa alone, but she couldn't babysit a grown woman 24 hours a day. And besides, her mum could use the company. Also, Vanessa could use a bit of time to think about her own life. Her savings were nearly depleted. She would need to find a job soon. She wanted Jessa in her life, but honestly, the girl was hurtling toward self-immolation. Vanessa couldn't see how much help her loving words would be in the coming days. Only a professional could help Jessa now and maybe a fat sack of happy pills.

It had been a few minutes since Jessa's dramatic exit, but Vanessa wanted to give her a little more time before confronting her. Vanessa threw another log into the wood burner and picked up Jessa's computer. It wasn't like Jessa could get doubly angry for catching Vanessa snooping a second time. She opened the browser and went into the search history. First on the list was: *Names of towns and cities in Poland.* On the page were all the towns starting with W. It must have had something to do with the scribbling in Jessa's notebook, the letters she had seen on the water tower in her dream: *Win???*

But there were no towns in Poland starting with those letters. There was Wiejce, Wieliczka, Witow, Wisla, and a few others, but nothing that started with 'Win.' Still, that hadn't stopped Jessa from digging even further. In another tab was a picture of a large red-brick water tower overlooking the Wisla River, a satellite image of the town itself below.

71

"Fucking crazy," Vanessa muttered, shaking her head in disbelief.

The next tab Vanessa clicked made her heart just about stop. The page opened and dozens of images of handguns stared her in the face. She remembered the note Jessa had made: *Why was I in possession of a gun? Whose house?* But what did it mean? There was another link that showed a Smith & Wesson M&P Shield 9mm. It looked just like the sketch Jessa had scribbled in her notebook, a small silver gun with a short muzzle.

Delusional disorder is a type of serious mental illness called a psychosis in which a person cannot tell what is real from what is imagined. The main characteristic of this disorder is the presence of delusions, unshakable beliefs in something untrue or not based on reality. People with delusional disorder generally experience delusions which involve situations that could occur in real life, such as being followed, poisoned, deceived, conspired against, or loved from a distance. People with delusional disorder often can continue to function normally and do not behave in an obviously odd or bizarre manner. In some cases, people with delusional disorder might become so preoccupied with their delusions that their lives are disrupted. Delusional disorder is slightly more common in women than in men and can be brought on by severe stress.

"Huh," Vanessa said, staring at the medical definition she had searched up. "Maybe you've got delusional disorder, babe. We really ought to get you some help."

It was certainly a possibility. Jessa's recent behaviour did show some of the indicators described in the text, and she was certainly preoccupied with the whole Kozlowski theory. Stress, too, was a major factor. She was thinking about calling DI Radisson and asking him about it. Vanessa knew the deeper she delved into the world of internet diagnosis, the more worried she would get, eventually concluding that Jessa was a paranoid schizophrenic suffering from a bipolar disorder and rampant night terrors. DI Radisson had told Vanessa to call him day or night if something happened. She had his number. Maybe she would text him.

Vanessa reached for her phone, and that was when a great crash and a piercing scream erupted from the kitchen.

Vanessa sprang to her feet, then ran across the lounge as another cry of pain resonated through the house. She nearly tripped over her own feet as she skidded into the hallway. Then she launched herself into the kitchen, where she found Jessa doubled over on the floor, gripping her side, jerking and crying out. The kitchen table was tipped on its side and papers were scattered everywhere. "What the fuck!" Vanessa screamed.

Jessa winced, cried out again and clung to her ribs.

"What's going on, Jessa?" Vanessa crouched beside her, unsure what to do. Jessa was jerking and spasming, teeth clenched as if someone was drilling into her spine, jaw muscles looking ready to split through her skin.

"That's it," Vanessa said, getting up, "I'm calling a fucking ambulance right now."

But before Vanessa could race into the lounge to get her phone, Jessa stopped twitching. Her screams ceased and her body relaxed. Her jaws unclenched. She looked oddly calm as her eyes rolled up to meet Vanessa. "I'm alright," she said, out of breath. She looked almost at peace, almost smiling as if she had enjoyed whatever the fuck just happened to her.

"For fuck sake Jessa," Vanessa said. "This is hardly alright."

Vanessa was about to storm out of the room and get her phone. She was going to call an ambulance, a paddy wagon, a fucking loony truck—anything that could get Jessa some help. She was fucking done. Finished. Enough of the fits. But Jessa lifted her hand. "Wait." Her voice was so damn feeble, causing Vanessa to pause in the doorway. Jessa had propped herself onto one elbow and was lifting her jumper.

Vanessa scoffed. "Getting naked isn't going to solve any—"

Then gasped and covered her mouth. "Oh my god." Jessa's ribcage was black and blue and purple, bruised as though someone had bludgeoned her with a club. Vanessa might have accused Jessa of self-mutilating herself, but she hadn't had the time. Jesus, she didn't even have the power to do that kind of damage. And it hadn't been there earlier. The girls had been naked together only

73

hours ago, Vanessa licking Jessa's pale, perfectly smooth skin. And now it was distorted and ugly as though she had just received a vicious kick-in.

Jessa chuckled—a helpless chuckle, sad and desperate. "What the fuck is happening to me, Vee? What in the holy fuck is going on?"

Chapter 21

They were in the lounge now, the only warm room in the house. Jessa was squirming while Vanessa touched around the bruises on her side, trying to determine if there was any serious injury.

"That hurts," Jessa complained.

"You're lucky it only hurts. Nothing appears to be broken, babe. But there's no telling what kind of damage has been caused internally. We really need to get you to a hospital."

"It's just bruising," Jessa said, yanking down her jumper.

"Jessa, you need to get it checked out. God knows what kind of internal damage you caused."

"I said I'm fine, damnit. I'm not going to the hospital. It's just bruising. All I did was catch myself on the table when it fell. Stop making a fuss."

Vanessa bit her tongue, watching Jessa wince and move uncomfortably on the sofa. She was clearly not fine. "I'm not fussing, babe. I'm just concerned about you. You didn't get that fucking bruise from falling on the table."

"Then how else do you explain it, huh?" Jessa asked. She wasn't willing to talk about what happened in her dream yet. She didn't want to admit the shocking truth she feared, that the beating in her dream had hurt her in the real world.

Vanessa's throat tightened. "I don't know," she said. "I really don't know."

Mid-afternoon and the painkillers Jessa had taken were starting to wear off. The room was getting chilly, the flames in the wood burner petering out. She really wanted to go for a jog to clear her mind, but Jessa was in no fit state to be running, and her immobility was worsening her mood. Vanessa's insistence that she go to the hospital was also adding to her anxiety and irritation.

Vanessa, irritated herself because of Jessa's refusal to seek medical attention, gave up and retreated to the kitchen.

Leafing through her notes, Jessa felt more frustrated than ever. She had convinced herself her dreams were a prophecy, yet she couldn't make sense of them. She exhaled slowly, trying to calm, trying to organise her thoughts. Maybe if she relaxed and tried to meditate she could earn some much-needed clarity. She became very silent, focusing on the sound of her breathing. Soon, the chill in the air and the pain in her side ebbed away like a receding tide. Her chaotic thoughts dissolved and a strange swirling aura of colour surfaced at the forefront of her mind. She focused on this, eyes flickering madly beneath her eyelids. The colour pulsated and flexed, and Jessa was overcome with nausea. An explosion of white light erupted inside Jessa's mind and she squealed in surprise, slumped into the soft pillows on the couch as a lightshow of colour and pulsing images flashed in her brain. She was overwhelmed by a strange sense of longing, as if someone was trying to connect with her. In between the flickering images was the tree, the water tower, the hotel room, the stranger writhing on top of her; and another image that crept from a dark recess in her mind. It was faint at first, but quickly came into focus. The image was her. She could see it clearly as if looking at a photograph of herself. Only, she looked terrified. Jessa sensed something sinister lurking beyond it. She grew afraid, dreading something terrible was about to happen. The facial features on the image distorted and became grotesque, and in an abrupt movement her jaw dropped unnaturally and she screamed.

Hovering on the edge of consciousness, Jessa clasped her hands over her mouth to stifle the scream. She could see gnarled fingers with sharp talons claw their way out of her mind's obscurity and spider around the image of herself, clutching at her skin and hair and dragging her violently backwards into the horrifying darkness.

Jessa's eyes snapped open. A wave of heat coursed through her blood and her lower back screamed in agony. She let out a tormented yelp of pain and fell back onto the cushions, and Vanessa burst into the room in a panic. Jessa was sticky in sweat, eyes sunken, skin sallow. She was in incredible pain. "Fuck," she cried. "Fuck fuck fuck." Clawing at her hair in frustration.

"Stop it," Vanessa said, pulling Jessa's hands away from her hair. "This can't go on. You need help. It's killing me seeing you like this and I really can't take much more, babe."

Jessa smiled through the pain, reached out to stroke Vanessa's cheek and said, "I love you, Vanessa. I really do. If you need to leave, I will understand. But I don't need any help because I'm not going crazy. I just need to understand what these dreams are trying to tell me. There is a connection. Someone is trying to connect with me, to warn me about something."

"Who?" Vanessa asked. "Who is trying to warn you about what?"

"I don't know," Jessa said, voice soft. "My mind is a fucking mess. I can't clear my head enough to make sense of it. I see all this scary shit and I don't know why, or where it's supposed to happen. I thought I was a damn good detective, but I can't make sense of what's happening to me." Jessa sideswiped the papers of the couch in anger. "None of it makes any fucking sense!"

"Let me help," Vanessa said, letting out a sigh. "You and me, one search engine, the rest of the day. Let's puzzle this thing out together."

"You mean it?" Jessa said, looking up at Vee with big, surprised blue eyes."

"Yeah." Vanessa thought that by changing her tactics—instead of badgering Jessa, if she went along with her craziness, she could subtly convince Jessa her dreams had no connection to Kozlowski or anyone else and her life was not in any danger, not now or in the future. She hoped to convince her the voices and visions she was experiencing in her head were just pure fantasy and nothing more. It was worth a shot. "Where do we start?"

"You can start by giving me some more painkillers. My back is fucking killing me. Oh, and toss another log into the burner. I'm freezing my tits off in here."

Chapter 22

By early afternoon, the winter sun was burning away the clouds and the temperature had risen slightly, melting the frost. Flames licked the logs in the wood burner and the lounge emanated a warm orange glow. Jessa lay on the sofa staring up at the ceiling, thinking about her dreams, trying to recall the detail.

It felt good to talk about what she remembered. Vanessa sat on the floor making notes on Jessa's laptop while Jessa rattled off everything that had happened and what she thought it all meant. Vanessa challenged certain aspects, debated from a logical standpoint, but Jessa believed firmly in her theories. She was positive her dreams were premonitions of her own deadly future.

"Right," Vanessa said, eager to begin. She had her fingers poised above the keyboard, ready to delve into the depths of the internet. "So, we have a stranger—male—in a hotel room. We've got a painting of two peacocks above the bed. There's some violent sex going on. I can assume the sex isn't consensual?"

"Of course not, Vee. I would never willingly have sex with a man." Jessa was repulsed.

"Right," Vanessa said. Truthfully, dream or no dream, the thought of Jessa having sex with anyone else made Vanessa sick to her stomach. "Then we have you being chased by an SUV. We can safely assume it's the rapist from the hotel room. And you're sure you don't know who this guy is, right?"

"Right. I have no idea. If I did, I would have told you. I still think there's a connection to Kozlowski, but I swear I've never seen this man before in my life."

Vanessa nodded, trying to put aside her reservations. "Okay. So, we have a stranger chasing you. In another dream, you're in the boot of a car, and another dream where you're in a car accident. Maybe if we can figure out where all of this is taking place, we can edge a little closer to discovering the mystery asshole's identity."

"Yes!" Jessa said excitedly. Now her detective gears were spinning. "It's a simple process of elimination. We find the location and it will lead us to the culprit. I was sure before the location was in Poland, but maybe it's not. It could be here in the U.K. It could be anywhere."

"Let's start with the letters on the water tower," Vanessa said. She typed in: *Water towers in Poland.* But after looking at some water towers and satellite images of the countryside, nothing looked right to Jessa. Too vacant, not the right trees, not the right road.

"Let's try the tree instead," Jessa said after watching Vanessa scroll through twenty pages of unfamiliar water towers. "It's a tree that gives off the scent of honey butter. Type that in!"

Vanessa typed into the search bar: *Trees with honey butter scent.* A ton of results came up for honey cosmetics and body butter products. There was a link for a website called: *Fragrant and Odiferous Trees – These Trees are Beautiful to the Eye and Their Honey Butter Fragrance can be Intoxicating.* Vanessa clicked the link and the screen was filled by a photo of a beautiful tree with white flowers in bloom.

The description under the photo read:

Almond originates from Western Asia and Northern Africa, and today is cultivated at the Mediterranean region, Israel, and California. It grows as a tree that can reach 7 meters of height. The almond blossom covers the tree in little white balls and an intoxicating, buttery, honey-like vapour radiates out for meters around.

"That's it, Vee!" Jessa said, shaking Vanessa's leg in excitement. "That's fucking it. That's the tree in my dreams."

Vanessa kept her doubt to herself. She found it hard to believe that finding one species of tree among 60,000 could be so easy. She wondered if Jessa was so desperate that she would have pointed to any tree and said it was the one. "Are you sure, babe? Are you sure it's the one?"

"Yes, Vee. One hundred percent. It's the tree from my dreams, the tree I saw in the oil painting. It's the almond tree."

"What about the locations where it grows?" Vanessa asked. "Asia, Israel, California. Do any of these places make sense?"

"No," Jessa said. "I really have no idea. I was sure the link was in Poland with Kozlowski."

"Maybe Rads was right," Vanessa said. "Maybe your dreams have nothing to do with Kozlowski."

"It could be," Jessa said, rubbing her chin, eyes focused on the computer screen. "Maybe these dreams are about a case I haven't worked yet, some international case I'm going to tackle in the future. That's why the scenery is so unfamiliar."

Vanessa felt a twinge of panic. She had managed to change Jessa's mind about Kozlowski, but now she was raving about future international investigations. Maybe she really was going nuts. Still, Vanessa had promised to help. She would see the day through. But tomorrow… maybe tomorrow she would go to her mum's.

"What does the almond tree produce?" Jessa asked, mostly to herself.

"At a guess, I would say almonds?"

Jessa gave Vanessa a look. "Thanks, smartass. Can you search what country produces the most almonds?"

Vanessa sighed as she keyed it into the search engine. "The United States," she said. "They produce 2,002,742 tons of almonds a year. The Golden State of California produces 82% of the globe's almonds, harvesting 800,000 acres of the tree nut across 400 miles in Northern Tehama County and Southern Kern County."

"California…" Jessa said, staring at the information on the screen.

Vanessa asked, "Does it mean anything to you?"

"Not a fucking thing, Vee."

Jessa kept thinking, *shrink the search area.*

"Now search for towns in California that start with 'Win.'"

Vanessa did as she was told, her belly grumbling with hunger. She hadn't eaten yet and was starving. "There are only two," she said, somewhat shocked. "A place called Winterhaven, population 894. And a place called Winters, population 7,273."

Excitement pricked the back of Jessa's neck. They were getting closer; she could feel it. But then Vanessa started to whine.

"I'm hungry, babe. Can we get some food?"

"Yeah, whatever," Jessa said hurriedly. "Order whatever you want. We can eat an Italian fuckin' stallion, Vee. But first, let's search these two towns."

Vanessa groaned and rubbed her stomach. "Fine, babe. Two towns and that's it. I'll start with Winters."

She punched: *Winters, California*, into the bar. The first image that appeared was the city of Winters, a reddish coloured road running between a row of flat, primitive American buildings. The tagline read: *Welcome to Winters Ca.*

Jessa studied the photo. A small blurb said Winters was a rural city situated in the Western Sacramento Valley in Northern California. But honestly, it didn't look at all familiar to Jessa. She scrutinized it hard, but there wasn't a goddamn thing she recognised.

"Wait!" Jessa leaned forward, crowding onto Vanessa's lap, swiping her hand out of the way and taking control of the laptop. "This one." She clicked on another link, transferring them to a page of photos of beautiful blooming trees in a row, their white flowers stretching long into the distance. The description read: *Winters CA, almond trees in the springtime.* A tingle spread from Jessa's neck down her spine. She recognised everything. The almond trees and the mountain range in the distance, its familiar ridge spanning the horizon.

She lay there stunned, half in Vanessa's lap staring at the screen. "That's it," she said. "My memory is a bit hazy, but that's fucking it." She scrolled further down the page, Vanessa grumbling about her hunger, until she spotted a photo of a lake. She clicked on the image to enlarge it. The photograph was of a lake, taken from the shoreline. The sky was a perfect shade of blue, the lake flat as a mirror. The reflection of the trees along the edges of the lake tinged the water a silvery green. Overlooking the lake was an elegant Victorian lake house, white like Jessa remembered. "It's the same one," she muttered. "It's the same lake house I saw from the hotel room window." Then she gasped. There was a link on the page for the hotel.

It was called the Almond Tree Hotel, and it was in Winters, California. Jessa could hardly contain her excitement as she read the name aloud to Vanessa, who didn't appear at all thrilled. She kept moaning about her fucking stomach. The hotel was located across from the lake house. She was on the booking website now searching through the photographs of the rooms, but she couldn't find any with an oil painting of peacocks. What she did find was a room with a lakeside view, and the room was a perfect match to what she remembered from her dream.

"I just need to do one more search," Jessa said. It seemed she was talking mostly to herself now. "Before I'm convinced, I just need one more search."

But then her mobile rang. "Oh, what the fuck." Jessa slipped back on the couch and grabbed her phone. It was DI Radisson calling. "One second, Vee," Jessa said, and she answered the call.

"Hey, Rads. What's up?"

The call only lasted a minute. Jessa spoke very little and thanked him before she hung up.

"What was that about?" Vanessa asked.

Jessa's expression was blank. "Kozlowski's dead."

"That's good news... right?"

"Good news," Jessa said, but her voice was hollow, as if she had whispered to herself. She had been betting everything on Kozlowski's involvement. But now he was dead. She had the link to Winters, but what was Winters without Kozlowski? Who else on Earth would have a murderous grudge against Jessa Summers? And why the fuck would she be working a case in the U.S of A? She had exactly zero answers.

"Vee," she said, "can you do one last search for me. One more and I promise we'll get some food."

"Seriously, babe?" Vanessa rolled her eyes. "Kozlowski is dead. We don't have to do this anymore. It's over"

Jessa narrowed her eyes at Vee. "It's obviously not fucking Kozlowski then, is it? And it's certainly not over. My dreams are trying to tell me something. Something important and I need to find out what. One more search and we'll stop. Now key in images for water towers in Winters."

Vanessa did as she was told. The first image that came up was of a grey, barrel-shaped water tower standing on spindly legs with **WINTERS** printed in blue across its metal belly.

Jessa sat back with a smug grin on her face. "So," she said, "we've found the where. Now we just need to find the who."

Chapter 23

Too many thoughts circle in my mind, each more frightening than the last. I sit in the silence of my glass prison waiting for the light. I haven't seen any of the smoky silhouettes in a while and I wonder if I merely imagined them before. What started as a tiny flicker of light has now grown into an expanse, continuously growing in the pitch of darkness. I ask myself if this light is Heaven waiting to open its doors and welcome me.

The explosion of white light blooms without warning and I close my eyes against it, opening them a moment later to find myself standing in a brightly lit room full of people. It's loud with conversations and laughter, people milling about the place and chatting with each other. It's a relaxed atmosphere, although I feel nervous as smartly dressed people drink champagne from glass cups and nibble on canapes, admiring the paintings on exhibition here.

I'm wearing an elegant blue lace cocktail dress and matching heels. My delicate curves are sensualised in this costume, though I feel uncomfortable in it. The heels are too tall and the dress is too short. I feel self-conscious. I'm fidgeting with my dress when someone creeps up beside me.

"Absolutely stunning," he says.

His voice is warm and friendly. I blush, look up at the tall, handsome man. He has greying hair. He's wearing an expensive suit.

"Exceptional," he says.

He's looking at the oil painting on the wall behind me, the painting of a beautiful tree in full bloom, its details so sharp and the oil so slick that the tree appears lifelike. He turns to me and smiles, and his piercing blue eyes almost take my breath away.

"Truly beautiful."

In a flash of light, I'm back in the hotel room, staring again at the peacocks above my head. I arch my back and reel against my bonds. Ecstasy washes through me. I moan in pleasure, tense my muscles, and throttle on the edge of orgasm. And then it comes, bliss pouring into me as I tug on the bindings; they rip into my flesh with satisfying pain. I see his head between my legs, feel his tongue gently massage my clit as he wriggles one finger inside me. I'm screaming with intense pleasure. He looks up at me with his hungry blue eyes and I shudder, rock my head back onto my pillow and scream from orgasm.

Chapter 24

Jessa woke up panting, her body still tingly from the rush of her dream. She was lying in bed blinking at the ceiling. This dream was the most intense yet, realer than life. The orgasm had certainly been real. Jessa had experienced her first wet dream. She reached between her legs and felt the moisture through her panties, the fleeting warmth of the orgasm. Then she remembered the man giving her oral and wanted to barf. The thought of a man's tongue between her legs made her cry into her pillow. She was revolted. The sex had clearly been consensual this time. She had been moaning in pleasure. But if the dreams were premonitions...

No, it didn't make sense. She would never fuck a man. Never mind enjoy it!

Vanessa slept peacefully beside her, the softness of her breath and the closeness of her body making Jessa feel unfaithful, even if it had only been a dream. In the year Vanessa had been gone, Jessa never had sex with another woman, though there had been plenty of opportunities. And now that she was back, Jessa couldn't imagine being intimate with anyone else. And never with a man! She wanted to erase the dream from her mind and forget all about it.

She needed to feel the love of a woman.

Jessa moved slowly to avoid hurting her back, turning on her side and slipping her hand under Vanessa's nightshirt to feel her breast. She circled Vanessa's nipple, kissed her shoulder, licked the side of her neck. Vanessa stirred at the touch, let out a soft whimper. Jessa wanted to kiss her all the way down to her navel, but her ribs still hurt. Instead, she glided her hand along the flat of Vanessa's stomach and slid it under her panties, then used her two long fingers to massage Vanessa's clitoris. Vanessa moaned and pushed her ass into Jessa's hips, squirming at the sensation. She craned her neck to try and kiss Jessa, and accidentally kissed her cheek. She tasted the salty tears pouring out of Jessa's eyes.

"Babe, what's wrong?" Vanessa asked, suddenly awake and realising Jessa was crying.

"Hush," Jessa said, her eyes glistening in the dark. She moved her fingers down and slid them inside Vanessa. "I don't want you to talk. I want you to fuck me."

Jessa's sexual fervour warmed her against the cold night air. She had the light on, lying beneath Vanessa as she kissed her breasts and slowly licked down her stomach. Jessa wanted to watch. Her body shivered from Vanessa's horny touch. Her skin prickled. She didn't care about the pain in her ribs anymore. All that mattered was Vanessa as she pulled down Jessa's panties and began to lick her. Jessa spread her legs as far as they would go, writhing, fingering Vanessa's dark hair. Jessa pushed her chin against her chest and looked down her front. She wanted to watch Vanessa devour her. They made eye contact, Vanessa slurping and fingering Jessa while leering at her with those sexy dark eyes.

It felt amazing. Jessa closed her eyes as the second wave of orgasm crashed against her. "Fuck yeah, Vee. Like that. Like that," she rasped, pushing Vanessa's head into her. Then Jessa opened her eyes and gasped. It wasn't Vanessa between her legs anymore. She was looking into the piercing blue eyes of the man from her dream.

"Get the fuck away from me!" Jessa screamed, scuttling backwards on the bed, pins and needles stabbing her bruised side. "Leave me alone!" She attempts to kick out at the man in front of her and screamed again, this time from the blind pain shearing through her side and back.

"What the fuck?" Vanessa reeled back in shock, wiped wetness from her mouth and gaped at Jessa. "Babe, it's me."

But Jessa's eyes were gaped in horror. She stared straight through Vanessa and sank her teeth into her bottom lip, drawing blood, quivering. She was in a trance, terrified, trapped in another one of her psychotic visions. The room suddenly plummeted in temperature and Vanessa shivered. "Babe, what's wrong? You're really scaring me."

It was like someone flicked a switch in Jessa's mind. She blinked, looked around slowly, then came back into focus. The man with the piercing blue eyes was gone. Her orgasm was replaced with a hollow feeling of desperation. Blood trickled down her chin. She saw Vanessa poised at the edge of the bed, looking like a wounded animal. She looked terrified.

"Oh god," Jessa said, "what have I done?"

Chapter 25

The feeling was just now coming back into Vanessa's cheeks as she sat in the little rustic café overlooking the River Exe. It was bitter cold outside and the walk from Jessa's house to the quay had left Vanessa frozen, her face cold as if she had been slapped a few times. The café had just opened, and Vanessa was happy to be their only customer. She was whispering into her mobile,

"I'm really worried about her, Paul. Her behaviour is getting more peculiar by the day. She's starting to scare the hell out of me."

There was a long moment of silence. Vanessa thought DI Radisson had hung up the phone. "Are you still there?" she asked.

"Yeah, sorry." He sounded distracted. "I'm just thinking about what we should do. Where's Jessa now?"

"At home in bed. She fell in the kitchen and her back is bruised. She can't move very well."

"Is she okay?"

"She's in pain," Vanessa said. "But she won't go to the hospital. She won't listen to anything I say."

"Jessa always has been bloody stubborn."

"I don't think stubborn is the problem," Vanessa said. She paused a moment while a purple-haired barista placed her americano on the table. "I think she's sick, Paul. Sick in her mind. She's seeing things that aren't there. She's hearing things that aren't there too."

DI Radisson breathed heavy into the phone. "We should talk to her about bereavement counselling," he said after a few seconds. "It would have been offered to her when she went on compassionate leave, but I guess she never took the offer. The mind is a powerful thing, Vanessa, especially when it comes to grief. I read somewhere that it's quite normal for people to experience hallucinations, particularly of loved ones after bereavement."

"It's more than just grief, Paul," Vanessa said. She couldn't keep the stress from her voice. "She's not even been hallucinating her father. She thinks her dreams are premonitions of the future. It's so ridiculous, but Jessa really believes her dreams are trying to warn her that something bad is going to happen. She thinks someone is going to hurt her."

"Does she still believe it's Kozlowski, even after I told her he's dead?"

Vanessa took a gulp of coffee, rolling her eyes at the deliciousness of it. "I don't know what she's thinking," she said, staring across the icy cold waters of the river. "But Kozlowski is dead, right? You didn't just make it up to put her at ease?"

"Yes, he's dead," Radisson said. "Dead as a fucking door nail. He never made it out of intensive care. Fuck him, is what I say. He lost too much blood. The sick fucker is dead and good riddance."

"I'm sorry, Paul," Vanessa said, sensing annoyance on the other end of the phone. "It's just, this is getting too much for me. Jessa has a notebook with all sorts of weird stuff written in it, and scraps of paper with notes and drawings. None of it makes any sense. And now she's got it in her head that the dreams are to do with a case she hasn't worked on yet, a case in America she'll be working on in the future."

"Really?" Radisson asked. "You're serious?"

"Really. And now she believes it's connected to a place called Winters, in California."

DI Radisson barked dryly. "Winters? Why on earth does she think her dreams are in California? That really does sound crazy."

"Jessa asked me to help her search for some stuff on the internet to try and find out where the events in her dreams are taking place. I was reluctant to help at first. I didn't want her to think I believed in her craziness. But she was adamant. So, I thought if I played along and the searches led to nothing, she would realise her dreams were nothing but fantasy."

Vanessa paused for breath, recalling Jessa's notes and the information they found on the internet. "Jessa had written down words and notes and sketches from her dreams in her notebook. Things like a water tower with the letters: 'win' on it, a lake house, trees that smelt like honey butter. She was sure it had something to do with Kozlowski in Poland, but we figured out the trees are from California. We found two towns starting with 'win.' Winters and Winterhaven."

"Sounds pretty fantastic," Radisson said, "but bloody ridiculous. Now I'm no expert in mental health, but I might have a theory. See, she acted strange during the Kozlowski case too, particularly when she was under a lot of pressure. She even admitted she was starting to have surreal dreams. I got worried. But after we solved the case, Jessa's weirdness went away. I put her erratic behaviour down to the pressure of the job. Anyway, I think her mind is fabricating its own case to keep her focused, to keep her playing detective so she doesn't have to cope with losing her dad or finding out she's adopted."

Vanessa looked up as the doorbells jangled and an elderly couple walked in dressed like Eskimos. "You might be right," she said, almost whispering. "But there are a few things still bothering me. If Jessa's fabricating a far-fetched case to mask her grief, I would understand the focus on Kozlowski and Poland. There is a history there. But Winters, California! What the fuck, Paul? She has no connection to that place. Why would she dream of a place she's never seen or heard of?"

"The mind can do funny things, Vanessa. Look at how easy it was to find some random place in California by searching the internet. It's clear Jessa is unwell. Her mind is open to suggestion. She wants to believe her dreams mean something, and so she latched onto the first thing she saw. I don't believe for a second that she's foreseeing the future in her dreams, nor that she has any connection to Winters or any other place on the planet. She's not well and we need to get her the right help."

"What about the sketches in her notebook?" Vanessa asked. "There were references to the lake house and the almond trees—all before we found them on the internet. Her sketches look dangerously similar to some of the photos we found."

"Coincidence, Vanessa," DI Radisson said. "Nothing more. You can find pretty much anything on the internet. If Jessa said she dreamed of waking up in a haunted house in the middle of a forest, she would have found the images on the internet that most resembled what she had claimed to have seen. It doesn't mean she is going to find herself waking up in a haunted house anytime soon."

Someone in the background called DI Radisson's name, and at the same time the bell over the door jangled and another elderly couple shuffled inside, their small dog bundled like a rat in a blanket.

"Give me a minute," DI Radisson yelled, the phone away from his mouth. "Look, Vanessa, work calls, so I've got to dash. Let me talk to my HR colleagues and the sergeant. They aren't going to discuss intimate details about Jessa with me, but at least I can make them aware of the situation. There are all kinds of support programs for officers. They may even make a referral for Jessa to have a psych evaluation."

Vanessa smiled at the phone, feeling like half her burden had been shouldered onto Radisson's shoulders. "Thanks," she said, "I appreciate the help."

"Hang in there, Vanessa. Jessa needs you now more than ever."

"Rads!" someone yelled again in the background.

"Look, I've got to go," he said. "I'm working on a serious case and don't have much free time, but I'll pop around as soon as I can to see how Jessa's doing. Okay? Give me a call if you need anything. Bye."

DI Radisson hung up, and Vanessa placed her mobile on the table and drank the last of her coffee.

Looking across the room at the elderly couples quietly enjoying their teas and cakes, Vanessa realised they were old enough to be her grandparents. Vanessa's own grandparents— whom she had loved dearly—had passed away a few years ago. She remembered them fondly. Then she thought of her nameless father, a man she'd never met. Then of her mum, whom she could only tolerate in small doses. It occurred to Vanessa that Jessa was the only person she really had in the world, the only one who cared about her. And she was suddenly determined to help Jessa through whatever torments she was experiencing.

Even if Vanessa went crazy in the process.

Chapter 26

The smoky wisps floating in and out of the light are becoming denser, like dark stains on a freshly laundered bed sheet. I still can't make out what they are, but as they drift and stretch in the bright light I'm wondering if they are other lost souls like me, trapped in their own blackness, searching for acceptance into an unknown world. I also hear whispers. They fade in and out of range, echoing eerily through the darkness around me. Are they ghosts beckoning me to join them?

If they are, I'm not ready. I am on a journey of discovery, a quest to find out why I'm here, why I was murdered. The Kaleidoscope of colour expands in my peripherals and I embrace the explosion of light.

I'm leaning on a wash basin, staring into the mirror on the wall. My arms tremble as I brace myself on the basin and watch my reflection stare back at me. My eyes are red with tears, the side of my face swelling. My long blonde hair falls around my oval face, my blue eyes bright with long, delicate lashes. I have an elegant nose and sensuous lips. It's obvious I'm attractive. I'd even say beautiful.

I'm in the fancy washroom like before. The details are clearer now. I can see the name of the hotel printed on the complimentary toiletries on the glass shelf. I'm in a place called the Almond Tree Hotel. It's printed on the small bottles of shampoo and conditioner. I don't recognise the name.

Looking at my fingers, they are smeared with blood and there's skin flakes under my nails. The voice is echoing outside the door when a flash goes off, a sudden memory of myself scratching at a man's face. Now I'm scrubbing my hands and fingers under hot water, wanting to remove every trace of the man from me. He calls again and I move slowly to the door. I take a deep breath before opening it. I tremble with fear. The only way out is through the hotel room—through him. I turn the handle and open the door.

I step into a garden. I know I've been here before. Behind me is darkness and dense foliage, no door, no washroom. Abrupt fear has me fumbling the gun in my hand; it shakes uncontrollably.

I'm standing in the cover of darkness as I watch the house, feeling anger, hatred, a deep-seeded loathing for the stranger within. I stand in the rain and watch him move unsuspectingly through the kitchen. He has his back to me, built strong with greying hair. I can't see his face but from his stature I'm sure he's the man from the hotel room.

He has a plate of food, a bottle of wine, and he makes his way casually from the kitchen to the living area. I watch him sit down in front of the television. My grip on the gun is firm as I begin to weave through the darkness of the garden. I must reach the back door without being seen. I must kill him.

Chapter 27

Jessa came to her senses, slumped over her desk, face down on her laptop. The last thing she remembered was pressing the print icon, then the dream. She slowly lifted herself up, reminded rudely of the pain in her side as it shouted at her. Jessa winced, sat back and took some steady breaths.

The weight of the gun had left a tingle in her palm. She flexed it to rid herself of the odd feeling. The hatred she had harboured for the stranger lingered like a bad smell. She sat in the chair thinking about how she had crept through the darkness with the handgun, moving towards the house with the intent to kill. It was an unsettling notion.

The laser printer hummed and pumped out an A4 sheet. It was a replica of the image on her computer screen, which meant Jessa had only blacked out for a few seconds. Ten at the most. She shifted in her chair, the cold from outside seeping through the single-paned window. Nearly an hour had gone by since Vanessa went out, since Jessa had made the agonizing trip upstairs to the spare bedroom she had set up as an office. It was a tiny room but not even the electric heater in the corner seemed able to warm it.

Small mounds of ice had formed in the corners of the old sash window frame and condensation peppered the glass. Jessa squinted through it at the neighbouring gardens, lost in wandering thoughts. She was trying to piece together the fragments of her dreams. They were getting clearer. The experiences felt more real as gaps in the story were filled, yet so many questions still lingered. The only thing Jessa was certain about was that Winters, California was the location of these events. There was no doubt in her mind.

She took the sheet from the printer, moaned as she stood up and crossed the room, then inspected the wall. Using Blu-tack, she stuck the page to the wall and slowly lowered herself back into the swivel chair, then studied the collage she had made. Twenty-seven pieces of A4 paper were displayed like a puzzle, showing a detailed bird's eye view of the town called Winters.

Chapter 28

Jessa was at the top of the stairs when she heard the front door open and Vanessa call out to her.

"I'm here, Vee," Jessa shouted back, climbing her way slowly down the stairs.

"What were you doing up there?" Vanessa said, frowning up the stairs at her. "You shouldn't be moving about, Jessa, and you certainly shouldn't be climbing the stairs."

"I needed the loo," she lied. Jessa had no intention of telling Vanessa about her latest blackout, nor about her photo wall. As she reached the bottom of the stairs, she bent down and gave Vanessa a kiss on the lips. "You're freezing."

"It's cold outside," Vanessa said. "And it's not much warmer in here." She kept her coat on as she walked to the kitchen, where she unpacked the items from the carrier bags. "Do you want a coffee, babe?"

"I'd love one," Jessa said, limping down the hall.

Vanessa peered out from behind the fridge door. "Go sit in the lounge, babe. I'll bring the coffee in when it's done. You really need to rest up."

"Yes, mum!" Jessa said with a smile, then hobbled into the lounge.

They sat on the sofa together, mugs of coffee in hand as the warmth from the wood burner put the colour and feeling back into Vanessa's cheeks. "I was thinking we could go for a meal this evening," Jessa said. "I could really do with getting out of the house for a few hours. I'm going stir crazy."

Vanessa smiled. "That does sound lovely, but are you sure you're up for it? You can hardly move."

"I'll be fine. If I sit around here all day my body is going to seize up and I'll be in even worse shape."

"Deal," Vanessa said. She gave Jessa a big smooch and wrapped her arms around her. "You've got yourself a date."

Jessa sucked in a gulp of air, flinching from Vanessa's hug.

"Oh shit!" Vanessa let her go. "Sorry, babe."

"It's fine, Vee." But Jessa's gritted teeth said otherwise. "Pass me the phone and I'll book us a table. How does French sound?"

Before Jessa took the phone, she popped two painkillers out of an almost empty blister pack and shoved them in her mouth. Then she called to make the reservation.

Although it was a relatively short stroll to the quay, they had decided to take a taxi. Jessa was in no shape to be walking anywhere. The restaurant was busy for mid-week, and Jessa was glad she had booked a table. The freezing cold hadn't kept away the punters wanting to try out the new French style bistro. As the taxi pulled away from the curb, Jessa drew Vanessa close and gave her a kiss on the lips. "I do love you, Vee," she said. "I want you to know that."

Vanessa was a little surprised, not by what Jessa had said but by the fact that she had kissed her in public. Vanessa knew Jessa wasn't ashamed of her sexuality, but she didn't generally show affection in public. "I know," Vanessa said. She beamed her gorgeous smile. "And I love you, babe."

They were greeted by a young, acne-pocked waiter dressed like a butler with a very dodgy French accent. "Right this way, madams." He escorted them to their table, the atmosphere relaxed with soft French music playing in the background. As they walked through the restaurant, they passed an old couple eating side-by-side at a table, bent over their meals; a group of middle-aged women laughing and talking loudly, their noise drowning out everyone else's conversations; and a young couple who sat staring at their phones and ignoring each other. When they sat down in a small alcove of the restaurant, Vanessa noticed a middle-aged couple digging into a lovely French dish. The smartly dressed man with his gleaming bald head glanced over, looked at them a little too long, then averted his attention back to his lady friend.

"This is quite nice," Vanessa said, frowning at the man and then looking around the place. The restaurant had obviously spent a fortune on the interior furnishings. The curtains were embroidered, hung in front of large mullioned windows, oak panelling and large, French-themed oil paintings, a flagstone tiled floor. Each table was swathed with a thick white tablecloth and decorated with a vase of fresh flowers.

"It looks expensive," Jessa said, using her naughty accent. "I hope my date puts out."

The waiter introduced himself in his obnoxiously bad accent. "My name is Antoine, mademoiselles. Here is the menu for the wine. I will return for your order."

"Antoine," Vanessa hissed when he left. "I bet his real name is Dave or fucking Wayne."

"I bet he's never even left Devon," Jessa said in a posh French accent, "let alone pied foule en France."

Vanessa blinked. "Uh, what?"

"Never stepped foot in France," Jessa said with a wink. "I did A level French."

The food was delicious. The Clafoutis dessert was to die for and the bill was extortionate. After finishing their second bottle of Louis Jadot, they decided to leave the cackling group of women—who were becoming more and more annoying—to argue over the cost of their bill with their petrified waiter and leave. The luscious red wine had turned Jessa's head fuzzy, but the pain in her side had at least been numbed. She managed to persuade Vanessa into a gentle walk home along the river instead of taking a taxi.

The evening was bitter. The cold stung their faces as they walked arm-in-arm along the path close to the riverbank. The night sky was perfectly clear and awash with glistening stars like glitter on black paper. The demons slept and chaotic thoughts were in abeyance for the first time in days and Jessa felt at ease. She knew the contentment would be short lived, but it was nice to enjoy it. She just wanted to snuggle with her beautiful girlfriend on a bench and overlook the river.

Moonlight shone across the dark water like streaks of silver, illuminating the ripples and causing the water to look like it was shivering. They sat in silence, wrapped in thick coats and scarves, enjoying each other's warmth, looking over the river at the distant lights of the city. And that was when the fragments of Jessa's dreams began to crowd her thoughts. The feeling of contentment she had been enjoying was slowly devoured by a creeping shadow in her mind, a sinisterly dark presence encroaching upon her. She knew it was insanity to go on like this, with the mysterious puzzle of her dreams driving her mad, her nerves shot every day, a fucking timebomb ready to go off. She knew it was time to act. She needed to solve whatever it was going on in her head before it was too late. Waiting around was useless. She'd just slip into a mental catastrophe. Or the visions would somehow become reality and she would be murdered in Winters, California. How, she didn't know. It wasn't as if she would accidentally get on a plane and go there and dress up in a fancy gown and be raped and beaten by a lunatic. Still, she had to act. She had to change the future. And Jessa had made up her mind on how to do it.

They arrived home and clambered straight into bed, curled up against each other with glasses of red wine. It didn't take long for Vanessa to fall asleep in Jessa's arms. Jessa sipped wine slowly, and softly stroked Vanessa's head, playing with her thick black hair. Jessa was once again engulfed by dark, turbulent thoughts. She was dreading what would happen when she fell asleep. She couldn't escape the thoughts that only became more real when she slept.

Jessa burrowed into the pillows and closed her eyes. Sleep came quickly and so did the fragmented dreams.

Chapter 29

It is most bizarre, but for a moment I'm sure I feel a tingle flow through my arms to the ends of my fingertips. It's the feeling of falling asleep on your arm, the deadened sort of pins and needles.

But now it's gone, nearly as quickly as it came. I've had no physical sensation since arriving in this glass prison, and so I do not believe the experience was real. How could it be if I'm dead? Perhaps it was a phantom limb situation, my spectral mind missing its old, physical body.

I pace the glass box, walk to all four corners, wait for the light to take me to another place. I see the colours forming and stretch my arms wide in welcome, arch my back and stare into the flood of light.

My vision comes in and out of focus, alternating between nothingness and a painful blur. My head is pounding as if someone's cracked me on the skull with an axe, and my cheekbone screams with hurt. The muscles in my neck are threatening to tear asunder from the weight of my hanging head, my chin bumping against my collarbone. My heels scrape across the ground. I'm being dragged.

I want to struggle, but I can't. I've been drained of my strength. I slur my words trying to speak, murmuring dumbly in a dazed confusion. With a jolt, I'm lifted onto my feet, the ache in my head intensifying horribly. My assailant takes my full weight and I hear them cursing under their breath as they try to keep me upright. A warm breeze tickles my face. I'm outside, a gravel tarmac fuzzy through my vision. Then it all goes black.

I'm startled by the wham of a slamming door, jarred into awareness. It's a fight just to open my eyes. I'm in the driver's seat of a car. Someone's clicked my seatbelt into place and the fabric slices into my neck. The car is moving slowly. My useless body won't respond. Outside the windscreen are silhouettes of swaying trees like a troop of dancing forest people. The car lurches and picks up speed and, with an agonizing grunt, I smash the brake. But it's jammed. I grip the wheel and take a fleeting glance into the rear-view mirror, spying the outline of a man with broad shoulders standing on the roadside in the moonlight. He looks oddly innocent.

I'm shaking violently as the car veers down a steep bank towards a chasm. My arms are flung from the steering wheel and the seat belt rips my skin and warm blood squirts onto my neck. The car vaults and my head smashes through the driver's-side window. The noise of crunching metal and splintered wood is deafening. The car spins and flips and my screams fill my head. Then all goes quiet.

Chapter 30

Everyone in the vicinity stopped what they were doing and looked at the screaming woman, who only moments ago had been asleep on the bench. Now she was upright with a stunned look on her face. Some people stared at her in confusion, alert for danger, while others glanced about nervously. It was like time had stopped. Then it rushed forward and everyone went back about their hectic business, their attention reverting to their phones or their books. A few people kept watching Jessa, the attractive and eccentric woman sitting on the bench.

"You alright, love?" a man asked. He looked genuinely concerned.

Jessa didn't respond. She was rattled in the aftermath of her dream, suffering a splitting headache. Her body felt like it had just gone through the rack.

"Love?" he asked, leaning forward in the aisle and looking at Jessa, careful not to get too close. "You look dazed. Can I get you anything?"

"I'm fine," she said without looking up. "Thank you."

"Are you sure? I have a spare bottle of water."

She smiled but didn't look at him. "I'm fine. Thank you very much."

"Alright." The man shrugged and went back to tapping on his laptop.

Jessa stretched, flexing her shoulder to try and liberate herself from the aches seizing her body. She was half aware of the curious peaks of those seated on the benches close to her. She acted like nothing strange had happened.

It had been almost a week since Jessa fell in the kitchen and she was starting to feel better. Her side and back still ached dully, and now and again a sharp pain would catch her breath in her chest, but she was mostly back to full mobility.

A message was broadcast over the PA system, but the announcement was drowned by Jessa's thoughts. She opened her rucksack and took out a couple of painkillers and her black notebook. She washed the pills down with what remained of her water and thumbed through the book. She was starting to piece together the mystery; at least, a small part of it. The crash was obviously not an accident. She was followed, forced off the road, attacked, and then dragged half-conscious into the car and pushed over the bank to make it look like an accident. There was no other way to look at it.

But there were still questions to answer: Where? Why? Who?

Hopefully, she'd find out soon.

Jessa's mobile rang, buzzing in her pocket. It was Vanessa's name on the display. She had avoided answering her girlfriend all day but knew she couldn't put it off any longer. It was almost time.

"Hello," she said as she put the phone to her ear.

Vanessa was hysterical, rattling a million miles a minute. "Thank god you answered," she said. "I've been worried sick. I've been ringing you off the hook for hours. I thought something bad happened. Why weren't you answering me? Where are you? Are you okay? What is going on?"

Jessa wasn't sure which question to answer first. She pulled the phone away from her ear and took a deep breath. "Vee, I'm okay." She saw the man who had offered her water was looking over his laptop at her. He had a pleasant face with deep laugh lines around his eyes. She raised her eyebrows as if to say, *yes, I see you too,* and smiled. Then the man returned to his computer.

"Okay?" Vanessa's angry voice on the other end of the phone. "Where are you?"

"London."

"London? What the fuck are you doing in London? Paul has been out looking for you. I've been going out of my fucking mind. You've been gone a full day and you've not sent me a single text to let me know you're okay." Now she was sobbing into the phone. "Do you even realise how goddamn bloody fucking selfish that is?"

Of course she did. Jessa knew full well how selfish she was being, and she was as guilty as a nun in a brothel for putting Vanessa through it. She had wanted to tell Vanessa her plan. She really had. She had been going to tell Vanessa her intentions at the French restaurant, but the moment never came. They had been

103

having too much fun and then Jessa lost her nerve. Anyway, she knew Vanessa wouldn't have understood. Vanessa would have said anything to stop Jessa from going, and she might have succeeded.

For a long time, Jessa didn't speak. She was trying to hold it together while Vanessa cried down the phone. There were too many people near her to cause another scene.

"I can't carry on like this," Vanessa croaked.

Jessa spoke to her softly. "I'm sorry, Vee. I really am. I know you won't understand, but I've got to do this. I've got to figure it out before it's too late."

"Figure out what, Jessa? What could possibly be so important?"

"The dreams, Vee. I need to find out what they mean."

"You've got to stop this, Jessa!" Now she was mad. "They're just dreams. Nothing more. All this stuff about dreaming your future, about someone wanting to hurt you, it's all in your head. It's not real and it's never going to be real. You need fucking help, Jessa. Real, professional help."

Jessa said nothing while another announcement blared over the PA, another useless security reminder not to leave your luggage unattended. Then she bolstered herself. "I've got to go, Vee."

"Go where? Where the fuck are you going? Is this because of me? Is it because I walked out on you, and now you're walking out on me? This is torture, Jessa. Where are you going?"

"I'm at Heathrow, Vee. I'm getting on a plane to San Francisco."

Part 2

Sometimes you wake up from a dream.

Sometimes you can wake up in someone else's dream.

Chapter 31

I sit here staring into the white light when the tingling sensation prickles the ends of my fingers and toes. It feels real but I know it's just my mind playing a cruel game. I tell myself I'm dead. I tell myself I no longer have a physical presence and no matter what my brain says, my predicament won't change.

The grey shadows floating in the whiteness have gotten busier. They emerge faint and then become darker and less translucent. At one point, I was certain the shadows took on human forms. I thought I saw one turn into a head with shoulders; thought it looked at me out of the white. But after a few blinks, the ghostly form dissolved into a wisp of smoke and evaporated.

I continue to stare. I'm waiting for the colours, for the swirling aurora of colour.

Sitting and waiting is all I can do.

Chapter 32

The inside of the Freedom in Christ Evangelical Church in the North Beach area of San Francisco looked more like a movie set than a place of worship. There was a large flamboyant stage at the back surrounded by lights. Microphones and cameras and huge black speakers hung from the ceiling that would have looked more appropriate at a rock concert. The portable seating area, which could accommodate 250 people, was set up in tiers in a semi-circle facing the stage. Just left of the stage was a smaller podium with microphones and lighting for the gospel choir.

Robert Flores, also known as the 'Holy Man,' was becoming quite the celebrity. His TV show, which had been running for almost a year now, had grown in popularity week after week. Robert was not a typical reverend. He was tall, athletic, and curiously handsome. He was fashionable too, his hair styled grey, symbolic tattoos covering most of his arms. He looked more like an aging rock star with a receding hairline than a man of God. His charm and charisma, together with his passionate and sometimes controversial (though very entertaining) sermons made his Sunday morning television show, The Holy Man, one of the most watched religious television shows on the network.

Every Sunday morning since the first live broadcast of The Holy Man, the church had been full. This Sunday morning was no exception. Robert sat in his private office in the back, same as he always did before a live TV performance, preparing himself for the show as the choir warmed up with the church band in one of the function rooms down the hall. The expensive high-backed leather chair creaked as Robert leaned back and thumped his shiny black shoes onto his mahogany desk. He was wondering the same thing he wondered before every live performance, a thing that made him almost want to pinch himself: *How on earth did this happen?* He had never intended to be a celebrity. In fact, it was the worst thing that could have happened to Robert. He had been perfectly happy keeping a low profile, going about his business undetected, preaching between his church in San Francisco and his church in Winters. But after the network executive attended one of his sermons, that was it. Robert got tied up in the hype and before he knew it, he was one of the biggest religious TV celebrities on the west coast.

Robert uncapped the small hip flask he was holding and took a long swig of bourbon, just enough to warm his throat. Then a series of short knocks rattled his door.

"Robert, you're on in five," one of the crew called to him.

Robert calmly screwed the cap back on his flask, plunked his feet on the floor, and put the little metal container into the top drawer of his desk. Slowly, he adjusted the expensive, tailor-fitted navy suit he was wearing (a suit he could not have afforded a year ago) and stood up. He was running the sermon he was about to preach over quickly in his mind. He picked his bible up off his desk and remembered the prayer he had promised to give for Susie and her family. Susie was a smoking hot twenty-three-year-old blonde from Winters and an active member of the Freedom in Christ Evangelical Church choir. Her family had reported her missing a week ago, and there had been little news coverage of her disappearance. Susie's family wanted Robert to say a prayer on television in the hope someone watching would come forward with information on her whereabouts. They had no faith in the police to find their daughter. All their faith was invested in God.

Robert gave his bible a kiss, a little ritual he liked to do in the privacy of his office before every show. As he opened the door and walked out into the circus of network folk rushing around like headless chickens, he knew God wasn't going to bring Susie home safely. It made him laugh to himself. No one was going to bring Susie home.

Chapter 33

Jessa rented a car from the San Francisco International Airport and took Interstate 80 north to Sacramento. As she headed past Vacaville City, she took the west exit onto Interstate 505 and headed onto E. Grant Avenue. Her mind was clouded by apprehension. It was late morning when she finally approached Winters, and the fields of almond trees sprawled on either side of the road, the mountain range in the distance instantly familiar. It was cool outside, and the breeze skirted in through the window as she drove towards Main Street under a clear blue sky. The scent of honey butter filled her nostrils.

The town was like most other small towns across America (or at least Jessa assumed so), its wide main strip lined with shops and cafes. As Jessa drove past the town square, she didn't notice the missing person posters tied to every other lamppost, a pretty young girl with blonde hair by the name of Susie.

Her GPS system guided her left off Main Street and onto Putah Creek Road. And that was when she saw the water tower rise in the distance, the blue letters printed boldly on its metal hull. The sight of the ugly thing gave her an unanticipated fright; its blue letters glowed like neon. She panicked and pulled the car off the road, skidding into the dirt outside an empty Mexican restaurant. She gripped the wheel, head spinning as fragments of memory tumbled inside her head. She had come to Winters for a reason; she was certain of it. But what if she was wrong? What if all her dreams were just by-products of her anxiety, her unstable mental health? Or what if the dreams were insights into her future? Was she putting herself in imminent danger? Now she was in Winters. Now the future could unfold.

"Excuse me, ma'am. Ma'am, are you okay?"

There was a woman standing beside her car, looking in through the open window. She gave off the pungent smell of cheap perfume. Jessa didn't look at her. She was considering turning the car around and driving straight back to the airport.

"Ma'am, are you okay?"

"I'm fine," Jessa said, and without looking, she put the car into drive and screeched back onto Putah Creek Road.

She was feeling sick, on the verge of a panic attack. But she willed herself on. Even though she had crossed the ocean and travelled thousands of miles, this was the true start of Jessa's journey. She knew she must carry on, even if it killed her. "Please don't lose it, Jessa," she whimpered to herself. "Hold it together girl." Her anxiety threatened to consume her. She desperately wanted to reach the hotel and curl up in bed.

Putah Creek Road stretched off into the distance and she took a right onto Lake Side Lane. As she turned, Jessa glimpsed Lake Solano glittering behind the thick row of western sycamore trees lining the road. She knew the hotel was close. Farther on down the road, the sycamore's thinned to reveal the lake. It was magnificent, spanning as far as the eye could see, its majestic blue water still as glass. The reflections of the trees and hills tinged the water in oranges and yellows. A short distance ahead, beyond a boating marina, the Almond Tree Hotel came into view.

The hotel looked exactly like the posh, 5-star hotel portrayed on the website. It had the feeling of a picturesque country home for the rich, tastefully decorated shades of whites and yellows adorning its exterior. It almost had a Mediterranean feel. The hotel grounds were nestled on the edge of Solano Lake Country Park, breath-taking views of the mountain beyond and the surrounding forest.

Jessa sat in the rental and stared at the entrance of the hotel. A groundskeeper busied himself watering the flowers and plants in front of the lobby, and a porter stood by the entrance speaking with a guest who looked dressed for the golf course. Checking herself in the mirror, Jessa saw a pale and exhausted woman with circles like bruises under her eyes. She was overcome with angst at her own reflection and it made her feel sick.

"What the fuck are you doing?" she asked herself. Jessa felt guilty for leaving Vanessa. Her heart wrenched with guilt for what she was putting Vanessa through, leaving her the way she did. Vanessa didn't deserve such cruelty. She was remorseful for not spending more time with her dad when he was alive. Maybe if she had been a better daughter, her father would have told her about the adoption. She felt imprudent for travelling thousands of miles because of some fucking weird dreams. Now that she stopped to think about it, she felt ridiculous. Maybe she was crazy. She wanted to drive back to San Francisco and get on the first flight back to London.

But she was in Winters now and she knew the dreams had meaning. She could feel it. She couldn't deny their power. All logic had evaporated. Jessa's paranoiac mind had smothered any rational thinking she had left.

Chapter 34

The live audience in the Freedom in Christ Evangelical Church, along with the thousands of worshippers tuned into The Holy Man at home, clung to every word of Reverend Robert Flores' sermon. The atmosphere inside the church was electric, and Robert relished the power gained by his followers' admiration. Tears of joy fell from the eyes of those in the audience, while others held their heads in their hands and cried, or raised their arms to the heavens as though witnessing a miracle.

They were being worked into a frenzy. Robert strutted around the stage, waving his bible, the gospel choir singing the end of 'God of Miracles.' As the last notes petered, Robert held his hands in a gesture for the audience to calm. The singalong lyrics of 'God of Miracles' faded from the large white projector screen behind Robert and was replaced by the photo of a beautiful young woman with blonde hair and perfect white teeth.

Robert paused for a full minute, looking at Susie Morgan's photo, listening to the hushed scuffles of the crowd and the pained sobs from Susie's family in the front row. He turned to the audience and spoke.

"A week ago, our friend, Susie Morgan, disappeared without a trace. No one has seen or heard from her since. I know, my God-loving brothers and sisters, that Susie is in all our thoughts and will be in our prayers tonight. We must pray to God for Susie's safe return home."

A loud sob escaped Susie's mother and she buried her face into her hands. Susie's aunt patted her on the back, trying to lend comfort.

"We lift our eyes to you," Robert said, "Heavenly and Most Gracious Father, from whom our hope and help comes." He paused, looked into camera 2 and lifted the bible above his head as though the Holy Spirit might burst out of it. "Today, Lord, we cry out to you on behalf of Susie. We, her family, her friends, and our whole blessed community anxiously await her safe return. Even though you said be anxious for nothing but in everything by prayer and supplication, with thanksgiving, let our request be known."

Robert slowly started to raise his voice, clenching his fist for added effect as he paced the stage. "Please Lord, give us peace that surpasses our understanding, so that our hearts may be guarded from negative thoughts. You are our great, all-knowing god, and you know Susie is somewhere out there needing to be touched by the Holy Spirit to find her way back home. If she has absconded, remind her how much she is loved by her family, friends, and community. If, for some reason Lord, she is being held against her will, we compel the abductors to release her unharmed in the name of Jesus Christ."

Robert paused, mindful not to be overdramatic. He lowered his voice, closed his eyes and clutched his bible to his chest. "We declare today, oh Lord, that we continue to stand strong in faith. We continue to trust and hope in the mighty workings of the Holy Spirit, and we continue to trust in you, Lord Jesus, for the safe return of Susie Morgan, and for you to lead her gently home. In the name of Jesus, we thank you for your everlasting mercies. Amen."

The church band started to play the intro to 'Lead Me Gently Home Father,' as Robert walked across the stage. As the words of the first verse filled the church, Robert turned and faced the audience and the camera. He crossed himself, kissed the bible, then walked off stage while Susie Morgan's photo slowly faded from the screen.

Chapter 35

I thought I would never see the swirling aura of colour again. I must have been sitting here for hours, if not days, staring into the nothing, hoping the colour would appear and transport me to another chapter of my sad saga. And so, it is with great relief when the colour finally appears and pulsates with an energy I have yet to witness. I ready myself for the light, for the next step in my journey.

I'm back in the hotel room, standing at the edge of the bed. The bed's empty. The peacocks hang over the headboard and through the window I see the boathouse and the lake. There's no sign of the man I was with before. Yet I sense a strange presence in the room with me, and am overcome with a peculiar, inexplicable feeling. It's as if someone or something is trying to reach out to me, and my subconscious is reaching out to them. I look down at the bed and see a rake of a woman asleep. Her image is transparent, ghostly. Her face is gaunt, skeletal, dark pools around her gruesomely sunken eyes.

For a moment, I don't recognise her. Then I recoil in disgust as I realise it's me. I'm looking at the withered spectre of myself! She's certainly not the image of beauty I saw in the washroom mirror. Is this my true self? My other self flickers like a hologram and stirs from sleep. In the blink of an eye, I'm hovering above her, suspended parallel to the phantom below me. I'm inches from her face and unable to move. The world is on pause. The eyelids of my skeletal shadow snap open and I'm staring into deep, black, bottomless pits. I try to move but I can't, so I try to look away but am transfixed. Her face starts to transform. Her jaws become disjointed. The end of her tongue tears and flaps onto her chin, held on by a shred of skin. Her teeth are replaced by black, bloody gaps, and cuts and gashes zigzag across her face and head as if she's being slashed by a furious demon with a knife. The image is so horrific I crave my glass prison. Is this how I died? Was I stabbed to death in a frenzied attack?

I see a white spot of light appear deep within the blackness of her eye sockets, followed by the dazzling aurora of colour. She screams a death wail from her mutilated mouth just as the colours burst from her eye sockets and explode around me.

Chapter 36

Even though the room was warm, Jessa woke in a cold sweat. The thin fabric of the hessian curtains fluttered gently as the warm breeze flowed in through the open window. Her eyes darted around the room, her hands fumbling over her face for cuts and gashes that weren't there. The vision had been so vivid, more real than any of the others. The dream frightened her, yet somehow, she wasn't left horrified. Instead of being scared or numb, Jessa felt energized, even sanguine. An extraordinary sense of connection clung to her like a vine around a tree. She felt a thread linking her to someone in an oddly beautiful and sophisticated way. It was strange, suffocating… and yet captivating.

Her suitcase was at the end of her bed, where she had left it after staggering into the room exhausted and flopping onto the bed, wanting to rest her eyes before unpacking. That was two hours ago. Now it was nearly 12:30 in the afternoon. Her stomach rumbled and she felt ravenous hunger for the first time in a while. Jessa had hardly eaten for days. She hadn't touched the food on the plane and knew she was becoming unhealthily thin. Somehow, the dream had injected her with renewed energy. She wanted to eat.

She ordered room service and sat on the bed with a folder full of papers, her laptop, and a bowl of Mediterranean salad with chicken and a side of chili fries. The sliding doors were open, the curtains pulled back. Outside were the beautifully hedged gardens, and the view of the boathouse and the lake. She had specifically requested this room and would have arrived a few days earlier if it wasn't for the room being already occupied.

The warm breeze flowed constantly inside, the air laced faintly with the scent of honey butter. Rays of afternoon sun shimmered off the still water of the lake, birds chirping in the garden. For the first time in a long while, Jessa's mood was lifted. Any underlying doubts she had about her visions or about travelling to Winters lay momentarily dormant as she shuffled through her printouts and notes, between mouthfuls of food.

She was scrolling through satellite maps, trying to refresh her bearings. She needed to plan her next move. Her focus was on finding the man from her dreams. She needed to find the man who wanted to hurt her before he found her first. To do that, Jessa needed to get a real feel for the place. She needed to find out as much as she could about Winters, not just what was on the internet. She needed to experience the real Winters and immerse herself in her new surroundings. Jessa forked the last of her meal into her mouth, closed her laptop, then slid off the bed. She didn't have much to go on. The only usable reference points were the hotel and the water tower. However, Jessa was convinced that by exploring Winters, she would find a lead. A location or a situation would trigger a memory or give her a vital clue.

First, she needed a shower and a clean pair of underwear. Jessa headed for the washroom. She never did notice the spots of blood speckled over the oil painting of two peacocks that hung above the bed.

Chapter 37

It was pissing out. Rain gushed from the broken gutters and soaked DI Radisson as he walked to the front door of Jessa's house. He was in a foul mood, cursing under his breath, "Fucking brambles." Cold rain trickled down his back. He had been working for twelve hours straight. What a horrendous day. All his leads had gone stale, another double murder with no suspects. Radisson was tired, hungry, and just wanted to go home and down a few beers before crashing into bed.

His mood improved when Vanessa opened the door. The girl's eyes were red from crying, glazed from too much alcohol. She looked sexy as hell. She was wearing a pair of tight black jeans and a long-sleeved sweatshirt. Her tits pushed through the fabric like two juicy melons. Her hair was upbraided, hanging just above her shoulders. And the little makeup she usually wore wasn't applied. She smiled at him as he walked into the house, then stood dripping in the foyer.

"Sorry I couldn't get here sooner," he said as he hung up his wet coat. "I've been swamped with work."

Vanessa embraced him with a hug. "Thanks for coming. I didn't know who else to call."

She was drunk, slurring her words. It was sexy enough without her large breasts pushing against Radisson's chest as she squeezed him, making him even hornier. He had to force himself to think of Shelia.

It was a relief to be sitting on the sofa for once instead of in the uncomfortable bucket seat. Vanessa sat next to him. She held a glass of red wine and expanded on what she had already told him over the phone, about Jessa and her escape to California. Vanessa was clearly distressed and worried about her girlfriend.

"I really don't know what to do, Paul," Vanessa said, half sobbing. "I really think she's going out of her mind, and now she's on her own halfway across the fucking world and there's nothing I can do."

DI Radisson wasn't quite sure what to do about Vanessa's face buried in her free hand. He took the wine glass from her before she could spill it all over the sofa and put it on the floor next to the empty bottle. Then he shuffled closer and gently rubbed her arm.

"She's so fucking selfish, Paul. She's so absorbed in this ridiculous theory. I really don't think I can carry on like this. She's driving me crazy with worry. I don't think I'm strong enough. I'm obviously not helping her." Vanessa reached for a tissue and dabbed at her eyes. "Her mental state is getting worse. She needs help and I don't know what to do."

Even upset with tears streaming down her face, nose dripping like a faulty tap, Radisson still wanted to bend Vanessa over and fuck her from behind. The thought of his bollocks banging against her plump arse made him all hot under the collar. He realised he was still rubbing her arm tentatively and quickly stopped.

"Is there anything you can do, Paul?" she pleaded. "Anything at all?"

Radisson looked into Vanessa's watery eyes, hypnotised by their rich brown colour. She was truly stunning. Being too close to her had him tingling with lust. Her coffee skin, perfect tits, tight arse—even the cute gap in her front teeth. He almost creamed in his pants right there. He was wondering if she'd ever been with a man.

Vanessa frowned, seeing the way Radisson was staring at her. He blushed, quickly blinking away the thoughts of him ramming her against the arm of the sofa. He seriously hoped Vanessa couldn't read his thoughts.

"I'll make some calls," he said, crossing his legs. "I'll contact the police department in Winters to give them a heads up about Jessa. I'll ask them to contact me if something happens."

"Thank you," Vanessa said. She dabbed at her eyes again, then picked up her wine glass and took a gulp.

Radisson asked, "When was the last time you had contact with her?"

"I spoke to her on the phone when she was at Heathrow. I keep texting her, but she won't reply. It's fucking bullshit." Vanessa looked dejected.

"Does Jessa still think this is linked to Kozlowski?"

"No." Vanessa shook her head. "I don't know what she's thinking. Most of what she was telling me made no fucking sense. I think she's fucking crazy."

They stood in the hallway as DI Radisson put on his damp coat, Vanessa swaying from too much wine.

"Hang in there, Vanessa," Radisson said. He smiled and placed his hand on her shoulder. "I'm sure Jessa will be fine. I don't believe anyone wants to hurt her. The only person she's in danger from is herself."

"Yeah," Vanessa said, "that's what worries me the most."

"She'll be fine," he repeated. "I'll let you know when I've contacted the police in Winters. If you hear from Jessa, let me know. Okay?"

"Okay, I will."

Radisson was about to go. He had his hand on the door, ready to walk out into the pissing rain. But Vanessa staggered towards him. "Thanks again, Paul." And before he could react, Vanessa had wrapped her arms around his neck and planted her lips on his. Her kiss was passionate and so goddamn sexy. Not even Shelia standing in the hallway with her floppy tits out could have quashed his desire.

Chapter 38

It was a beautiful Sunday afternoon when Robert Flores drove his SUV along Highway 505 towards Winters. The moment they finished filming The Holy Man, Robert couldn't wait to get away from the church. But he always had to hang around listening to the production team kiss his arse and tell him how great he was—tell each other how great they were and how great the show was. Everything was just fucking great.

Then there were the cocksuckers from the audience. There were always a few who wanted to hang out after the show and get a photo with Robert, sometimes ask for his autograph on their bible. He had relished the attention at first, but the novelty quickly wore off. Especially when he started getting stopped in the street by people who recognised him from the show. That wasn't his style. Being recognised wasn't his style. Robert loved the money he earned from the show (more money than he'd ever seen in his life), but being a local celebrity was making it difficult to go about his normal business. There was so much planning now. He couldn't just act on impulse anymore. And he couldn't afford to have any more loose ends hanging over him, like damn Elizabeth.

As he approached Winters, Robert checked the time. It was mid-afternoon. He still had a few hours before he said he'd be home. He had called Juliet on his way out of San Fran, telling her he needed to visit the office at his church in Winters before going home. They were having a BBQ tonight at the new 1860's Victorian estate Robert had bought with the royalties from his show, a place on the outskirts of Sacramento. Robert's daughter and her new jerkoff boyfriend were coming over, and Juliet didn't want him to be late.

Robert stopped at the lights on E. Grant Avenue and looked out the window. Missing person posters were everywhere. On every lamppost was Susie Morgan smiling at him with her perfect smile. It was the same photo he had used in his sermon that morning. As the light turned green, it occurred to Robert that Susie was the same age as his daughter.

The Freedom in Christ Evangelical Church was situated on a large plot of land donated by a wealthy and religious beef rancher. The rancher had passed on many years ago, but before dying had left a few hundred thousand in trust for the church's upkeep and future renovations. The area was isolated (which suited Robert perfectly),surrounded by nothing but fields of grazing cattle and almond trees, with only one access road that went several miles to downtown. It was busy during the weekly sermon, but the rest of the week Robert's church was quiet. He spent most of his time now in San Francisco. The rest of the church functions were held in the newly built community hall.

Robert drove past the empty community hall and then into the church's parking lot, then around the back to his private parking space. The afternoon sun was warm as he climbed out of the SUV. He unlocked the side door to the church and walked into the small, stuffy vestibule. There was a locked door opposite the entrance and another that led to the main church. Robert locked the entrance behind him, unlocked the door to his private office and went in.

His office was small and stuffy and scantily furnished. It was a complete contrast to his fancy office in San Francisco. But he didn't care. He didn't work much in his Winters' office anymore. In the corner was a floor-to-ceiling storage cupboard built into an alcove approximately six feet wide. He unlocked it using the key attached to his car fob. Inside were brown cardboard boxes, a few suits and shirts hanging from the rail, and a single pair of brown brogue shoes on the carpet. Robert knelt and removed the shoes, lifted the carpet and took hold of the small metal ring on the floor. A gentle pull triggered a section of the cupboard floor to spring open. He lifted it, revealing a wooden ladder and a dark hole in the floor. He pushed a light switch on the underside of the floor and his little basement room lit up. He shimmied his large frame into the hole and down the ladder, pausing to close the hatch behind him.

The single bulb glowed inside the windowless room. It was an underground prison cell, bare except for a plastic chair in one corner, a coat stand, and a small television monitor fixed to the wall. There was one door for the shower room and another door secured by a digital combination lock. There was also a final door no more than four feet squared.

Robert was buzzing with excitement as he sat down in the chair and untied his shoes. He stuffed his socks in his shoes and stowed them under the chair. The cold concrete was refreshing on his sweaty feet as he stood up and stretched. He felt good. Then he took off the rest of his clothes, letting his excitement build as he hung his suit on the coat stand, stripped off his underwear and threw them on the chair. Naked, he moved to the locked door and punched in the code.

The room was windowless, but bigger than the main chamber. The only piece of furniture was a large wooden bed in the centre. Robert closed the door behind him, the lock clicking shut with a loud beep. He was already fully erect when he walked to the bed, the ache in his groins like hellfire burning him inside. Poor little Susie Morgan squirmed naked on the mattress, tied spread-eagle. Her misery gave Robert joy. He stood there a moment stroking himself as he watched her wriggle and sob through the gag in her mouth. Her eyes were bright with fear. Robert loved it. He salivated as he climbed on top of her.

Susie Morgan closed her eyes, whimpered and hoped God would soon find a way to save her.

CHAPTER 39

Jessa hadn't noticed how elegant and luxurious the hotel lobby was when she first arrived. Standing in the reception area dressed in running shorts and a t-shirt, she admired the fancy décor as the other hotel guests went leisurely about their business. The floor was tiled with fine marble, the walls painted in shades of gold and green. The sofas were silk, a collection of them in the corner facing a flat screen television. Pendant chandeliers hung from the ceiling, light reflecting off their beads of glass. Even the door handles were engraved with motifs and elegant designs. There were also paintings from local and international artists on the walls, some available to buy. The website had boasted the hotel was renowned across America for its annual art exhibition. Artists and celebrities flocked to the rural hotel to congregate at its prestigious yearly event.

Jessa had never stayed somewhere so grand. She wasn't particularly enamoured by its extravagance, nor by the high-class artwork. The tasteful decorations clashed with her minimalistic idealism. She thought of the luxury as more of a sacrifice than an indulgence. She told herself she only had to endure it for a short time, at least until she solved whatever the fuck it was that she was trying to figure out.

She left the lobby and walked into the warm afternoon sun. Although still quite sore, Jessa's ribs were healing. The bruising had faded, turned a rotten bluish green, and the pain was bearable enough for her to run. She started from the parking lot and ran a few miles along Lake Solano, feeling invigorated by the exercise and the warm wind. She chased the mountains until reaching Putah Creek Road, which she jogged along until finding the water tower. Now it loomed above her, a big rusted barrel on spindly legs with faded blue lettering.

She had been holding onto a more impressive image of the tower in her mind. Now that she was standing in front of it, it was just a big ugly neglected bulk of metal. It was an eye sore. She had expected it to be bigger, had expected the blue letters to be somehow brighter. Although she had only briefly glimpsed the tower that morning before her minor meltdown, she was certain the lettering was brighter, almost neon like. As she shaded her eyes and squinted at the word: **WINTERS** in bold blue, nothing happened. She had hoped being close to the tower would ignite a memory or a vision, but there was nothing.

She walked over to the rusted metal structure and placed her hand on one of its legs. Taking slow breaths, she closed her eyes and bowed her head. She needed to focus, to clear her mind and allow her subconscious to melt into her consciousness as she tried to connect with her surroundings. The sounds of the world filled her head. The skin of her palm absorbed the rusty feel of the water tower. The smell of the lake and the grazing cattle filled her nostrils. She smelt it all. And she waited.   Jessa believed by visiting locations from her dreams, by touching, smelling, and soaking up the environment around her, it would prompt some intense visionary episode and give her the vital clues she was seeking. But nothing happened. The sun beat down on her back and the flaking metal stained her hand. She suddenly had an overwhelming feeling of loneliness and isolation, like she was the only person alive in the world.

*

Robert fucked Susie Morgan three times and then sodomized her. He ravaged the girl with such unrelenting force that she lay torn and bleeding on the mattress. Cum and blood leaked from her battered anus and bite marks scarred her tits. He stood in the room and admired her. God, she felt so good. She wasn't whimpering any more. She lay motionless. Her eyes stared vacantly at the stained ceiling.

An old pipe clanked and rattled as Robert turned on the shower. It took a few gargles before cold water gushed out in spurts from the shoddy rusted shower head. He felt incredible. There was no better feeling than dominating a beautiful woman in the most unholy ways imaginable. The best was when it was against her will. That gave Robert extreme sexual gratification. It wasn't just the sadistic sex that drove his perversion, it was the thrill of the hunt. It was knowing he could end their life at any time. He was the master, the alpha and the omega. He was God.

This was Robert's drug. It was his addiction.

Robert always chose his victims carefully, usually a beautiful blonde who lacked confidence and looked vulnerable, just like Susie. He liked them insecure. He liked to build relationships with them. Slowly at first—earn their trust, learn their most intimate secrets. Then the affair would start. Robert met his prey in secret, enjoyed their company for a while, fucked their brains out, lured them into a false sense of security. He liked to give them the self-confidence they were missing. That was what fuelled Robert's ego. He enjoyed lifting up these damaged, broken women and making them feel self-assured and important. Then he destroyed them. That was what really ignited his fire, when he took it all away.

He cleansed himself with cold water, humming 'Halleluiah,' one of his favourite songs. He knew that soon he would have to offer Susie to Heaven. She was like all the other women who struggled and fought and pleaded for their lives. When he fucked them, they resisted. Always they resisted at first. But in the end, they succumbed. They realised their life was forfeit, their fate sealed. They grew submissive and boring. And when Robert became bored, he needed a new toy. He disposed of his prey, sought forgiveness in God, and started the hunt anew.

*

Feeling dejected, Jessa was ready to jog back to the hotel. She had been sure the water tower would trigger something in the recesses of her disjointed memory, but it didn't. It only provoked her anxiety, and now she was drained. She hadn't realised how weak she'd become. The jog from the hotel was only a few miles. She should have been able to go the distance without breaking a sweat. She'd eaten well today, but it was the first decent meal in a while. Coupled with the raging sun, Jessa was beat.

She retrieved her water bottle from her backpack and took a swig, then stuffed it back into her bag. She took out some of the printouts of the satellite images of the area to try and orientate herself. The road to her left led back to the hotel, and the main road ahead went to Winters. The unmarked road she was looking for was about a mile north and to the right. She wasn't sure if the road bore any significance, or if she would find anything at the end of it. However, according to the map, it was one of the few roads that passed through the fields of almond trees and she needed to check it out. Jessa needed to find her tree.

The scent of honey butter filled the air as the fields of cattle turned to fields of beautiful white almond trees. Row upon row spanned the countryside, the landscape a sea of candyfloss. It was the same view in every direction, miles and miles of white candyfloss. Trying to find the tree from her incoherent memory was going to be next to impossible.

*

Robert was in exceptionally good spirits as he drove home from the church. His doting wife would be waiting for him, and his daughter and her jerkoff boyfriend would soon be arriving for the BBQ. It was a blissful early evening and Robert was actually looking forward to throwing a few steaks on the grill and spending time with his daughter. It had been another perfect day in the life of the Holy Man. He had put on another great performance, had spent a joyous few hours with Susie, and now he could sit back and relax in the comfort of his lavish new home. God was good to him.

*

Jessa was beside herself with frustration. She paced her hotel room after spending most of the afternoon jogging aimlessly through rows and rows of almond trees looking for 'the one.' But they all looked the fucking same. None of them were magnificent or looked remotely like the one she needed to find. Jessa knew there were over 800,000 acres of almond trees in California, but she was adamant her tree was in Winters. The reality was that the tree could be anywhere and the likelihood of finding it, if it existed at all, was next to none! Her earlier optimism was gone. Nothing was playing out the way she had imagined. And now she had thrown herself into another state of total despair. Jessa had just arrived in Winters and already what little hope she had left was lost.

She stood at the door of the balcony in her bra and panties, looking at the lake and the boathouse. Her thoughts were a twisted mess of unintelligible voices, a storm of destruction brewing inside her. She switched on her mobile for the first time since Heathrow and it pinged like crazy, dozens of text messages coming through.

They were all from Vanessa, a few from Rads. She suddenly realised how badly she missed her girlfriend. She wanted Vanessa there with her, to huddle together on the bed and allow her fears to be soothed. She dialled Vanessa's number, wanting to hear her voice and say everything was okay, but the call went straight to voicemail and Jessa threw her mobile on the bed in frustration. She felt utterly terrified, lost in her own darkness and consumed by an unknown fear.

Across the gardens, toward the boathouse, a couple walked hand-in-hand, enjoying the early evening sun. Another couple stood by the edge of the lake and basked in the glorious view of the mountains. Jessa… she stood forlorn in her hotel room staring blankly at the darkening horizon. It was just her, alone, lost in a strange place with strange people.

CHAPTER 40

Vanessa cursed to herself when she saw the missed calls from Jessa. She felt disgusted. Her head pounded from the hangover. Seeing DI Radisson asleep next to her in Jessa's bed made her physically sick. What the fuck had she done? She nearly passed out as she launched herself out of bed, head spinning as she dashed naked into the bathroom. She just managed to make it to the toilet; puke sloshed into the bowl. She wiped her mouth and flushed, then sat on the bathroom floor with her back against the wall and her knees to her chest. The room was cold, but she didn't care. She wanted the world to swallow her. She was humiliated and ashamed.

How had she allowed this to happen? Vanessa had been feeling miserable when DI Radisson showed up. And she had been drunk. Had he taken advantage of her? No... Vanessa was fully aware she had instigated it, jamming her tongue into Paul's mouth like a fucking teenage whore. She put her forehead on her knees and cried, remembering how she had whispered in his ear, "I want you to fuck me. Fuck my pain away, detective."

Of course, Paul hadn't declined—hadn't even hesitated. But Vanessa was the instigator. She had been lonely, scared, pissed off. Vanessa had just wanted to feel loved, to be intimate with someone. She'd slept with men many times before meeting Jessa. She'd even enjoyed a threesome. But she preferred women, and she had never been unfaithful to Jessa until now. Shagging DI Radisson, Paul, whatever the fuck she was calling him—it was inexcusable. How could she ever forgive herself? More importantly, how could Jessa ever forgive her?

DI Radisson was leaning in the doorframe of the bathroom, nonchalant in his boxer shorts. "It wasn't that bad, was it?" he said, trying to be funny and defuse any tension. But seeing her naked on the floor was getting him horny again. For a lesbian, she sure knew how to ride a cock. Feeling ballsy, Radisson offered her his hand. "Come back to bed, Vee."

Vanessa shook her head. "You need to leave, Paul. I'm sorry. This was a huge mistake. It's a fucking mess and I don't know what I was thinking."

DI Radisson felt a little awkward now, standing in his boxer shorts with a semi-on. But more than awkward, he felt horny. He wanted more. He wanted to slap his dick off Vanessa's tear-streaked face and cram it between her dark lips. "Come on," he said, smiling like he was being cute. "Let's go back to bed. You didn't think it was a mistake last night when you rode me like a cowgirl."

"Paul, get the fuck out."

He sighed. "Fuck, Vee, at least let me get you back into bed. I'll make you a cup of tea or something before I leave. Come on." He bent down to lift Vanessa up by her arm, but she lost her mind.

"Get the fuck off me!" She ripped away from him, sobbing like a child. "Just fucking leave. Get out of this house!" She buried her face in her arms and cried. DI Radisson was just like every other pussy-hungry man. She was so embarrassed and so fucking angry with herself.

DI Radisson dressed quickly and climbed down the stairs leaving Vanessa naked and crying on the bathroom floor. As he closed the front door behind him and prepared himself for a fight through the overgrown brambles there was only one thought on his mind. He smiled to himself, feeling proud. He had the most amazing sex with a beautiful lesbian. His dream had come true.

Chapter 41

Was that really me? Was that how I looked before I died? It was horrifying. I looked so bony and thin, so broken. My collarbones and ribs protruded from my skin like a fossil under a tarp, my cheeks and eye sockets sunken horribly. The last part scared me the most. It wasn't what I saw (which was certainly horrific), it was what I felt. It felt like something calling out to me, trying to connect with me. I felt a sensation like the steady pulse of electricity. The experience has left me tortured, yearning to know more. I must discover why I was murdered and what happened to my body. Out in the darkness, the whiteness blooms.

I'm slapped across the face, the room spinning as I hit the floor. My vision goes black. A drone fills my head. When I can see again, there is a man above me shouting a hurricane of insults. The venom in his voice is frightening. He spits words like 'bitch' and 'whore.' I'm lying on a hardwood floor. I see, as I try to lift myself, that it's shiny and polished. I can almost see my reflection in the glossy wood.

Then my hair is yanked back and my neck almost snaps. I grab hold of his wrists as he drags me backwards across the floor, the polished wood like an ice rink. I'm dragged through a kitchen and down a hall, into a reception area. A grand staircase sweeps around to the left. I get the impression I'm in a luxurious house. Then I'm being pulled up the stairs by my hair, my arse and legs thumping painfully on the stairs. There are picture frames on the walls, the photos within them too blurry to discern. We hit a carpeted landing and I wonder what I've done to make this man so angry. He throws me into a bedroom and I crumple into a heap beside the bed.

Before I can do anything, he's on me again, lifting me with his strong arms and tossing me onto the bed. My face is buried in a soft red pillow. I scream when he punches me in the side, in my kidneys, in my ribcage. I think I'm going to pass out from the pain. But then he stops to rip off my panties. He's calling me a whore, a slut, a bitch. My insides tear as the man's penis violates me. I shut off my mind and try to escape...

I'm relieved to arrive at my happy place. It's a beautiful day here and there is not a cloud in the sky. The smell of honey butter fills the air. The painting stands on an easel in front of me and up ahead is the beautiful almond tree in full bloom. The water tower is just there over the trees, the mountains beyond. I'm safe here. I'm at peace. I once again marvel at how natural and realistic the painting of the tree is. There's something new in the painting, something I haven't noticed before. The tree is the main focus, but obscured in the landscape is a building. It looks far in the distance, white, a bell tower protruding from its slanted roof.

Looking past the painting, beyond the fields, I see it. There is a little white church nestled between the almond trees.

Chapter 42

Jessa woke with a jolt and a sharp stabbing pain in her side. Another horrific dream, this one lathered in more violence than she cared for. It felt too real. She still never saw the man's face, but she sensed he was strong and full of rage.

She lifted her vest and checked her side for any more bruising, but there didn't appear to be any. Her old bruises were still tender, but no worse than before. She thought about switching on her mobile to call Vanessa but decided not to. Her moment of desperation had passed. Maybe she would try calling Vanessa tomorrow.

Jessa ordered room service and sat cross-legged on the bed with a small continental breakfast and her usual array of papers and notes. It was only 7am and the day was already warm. As she sipped her coffee and picked at a bowl of mangos, she reviewed the fragments of information she had. There was nothing new. Her only real clues were the water tower and the hotel room she currently ate breakfast in. Neither one had yet to yield results.

Jessa wondered if she was looking for one man or two. Was the man assaulting her in the house and the man forcing her off the road the same lunatic or two different people? The man fucking her in the hotel room and the man beating and raping her in the fancy house—is this the same man? It was hard to say. Either way, the culprit(s) were strong and violent. Were Jessa investigating the case in an official capacity, she would have requested the hotel's guest ledger for the previous six months. She would be particularly interested in who had stayed in the Peacock Suite. She thought about going to the local police, but what could she tell them? *"Yes, that's right, I travelled from England to Winters, California because I'm experiencing strange dreams about being murdered and I believe my future murderer lives in your town."*

Yeah, probably wouldn't go over well. They would certainly think she was as crazy as her theory sounded.

Jessa knew she was missing something. Her mind kept wandering back to the beautiful almond tree and the painting. She figured the tree was the key to unlocking the truth to her fucked-up, far-fetched mystery. She needed to find it. But how to find a single almond tree among thousands? She'd be digging for a needle in the world's largest haystack.

*

Robert kissed his wife on the forehead before leaving the house, then she waved him goodbye from the front door as he rumbled up the driveway in his SUV. He had his suitcase stowed in the back, ready and packed for his flight to New York. It was seven o' clock Monday morning and he had a few hours to kill before starting out for the San Francisco International Airport. Tomorrow evening he was scheduled to appear on a live television talk show to discuss his increasingly popular program, The Holy Man. Apparently, people wanted to know how Robert had managed to make religion popular again on the west coast. He wasn't looking forward to the interview. It was more publicity and more of his face exposed to the public than he wanted. But the money was good.

To calm his nerves, Robert decided to spend a few hours unwinding. He'd pay a quick visit to Susie.

The smell of shit and piss greeted him. The windowless dungeon smelt like a fucking outhouse. Robert stood naked with his hand over his nose, glaring at Susie in disgust. He had been so excited on his way to the church, stroking himself through his pants while he drove. Now his penis hung flaccid overtop his hairy, wrinkled balls and all his desire was gone, replaced by anger and repulsion. Susie had shit and pissed herself. Runny diarrhoea had been vomited out of her ruptured arsehole. Brown, runny muck was splattered down her inner thigh, a muddy pool of shit between her bound legs. The smell was vile, unbearable in the stuffy room. Robert was gagging. He looked down at Susie and scorned her. "You fucking dirty little bitch." She wasn't beautiful anymore. Susie was just a putrefied piece of meat covered in shit and piss and she repulsed him. She had served her purpose. It was time for her to disappear.

*

After breakfast, Jessa went for a jog. There was a walker's trail around the perimeter of the lake and the entrance to the trail was only a short distance from the lake house. She was still unsure if the lake house held any significance, but it was a feature she remembered from her dreams. She thought it was worth having a look.

The lake house was, in fact, a boathouse. It was a rather elegant boathouse. But from the hotel window it had looked like a Victorian manor, its turreted façade and balcony overlooking the lawns and lake. It wasn't so extravagant up close, and reminded Jessa of a hollow building on a film set. The interior was open, filled with boats, canoes—kayaks hung on ropes from the rafters. A set of wooden stairs led to the balcony, but it didn't look well-used. The jetty ran out of the boathouse on stilts, going a short distance into the water. It took Jessa half a minute of nosing around to see there was nothing of interest. Still, she went up the stairs to the balcony, which wrapped around the entire building like a ring. She walked it, taking in a 360-degree view of the area and the spectacular scenery. The lake was beautiful, surrounded by rolling hills and thick forests. The Vaca Mountains touched the horizon at the farthest extent of Jessa's vision.

Under different circumstances, Jessa would have leaned over the balustrade and enjoyed the view for hours, breathing the clean air, basking in the warmth of the California sun. She couldn't remember the last time she had appreciated the natural world around her. She'd been so engrossed in work, so lost in personal struggles and tragedy, she had forgotten how to enjoy life, how to be thankful for the simplest things, like a beautiful view.

But Jessa didn't come to Winters for a holiday. She wasn't about to waste time on scenic views of lakes and mountains. She needed to find out what the fuck was going on. She needed to find her own killer.

*

Robert stood in the shower with cold water pouring over his head. He'd been in there for almost thirty minutes in a sort of dull delirium. His fingertips were wrinkled, his cock shrivelled like a bloodless worm, his lips bluish purple. Coming down from a high after a kill usually left him feeling physically drained yet wholly fulfilled. Killing Susie Morgan had left him with an infuriating cavity in his soul. He had wanted to spend more time with Susie. She had still been making him feel good, still satisfying his sadistic sexual urges. Killing her so early hadn't been in God's plan.

Seeing her there covered in shit and piss... There was nothing else Robert could have done. He had been too disgusted. The thing he had adored, his perfectly beautiful plaything, was reduced to a repulsive, stinking, festering piece of garbage. The only sensible thing had been to throw it away.

Assured he had cleaned himself of the blood and excrement, Robert towelled off and got dressed. He needed to get going if he was going to catch his plane to New York. He studied the TV monitor in the main chamber, same as he always did before climbing the ladder. The monitor displayed surveillance footage of the church and its grounds. There was no one around for miles.

Before leaving, Robert said a quiet prayer of forgiveness. Then he climbed the ladder and left Susie's lifeless body on the bed, wrapped up tightly in plastic.

*

The route around the lake was just over ten miles long, and Jessa was back in her hotel room, showered and changed before 10am. Her plan was to go into Winters and spend a few hours wandering through the small city to see if anything alerted her interest.

She entered the lobby and was met with an air of excitement. A crowd was gathered around a closed set of double doors on the other side of the room, talking and laughing. Jessa approached the front desk. "What's going on?" she asked the woman behind the counter, a brunette with too much makeup, fake tits, and a faker smile.

"A famous artist from San Francisco is showing off his new painting today in our wonderful gallery," the woman said in a slow drawl. She gestured to the double doors. "If you're a fan of the arts, ya ought to stick around. The gallery'll be opening in a few minutes."

"Thanks," Jessa said.

"Alright, well you have yourself a wonderful day, miss."

Jessa really had no interest in art, but she was thinking about the oil painting from her dream. It was a long shot, but maybe the visiting artist knew something about it. Maybe he had seen an exquisite oil painting of an almond tree somewhere recently. Maybe he knew who painted it.

The crowd was buzzing as the double doors to the art gallery pulled inwards. They scuttled inside like maniacs on Black Friday. Jessa sauntered in behind them. The gallery was more of a large hall with huge, vaulted ceilings. A red carpet furnished the floor and paintings hung on the walls, little blurbs about the artists tacked beneath them. There were four rows of partitions set at varying angles that ran the length of the room, each partition displaying various paintings. The crowd migrated to the far end of the gallery at one of the partitions, where black curtains obscured what Jessa assumed to be the artist's new masterpiece.

Jessa tucked herself in at the back of the group and waited for the painting to be revealed. The artist, a spindly little grey-haired man with a large red nose, addressed the crowd, thanked them for coming. Then the artist whittled on about something Jessa had no interest in hearing. She tuned him out, losing herself to her own thoughts. She imagined the black curtains slowly being drawn back to reveal a beautiful oil painting of the almond tree. Then Jessa heard him say, "Well, that's enough of me yodelling on. Ladies and gentlemen, I present to you a piece I have titled, The Tree of Adoration."

Jessa leaned forward, suddenly very interested in the artist and his painting. Her heart seized in her chest. Could it really be the one? She almost had her chin on the man's shoulder who stood in front of her. Glimpses of white and pink appeared in the gap as the curtains began to pull apart. Jessa nearly shouted when the curtains got stuck. The artist looked embarrassed, his red nose glowing like a beacon. He kept yanking on the strings. "A little help here, please?" Two hotel employees rushed over to help. Jessa had to restrain herself. She wanted to push through the crowd and yank the fucking curtains down herself.

"Sorry about this," he said with a nervous laugh, reminding Jessa of Woody the Woodpecker. "A little technical hitch. A couple of faulty curtains."

The hotel staff resolved the problem and motioned to the artist to try again. The artist said, "And for the second time, ladies and gentlemen, The Tree of Adoration."

The curtains pulled back to reveal an abstract oil painting of two lovers, their bodies shaped from the trunks, branches, and roots of two entwined trees. The lovers' hair made the leaves in bloom. It was quite exceptional, encouraging a few gasps from the crowd. Everyone cheered and clapped. Everyone except Jessa, who was disappointed.

People bustled to get a closer look, while others crowded the artist and tried to grab his attention. He beamed, relishing in the admiration. And now a knot of anxiety was forming in Jessa's stomach. Being around so many people was making her flustered. She wanted to ask the artist about the almond tree painting, if he had seen it somewhere. Artists were in and out of galleries all the time and surely mixed in the same social circles, Jessa thought. But the guy was swamped. She wasn't going to get an audience with him. Not with all the fanatics trying to shake his hand and take selfies with him.

She hung back and looked around at some of the other works on display. She wandered between the partitions, observing the paintings of landscapes and portraits and abstracts. Maybe one day, Jessa thought, she could appreciate the arts and enjoy a painting or a sculpture or a beautifully composed piece of music. She rounded one partition displaying a very large and uninteresting painting of the Golden Gate Bridge and walked in between two other partitions. And there it was. She had to clasp her hand over her mouth to keep from yipping. Her legs nearly gave out from under her. An invisible fist punched her in the chest. Hanging on the wall in front of her was the painting of the almond tree. It was her fucking painting! The one she had dreamt of. It was as if the image in her mind had been captured and transposed onto the canvas. The vibrant colours of the oils made the tree lifelike in a remarkable way.

For a moment, Jessa couldn't believe she was physically seeing it, that the painting was close enough for her to touch. There was no question about its authenticity. It was definitely the one. She examined it closer and saw a little white church painted into the background, and an involuntary laugh escaped her throat. She had been at the cusp of losing hope in her sanity. But this proved she wasn't nuts. The painting proved Jessa wasn't going mad. It substantiated her dreams and visions.

Ignoring the 'please do not touch' sign, Jessa reached out and delicately floated her fingers over the smooth oils. She was so mesmerised that she almost forgot to look at the most vital clue. She saw it at the very last second. The plaque on the wall next to the painting had the artist's name on it. Her name was Elizabeth Foster.

CHAPTER 43

Was this the break Jessa had been looking for? What connection did she have with Elizabeth Foster? The name meant nothing to her. Jessa needed to speak with the artist, ask him about Elizabeth and it just couldn't wait any longer.

The crowd around the red-nosed artist had thinned. Most people had moved on and were walking around the gallery admiring the other artwork. Jessa pushed through the remaining few people still heckling the guy and said, "Excuse me, sir."

"Excuse me, lady!" a rather portly Japanese man said. "Wait your turn."

"Sorry, this can't wait."

The Japanese man muttered to his friends in Japanese while the artist twiddled his thumbs, looking a bit uneasy. "Sir," Jessa said, glancing at the plaque next to his painting. "Mr. Simmons, I need you to look at a painting over there for me. It'll only take a second. Please, it's very important."

Mr. Simmons gave Jessa a somewhat nervous look. He didn't quite know what to make of the gaunt-looking woman standing in front of him who appeared very agitated. He glanced uneasily at the hotel staff, who read his face and began to make their way towards him.

"Please, Mr. Simmons," she said. "It will only take a minute and then I'll leave you alone. I need your expert opinion on an oil painting over there."

"Oh, really?" Mr. Simmons motioned the hotel employees back, giving Jessa a boastful little smile. "Okay, show me the painting," he said, gesturing for Jessa to lead the way.

She took him over to the painting of the almond tree. "It certainly is a work of art," Mr. Simmons said, admiring the sharp details. "The intelligent use of colour almost gives it a fauvism feel and the detail is utterly sublime."

"Have you ever seen this painting before?" Jessa asked.

Mr. Simmons shook his head, not taking his eyes off the painting. "No, but I certainly would like to see more work from this…" He paused, reading the name on the plaque. "From this Elizabeth Foster."

Jessa was surprised. "You've never heard of Elizabeth Foster before?"

"There are many painters from around the world who have their artwork displayed in this gallery. I must say, lady, I don't know them all. Now, unless you have any further questions, please excuse me."

"I do have one more," Jessa said clutching his forearm. "Do you have any idea where this scene could have been painted? I'd like to find this tree."

The artist frowned. "Why is this tree so important to you?"

"It's complicated," Jessa said, offering a weak smile. "But it's very important that I find it. Do you know where it is?"

"No. I have no idea. This tree might not even exist. It could have been painted from the artist's imagination. The person you should speak to is the artist herself. Now really, lady, I must be going."

And with that, Mr. Simmons scuttled away back to his own painting.

And once he was gone, the room started to spin. A fuzz creeped into the sides of Jessa's vision. The painting looked as though it had come to life. The tree swayed and swirled with the landscape, the colours fusing together. A powerful headache stabbed the back of Jessa's skull, nausea filled her stomach. The room spun faster, and Jessa knew she was about to pass out. She thought the strangers in the room were laughing and pointing their fingers, ridiculing her. Even Mr. Simmons with his shiny red nose mocked her. She needed to take flight, overwhelmed by an immediate urge to escape and get away from all the onlookers. As she stumbled for the double doors, one of the hotel employees approached her. He'd been keeping a watchful on her ever since she first approached the artist with the shiny red nose.

"Excuse me," he called out.

Jessa kept walking, trying to get out of the room quickly.

"Miss," he said, "I overheard your conversation. I know where the tree was painted."

Jessa stopped dead. The significance of the man's words reached her just as she was about to walk out the double doors. But as she turned to look at the hotel employee, the room gave a mighty spin and everything went black.

CHAPTER 44

The blanket of white stretches far off in front of me. If I could step out of the glass, I would find myself amid the light. The whiteness is slowly devouring the dark, and I am mindful it won't be long before it completely erases the blankness. This concerns me, for I feel that once the blackness has been absorbed, I too will be erased. I don't think I have long left now to find out what happened to me... before I am consumed by the light forever.

I'm standing in the art gallery next to the painting of the almond tree. The painting hangs on one of the partitions. I feel anxious. The alluring clothes I'm wearing make me uneasy about myself and I'm not sure why. I can see I'm in great shape. My short cocktail dress accentuates my figure. Why am I here? I wonder. The vision is vivid and I see the other paintings on the walls. I can make out the features of the people wandering through the gallery with champagne glasses and canapes. Then I see him.

Excusing himself from a crowd of people, he slowly makes his way to me. He's tall and handsome, greying hair and crystal blue eyes. I feel like a schoolgirl with a crush on my handsome, older teacher. It gives me a tingling sensation. I like his strong build, his expensive blue suit. He looks like a million dollars. I blush as he approaches me with a smile.

"Absolutely stunning," he says, looking at the painting of the almond tree. "Exceptional!"

He takes a sip from his crystal champagne glass and turns to me. His eyes are clearer than a perfect blue sky. I notice him marvelling at my body.

"Truly beautiful," he says. His smile melts my heart.

Then the gallery and the handsome man evaporate and I'm standing in the field, in my happy place, looking at the beautiful almond tree. The honey butter smell fills my nostrils as I take a deep breath. I spy the little white church beyond the tree. It's the size of a postage stamp in the distance. I have the urge to walk to it. I start walking across the field, the soft grass caressing my bare feet.

The memory flickers and wilts, and a sudden flash of light, I am standing outside the white church.

The wooden panels have been freshly painted white. Above the door hangs a sign: Freedom in Christ Evangelical Church. Another flicker and I'm inside a small office, lying on a wooden desk. My head sags over the edge and I see a crucifix hanging on the wall. I'm shaking, being throttled to and fro on top of the desk. Every nerve is electrified. I'm gasping in pleasure. My vision is blurry as I lift my head, seeing the handsome man from the art gallery humping between my legs. He penetrates me with force, a certain lack of emotion on his face. As I orgasm and scream with pleasure, he's staring at me with a look that pierces my soul.

CHAPTER 45

When Jessa came to, she was looking up into a throng of concerned faces. "Huh?" she moaned, trying to pick herself up. Her vision was murky.

"Take it easy, miss," the young hotel employee said. "The paramedics are on their way."

Jessa rubbed her temples, remembering the church, being fucked on the desk, and the man. For the first time, she had a clear memory of his face.

"Are you okay?" the young man asked.

"I'm fine."

"Just stay where you are, miss. The paramedics won't be long."

"I'm fine," Jessa repeated. "I don't need paramedics."

The hotel clerk twisted his face. "Well, they're on their way, miss. There ain't nothing we can do to stop them now. Let's have them check you over, okay?"

Jessa clambered to her feet. "I said I don't need the fucking paramedics. I'm fine."

The crowd gasped. A few of the onlookers backed away uneasily, afraid of the hysterical woman. The hotel employee looked around like he was lost, hoping a colleague would come to his rescue.

"I'm sorry," Jessa said, holding her hands up in surrender. "I'm fine, honestly." She checked the young man's nametag. "Juan, you said you know where the tree was painted."

"Yes," Juan said. "It's just outside town."

"And you're sure it's the tree from the painting?"

"I'm sure, miss. I see it from the road when I go to the church on Sundays. There's no other tree like it. I recognised it as soon as I saw the painting."

"Where is it, Juan? How do I find it?" Jessa was getting urgent, demanding more than asking.

"You go east out of Winters and follow the signs for the Freedom in Christ Evangelical Church. You'll see the tree a few miles down the road on the left, beyond the first few fields. You really can't miss it."

"What about the artist?" she asked. "Do you know who the artist is?"

Juan shook his head. "No, miss, sorry."

"Thank you, Juan." Jessa hugged the young man, then whispered in his ear. "Thank you so, so much."

And then Jessa was gone, leaving the crowd and the young Juan in shock as she rushed out of the gallery, passing the reception desk with the brunette and her fake tits, and a couple of bemused looking paramedics.

"Miss!" the receptionist called.

But Jessa kept going, damn near sprinting for the hallway. "I'm fine. I don't need paramedics." And she was around the corner and dashing to her hotel room.

*

Robert loathed airports even more than he loathed flying. He hated the hassle of the security checks, the queuing, and most of all, the waiting. Even the first-class executive lounge with its complementary food and drink didn't appease Robert's restlessness. The waiting was torture.

He presented himself as calm and relaxed as he perused the daily tabloids, sitting in a leather armchair overlooking the runway. But underneath Robert's calm exterior was rage. A fury boiled his blood. His insides felt like a pressure cooker about to explode. He wanted to scream and shout and rip someone's head off. He had been cheated by that stupid bitch, Susie. Why did she have to go and spoil what they had? She'd been so perfect. Robert had been looking forward to abusing her in ways she'd never allowed during their short affair. Her survival instinct, her determination in the face of Robert's abuse, had intensified his sexual deviance—he was angry that it was over. The filthy, stinking whore had gone and fucked it all up by shitting herself, denying Robert his ultimate orgasm. There was no way Robert would have stuck his dick into her after seeing and smelling all that rankness. Fuck, he could still smell it, the pungent aroma of shit stuck in his nostrils, making him feel sick.

Robert's plane was ready to board. He left the executive lounge and made his way to gate 50, not knowing how long he could contain his frustration.

*

There was a knock on the door as Jessa booted up her laptop.

"Miss Summers," a female called through the door, "please open up. It's the paramedics. We can't leave until we know you're okay."

"I'm fine," Jessa called.

"Miss Summers, please open the door. Once we've seen you're okay, ma'am, we can leave." The woman had that annoying American twang in her voice.

"Fuck sakes." Jessa jumped off the bed and walked to the door. "Thank you for your concern, but I really am fine," she said, undoing the lock and swinging the door open. She tried her best to smile.

There were two female paramedics standing in the hall in their bulky uniforms, one tall and dark, very attractive—her nametag said Candice on it. The other was short and dumpy with an arse as wide as the door; she looked totally pissed off.

"I'm sorry," Jessa said, looking only at Candice, "but you came out for nothing. I'm fine. I just had a funny turn, that's all. It must have been the heat."

"Are you sure you don't want us to check you over, Miss Summers?" Candice asked with a sincere smile. "It really would be no trouble."

"Thanks, but no. I'm fine and I must be getting on. So, if you'd excuse me..." She slowly closed the door, leaving Candice looking slightly perturbed and the dwarf with the arse the size of a small island looking like she was chewing a nest of wasps.

Before setting off in search of the almond tree, Jessa wanted to find out more about Elizabeth Foster. Sitting back on her hotel bed with her computer in her lap, she typed: *Elizabeth Foster, Winters CA* into the search engine. The first link was for an article written by the San Francisco Chronicle.

Local Artist in Critical Condition After Car Accident

Elizabeth Foster, a local artist from the San Francisco Bay area, is in a critical condition after swerving off Route 179 late Saturday evening as she drove home from Winters. The cause of the accident has yet to be confirmed, but no other vehicle is said to be involved. It is believed Mrs. Foster lost control of her vehicle, careened off the road, and plummeted 40 feet down an embankment. The vehicle rolled several times before becoming lodged between two trees. The trees saved the vehicle and Mrs. Foster from plummeting a further 150 feet down to Pleasants Creek and certain death. Mrs. Foster was found unconscious and in horrific shape by a pair of hunters who were alerted by the sound of the crash.

'The sound was deafening and horrifying,' said Mr. Bryant – a local man from Winters. 'It sounded like a bulldozer crashing through the forest.'

The Emergency Services were called and Mrs. Foster was cut from the wreckage and airlifted to Zuckerberg San Francisco General Hospital and Trauma Centre, where she is in critical condition with life threatening injuries.

The article was just over two months old. There was no photo of Elizabeth Foster with the news story, but there was an image of her car lodged between two trees. Judging by the crumpled mess of metal and rubber, it was a miracle Elizabeth Foster had survived the accident at all. The only other relevant link Jessa could find was for Elizabeth's art website. It showed photos of paintings she had for sale, although the painting of the almond tree wasn't anywhere on the page, and there was no photo of the artist herself. Jessa thought this was a little odd. The website did give the address of a small, independent gallery in downtown San Francisco where Elizabeth's paintings could be viewed and purchased.

Jessa scribbled down the address of the gallery in her notebook, added a few more notes, and even more unanswered questions. Jessa wrote:

Who is Elizabeth Foster and what connection do we have, if any?
- *Is she still alive?*
- *Zuckerberg San Francisco General Hospital and Trauma Centre.*
- *Visit the art gallery in SF?*

Where does the painting fit in all this?
- *Find the tree?*
- *Visit the church?*

Who is the male?
- *Description – Caucasian, tall, athletic, handsome. Approx. 35 years of age. Grey, slightly receding hairline, high cheekbones, square jaw, piercing blue eyes.*
- *Same male as the one in the hotel room? The car accident? The house?*

The article about Elizabeth Foster's car accident troubled Jessa. She wondered if it was coincidental that Elizabeth was involved in the same sort of car accident Jessa had dreamt of. Even though the article hadn't said much in the way of details, something about the accident didn't sit right with her. She needed to find out where the accident happened and visit the crash site.

Plenty of questions were still unanswered, and a lot of what Jessa remembered was vague—jumbled memories floating inside her head. But she was getting somewhere. Jessa was sure of it. She had the name of the artist, she had the painting, its location, and she had the man's face now engrained in her mind. His handsome features were imprinted on her brain. She was sure she'd recognise him if she saw him in the flesh. Jessa was also sure it was the same man in all her visions.

An involuntary shudder shocked Jessa as she thought back on her dream. It was not so much being fucked by him that haunted her the most, not even the pleasure of it. It was his piercing blue eyes boring into her core as he pounded her over the desk. His cold hard stare had been void of emotion, almost murderous.

CHAPTER 46

The first-class air cabin had no shortage of luxury, but to Robert it felt like he had been placed inside a time capsule, about to be put to sleep for the next five hundred years. They weren't stuffy seats like back in economy class. Each seat was its own spacious cubicle, private flat screen, nice headsets, leather reclining seat that could lay flat. He was an hour into the flight, and if it wasn't for the blonde stewardess with the nice arse and supple tits, Robert would have been climbing the walls in frustration.

Patsy was her name. She was stunning, and in some ways reminded Robert of Elizabeth. She was tall, sensuous, sexy in her unappealing uniform. Her hair was tied into a ponytail, a tumble of golden curls draped down the side of her pretty face. She wore a little too much makeup for Robert's liking, but he could still see Patsy's flawless skin underneath all the muck she had smeared on. And she kept glancing at him. Each time she toddled to and from the staff area, he returned Patsy's curious glances with a warm smile, making her blush. Patsy's red cheeks glowed through her overly applied foundation.

Robert pressed the call button on his seat. Patsy sauntered over to his cubicle all sexy like, bent down to turn off the button, and as she did, Robert breathed her scent. She smelt delicious. Although he had already seen her nametag, he made a point of looking at it, since it was pinned just above her breast. "Hello… Patsy. I could really do with a bourbon."

He looked into her eyes, holding her gaze while Patsy appeared lost in a sudden reverie.

It was a few seconds before she snapped out of it. "Certainly, sir." She was blushing. "Give me one moment, sir."

"Sure thing."

While Patsy went to fetch Robert's bourbon, his thoughts drifted to Elizabeth. She had been one sexy bitch. From the moment he set eyes on her, Robert had fantasised about all the filthy things he wanted to do to her. There had been so many women over the years, most of whom Robert had no inclination to remember. But Elizabeth haunted him.

The seatbelt sign pinged as the plane hit turbulence. Robert was distracted from his thoughts as an announcement blared inside the cabin, advising passengers to remain in their seats with their seatbelts fastened. Robert shrugged it off and went back to daydreaming about Elizabeth. The first time he saw her had been after he was invited to the annual art exhibition as a guest of honour at the Almond Tree Hotel in Winters. She looked awkward standing in front of a painting of the almond tree. Robert instantly sensed her vulnerability and made his approach. She was wearing an elegant slim-fitting cocktail dress. She looked like a million dollars, damn sexy, and every man in the room stole glances at her, fantasising about what they would do to her in their dirty little minds. The women leered at her enviously.

Again, Robert was disturbed from his thoughts. Patsy had returned with a crystal tumbler of bourbon. The seatbelt sign had been turned off.

"Sorry for the delay, sir." Patsy put the tumbler in the cup holder and a napkin on Robert's table.

"No problem at all, Patsy. It will be worth the wait."

Patsy hovered while Robert sipped his bourbon. "Sorry, sir," she said, crouching beside his cubicle, a little nervous. "Can I ask, are you the Holy Man from TV?"

"Yes," Robert whispered with a cheeky grin, "but don't tell anyone."

Patsy giggled. She glanced quickly at the curtain that separated the cabin from the staff area. None of her colleagues appeared to be watching. Robert wondered if there were any other stewardesses in first class. He hadn't seen any.

"I love your show," she said. "I try to watch it every week, you know, when I'm not flying. Your sermons are so wonderful, so powerful. You have so much passion."

"Why, thank you, Patsy. Have you ever been to one of my live sermons?"

She looked a little embarrassed. "No," Patsy said. "I tried once, but I couldn't get in. There were too many people. I honestly wasn't touting for a free pass, sir."

"I wasn't suggesting you were," Robert said, smiling politely. "But I will happily get you a free pass for any Sunday service. It would be my pleasure."

"Really?" Patsy stood up, her face beaming. "Thank you, sir. Thank you so much. That would be wonderful."

"It's no problem at all." Robert looked deep into her eyes. "And Patsy?"

"Yes?"

"Call me Robert."

CHAPTER 47

Jessa switched on her mobile. She wanted to make sure it had enough charge to take any photographs she might need—for evidence or reference. She was in surprisingly good spirits and eager to carry on with the investigation. She had already planned her day. The first task was to locate the almond tree and the church. Hopefully, one of these places would reveal a truth that Jessa desperately needed. Then, if time allowed, she would drive to San Francisco and find out more about Elizabeth Foster.

She looked at the time on her phone and wondered where the hell the day had gone. It was already mid-afternoon. The dual clock showed 6:30AM in the U.K. Her thoughts wandered to Vanessa. She really should ring her girlfriend and let her know everything was alright, assure her that she wasn't going crazy and that there was no need to worry. But Vanessa was probably still asleep. She never had been an early riser, Jessa thought with a smile. She sent Vanessa a quick text instead: *Hi, babe. I'm fine. Ring me xx J.*

It was a hot day, rays from the sun reflected off the lake, the water shimmering like a bed of diamonds. Just a short walk across the car park and Jessa was sweating. She never had liked the hot sun and was thankful for the air conditioning when she got into her rental car and started down Lake Side Lane. The hotel slowly faded from the rear-view mirror.

Driving through downtown Winters was like driving through a town made from Lego blocks. Winters was a patchwork quilt of square buildings, all different coloured façades lining the main thoroughfare. Even the road was paved with small red bricks. Jessa passed city hall, heading east, and came to a standstill at a stoplight outside the Putah Creek Café. Tables and chairs lined the walkway, happy customers enjoying coffee and beer in the afternoon sun. As the car idled, Jessa assumed the café was the bustling hub of Winters, since everywhere else looked dead. She wondered if it was worth a visit. And that was when she saw the missing poster on the lamppost.

She had just read the name: *Susie Morgan*, when the car behind her blared its horn. Some arsehole in a cowboy hat was waving his hand at her. The light was green. Jessa accelerated in a panic, tyres screeching through the intersection. In her rear-view mirror, the arsehole in the cowboy hat was shaking his head in annoyance before turning left.

Driving out of Winters, Jessa counted at least fourteen missing person posters tied to posts or taped in windows. She figured they had been put up recently since she didn't remember seeing them yesterday on her way through town. There were so many, they would have been hard not to miss.

Juan's directions were spot on. The signs for the Freedom in Christ Evangelical Church appeared as she continued her journey east out of Winters. **Believers, This Way – Evangelical Church** printed on a big arrow pointing down the road.

A few miles out of the city and there was nothing but fields. Another sign for the church directed Jessa left. Soon, the fields full of cattle turned into fields full of almond trees. Blankets of whites and pinks stretched along either side of the road like infinite oceans. Another sign stapled to a wooden post indicated the church was five miles ahead. And that was when she saw it. Even from the road the tree looked magnificent. It stood proud in the centre of a small clearing, overlooking hundreds of smaller almond trees like a queen standing amongst her army. The clearing was higher than the fields surrounding it, making it easy to spot. Jessa pulled the rental off to the side of the road and got out.

She felt a tingly sensation all over her body as she stood and admired the tree from the roadside. It was obvious why the artist had chosen to paint that tree rather than any other. It was stronger and bigger, and its bloom was fuller and more splendid. A white post and rail fence separated the field from the road, but Jessa climbed over it easily.

The rows of trees ran vertical adjacent to the one she needed to get to. There was no visible path directly ahead so it would be a matter of walking across the field for about a mile or so blind. She set off in the general direction of the almond tree. It was like being in a perfume store that only sold one fragrance. The smell was intoxicating; a little too much and Jessa began to feel a little nauseous.

Just when she started thinking the rows of trees would go on forever, she made it through to the clearing. Jessa walked out of the forest and up a steep incline, to a plateau, the almond tree even more spectacular up close. It stood solitary on the mound, the grass around it seemingly greener than the grass below. It was as if the tree was meant to be on display.

Jessa was tired from the walk and incredibly thirsty. The almond tree creaked and whispered above her as sunlight flashed through its white leaves. From where she stood, Jessa could make out the water tower far off and the mountain range beyond. In the other direction, she saw the sheen of the church's bell tower through the mist of cloud. It was almost camouflaged by the sea of white. Jessa would have missed it if she didn't already know it was there.

It was surreal now. Jessa had finally made it to the tree. She knew she was meant to find it, but still wasn't sure why. She'd been brought here for a reason. Why else would the tree keep reoccurring in her dreams? Something had brought her here. It was the key to solving her mystery. The only question was: why?

*

Vanessa sat cross-legged on the sofa. She was wrapped in layers of clothes, yet she still shivered from the damn cold. She had shed enough tears in the morning to fill an ocean and was finally done crying. Jessa's text message glowed on her phone screen. She had been debating for nearly an hour if she should reply. She decided to call instead. She hit the button and put the phone on speaker. It rang twice before Jessa picked up.

"Vee," Jessa said. She sounded excited. "I found it, Vee. I found the tree. I found the painting first in the art gallery at the hotel, then I found the tree. I'm standing in front of this beautiful, beautiful almond tree."

Vanessa had been rehearsing what she would say, how she would break the news to Jessa. She knew her mental state was fragile, and she wanted to let Jessa down easy. But her anger instantly flared and all Vanessa's frustration came rushing out of her mouth like a toxic avalanche. She lost her fucking mind.

"I'm leaving you, Jessa. I've had enough of your crazy talk. I'm done. I thought I was strong enough to help you, but I'm not. Your fantasy, your crusade—whatever the fuck—it's ridiculous and I can't take it anymore. You have no consideration for me or how I'm feeling. You just fucking left me here to stew and worry. I need to get on with my life, Jessa. I can't deal with you anymore. I'm done."

"Vee... Babe, listen to me. I'm sorry for leaving you the way I did, but I'm getting close. I know I am."

"Close to what?"

"Close to finding out who wants me dead, Vee. I'm getting close to understanding what my dreams mean."

Vanessa rolled her eyes, getting even angrier. "For fuck sakes, Jessa. You're sick. You're fucking sick and you don't even know it. You're mentally unwell. You need help. Don't you realise how crazy this all sounds?"

Jessa sighed down the phone. "I'm not going crazy, Vee. I'm not. Please, just give me a few more days and I'll prove the dreams are really trying to tell me something. They really do mean something. I just need to—"

Vanessa cut her off. "I fucked Radisson," she said.

Silence on the other end. Vanessa listened to the soft rasping of Jessa's breath. Then finally, "What?"

"I fucked Radisson. I feel terrible about it. It was a mistake. I was angry with you. I was scared, lonely. I'm not making excuses. I felt abandoned and I fucked Radisson. That's it."

Again, excruciating silence from Jessa's end of the line. Then she asked, "Where?"

"What?"

"I said, where did you fuck him?" Jessa's voice was ice cold.

"Does it matter?" Vanessa asked. "I had sex with him. Why does it matter where we did it? It shouldn't have happened, but it did, and I feel ashamed and stupid and—"

Jessa was gnashing her teeth. "Did you fuck him in my bed, Vanessa?"

Silence crept through the phone like a poison.

"Did you fuck Radisson in my bed Vanessa?"

"Yes. We had sex in your bed and I'm sorry. I'm really, really sorry."

More unbearable silence.

"Where are you now?" Jessa asked, her voice unnervingly calm.

"I'm at your house."

"Right. Pack your shit and get the fuck out of my home. I mean it Vanessa. You better not fucking be there when I get back."

There was a click as Jessa hung up the phone.

Vanessa let out a sob and dropped her mobile into her lap. But really, what else had she expected? Did she think Jessa would forgive her and tell her everything was okay? No, of course not. Vanessa knew there was no coming back from this. And all for what, a shag she didn't even enjoy? She had once again let down the only person who really loved her, betraying Jessa in the worst way possible.

"Fucking selfish," Vanessa hissed at herself through tears. "Fucking weak, selfish, narcissistic slag."

Jessa was disturbed, grief-stricken, and quite possibly delusional. Jessa had just found out she was adopted. She was alone in America and Vanessa had gone and fucked her work colleague. "Disgraceful," Vanessa muttered to herself. She got off the sofa and walked into the hallway. She retrieved her coat from the hook and put it on, bent down and picked up her packed holdall. As she did, she noticed the small photo frame on the oak table. It was one of few photos in the house, one that had always been there. It was a snapshot of Jessa and Vanessa outside the Greek restaurant on the quay. She remembered Jessa's dad had taken the photo. They looked so happy together, smiling in the glorious summer sun.

Tears streamed down Vanessa's face as she looked at the photo for the last time. Her heart ripped to shreds. Vanessa slung the holdall, the little bag filled with all her worldly possessions, across her back and quietly left the house. She pulled the front door shut, locked it, then slipped her key through the letterbox.

Vanessa's words echoed in Jessa's mind. Her knee's buckled and she had to bolster her feet to stop from falling. Ever since Vanessa left her last year, Jessa had hidden behind an emotional barrier to keep herself safe, to protect herself from getting hurt again. She had known it was a risk allowing Vanessa back into her life so quickly. But she really had missed her and needed her. With Jessa's dad gone, she hadn't had anyone else to love.

Tucking her phone in the back pocket of her jeans, Jessa looked up at the almond tree. Its branches reached across the cloudless sky like gnarled arms twisting and contorting beneath the canopy of colour. Something about this place made Jessa happy. She felt tranquil. It was strange to feel at peace when she should have felt angry and sickened by Vanessa's admission of fucking DI Radisson. But Jessa was calm. She thought about the fine line between love and hate. She thought that one moment you love someone unconditionally, and the next you hate them more than anything in the world. But Jessa wouldn't let herself be consumed by hate. She didn't want to waste her much-needed energy. She had more important matters to focus on than her cheating girlfriend, priorities that meant life or death. She needed to make sense of her dreams before she wound up dead. Nothing else mattered to her right now.

Jessa placed her hand on the trunk of the tree, fingers tracing the ridged patterns on the bark. The moment she felt the tree's woody surface, images flashed in her brain like jolts of intense energy. It felt like someone had attached live wires to her temples. A high voltage surged through her brain and the world faded to black.

CHAPTER 48

I'm not sure which I find more unsettling, being surrounded by complete darkness or what I now see before me. The expanse of whiteness has totally engulfed three sides of my glass prison and I feel trapped in a whiteout. The dark shadows glide like a choreographed dance through the light and pause occasionally in the air before floating off again. I have seen the occasional shadow emerge out of the whiteness like a spectre in the shape of a human form, before disappearing again into the ether. I am still unsure if they are other trapped souls or servants of the realm of which I am destined for. Whoever they are, I sense they are becoming restless. It feels like I'm on death row.

I sit with my back to the shrinking blackness and stare into the light. And then the colours come.

I stand as still as the tree before me, allowing myself to be smothered by the cool air. I inhale deeply and breath in the fragrance of honey butter. I think this is one of my most favourite places in the whole world.

I step closer to the almond tree and place my hands on its rough skin, my fingers caressing the coarse creases of the bark. I close my eyes and feel the texture through my fingertips. The rough, irregular patterns feel like a map of wrinkles, each one with a story to tell. As I move my hands slowly down the trunk, I feel the surface smooth and become warm as if the tree itself is alive.

I open my eyes. The tree is gone. I'm crouched in front of a man with my hands on his hips. He's leaning back against a desk, one hand supporting him and the other hand resting on top of my head. He's moving me in a gentle rocking motion. His cock expands deep in my throat as he ejaculates. The taste of his cum splatters my tongue. I wait until he finishes groaning before I take him from my mouth, his semen dribbling off my lip. I wipe it away with the back of my hand. I look up at him and see his toned body, his muscular arms riddled with tattoos. He watches me with those piercing blue eyes, a savage sort of expression on his face. Just above his shoulder I can see Jesus on a crucifix hanging on the wall and that's when I suddenly remember.

I remember his name.

CHAPTER 49

Robert had been struggling to contain his pent-up frustration all day. The last thing he wanted was to sit down for a meal with a bunch of arse-kissing, egocentric morons from the television network. But here he was, eating mediocre food in an expensive restaurant in the middle of New York City, enduring mindless conversation with a group of turds.

As the coffees were served, Robert's cell phone buzzed against his chest. He took his phone from the pocket of his blazer and looked at the text. *On my way*, it read. Robert waved the waiter away before the guy had a chance to place Robert's cup and saucer down on the table. He had no time for coffee, and no desire to spend any more time with the network arseholes.

"A secret date?" Rick asked, laughing like an imbecile and slapping Robert on the arm. The little fat man had been sweating since the moment he sat down at the table, his ugly bald head covered in perspiration. He was one of the top executives from the Late Show and was a total prick.

Robert tried to hide his disdain for the man, sliding his phone back into his jacket. He had only been acquainted with Rick for a few hours and already hated him. "Just my daughter wishing me luck for tomorrow," Robert lied.

Rick slapped him again, as if they were old chums. "You'll be fine," he said. "A strong, handsome man like you, they'll love ya."

Robert smiled, thinking, *if you slap me one more time, I'm going to rip your arm off and shove it down your fat fucking throat.* Then he stood up. "Gentlemen, thank you for your hospitality, but I really must call it an evening." He refrained from saying, *"I can't stand you fucking pricks any longer."*

Rick stood up, a good foot and a half shorter than Robert. "Rob, my man, the night is young. Are you sure you won't join us for a night cap? Some of us were thinking about heading over to the Slipper Room. They have a lesbo action variety show on tonight." Again, Rick chortled his annoying laugh and slapped Robert on his arm.

Robert saw himself grab hold of Rick's fat sweaty head and crash it hard onto the table. He would have loved hearing the little prick's skull crack. "Thanks for the offer," Robert said, looking calmly up to the heavens. "But I don't think the Slipper Room is my kind of thing."

"Yes, of course," Rick said, entirely missing the point. "You don't want to upset the big guy upstairs, do you?"

Robert couldn't get out of the restaurant and away from Rick and his cronies quickly enough. One more slap—one more stupid fucking remark, and Robert was sure he would have punched him into next week. It was hard to tell if Rick was joking or just plain dumb. Whichever it was, Rick clearly hadn't done his research. Inviting a reverend to a lesbian action show was one thing, but inviting a controversial reverend who had openly spoken out about homosexuality being a sin was just plain fucking ignorant.

The New York evening was cold, and Robert was thankful it was only a short walk to the Baccarat Hotel. The network certainly spared no expense with the first-class travel, the posh restaurant, and the 5-star luxury accommodation. Robert didn't think things could get any better, although he could do without all the pretentious bullshit.

Robert barely had enough time to shower and change before there was a light knock at his hotel room door. He checked his hair in the mirror, flexed his muscles, then went to answer it.

"Come in," Robert said, smiling warmly. "You look exquisite."

"Why, thank you," Patsy said. She strutted into the room like a model on the catwalk. "You look great yourself, handsome."

During the five-and-a-half-hour flight, Robert had applied his charm, amused at Patsy gushing over him the whole way. By the end of the journey, she had practically been eating out of his lap. She'd probably have sucked his cock there and then if he'd asked. She had made a point of telling Robert repeatedly that she was staying over in New York, not flying back to San Francisco until tomorrow. When Robert had suggested Patsy come over to his hotel for a drink, she agreed without hesitation. It was almost too easy.

"Wine?" Robert asked, stepping over to the wine cabinet. "Red or white?"

"Red please." Patsy was looking around the hotel room as if she'd never been in such a luxurious place before. "This room is amazing. It's almost as big as my apartment."

Robert poured two flutes of Pinot Noir and handed Patsy a glass.

"Thank you," she said. She bit her bottom lip. "Are you drinking too, Mr. Preacher?" Patsy was toying with him, raising her eyebrows.

"Of course. Wine gladdens the human heart." He smiled, then clinked Patsy's glass.

"Really?"

"That's what the bible tells me," Robert said, his smile devilish as he took a sip of wine and Patsy giggled.

Patsy walked over to the glass table, gulped her wine and put the flute down.

"Please," Robert said, "let me take your coat." He followed her to the table and put his own flute down, unwrapped her wool coat, then watched as she finished the rest of her wine. She looked amazing, even more now that she wasn't wearing her dour stewardess uniform. She was dressed in a tight pinstripe jumpsuit. Her breasts were fairly average, but perfectly shaped for her slim frame. Patsy's golden ringlets fell softly over her shoulders, a cute diamond stud in her nose. She was still wearing too much makeup, but Robert could look past it for now. She was also a bit too confident for his liking, but she did remind him of Elizabeth. Not so much her personality. In fact, she was the total opposite. But she did bare a remarkable resemblance.

Patsy walked over to the wine cabinet and took out a $200 dollar bottle of wine. "May I?"

"Of course." Robert put her coat over the back of a chair, thinking, *you are one confident little bitch, aren't you?* She was certainly different outside her work environment, confident and privileged. How often did she fuck the first-class passengers?

Patsy poured herself a glass of the expensive wine, then walked over to Robert and went to fill his glass, but he refused. "No, thank you. One is enough. Anymore and the big man wouldn't approve." Robert look skyward, as though blushing before God. He looked into Patsy's glazed eyes. She had either been drinking before she arrived or had taken something illicit.

With a playful huff, Patsy placed her flute and the bottle on the glass table. She stepped back and lifted herself up on her tiptoes, giving Robert a soft kiss on the lips. Before Robert had a chance to react, she crouched and began to unbutton his pants. As she took his cock out of his underwear, she looked up with a mischievous grin, then cupped his warm balls in her hand.

"Would God approve of this?" she asked, putting his penis in her mouth.

Robert leaned his arse on the glass table, closed his eyes and let his thoughts drift to Elizabeth, enjoying Patsy sucking him off. There had been many women over the years Robert had preyed on, abused, killed to appease his sexual desires. Elizabeth was the only one he always came back to. She was the only one who haunted his dreams.

But Elizabeth wasn't like the others. Yes, she was shy and quiet, reserved and lacking in confidence, but she was sexy as hell. She could walk into any room and make other women feel inferior without even knowing it. The most appealing thing about her (for Robert) was her vulnerability. Elizabeth was exceptionally beautiful, but she didn't realise it. Somehow, this had earned her real, emotional feelings from Robert, when he had never exhibited feelings for one of his victims before. It wasn't love. He was incapable of that. But it was something, some strange feeling he hadn't felt before with anyone else. He had wanted to string Elizabeth along for as long as possible, and he knew that when it came time for their final act, it would be pure heaven.

Shutting his eyes, Robert pictured Elizabeth. She had a look of vulnerability, so fucking beautiful. He looked down and it was Elizabeth sucking on his cock, not Patsy. His body stiffened and his erection expanded, and his orgasm exploded into the blonde whore's mouth. Patsy stood up, looking pleased with herself, and

164

began unzipping her suit. Robert stared absently through her, as if Patsy wasn't there. Thoughts of Elizabeth were haunting his mind. Elizabeth was the only one who got away.

CHAPTER 50

It was just past nine when Jessa woke up. She looked around the hotel room, disoriented and confused. The last thing she remembered was standing in front of the almond tree. She had no recollection of waking up after passing out, nor of arriving back to the hotel.

Jessa sat up in bed, fragments of her dream coming into focus. She suddenly wanted to vomit. She jumped out of bed and sprinted to the washroom and barfed into the toilet. She slumped beside the bowl and wiped spittle and puke from her mouth with toilet paper. She was disgusted. The thought of performing oral sex on a man revolted her. There was no way she would do it, not ever! Not even if someone forced a gun to her head. She'd rather die. And yet in her dream she had sucked the man's dick willingly.

She leaned over the toilet seat again and gagged and heaved. It made no sense. There was no way she would ever perform such an act on a man. It just made no sense.

Jessa stood at the wash basin and splashed cold water onto her face, trying to wash away the revolting memory. She cupped her hands and slurped some water. Her throat burned. She looked at herself in the mirror. She had lost more weight, her face a little gaunter and her skin a little paler. As she looked at the small bottles of toiletries next to the basin, her vision flexed and ebbed, and she had to brace herself on the porcelain bowl to keep from falling. She thought she heard a voice call out from the bedroom, and she spun around to look, almost losing her balance. For a split second, she saw him sitting on the bed. It was so brief, then the vision was gone. But there was no mistaking it. She knew now the man from her dreams was called Robert.

Jessa was worried she had left the rental car in a ditch somewhere. She had no memory of driving back to the hotel. What the fuck had happened? Yet to her surprise, the rental was in the car park, neatly tucked into a space at the front of the hotel without a scratch on it.

It was another warm morning as she climbed into the rental and drove south down Highway 80 to San Francisco. She had keyed in the address of the art studio she had found on the internet and was on her way to find out anything she could about Elizabeth Foster.

*

Patsy was as confident in bed as she was out of it, and it wasn't long before Robert lost interest in her. After finishing the expensive bottle of wine, she was willing to do almost anything. But Robert wasn't feeling it. Elizabeth weighed heavy on his mind, and Patsy's exaggerated, pornstar moans made Robert want to suffocate her with a pillow.

When she finally fell asleep naked beside him, she started to snore. This pissed Robert off to the extreme. She didn't look sexy to him anymore. She looked dirty and smutty. He had to will himself to keep his hands from strangling the life out of the filthy whore while she slept.

Just past 9am and Robert was showered and changed. He stood at the edge of the bed looking Patsy over as she lay on her front, naked and snoring. She had one leg bent up, and Robert could see a small tuft of blonde pubic hair between her legs. Just above her buttocks was a small tattoo of an angel with its wings in a V shape and a halo over its head. In that moment, nothing would have pleased Robert more than plunging a knife deep into her back and splitting her from neck to sacrum. He got an erection just thinking about it. Instead, Robert left the hotel room quietly, hoping he'd never see the slutty stewardess again.

*

The drive from Winters to the outskirts of San Francisco was uneventful with light traffic most of the way. As with most big cities, the traffic in and around the downtown area was horrendous. It took Jessa almost an hour to drive a few miles through bumper-to-bumper traffic before the Sat-Nav finally announced she had arrived at her destination.

The Minna Art Gallery and Studios looked completely out of place nestled on the corner of Minna Street. It was close to the city's financial district, and the single-storey building was swamped by towering office blocks for multi-million-dollar companies. Jessa found a parking space half a block away and walked. Even though it was warm and bright, the towering skyscrapers blocked most of the sun and made it cool and overcast.

The art gallery wasn't spectacular to look at from the outside. It had a single glass door and a gunmetal-framed window, a single painting on display. Before entering the gallery, Jessa studied the singular piece of art in the window and tried to work out what it represented. It had a 3D look to it. Jessa didn't know the first thing about art (she didn't care to know either), but she could see the artist had applied layers of oils to build mounds that jumped out of the painting, giving it deep, realistic crevices. Swirls of dark blues, blacks, greens, and whites littered the canvas, and after a minute Jessa gave up trying to figure out what it was. The title hanging beside the painting read: *The Deepest Sea*. The artist's name was Will Phelps, and the price tag was an astronomical $31,000 dollars. Even if Jessa did have an extortionate amount of money to waste on a painting, there was no way she'd spend $31,000 on one she needed the name of the artwork to give any kind of inkling of what the fuck it was all about. But what did she know about art? Not a damn thing! Jessa pushed open the glass door and entered the gallery.

The interior of the gallery looked like the Tardis. It spread far and wide and the floorspace was almost as big as the art gallery at the hotel. An expanse of light oak wood covered the floor and skylights lined the low ceiling, allowing much natural light inside. A café/bar area with table seating was just off from the main door, currently vacant. Paintings hung from the walls, sculptures of all sizes on display. And there was a woman in her fifties with short grey hair and enough foundation to fill Putah Creek, dressed elegantly in a dress too tight in all the wrong places.

"Good morning, ma'am," the woman said. "I'm Sandra, and how are you this morning?" Her smile was warm, but she had one of those annoying American accents.

Jessa forced a smile. "Hi." But she didn't offer her name. "I'm looking for paintings by Elizabeth Foster."

"Great." Sandra walked over to her counter and picked up a tablet. She tapped and swiped a few times, humming to herself.

"Ah yes, we only have a few of her paintings. If you would like to follow me, I'll show you where they're displayed."

"Thanks," Jessa said. She followed Sandra across the gallery, glancing at the various paintings and sculptures, paying close attention to the insane price tags for her own amusement. Many of the paintings were a few thousand dollars. A sculpture made from a jumble of old nuts and bolts and used tools had a price tag of $16,000, and a rather ugly painting of a fat woman with overly proportioned breasts was selling for $67,000. Jessa couldn't believe anyone would spend $67 dollars on such a ghastly painting, never mind $67,000. The painting looked amateurish and would only look good with the lights off. The artist was either taking the piss or completely insane.

Sandra noticed Jessa's interest in the painting. "Beautiful, isn't it? We've only displayed this piece for a few days and it's already sold."

Jessa continued to follow Sandra to the back of the gallery, thinking to herself she really didn't know the first thing about art.

"Here we are," Sandra said, standing in front of two small paintings and one slightly larger. "Are you familiar with Elizabeth's work?" Sandra touched and swiped the tablet.

"Not really," Jessa said. "I'm staying at the Almond Tree Hotel in Winters and saw a painting of hers there."

"Ah yes, the painting of the almond tree. Such a stunning piece. It's a shame we only have these three paintings of hers in the gallery. As you can see..." Sandra motioned to the paintings. "...Elizabeth is quite talented."

"Have you ever met her?" Jessa asked, pretending to take interest in the three paintings.

"No, I rarely get to meet the artists. I only work a few days during the week, you see, and the paintings are usually delivered by a courier. If the artist does bring their work in themselves, it's usually when I'm not here."

Sandra paused while she referred to her tablet. "So, it says here Elizabeth Foster is a local artist from the Bay Area. She likes to paint landscapes, as you can see from the pieces here. Also, she's only been painting for a few years. The small piece on the right is called 'A Winters Summer,' and I believe the landscape is not far from the Hotel where you're staying."

Sandra was still looking at her tablet. "It says here the piece is on sale for $1600. The other small painting..."

Jessa interjected, "I heard Elizabeth was in some kind of car accident."

"Yes," Sandra said, looking up from her tablet, a little taken aback. "It was a terrible incident."

"Do you know anything about what happened?"

Sandra looked hesitant, not offering a response.

"I've been looking for an artist," Jessa said, thinking fast, "to commission a painting for me. It's for a very special friend and I just love Elizabeth's work. Do you have any idea how I could contact her? I assume she's feeling better now."

Sorrow stretched down Sandra's face. "I don't think that will be possible, Miss..."

"Jessa. My name's Jessa. And why wouldn't it be possible? Money is not an issue. Even if she's still in recovery, I'd like to talk to her about working in the future, once she's better."

"It's not possible," Sandra said, truly looking sad. "Because the poor girl is in a coma. She's unlikely to ever recover from it."

CHAPTER 51

As the air-con cooled the car, Jessa's head ached from a disarray of thoughts. Who was Elizabeth Foster? Jessa was still unclear what connection they shared. It seemed unrealistic that they would have any future connection, since Elizabeth was deep in a coma. Sandra had told her that Elizabeth was in a private hospital somewhere in San Francisco on life support, and Elizabeth's family were from a wealthy generation of farmers and landowners. Sandra had also told Jessa that Valance, the gallery owner (who was generally away on business) was good friends of the family. Jessa had given Sandra her mobile number and asked if she would have Valance call her when he returned. But really, Jessa had left the gallery with very little hope of ever receiving a call from the owner.

Jessa's leads were quickly running out as the day crept toward early evening. She needed to find out more about the man, about Robert. She hoped the Evangelical Church in Winters would give her some clues. On her way back to Winters, Jessa ignored Highway 80 and opted for the scenic route, Route 179. She wanted to drive the road where Elizabeth Foster had suffered her tragic accident.

*

Robert returned to the Baccarat Hotel shortly after 11:30 in the morning, freezing his balls off. He hated the cold weather. He had chosen to have breakfast away from the hotel to avoid Patsy and had found a lovely eatery on 55th Street named Michael's, which served California cuisine. He was relieved when he returned to his empty hotel room.

The room was pretty much how he had left it. The bed was unmade, and the empty bottles of wine were on the table. Patsy had left a note on a sheet of hotel paper. It rested on the stained bedsheet, alongside her used lace panties. The note read: *Something to remember me – Thank you for a wonderful night, Mr. Preacher. Let's do it again. Call me anytime, you have my number. Patsy xxx.*

Disdain crept into Robert as he saw a single curly blonde pubic hair stuck to the black lace panties. If Patsy came back into the room at that moment, he would have strangled her with her own fucking lingerie. Did Patsy not know she was causing him a slight inconvenience? Although it was not a huge problem, Robert would have to dispose the panties appropriately. He couldn't leave them in the hotel for an employee to find, someone who may have recognised him and would go blabbing their mouth off. He certainly couldn't take the panties with him. He didn't want to risk forgetting he had them and his wife finding them. He had one more night in the hotel room, and it was due to be cleaned in a few hours. He needed to get rid of the panties fast. Robert was always overly paranoid when it came to disposing things he no longer wanted. As soon as he finished with them, they were just flotsam and jetsam.

Once Robert decided how he was going to dispose of the dirty underwear, it occurred to him he had a slightly bigger piece of garbage to get rid of back in Winters: the lifeless body of Susie Morgan.

*

The drive out of San Francisco was a blur. Jessa was on autopilot. She was wrapped in a dark blanket of angst and couldn't remember leaving the busy, four-lane highway and exiting onto Route 179. And now the urban sprawl of the city was turning into countryside. According to the news article, Elizabeth Foster's accident occurred on Route 179, somewhere near Pleasants Creek. The river flowed alongside the road for five miles before disappearing into Putah Creek. Elizabeth's accident could have happened anywhere on the five-mile stretch of road. The place was unfamiliar to her and finding the site of the accident, especially after two months (there would unlikely be any leftover evidence) was highly improbable.

Route 179 was much quieter than the busy highway, and the scenery was pleasing. Farms and small clusters of residential homes drifted by, the rest of the roadside blanketed in sprawling fields of cattle and crops. Most of the way was flat, but then the road started to climb and Jessa saw a blue undulated line on the GPS showing Pleasants Creek. She glanced out of the window but the creek was hidden by trees and foliage. The road kept climbing and then flattened again and Pleasants Creek was lost deeper in the valley. Tall trees replaced the fields, growing out of the valley below. A yellow convertible raced past Jessa in the opposite direction. She watched it vanish in her rear-view, realising it was the first car she had seen since driving the road.

Jessa's anxiety was subsiding. Her senses were becoming more attentive. She scanned the road and the verges, hoping to spot a broken or missing barrier, maybe a newly replaced one. Even tire tracks left on the road by a vehicle skidding across the tarmac. But a mile on and there was nothing noticeable. She hit a bend in the road and the familiar mountain range came into view in the distance.

As the road started to straighten out, a flash of memory hit Jessa behind her eyes, causing her to reel in surprise. Her head snapped back and hit the seat. Her vision went blank for a split second and she lost control of the car. Another jolt of memory hit her and this time she tensed, involuntarily pressing the accelerator. The car kicked forward and sped up and Jessa passed out.

CHAPTER 52

The explosion of light takes me by surprise, and suddenly I'm driving down a remote stretch of road. I know that it's Route 179 and I'm bound for San Francisco. My cheeks are sticky from crying. I feel angry and stupid. Air flows in through the windows but does little to cool the burning sensation on the side of my face. In my rear-view mirror is a full moon. I remember why I'm here, driving down this desolate road in the night. I'm getting away from the man in the hotel room. I'm getting away from Robert.

A car's headlights glare in my side mirror as a vehicle speeds towards me. It's him. It's Robert! He's coming for me. My heart jumps as his SUV almost ploughs into the back of my car. He's driving erratically behind me, speeding up, braking like a mad man, flashing his lights. Then he swerves into the oncoming lane and accelerates beside me. He's shouting and pointing through the open window. Robert's face is full of rage. I have to get away, but his SUV is too powerful. He speeds past me and swerves, then brakes hard. My tyres screech as I hit the brake. I skid and snake across the road, breathing in gasps as my heart races. I spin out of control and it's a miracle I avoid careening over the bank.

Robert opens the SUV. I remember our fight in the hotel room. I remember clawing and scratching at his eyes, and I remember him backhanding me across the face. As he walks to me, I want to press the ignition. I want to go, but I'm paralysed. He's getting closer. I suddenly remember running from the hotel room, running away from Robert with his baby inside me.

CHAPTER 53

She heard a burring noise. It was faint at first, then it quickly grew louder and louder. Jessa jerked awake, eyes snapping open. Instinct took over and she pulled hard on the steering wheel. The car screeched and snaked across the road, narrowly missing an oncoming car and hitting the verge. For one terrifying moment, she thought the car was going to crash through the metal barrier and dive into the valley below. She stomped hard on the brake, fought with the steering wheel, and another oncoming car blared its horn. Jessa skidded to a halt on the side of the road. The car passed and kept going. Jessa kept gripping the wheel as if her hands were soldered to it. She shuddered, hyperventilating, staring out the window. She had narrowly escaped death and the sheer thought of it made her burst into tears.

"What the fuck is going on?" she asked herself through deep sobs. The vision had only lasted a second, but it was long enough to leave a disturbing impression in Jessa's mind.

I was pregnant, she thought. *I was fucking pregnant.*

Jessa slammed her palms down hard on the steering wheel. "What the fuck am I doing?" she screamed. "Why am I here? None of this makes any sense. If my dreams are prophecy, how am I going to get pregnant? There's no fucking way. It's inconceivable."

She felt desperate and alone... so fucking alone. Jessa was in the middle of her own living nightmare and the few people she could rely on in her life were either dead or may as well be. She was on her own.

Unbuckling her seatbelt, Jessa scrambled out of the car, leaving the door open and the keys in the ignition. The car pinged at her as she walked away, hands on her hips, a few yards along the verge, sucking in deep breaths. She was distraught, trying to console herself. Jessa had no one to turn to and nowhere to hide. She was terrified the dreams of her future would play out, and she didn't want to wait for that to happen.

Stepping close to the safety barrier, Jessa looked down into the ravine. It was a steep drop into a ridge of trees, then the bank fell away into the creek. She felt a sudden urge to jump. She could end her misery here and now. Her future could change with one fatal leap. It would be so easy.

Instead, she stepped away from the edge and screamed hysterically.

Jessa didn't remember going back to her hotel room. She woke on her bed with an empty space in her memory. It was early evening and her stomach ached from hunger. She hadn't eaten a single thing all day. Jessa went to take a shower to rid herself of the weird, groggy feeling bogging her down. She would freshen up before heading into Winters.

*

The thought of having to meet the fat little prick again made Robert's skin crawl. Luckily, Rick couldn't make it, and Robert arrived at the television studio and was met by Brad, one of Rick's assistants. Brad reminded him of a certain black comedian, and was thankfully more amiable than his sweaty, overweight boss. Brad explained Rick had been delayed by 'technical issues,' but would hopefully catch up with Robert before the show. Robert hoped he wouldn't.

There were still a few hours before the show started, and Brad showed Robert to the guest lounge, where he could relax and enjoy complimentary food and drinks and meet the other guests on tonight's broadcast. Honestly, Robert couldn't have imagined anything worse. Mingling with a rock star he'd never heard of, who had apparently just gotten out of rehab, and an English actor promoting a new film he'd never watch, was going to be intolerable. But it was something Robert had to do to satisfy the TV network that sponsored The Holy Man. They told him the exposure would be good for the show, and more viewers meant more money.

The guest lounge had three large leather sofas lined before an enormous flat screen, a bar attended by a beautiful Asian woman, and a few tables covered with food. Apart from the hostess behind the bar, the lounge was empty. Robert figured he was the first guest to arrive. Brad told him to make himself comfortable and ask Rosa, behind the bar, if he needed anything. Robert would be called for hair and makeup shortly, and when the other guests arrived, they would all get to meet the host, David O' Carra, before the show went live on air. Robert went to use the toilet before asking the Asian girl for a drink.

The restroom was nice, the air scented with aromatic perfume. Expensive tiles gleamed from the floor to the ceiling, modern bathroom furniture and fancy décor. Robert went into one of the cubicles and locked the door. From the inside pocket of his suit, he took Patsy's used panties and dropped them into the toilet. It took three goes to flush the rancid things away.

When Robert walked back into the guest lounge, he saw a tall, scrawny, long-haired man in white leather pants and a ripped t-shirt leaning unsteadily on the bar, chatting up the Asian hostess. The man was a throwback to the rock stars of the early nineties. Rehab clearly hadn't done him any favours.

*

The Putah Creek Café was busy. It was certainly the place, if not the only place, to go for an evening out in Winters. The outside patio was crowded with rowdy customers, everyone laughing and enjoying the last of the evening's warmth. Even the bar was busy with standing patrons, dozens of conversations echoing inside the café. The music from the jukebox was barely audible over the clamour. A basketball match played in silence on the TV screens over the bar.

Jessa managed to find a vacant stool at one end of the bar and perch herself on it. The young bartender with fiery red hair came over and placed a menu on the bar, then raced off to serve other customers. Jessa wondered if the café was always so full. It was only midweek. She had hoped to strike up conversation with a few locals, or even the bartender. She wanted to know if anyone knew Elizabeth or Robert, and was planning to ask some questions about the Evangelical church, but the bar staff were clearly too busy for a chat. The noise in the café was too loud, and the customers were too absorbed in their own conversations. There was nothing Jessa could do but to wait for the raucous atmosphere to die down. She decided to eat something and ordered a California chicken salad and a glass of house red. She sat staring absently at the TV screen, lost in her own thoughts when someone touched her arm.

She ignored it, thinking someone had only brushed past her. Then they touched her again. It startled Jessa and she almost knocked over her glass of wine turning to see who it was.

"Miss Summers."

She was tall, dark, and very attractive. She smiled amiably at Jessa, but Jessa didn't recognise her.

"Miss Summers, it's Candice, the paramedic from yesterday. We met at your hotel room."

"Oh, yes." Jessa had to shout above the noise. "Sorry, I didn't recognise you out of uniform."

Candice indeed looked different without her uniform on. Her hair was down and she had tasteful makeup around her eyes. She wore a bright, casual dress. Candice was attractive. She said, "I saw you come in and thought I'd say hello, see if you were okay. You know, after yesterday."

"I'm fine," Jessa said, trying to sound convincing. Candice was a pleasant distraction and her cute smile made Jessa blush. "I'm not used to the heat. We don't get this much sun in England."

A loud burst of laughter erupted from a group of middle-aged men standing behind Candice, and a few of the men threw glances at her. Candice raised her eyebrows, winked at Jessa, then turned to the group. "You're going to send that old heart of yours into cardiac arrest with talk like that, Frank. And you know you're not my type."

Frank's nose was tinged purple. He had a port belly and was clearly no stranger to beer and greasy cheeseburgers. He gave Candice a huge smile. "One day, my luscious stick of candy," he said in a drunken slur, "you won't be able to resist the charm of this body." Frank's friends laughed as he patted his bulbous belly.

"Don't encourage him," Candice said to them, laughing as she turned back to Jessa.

"Luscious stick of candy?"

Candice raised her eyebrows again. "Frank has always called me candy, ever since I saved his life after his heart attack last year. I hate it, but I have given up trying to correct him. He's harmless, really, and kind of sweet."

"As sweet as candy." Jessa remarked

"I certainly am," Candice said. She gave Jessa an alluring smile.

*

Robert had just witnessed the rock star, Hudson Hood, from the band the Hoods, make a total jerkoff of himself on live TV. Hudson was listed as the last guest to be interviewed, so he could play the show out with his band. But he was wasted before the show even started. He was a total embarrassment, and Robert found it highly entertaining to watch it on the large screen in the guest lounge as Hood's band looked on in horror. At the start of the interview, Hudson almost fell asleep, and at one point nearly slipped out of his chair. David O' Carra tried his best to carry on with the interview, but Hudson couldn't give an intelligible response, and the interview was swiftly ended. The TV network cut to commercial and one of the band members had to rush onto the set and drag the singer away from the cameras.

Robert was now sitting in the big leather armchair beside David's desk, beaming in front of the cameras and live audience. He felt calm and relaxed. No matter how controversial his interview was going to be, Robert knew it would be insignificant compared to Hood's. Hudson had done him a favour and the media and tabloids would have a field day tomorrow exploiting his antics. No one would remember Robert.

*

Most of the rowdy clientele had dispersed, leaving the Putah Café less crowded and far less noisy. Jessa had finished her salad and was starting to relax. She liked Candice's company. They had moved to a table opposite the bar and were sharing a bottle of red and enjoying light conversation. Jessa hadn't offered too much in the way of her life story, saying only she was on vacation from England for a few weeks. Candice had been a little more open, telling Jessa she had grown up in Los Angeles and moved to Winters a little over a year ago to get away from the city and a bad relationship. She moved to Winters because it was generally a safe place to live,

179

although the recent disappearance of poor Susie Morgan was the talk of the town. The tragedy was on everyone's minds. Candice knew the Morgan family reasonably well. They were good, honest, church-going people and she really hoped Susie would return home safe and sound.

"I've seen the missing person posters all over town," Jessa was saying. "Any idea what could have happened to her?"

Candice took a sip of wine; a small droplet hung on her bottom lip. "No," she said, and licked the red droplet away. "Some people think she's run away. Her parents are devoted to the church, as was Susie—or so it appeared. But the rumours are that Susie had had enough and just left the area. I hope the rumours are true, but I don't buy it. Susie was an active member of the Evangelical church and was always involved in the community events and fundraising. She would do anything for anyone, and she loved her family. I doubt she left them high and dry."

"She looks pretty in the photos," Jessa said. "Did she have any boyfriends?" Jessa was starting to feel like she was interviewing a witness.

Candice shrugged. "Not that I'm aware of. If she did, she was keeping it a secret."

"So, you think she could have been abducted?"

"I honestly don't know," Candice said. "I saw her a couple times in passing a few days before she disappeared. She didn't look like her usual self. Something about her was different, wrong. I told this to the police after she was reported missing, but they weren't interested in my feelings. I'm pretty sure they think Susie ran away."

Candice looked troubled by her thoughts. Then she smiled across the table. "Anyway, I'm sure she will turn up safe real soon."

"Do you ever go to the church?" Jessa asked.

Candice said, "No," a little too quickly. "The church has turned into a bit of a circus. Anyway, I'm not really into all that praise the lord stuff."

"What do you mean a circus?"

"Well, the reverend has become a bit of a celebrity. His preaching has gotten so popular that he now has a TV show every

Sunday morning, and some of his more controversial sermons have even been supported by Donald Trump." Candice shook her head in disbelief as she said this.

Jessa asked, "Controversial?"

"He openly supports anti-abortion and believes anyone who aborts a child will go to Hell. And he believes all homosexuals are sinners." She looked hard across the table and Jessa. "And I ain't no sinner."

Jessa took a gulp of wine, holding Candice's gaze. "Nor am I."

They looked across at each other, repressing their grins. The background music was suddenly silenced as the volume on the TVs was turned up. The bartender was fiddling with the remote. Conversations hushed as the other customers focused on the TVs.

"Fuck," Candice whispered, nodding at the screens. "There he is now. Our famous reverend is on the David O' Carra Show."

Jessa's heart stopped beating for a few seconds. It felt like time had stopped. On the televisions was the man from her dreams. Robert Flores sat in a chair on live TV, being interviewed by David O' Carra.

*

Somehow, Robert was enjoying his experience. The interview was going well. He felt the live audience was responding kindly to him. David O' Carra, whose face was unusually orange under the lighting, hadn't asked any thorny questions yet. But Robert was sure it was only a matter of time before he did. Still, Robert wasn't worried. He knew the contentious questions were coming and he was prepared for them.

"The Holy Man is becoming quite a phenomenon," David said, smiling at Robert. His white teeth gleamed. "Your last show reached nearly four million viewers." David turned and beamed at the camera. "And I didn't think religion was fashionable these days!" Then, back to Robert. "So, tell me, why do you think your show has become so popular? Do you think our fearless leader has anything to do with it?"

Laughter spilled from the audience.

Robert smiled warmly before answering. "Well, David, I think religion has lost its way over recent years. Too many people are afraid to be open and honest about their faith. In this world of political correctness, the word of God has been watered down so not to offend people. I preach from the heart and I speak God's word as it was intended. So many people have had their true beliefs suppressed for too long, simply to concur with society, feared of being ostracised. I believe that through the true meaning of God's word I give people their hope back. I give them the encouragement and strength to stand up in their own social circles and express their beliefs without feeling restrained."

The audience erupted in applause. Robert waited for the cheering to dissipate, then leaned to David, pretending to speak inconspicuously. "And it has nothing to do with Trump."

More laughter from the audience.

"Well," David said, "you're certainly no stranger to controversy. You've had some bad press recently, particularly about your homophobic views and support for anti-abortion. We know Trump is a fan of yours, but what do you say to those people who have referred to you as…" David picked up a newspaper and read aloud to the camera. "A fascist, a homophobe, and a traitor to God."

"I am simply repeating the words of God," Robert said, "from the bible and elucidating HIS message. Everything I preach is from the holy book. It's all there in black and white. Some people fear God's word. Fear has been planted in all our lives by the Devil. Anyone can overcome their fear by putting their trust in God's word, knowing his words are altogether true. I am neither a fascist nor a homophobe, and I am certainly not a traitor to God." Robert looked straight into the camera. "I simply preach the word of the Almighty One as it was intended."

"But didn't you say homosexuality is a sin and all gay people will burn in Hell?" David asked, receiving a jeer from the audience.

For a split second, anger flared in Robert's face. But he quickly regained his composure. "This is just untrue, David. I have never said gay people will burn in Hell, and there is no such reference in the bible. Yes, homosexuality is a sin because the bible condemns it as a sin. God created a man and a woman to carry out his command to fill and subdue the Earth. Homosexuality cannot fulfil that mandate and anyone who commits or supports homosexuality will have a heavy judgment administered by God himself."

There was a mixed response from the audience, boos and hisses mixed with cheering and clapping.

"Sounds like you've split the opinion on that one, Robert," David said. "You've also received mix reactions about your belief in abortion. Although, the president does support you on this and even took to the internet recently after one of your sermons. He wrote: *Abortion is murder and murder is sin. Thou shalt not kill!*

Robert shifted in his chair. "God gave us the miracle of life, David, and when God creates the miracle of life inside a woman's womb, not one of us has the right to extinguish that life. It is sacrilege to decide an unborn child must die just so people can continue to live their lives as they wish. Abortion is murder against the innocent and if we accept that a mother can choose to kill her own unborn child, how can we tell other people not to kill one another?"

David addressed the camera, shining his white smile. "Some strong views here from a reverend whose television show is becoming almost as popular as mine. Ladies and gentlemen, join me after the commercial break."

CHAPTER 54

I'm lying on my back, looking into Robert's electric blue eyes as he lies over me. My legs are propped over his muscular shoulders and my wrists are extended above my head, tied to the bed posts. He thrusts into me hard and his thighs slap against my buttocks. I scream in pleasure. He thrusts again and again and I pull on my bindings. The fabric bites into my skin, the pain pleasurable. I stretch my head back and expose the full length of my neck, looking up at the peacocks before I close my eyes. Robert's strong hands close around my neck. My air is restricted, and I quickly get lightheaded. Robert drives his big cock into me and clamps his hands tighter around my windpipe. I'm on the brink of passing out. Then he lets out a roar and releases my neck, cumming inside me. An earthquake of pleasure spreads throughout my body. Every muscle stiffens as I relish my most powerful orgasm.

Now I'm lying on the bed next to Robert. My arm rests across him, my fingers playing with his hairy chest. His heavily tattooed arms are crossed behind his head, Robert staring up at the ceiling. It feels like the right time to tell him. I say to Robert that I love him and that I'm carrying his baby inside me. I kiss his shoulder. At first, he doesn't respond. I think I may have spoken too softly. But then he explodes. He lifts himself up and gives me a pitied look. It's now I remember the promises he made to me. Robert promised he would leave his wife so that we could be together. Robert promised to protect me. I see he's disappointment and even repulsed.

I realise his promises were lies.

CHAPTER 55

Candice leaned across the table and clasped Jessa's hand. "Jessa, are you okay?"

Jessa looked dull, confused, and totally absent. She was lost in the aftermath of the dream. Consensual sex with the preacher or with any other man would never happen, not fucking ever. And falling in love with a man was impossible. Getting pregnant was physically possible because Jessa wasn't on any contraceptive medication. But then why would she be? She was a lesbian. Jessa felt fear clawing upwards from the pit of her stomach. Nothing was making sense. She suddenly wondered if Vanessa had been right all along. Maybe she was going crazy.

"Jessa," Candice said, a little sharper, "are you okay?"

The dreaded black mist began to form behind Jessa's eyes. She felt the blackness coming.

"Jessa?" Candice got up and moved over to her.

"Yes," she said, staggering back into reality.

"Are you okay? You look like you've seen a ghost, Jessa." Candice put her fingers on Jessa's wrist. "Jesus, girl, your heat is racing."

Jessa shrugged it off. "I'm fine. Honestly, I'm fine. I think I drank a little more wine than I should have." Jessa glanced at the nearest TV screen. The host was talking to a different guest, some guy she didn't recognise. "Sorry, Candice, but I need to go."

"Okay... Where do you want to go?"

Jessa hadn't intended on drinking any more than a single glass of red wine, but between them, they had finished two entire bottles. Jessa was in no state to drive, so Candice suggested they walk the few blocks back to her apartment. She said the fresh air would do them both good. She promised to call Jessa a cab from there.

They were sitting on the sofa in Candice's second-floor studio apartment, overlooking Main Street and drinking soda water. Candice's apartment had an African theme, the paint a warm orange, prints of elephants and zebras on the couch, African masks hanging from the walls, a cluster of wooden giraffes in the corner. There was a statue of a tribal woman on one of the console tables.

"So," Jessa said, "you like Africa then." She had never seen so many ornaments in one small room.

"Just a little," Candice replied with a smile. "My dad is originally from Kenya. He took me on vacation there after I graduated and I fell in love with the country. He goes back nearly every year and always brings me back one or two souvenirs. Have you ever been?"

"To Kenya!" Jessa laughed, shaking her head. "California is my first trip outside the U.K. I mean, my parents used to take me on holidays to Europe when I was little. But as an adult, this is my first trip abroad."

"Wow, and you chose Winters of all places?"

"I'm a bit of an art geek," Jessa lied. "I found out the Almond Tree Hotel is quite famous for its art exhibitions, so I decided to check it out. Besides, I've always wanted to visit San Francisco."

"You know what," Candice said, a sly smile spreading her dark lips, "I have a few days off next week. If you're still around, I'd be happy to show you the sites."

"Sounds good. I may take you up on the offer. There are a few galleries I'm interested in checking out. There's a local artist. Her name's Elizabeth Foster. I really love her paintings and I want to buy one before heading home. Have you heard of her?"

Candice shook her head. "No, can't say I have."

There was an awkward pause. Jessa checked the time. "It's late. Maybe I should go. I really don't want to keep you up."

"It's fine," Candice said, a little too fast. She clearly didn't want Jessa to leave. "I'm on late shift tomorrow, so I don't have to get up early." She hesitated. "You can stay, if you want..." She touched Jessa's hand. "I'd like you to stay."

Jessa didn't say a word. She looked at Candice's hand folded over hers and was plunged into a sudden vision of Vanessa grinding on top of DI Radisson. This was followed by a flash of the Reverend fucking her on the hotel bed.

"Or... I could call you a cab."

"No." Jessa was firm. "I want to stay with you." She leaned over, heart fluttering, and kissed Candice.

They kissed tenderly, and Jessa pushed Candice flat on the sofa and licked her lips. As she did, she cupped one hand around Candice's breast and caressed her nipple through the thin fabric of her dress. Candice moaned softly as Jessa's other hand slipped up her thighs and pulled aside her panties, wriggling her finger into Candice's wet slit. Jessa was desperately trying to block out the images of Robert. She kissed Candice harder, fucking her vigorously with two fingers.

"Slow down," Candice whispered. "We have all night."

But more images were corrupting Jessa's mind. She saw herself kneeling in front of Robert, giving him a blowjob. Jessa had to fight back tears as she lifted Candice's dress above her hips and pulled down her panties, exposing Candice's dark, moist vagina. She wanted to feel the love of a woman. She needed to reassure herself she was gay. Jessa licked the soft dark skin around Candice's inner thigh, the fire igniting between her own legs. Candice groaned with pleasure, intensifying Jessa's arousal. Like an erupting volcano, sexuality surged through Jessa's body.

And that was when the revelation dawned. Maybe the dreams weren't insights into Jessa's future. Maybe they weren't her dreams at all.

*

The smell of fried eggs and bacon filled the room, rousing Jessa from sleep. Her head ached from the wine and she would have happily lay in bed all morning, but the smell of sizzling bacon pulled her out of it. She always felt remarkably hungry the morning after a night of rampant sex.

Candice was in the alcove kitchen, cooking in a t-shirt and panties. "Morning," she said as Jessa walked in. "Take a seat. Breakfast is almost ready." She motioned to the dining table. "Help yourself to some juice. Would you like a coffee?"

Jessa was already pouring herself a cup of orange juice. "Coffee would be great. Thanks."

"You never told me what you did for work," Candice said. She brought a mug of coffee and placed it in front of Jessa.

Jessa took a gulp of juice, then smiled and wiped her lips. "You never asked."

"No, I didn't. But I'm asking now. So, what do you do for a job?"

"I'm a detective inspector," she said, trying not to leer too hard at Candice's firm arse in her black panties. She wanted Candice to wrap her long dark legs around her waist again.

"Wow," Candice said. She came over with two plates of eggs and bacon. "A police detective who loves art. Who would have thought?"

Jessa smiled, was about to fork some bacon into her mouth when someone's mobile began to buzz. Candice glanced at the table with the wooden giraffe standing on it. "I think it's yours," she said.

Jessa got up and checked. She didn't recognise the number calling her. "Hello," she said, phone to her ear.

"Hello, is that Miss Summers?" It was a very camp male on the other line.

"Yes, who's calling?" Jessa said defensively

"Hello, my name is Valance from the Minna Gallery. You spoke to Sandra yesterday about commissioning a painting from Elizabeth Foster."

"Yes. Wow. Thank you for ringing me back." She couldn't believe Valance had actually phoned her.

"Well," Valance said, "as you saw yesterday, we only have the three paintings for sale at the gallery. The painting of the almond tree you enquired about, unfortunately, is not currently for sale. And as for Elizabeth taking a request, I'm afraid it isn't possible due to her terrible accident. I can, however, put you in touch with a number of other artists who offer commissions."

"Thank you for the offer, Valance, but I'm only interested in Elizabeth Foster. You said the painting of the almond tree is not for sale. Why is that? I would certainly be interested in buying it. And I can assure you, Valance, money is not an issue." She winked slyly at Candice.

Candice looked back at her with raised eyebrows, chewing on her last piece of bacon.

"None of the work displayed at the hotel gallery is for sale," he said. "They are sold eventually, but only when the artists decide they no longer want that particular piece on display."

"Well," Jessa said, "considering Elizabeth's current position, she isn't able to decide on anything. I really don't want to sound rude or insensitive, but I am interested in purchasing the painting of the tree. I am willing to pay the asking price."

Valance sounded irritated now. "I am truly sorry, Miss Summers, but the family have explicitly requested the painting not be sold. And that's final."

"Sandra told me you're a close friend of the family. Maybe I could contact them, or you could pass my number on to them so—"

"Miss Summers, the family have made it quite clear they do not want any communication from anyone regarding Elizabeth's art. This is a very traumatic time for them. Their only interest is in Elizabeth's recovery. You can purchase any of the other paintings on display in the Minna Gallery, but not the almond tree. And contacting the family is out of the question. Now I must say goodbye to you, Miss Summers. I have a very busy day ahead of me."

Without saying another word, Valance ended the call.

Candice looked across at Jessa. "Everything okay?"

With a half-hearted smile, Jessa placed her mobile back on the table. "Fine. I was just enquiring about a painting." She sat down at the table, looked down at her bacon. "Thank you for breakfast."

Although Jessa was no closer to understanding what her dreams really were, she was now confident they had nothing to do with Kozlowski. Robert Flores was the mystery man. But what did he want? Why did *he* want to hurt her? Was it because they were having an affair and she was pregnant with his baby? Impossible! And where did this Elizabeth Foster fit into the puzzle? Her instincts were telling her there was a connection—Robert, her, and Elizabeth all linked somehow. She only needed to figure out *how*.

Jessa ate the rest of her breakfast in silence, contemplating her next move. She wanted to confront Robert Flores and find out more about Elizabeth Foster. If Valance wasn't willing to give her the information she wanted over the phone, maybe she would have to meet him face-to-face.

CHAPTER 56

The early flight from New York landed in San Francisco at midday. The drive from the airport to Winters was uneventful. It was two by the time Robert pulled in behind the church. He had telephoned his wife and told her he needed to pick up some things from the church before heading home. He was due to give his weekly sermon to the local congregation that evening and needed some literature. She didn't question him. Robert's wife never did.

Robert stood naked in the basement looking at Susie Morgan's lifeless body on the bed, her ugly face pressed against the plastic. He hauled her off the bed and dragged her across the room and into the smaller room. The hatch was open on the other side.

Crouching, Robert crawled backwards, squeezing his bulk through the small opening. The cool dank air was a relief from the stuffy cellar. He flicked on the light and a string of bulbs sputtered to life, illuminating a large floorspace of dirt and foundation beams. There wasn't enough room for Robert to stand, so he had to hunch as he pulled Susie's corpse into the under croft. A newly prepared grave waited to be filled. He kicked her ragged corpse into the hole. The sound of soil splattering plastic stimulated him as he buried the stinky bitch; it aroused him. Robert knew it was time to find a new victim. The hunt was nearly as exciting as the kill.

*

Valance looked as camp as he sounded on the phone. Jessa found a photograph of him on the Minna Gallery website and saved it to her phone. He had quite a distinctive look, and certainly stood out from the crowd. He wouldn't be difficult to find.

The gallery was due to close by the time Jessa battled her way through the rush hour traffic and pulled into a parking space. She would have gotten there sooner, but Candice had kept her occupied for a few hours after breakfast. The gallery looked empty as she looked across from the rental car. Jessa couldn't see any movement inside, but the lights were still on. She really hoped it hadn't closed early. She wasn't hopeful in the first place, thinking Valance would refuse her the information on Elizabeth that she wanted. If the gallery was closed it would be another lead lost.

Jessa jogged across the road, narrowly avoiding a speeding taxi, tried the door and went inside. She had no idea what she was going to say to Valance, and even less of an idea what she was going to do if he refused to talk. The place was empty of customers. She checked her watch. It was ten minutes before the gallery was due to close. A faint trickle of classical music wafted from somewhere deeper in the gallery. Jessa walked slowly past the ghoulish painting of the fat woman with humongous tits, seeing it now had a *'sorry, this painting is sold'* card over the ridiculous price tag. She stood in front of the three paintings by Elizabeth Foster. W*ho are you? Jessa thought.*

"Hello," Valance's camp voice said from behind her. "Sorry to keep you waiting."

Jessa turned and faced him, and Valance stopped dead as if he'd been frozen in time. The colour drained from his flushed complexion and his cheery expression fell flat as he stared open-mouthed. He tried to speak, but no words came out. He moved his mouth soundlessly, Jessa standing awkward before him. It was a full minute before he finally stuttered a word.

"Elizabeth? he said.

*

Robert was relieved when he finally parked his SUV outside his lavish house. Susie Morgan was gone. Her body was covered in earth, buried where no one would ever find her. Susie's spirit was now a disciple of God.

Robert looked around the interior of the SUV, glanced at his expensive new house, where his doting wife who never asked any questions was waiting for him. He thought, *God, how far I've come over the last twelve months.* At first, Robert hadn't wanted the attention or the money, but he was starting to quietly enjoy it. He had been concerned his new, semi-celebrity lifestyle would hinder his clandestine existence, but it had in fact given him more opportunities to meet beautiful women and explore his desires. Robert knew if he continued being devoted to God, then God would continue being kind to Robert.

He smiled at himself in the rear-view mirror. Robert felt indomitable. With God as his mentor, he could do anything he wanted and no one would stop him.

*

When Valance realised who Jessa was, he asked her to leave. She shouted at him, "Why did you call me Elizabeth? What the fuck? Tell me why you said that!" But Valance only puckered his lips and told Jessa to leave. He looked at her like she was a freak. But he also looked at her with disturbing recognition, somewhat mystified. "Tell me why you said that," Jessa said, close to throttling the little twerp. But he wouldn't answer. He threatened to call the police. Jessa had no choice but to leave when he picked up the phone and started to dial.

She just didn't understand. Jessa was driving back to Winters now, angrier than hell and full of angst. Why had Valance acted so defensive and suspicious when he realized Jessa wasn't Elizabeth at all? But for a moment, he had obviously thought she was. It made no sense. Jessa wished she hadn't gotten so aggressive. Valance was keeping something from her. She damn well knew it. He had some vital piece of Jessa's puzzle and the camp little bastard wouldn't give it up.

Heading through downtown Winters, Jessa passed the Putah Café, less busy than it had been the day before. She passed the fading missing posters of Susie Morgan and continued east, following the signs for the Evangelical church. Several miles beyond the great almond tree, the church spire came into view, followed by its bell tower. Another mile and the church's body started to appear as if being pushed up from the ground. The road swept left, then straightened for another mile, then exited into a parking lot full of vehicles. Jessa squeezed into one of the few free spaces. Judging by the number of vehicles, half the population of Winters had come to the church.

Jessa got out, stood beside her rental car as a cool breeze blew across the lot, bringing with it the faint scent of honey butter and the sound of gospel music. Up the way was a large community hall that looked brand new, and beyond that, up a slight incline, the church; in the far distance the mountaintops touched the sky.

Jessa walked to the church, and as she approached saw a large gathering outside. The double doors were open, but there were so many people packed inside the church that they spilled out onto the grounds. Black speakers had been set up outside, gospel music blaring out of them, the whole crowd singing along. Jessa stood at the back of the worshippers trying to catch a glimpse of the reverend, but the place was too congested. The worshipers were a singing, swaying legion in their finest clothes. The last notes of the song faded to silence, and a few seconds later, the reverend's voice came through the speakers.

His voice punctured the silence and boomed out of the speakers. Everyone listened intently, the man's voice thick with power and command. His words vibrated Jessa's bones. She thought she would be physically sick as she remembered the reverend fucking her. She started getting anxious. There was no way she'd get through the crowd and into the church, but she needed to see him, needed to confront Robert. The reverend was the villain and she knew he had the answers she so restlessly sought.

The people were a throng of cult members transfixed by the reverend's voice. Jessa moved behind them, came to a gravel path and followed it around to the side of the church. Scurrying down it unnoticed, she came to the rear of the church and a wooden door, an SUV parked alone in the dirt. She studied the SUV, trying to remember if it was the same vehicle from her dreams. It must have been, but she couldn't tell for sure. Taking a quick glance around, confident no one was watching, Jessa entered the church through its back door.

She found herself in a small, stuffy vestibule. The reverend's voice emanated from behind one of the closed doors. She tried the one in front of her, but it was locked. She tried the other and it opened with a creak, bringing Jessa into the main church, to the backside of the pulpit. The choir stood on a small stage in front of her, while to her immediate right was Robert Flores. He walked the length of his stage, addressing the congregation.

No one noticed Jessa standing there.

The mere sight of Robert Flores repulsed her. He had an assured manner, conceited and smug. Now that she stood close enough to touch the slime bag, there was no question about it. The man in her dreams was Reverend Robert Flores.

The reverend's strident voice boomed throughout the church, followed by a cacophony of applause and cheering, the worshiper's charged and electrified. He walked across the stage while the crowd surged and shouted their emotion. Jessa had a strong urge to jump onto the stage and confront Robert in front of his flock. She was about to do it, too. Then Robert walked across the stage in her direction and stopped. His face twisted in fright and horrible recognition. Just like Valance, Robert recognised her.

*

The crowd whooped and cheered and held their hands to the heavens as Robert paced the stage. He preferred holding his sermons in the small Winters church, away from the cameras and the media circus. It wasn't the cheering or the applause, nor the admiration from his followers that gave Robert his biggest buzz. It was knowing all the people standing in front of him didn't have the faintest idea that beneath their feet, buried in the foundations of their beloved church, were the rotting corpses of thirteen women.

Robert was about to deliver the final message of his sermon when he saw her standing at the side of the stage. He stopped, momentarily stunned at the sight of Elizabeth staring back at him. She had been a reoccurring ghost ever since the incident, but Robert had yet to experience a hallucination like this. For the first time in a very long time, he was frightened. Elizabeth looked real, and her expression was full of hate and revulsion. He tried to compose himself, to blink away the apparition, but she wouldn't vanish. He looked out to his congregation and saw a sea of bemused people. Then Elizabeth was jumping on the stage. She was no fucking ghost. She was real! But how could it be? Elizbeth was supposed to be in a coma, never to awake!

*

Before Jessa even thought about what she was doing, she had jumped onto the stage and was standing face-to-face with Robert Flores. Nothing mattered to her more in that moment than finding

195

out why Robert Flores knew her, why he gaped at her like the returned ghost of some departed lover.

"You know me!" Jessa said, her voice echoing over the speaker system.

Robert was dumbstruck. The audience muttered amongst themselves. He tried to appear unfazed. "I'm sorry, miss," he said, "but I have never seen you before. Please, if you wouldn't mind—"

"You're lying! You know me. How do you know me?"

Robert blinked, looking like he didn't know how to process the situation. "Please," he said, "if you would like to leave the stage and kindly wait until I've finished my sermon, I will happily talk to you. But I assure you, miss, I have never seen you before."

Two big black male choristers got up from the choir and began making their way to the stage. Jeers were erupting from the crowd. "Get her off the stage!"

"Why are you lying?" Jessa shouted. "You recognised me. I knew as soon as you saw me. Tell me why!"

One of the choristers was trying to take Jessa by the arm. She screamed at him, "Get the fuck off me!" and the crowd gasped.

"Miss," Robert said, "if you don't leave, we will have to call the police."

Jessa was crying in anger. "Why are you lying?"

Robert held his hand up and spoke assertively. He seemed to have found his composure. "Submit yourself to God, miss. Resist the Devil and he will flee from you." And before Jessa had the chance to say another word, everyone and everything faded and she fell into swirling darkness.

CHAPTER 57

I feel it is not long before I am totally engulfed by the whiteness. What ensues is anyone's guess. It is strange, but the tingling feelings are becoming more intense. The sensations are too real. I feel they are more than a phantom tingle. I am becoming more of a presence, more than just a soul. But how can this be possible when I'm dead?

Waiting for the colours is torture. I worry that I will be taken by the white before I make sense of my fragmented memories—before I discover what happened to me.

And then they come.

I'm back in the hotel room next to Robert. No one has ever satisfied me like him before. When I'm with him, I feel safe and good about myself, feelings I haven't felt in a long time. I've fallen in love with this man and now I'm carrying his child. I remember his promises. Then I remember the look on his face after I whispered in his ear.

Robert climbs out of bed and looks at me, contorted in anger—agitated, disturbed. He is clearly disgusted by what I've told him.

"How can you be pregnant?" he asks me. His voice is dull and edged with anger. Robert's normal charismatic charm is replaced by a whole new identity. For the first time, I'm scared of him. I honestly thought he would be happy. He told me before he wanted to leave his wife and be with me. I thought he loved me. Looking now into his furious eyes, seeing Robert's supercilious personality, I know he was lying to me all along.

I say, "I thought you would be happy. I thought this is what you wanted, what we wanted. We can be together now, Robert, as a family."

"I didn't want to get you pregnant," he says, and the vileness in his voice shocks me to my core. "This spoils everything."

"What do you mean spoils everything? You told me you wanted to be with me. You told me you would leave your fucking wife so we can be together."

He's pacing the room now. I have never seen Robert act this way before. It's alarming.

"I lied," he says. "Did you really think I would give up everything for you?" He laughs, hurting me with his piercing stare. "How do you think it would look, huh? I've preached about adultery being evil and I've committed the very sin I condemn. The media would crucify me."

A great swell of anger propels me off the bed. I'm conscious about my nakedness and scramble for my underwear, screaming at him. "You should have thought about that before you started fucking me behind your wife's back, you self-righteous hypocrite."

He's towering over me as I pull on my panties. There is pure evil in his eyes, and for a moment I think he's going to kill me. But what do I care? I've spent too long being abused and demoralised. It's time I stand up, find my courage and spit back in the face of evil. Ironic, I suppose, that Robert is the one who gave me the mettle to believe in myself.

"And what do you think the media will say when I tell them I'm carrying your baby?"

Robert stares at me, face blank. It's the emptiness in his eyes that frightens me the most. But then he says, "I'm sorry," and smiles. "Of course I want to be with you. But really, it's just not the right time for us to have a baby." I can't believe it. Robert's wiping the tears from my cheek.

I want to trust him. I so desperately want to believe him, but the damage is done. His true self has surfaced and he's not the man I fell in love with. I've already spent a lifetime being told 'sorry,' being fed lies by bullies like him. I won't be taken for a fool again.

Robert's running his fingers through my hair. He says, "Look, we can make this go away and when the time is right, I promise, as God is my witness, we will be together. We will start a family of our own."

"Excuse me, Robert? What do you mean 'make it go away?' Are you suggesting I get an abortion?"

"I think it's for the best," he says, placing his hand on my shoulder. "God will forgive us."

"You fucking bastard!" I slap his hand away, rage fuelling me like never before. I lunge at him, claw and scratch his face. I want to dig his eyes from their sockets. "You fucking hypocrite!"

Through my flailing, Robert grabs my throat. He's bigger than me and stronger. He could snap my neck like a twig. I've felt these strong hands around my throat many times before, and it suddenly occurs to me he can only ejaculate when he's squeezing my windpipe. In blind anger, I lash out, but he's too strong. He jerks me backwards on my heels and backhands me across the face.

I slump to the floor, blood seeping from my lips, from my nose. My rage is extinguished. My fight is gone. I feel crestfallen. My vision is hazy as I look around for my clothes. I want to leave. Robert's standing above me and I can feel his hatred and violent malice. "I loved you!" I weep to him.

Robert leans over me, a look of pity on his face. His hands move again for my neck and I shout, "Leave me alone." I bat his hands away, hurriedly pick up my clothes and scramble into the bathroom and lock the door. Why didn't I just run from the hotel room? I'm washing the blood from my face, the bastard's skin from my fingernails. I don't want any trace of his scum on me. Looking at myself in the mirror, I know how foolish I've been. I tell myself I'm an idiot. As I put on my jeans, I hear him calling me from behind the door.

"Elizabeth, get out here!"

CHAPTER 58

"Where am I?" Jessa asked. A bright light shone above her. She was rocking lightly from side to side.

Jessa tried to sit up, but restraints bound her wrists and ankles and she couldn't move. Her restriction made her panic harder. "Where am I?" she screamed, fighting and thrashing.

"Jessa, it's okay," Candice said. "Take it easy. It's me, Candice. You're in an ambulance. We're taking you to the hospital."

Jessa blinked away the fuzz, seeing Candice's smiling face hovering above her like her guardian angel in the light. "What happened?" she asked.

"You fainted," Candice told her. "You've been out for a while. I was getting worried about you."

"The reverend," Jessa mumbled, her eyes darting about. "Where is he? Where's the reverend?"

Candice stroked Jessa's hand. "Don't worry about the reverend. The police have spoken to him and he's not going to press charges. Just get some rest. We'll be at the hospital real soon."

"I don't need the hospital. Can't you get these damn things off me?"

"No," Candice said. "The restraints need to stay on while the ambulance is in transit. Just lay still, we're nearly there."

"I don't need the bloody hospital," she said. "I'm fine. Please, take these off me."

"I really can't," Candice said, making a 'sorry, tough shit,' kind of face. "It would be against protocol. If you fell out of the bed while in transit, you could sue. I might lose my job."

"You don't understand," Jessa said. "I need to get back to the hotel. I need to find out where Elizabeth Foster is. It wasn't me. It was Elizabeth all along! The reverend didn't want to hurt me. He wanted to hurt Elizabeth."

The nurse was just finishing checking Jessa's vitals when a police officer walked into the small hospital room. He was short and stocky, the name 'Gonzalez' embroidered in gold lettering on his dark blue uniform. He had greased hair and a goatee. "Miss Summers?" he asked.

"What do you want?"

Gonzalez looked at the plump nurse as she unstrapped the sphygmomanometer from Jessa's arm. The nurse said, "Your blood pressure is a little higher than normal, but other than that, your vitals are fine."

"Thanks," Jessa said.

Gonzalez waited for the nurse to pack her equipment and leave, then he sat in the red plastic chair across from Jessa. "So," he said, "what was all the commotion about at the church?"

Jessa didn't respond. She didn't want to share her thoughts with anyone, especially not the police.

"You were screaming obscenities at Mr. Flores, interrupting his sermon. You said he recognised you. Now, I've spoken to Mr. Flores, Miss Summer, and he denies ever having known you." Gonzalez paused, waiting for Jessa to respond—but she kept her mouth closed, staring at him. "Luckily for you, Miss Summers, he's not pressing charges. But I would like to know why you think Mr. Flores knows you."

"Pressing charges?" Jessa choked out a laugh. "What a joke."

"You were disturbing the peace, Miss Summers. Here in California, that's a criminal offense."

"But I'm not under arrest, am I? And therefore, I'm free to go."

Gonzalez leaned forward and rested his elbows on his knees. He looked annoyed. "Miss Summers, I know who you are. You're a police detective from England. Your friend, DI Radisson, contacted me and told me why you've come to Winters."

"Rads isn't my friend." She could nearly taste the venom on her tongue.

Gonzalez shrugged. "Friend or not, DI Radisson tells me you're unwell. I understand you've been through some trauma recently, Miss Summers, but whatever crusade you're on must stop. Police or not, you can't come here and cause trouble. If you do, you'll be arrested."

"Do you know Elizabeth Foster?" Jessa asked. Fuck Gonzalez and his empty threats. She was police. Jessa knew her fucking rights.

"No, I don't."

"Well, Gonzalez, I believe Robert Flores knows Elizabeth and I believe he tried to kill her," Jessa said matter-of-factly.

Gonzalez sat up, looking even more irritated. "Do you have any evidence to collaborate this theory, Miss Summers, or is it all in your dreams?"

Jessa didn't answer. She knew it sounded crazy and already regretted telling the Hispanic cop anything.

He got up to leave, clearly uninterested in Jessa or her theories. "Go home, Miss Summers. And if you choose to stay in Winters, do yourself a favour, don't go anywhere near Mr. Flores again. Am I clear?"

Candice had left a message for Jessa, saying she had arranged for her car to be taken back to the hotel. Candice said she was working late but would call her sometime tomorrow.

The taxi driver told Jessa the journey from the Vacca Valley Hospital to the Almond Tree Hotel would take about twenty-five minutes. He gave up on small talk two minutes in, after Jessa showed no interest in chitchat. They drove on in silence. Jessa retreated into her thoughts, into her anxieties. All this time she had thought she was experiencing someone else's dreams. She had thought she was the one in danger. But no... it wasn't about her at all. It was about Elizabeth. But how exactly was Jessa experiencing someone else's dreams? And why?

The taxi pulled in front of the hotel lobby. Jessa barely had enough dollars in her pocket to pay the fare, and the driver drove away disgruntled without a tip. The evening air was cool, the clear sky pocked with stars. It was late and Jessa considered going for a run before ordering room service. The path around the lake was well-lit. She could really do with the physical exertion, the rush of stress relief. She needed to feel her muscles burn and ache, needed to clear out her muddled mind. As she entered the hotel, her phone rang. She frowned at the unknown number, but answered the call as she walked towards her room.

"Hello?"

"Yes," said a soft female voice, "is this Miss Summers?"

"It is. And who is this?"

"Miss Summers, my name is Rosemary Myers. I am Elizabeth Foster's mother."

CHAPTER 59

After the bitch had been taken away by the paramedics, Robert calmed his congregation and finished his sermon. Questions were asked, and he assured the crowd the woman had probably seen him on TV. He told his congregation she was probably a stalker sent by the Devil. The fucking idiots would believe anything Robert told them.

Robert now stalked his small office, full of anger and frustration. He was deliberating what to do next. The police had told him the woman's name was Jessa Summers, a mentally unstable visitor from England. They told Robert if Jessa caused him any more problems, he was to call them immediately. Seeing her had left him unnerved, a feeling he rarely ever felt. She looked so much like Elizabeth that Robert had been sure Elizabeth had come back from the brink of death, sent by the Devil himself to seize her revenge. But it wasn't. It was a stranger named Jessa Summers. Why had she known he recognised her?

Robert hadn't felt such anger since the last time he was with Elizabeth. He felt like a pressure cooker and if he didn't find release soon, the rage would become unbearable and his behaviour unpredictable. He'd turn into a beast. Going home wouldn't improve his mood. The last thing he wanted was his frigid Stepford wife fussing over him.

Robert settled on driving two and a half hours to Reno, taking Interstate 80 through the Nevada desert. Reno, 'The Biggest Little City in the World,' was renowned for its casinos and its filthy red-light district—and Robert had no desire to gamble. He had a hard time keeping to the posted speed limits as he drove. He couldn't reach the city fast enough, slowing every so often when the speedometer peaked at 100mph. When the lights of the city came into view, Robert's violent rage was still flaring. It wouldn't be long before he unleashed it, flushed the anger from his body and cleansed his soul.

Over recent years, millions of dollars had been ploughed into the downtown area of Reno, turning it from a sleazy shit hole into a glamorous one. Away from the glittering lights, the cocktail haunts, sushi bars, and the bustle of the casinos, a small area of town still existed to serve those who wished to score a good old fashion, cheap, dirty fuck. The area was only a few square miles, rife with drugs and prostitution. It was not uncommon for whores to turn up dead on the street corners, their bodies slashed inside seedy motels. Junkies dying in the gutters was a daily occurrence. It was Robert's kind of place. He used to frequent the seedy corners of town but hadn't been around in a while and the sleaze hadn't changed.

Robert parked his SUV on a residential side street and started walking. He marched down Arlington Street in a fiery rage with his fists clenched. He pulled his hood over his face, blocking the world and the wind, the noisy traffic and the late night revellers. Jessa Summers weighed heavy on his mind as Robert turned onto California Ave. She looked so much like Elizabeth, Robert couldn't get over it. They were almost identical. He was trying to remember if Elizabeth had ever mentioned having a sister. Had he ever really listened to anything she said? He was sure she had said something about being an only child.

Robert whispered under his breath, "Who the fuck is Jessa Summers?"

Turning off the busy California Avenue, Robert headed down a narrow side street between a pawn shop and a restaurant aptly named for the area, Dirty Dick's Crab House. The surroundings degraded each block onward he roamed, until the streets were seedy and smothered in a sinister ambience. Rows of dirty apartment buildings stood out like stained, broken teeth. Graffiti-marked walls and doors and dumpsters—used syringes and condoms kicked against the shoddy brick walls of subsidised tenements. Every corner stank like piss and shit and stale booze. Lowlifes shuffled through the shadows, itching for a fix; punters scrounged for a good time with a bad lady. Cars cruised slow and stopped, stuck out a hand and exchanged shakes with hooded bandits. Some slowed and whistled and welcomed street hookers into their passenger seats.

Robert blended with the shadows and the degenerates, his own deviant needs and sickening anger building as he scuffled through the dark alleys, passing bums and the bones of shopping carts. He was desperate to expel the maddening force inside him. He had to keep focused. Robert needed to remain in full control. But his impatience was starting to spew.

He crossed the street, stepped over a curled-up body, either dead or passed out on the pavement, and proceeded down an alleyway. Dim lights oozed through nicotine-stained windows, casting eerie shadows on the crumbling walls and darkness lurked in every corner. The alley was narrow, the buildings like giant neglected tombstones. Robert followed twists and turns and then entered a labyrinth of dark, cramped passages. A scream broke through an apartment window somewhere above, followed by shouting, a loud crash, and then silence. Robert walked on unperturbed, his only thought to extinguish his suffering.

A whore emerged from a gloomy doorway. She asked Robert if he wanted company. In the yellow light flickering above her, Robert could just distinguish her pale, craggy features. She looked about sixty, but was probably twenty years younger. Her badly applied makeup couldn't hide the years of substance abuse. She smiled and her teeth were shockingly white—probably dentures. Robert was looking her over when she opened her fake fur coat to show off the goods, tatty old lingerie and large, sagging breasts. Her body was as vile as her face.

Robert moved on without a word, the hooker muttering something about him being an arsehole. He continued through the alleyways, passing prostitutes viler than the sewer rats that scavenged through the garbage. The farther he went, the colder and more rancid the air became. And even though it was a dangerous place, Robert felt safe, invincible and invisible. The cops stayed away unless someone was killed, and even then their response was slow. It really was a shithole. Robert passed a boarded-up doorway, glancing through the cracks to see a fat black hooker squatting, giving some greaseball a cheap blowjob. Drum and bass music blasted from above in one of the apartments.

As Robert turned the corner, he saw a pair of prostitutes standing together under a streetlamp. One of them, a plump girl with dark skin, was engaged in conversation with an equally plump punter. After a few seconds of talking, they vanished into a derelict apartment building. Robert waited, eyes fixed on the lingering prostitute under the lamp. She was scanning the street. Young, mid-twenties, wearing a red leather skirt, white boots, and a puffer jacket; long blonde hair sleeked back into a ponytail. Robert approached her and she forced a smile. Her skin was like porcelain under the toxic streetlight, her lips tinged blue from the cold. She would have been attractive if it wasn't for the fact that she looked wasted and her drug-polluted body was stick thin.

Pulling back his hood, Robert revealed his face to the crackwhore. He wasn't concerned. She probably didn't even know what day of the week it was. It wasn't like she would remember anything after Robert had finished with her. Nervous energy heightened his senses as he stared into her dead, marble eyes. They were glazed, vacant, and wholly vulnerable.

She was perfect.

The whore hadn't noticed Robert pull his hood up again when he followed her up the old, creaking wooden stairs. Most of the balustrades were missing or broken, and old newspapers and other rubbish littered the steps. The dull thud of music quaked the walls. A baby was crying inside an apartment down the hall. The whore took a left at the top of the stairs and paused outside the front door. She took a key from her coat and unlocked it.

The apartment was sparse but surprisingly tidy. A single lightbulb hung from the ceiling, illuminating the room a dull yellow. There was one main room, which served as the bedroom, living room, and kitchen. A door led to the washroom. Patches of old plaster clung to the exposed brick walls and a badly stained carpet covered the floor. A small electric heater was next to the bed, giving off heat like a dog's wet breath.

As the skinny young woman walked clumsily to the bed, Robert locked the door. She sat down, swaying slightly, and began to unzip her boots.

"Leave them on," Robert told her.

She shrugged, zipped the boot back up and took off her coat. She had on a white crop top with a faded smiley face on the front. Robert walked over to the windows and covered them with the brown, moth-eaten curtains. As the whore took of her shirt and bra and showed Robert her small tits, Robert removed his hood. The girl's skin was blotchy and red.

"You want it front or back?" she asked, slipping out of her leather mini skirt. She had no shame showing Robert her pussy.

Now he was feeling the buzz. Robert undressed and folded his clothing neatly, placed them on the table. "Back," he said, "and let down your hair."

The whore removed her hairband and her blonde, greasy hair fell around her face and shoulders.

Robert smiled at her. "That's better, Elizabeth."

"Call me what you like, honey. Do you want me to get you hard first?" She was looking at his limp penis.

"I'll be hard soon enough," he said.

Robert motioned her to get up on the bed. She did as she was told, crawling in a way that was far from sexy as she positioned herself on her elbows, arse up in the air. She rested her head on her forearms and waited to be entered. Robert stood behind her, placed his large hands on her bony shoulders, then gently slid them down her body, fingers edging over the bumps of her spine. Resting his hands on her lower back, Robert bowed his head, closed his eyes, and whispered, "It is God's will that you be banished to the depths of Hell."

"What was that?" She turned her head back to look at him.

Robert punched her in the side of the head. She slumped onto the mattress without a sound. Robert felt aroused already, his dick twitching as it got hard. He looked at her feeble body. The girl was pathetic. He turned her over and lifted her closer to the headboard, then used the bitch's own bra to tie her hands to the post above her drooped head. He used two pairs of stockings he found in a cupboard to tie her ankles next to her wrists, trapping her in an ugly contortion. Then he scrounged in her ratty bag for a condom, opened it and rolled the rubber sheath down his erection. The prostitute was gaining consciousness.

Her head jerked and she started muttering nonsense, and that was when Robert entered her. He rammed himself into the whore with extreme force, causing her eyes to flick open. It took her a few moments to register what was going on, then she began whimpering and trying to wriggle free. Her head snapped left to right, eyes straining to look at her bound wrists and ankles. The fear in her eyes heightened Robert's excitement and he kept bashing into her. Even through her drug-induced stupor, the whore knew she was in danger. She tried to scream, but only managed to wheeze as Robert's hands clamped around her skinny neck.

He choked the life out of her. The harder Robert squeezed, the harder he fucked her. The prostitute's pale face went red, her eyes bulged from their sockets, and just as she forced out her last breath, Robert roared into her ugly, pained face. His anger, tension, frustration—all of it released as he came inside the dead girl.

After washing himself in the filthy shower and dressing, Robert stood by the door. He felt calm and satisfied. His anger had been quenched. He looked at the strung-up corpse and smiled at the yellow smiley face on her shirt, now covering the dead whore's head like a hangman's mask. He left the building and walked leisurely back to his car, safe in the knowledge that God was looking out for him.

CHAPTER 60

Jessa was up early. She couldn't contain her excitement. Rosemary Myers had agreed to meet her later that morning. She had tried to ask questions about Elizabeth over the phone, but all Rosemary had offered was that Valance was a close friend and he had told her they just had to meet.

Breakfast wasn't served for another hour, so Jessa decided to jog around the lake. It was another beautiful morning and she needed to pass a few hours before it was time to leave. She needed to figure out what to ask Rosemary. Should she give Rosemary the whole spiel, about the dreams, Robert, the almond tree, the crash—about everything? It would sound insane. But what did she have to lose? She might finally learn what had brought her to Winters in the first place.

Jessa's GPS guided her to the address Rosemary had given her. She parked outside a large iron gate, the white walls so huge she couldn't see the house beyond. Jessa even checked her GPS location to make sure she was in the right spot. She had driven for nearly two hours to a place called El Granada, twenty-five miles south of San Francisco. Noticing the intercom on the post by the gate, Jessa stretched her arm out the window and pushed the button. Seconds later, a female voice answered.

"Good morning, the Myers residence."

"Yes, hello, this is Jessa Summers. I'm here to see…" The gate was already opening. "…Rosemary Myers…"

The voice told her to drive to the front of the house. Jessa moved through the opened gate and followed the gentle rise of the brick driveway alongside massive, immaculately mowed lawns. There was a ball-shaped water fountain in the centre of a small lake on Jessa's left, the driveway hemmed by neatly pruned trees. The house itself was grand. Jessa parked her rental next to a shiny SUV that looked brand new and very expensive.

The house reminded Jessa of the White House, only smaller. It had a white exterior and four large pillars supporting the portico. Six steps led to a huge oak door, five rectangular windows along the ground floor and seven on the upper. Beyond the house, the view stretched to the North Pacific Ocean where sea met sky. The Myers were obviously wealthy. Jessa walked up the fancy stairs to the front door. She was about to hit the buzzer when one of the oak doors swung open and a middle-aged Thai woman appeared in its threshold. She was short, slim, had grey roots and was attractive. Her eyes were kind and her smile even kinder.

"Hello, Jessa Summers. I am Malee. Please, come in." Malee bowed, gesturing for Jessa to enter.

Jessa walked into a grand oval hallway. A crystal chandelier hung from the ceiling, and a sweeping staircase led to the second floor. Beige marble was everywhere.

"This way please, Miss Summers," Malee said, leading Jessa across the hallway and into a lounge. The place was spacious and airy and tasteful. On the wall above the black sofa hung an oil painting of an ocean view. Jessa paused to inspect it, assuming it was one of Elizabeth's pieces. The style was the same as those that were in the Minna Gallery, and a small EF was scrawled in the bottom right corner.

"This way, please," Malee said.

Jessa followed the little Thai woman through the lounge and into another room with windows stretching its entire length. The view from the huge windows must have been Elizabeth's inspiration for the painting in the other room. They were almost identical. "Please sit," Malee said, nodding at a cream-coloured sofa. "Mrs. Myers will be with you shortly. Would you like anything to drink? Perhaps some tea?"

Jessa sat down. "Yes, Malee, tea would be fine. Thank you."

Jessa had been a bit nervous when she arrived, but was even more nervous now. She was on her own in a damn palace. Jessa had no idea what to expect from Rosemary and was uncertain why she had even been invited to her grand residence. Surely something about Elizabeth, right? Jessa wondered if she should start straight with the dreams. She was also concerned about how much detail to give, how honest to be. The poor girl was trapped in a coma on life support. The last thing Jessa wanted was to upset Rosemary by talking about the kind of sordid sex her daughter had been performing with the reverend. Did she already know about the pregnancy? Surely the doctors had told Elizabeth's family after the accident. But did Rosemary know it wasn't an accident, but an attempted murder? And what if Rosemary called Jessa crazy and dismissed her dreams as nonsense just like everyone else did?

It was a tough spot. Jessa had no physical proof of her theories. She started getting nervous in that big lavish room by herself. Her vision began to waver, and she had to grip hard to her senses to stay lucid. She didn't want to pass out. *Not now, Jessa! Not fucking now!* She sucked in a deep breath and walked over to the window, where she focused on the beautiful view. The day was warm and sunny. *Deep breaths, girl. Just keep taking deep breaths.*

"Miss Summers," came Malee's voice.

Jessa turned to see Malee pushing a frail old woman into the room in a wheelchair. Her anxiety and nausea immediately began to fade.

"Miss Summers, may I present Rosemary." Malee helped the old lady out of her wheelchair and into a padded armchair. Rosemary wore a plastic oxygen mask over her nose and mouth, making it a real struggle to transfer between chairs. As rosemary settled, Malee placed a small oxygen cylinder beside her legs. A rubber tube connected it to Rosemary's facemask.

"Thank you, dear," Rosemary said, patting Malee's hand.

The Thai woman said she'd come back soon with tea and left the room.

Jessa and Rosemary were alone, Jessa standing awkwardly and studying the old woman. It was hard to tell how old she really was, but Jessa would have guessed ninety. Even so, she was elegant and well-presented. Her thin grey hair was combed and pinned back, and she wore tastefully applied makeup around her eyes and on her cheeks and lips. She wore a black dress with yellow flower print, which flowed to her feet. She had long, delicate fingers and bulged knuckles.

"Let me have a good look at you," Rosemary said, motioning Jessa closer as she took off her facemask. "My sight is failing, but I can still see good up-close."

Jessa took Rosemary's cold bony hand and crouched in front of her. Although Rosemary's body was old and crippled, she still had a sparkle in her eye. She had an articulate eloquence in her speech. Rosemary sucked in a deep breath at the sight of Jessa up-close. Tears welled in her eyes as she put a shaky hand on Jessa's cheek.

"Valance was right," Rosemary said, struggling through her tears. A dark sadness had shadowed her face. "If I knew no better, I would swear I'm looking at my Elizabeth."

A quiet whimper escaped Rosemary's wrinkled lips. She was tracing Jessa's jaw with her leathery finger, looking at her with an unfathomable amount of adoration.

"I don't understand," Jessa whispered, on the verge of crying herself.

Rosemary smiled. "It's simple, Jessa. Elizabeth is your sister. She's your twin sister."

Part 3

Dreams can become

reality and reality

can sometimes be nothing more than a dream.

Chapter 61

My name is Elizabeth. My surname alludes me and the name Elizabeth is nothing more than a word, but I know it's my name. I still don't know my past. I don't understand who I am. All I know is what the whiteness shows me. It's nearly taken over. The blackness is almost gone and when it fully disappears, maybe then I will be gone forever.

I've not had the chance to fully comprehend that I was pregnant... until now. I assume I've lost my baby. But before I can dwell on my dead, unborn child, the explosion of light hits me

I'm gazing into the dark night sky, rain falling onto my face. Looking toward the house, I remember the feelings from the last time I was here. Overcome with fear, I look down and see the gun in my hand, dripping with rain. I am here to kill someone.

Though my body trembles, I am totally focused and committed to what I've come here to do. I stare at the man in the kitchen from the shadows. I see the back of his head as he hunches over, preparing something on a worktop. I'm invisible in the darkness. I grip the gun tight; its cold metal feels heavy and good in my hand. I hate the man in the house. Nonetheless, as I go slowly through my covering of darkness, I hope I have the courage to pull the trigger.

I move towards the back porch, watching as the man goes from the kitchen and into his living room. There's no clear view of his face, but from his hair and strong shoulders he could be Robert Flores. I creep to the back porch and climb the steps very quietly. I try the door handle. It's locked. I take the key from my coat pocket, hand shaking as I struggle to insert it in the keyhole. I'm scared but my adrenaline spurs me on.

Quietly, with much care, I open the door, pausing a moment to listen. As I step inside, I pull back my hood and check the safety on the gun; it's off. The utility room is familiar. I know the door ahead leads to a washroom, and the door on the right to the laundry, another door to the double garage. I open the one on the left and creep into the kitchen. Spotlights illuminate the room, the

215

kitchen modern with black granite countertops. I tread softly and droplets of water fall from my coat. The television is on. The man I've come to kill waits unknowingly behind the partition wall.

I point the gun, let my finger hover over the trigger. I can't stop my hand from shaking. I'm halfway through the kitchen when a chime rings. I stop dead, my heart jumping in my chest. At first, I'm unsure where the sound is coming from. I soon realise someone is calling at the main door of the house. It's the doorbell ringing.

The TV shuts off and silence sweeps through the house. Someone's moving in the living room. I freeze, my heart threatening to explode. From the corner of my eye, I see him walk from behind the partition and into the hall. He didn't see me dripping in the middle of his kitchen with the gun in my hand.

Muffled voices from somewhere in the house. They're getting closer. I have no choice but to scurry back through the kitchen, closing the door quietly to the utility room and then leaving the house. I click the lock shut, put the key back in my pocket, and retreat through the darkness. I hide in the bushes and look back at the house.

He's in the kitchen with a woman. She's tugging at his belt while he smothers her with kisses. I can't see her face through his muscular frame, only the hint of brunette hair. They continue to grope and kiss, and he lifts the woman onto the kitchen counter. She wraps her legs around his waist. He's fumbling between her legs. Then the thrusting starts. She grabs the back of his head and pulls his face into her chest. Open-mouthed, she looks out of the window straight at me. I'm camouflaged in darkness. She smiles in pure joy as he continues to penetrate her.

The light starts to wither and before it fades completely, I recognise the woman.

CHAPTER 62

The dream burdened Jessa long after she opened her eyes. It took a few minutes for her to sit up in bed, a little disoriented and out of place. She forgot where she was and had to look around. The early morning sun crept through the blinds, casting streaks of light across the walls and ceiling. Then she remembered and all the emotion came rushing back at once. The significance of her meeting with Rosemary Myers yesterday struck her straight in the heart. After Jessa had left the old woman's house, the rest of her day passed in a blur. The truth was shocking. Jessa's twin sister was somehow communicating with her while in a coma. If it wasn't happening to Jessa, she would have never believed it possible.

Jessa rested her head in her hands and tried to recall the details of her dream, rubbing her temples with the tips of her fingers. She wanted to know if the man in the house was Robert Flores. His stature certainly matched, but she hadn't seen his face. Still, Jessa was almost certain it was him. Who else could it be? And who was the woman? Probably some other gullible soul Robert had made promises to and then betrayed. And the other questions: Why did Elizabeth want to kill him? Did Robert abuse her? Had he blackmailed Elizabeth and killing him was her only escape? Or had she finally had enough of the torture?

There was still a lot of uncertainty. The one thing Jessa knew for sure was that she wasn't crazy. Everything happening to her was real. Her dreams were fragments of her twin sister's life. They were the events leading up to her coma. All this time Jessa had thought the dreams were warnings about her own dismal future, but now she understood. It made sense—the strange feelings of longing, of being connected to someone. It was her sister reaching out for help.

Candice stirred beside Jessa, not quite awake. After Jessa's meeting with Rosemary, she hadn't wanted to be alone. She had needed company and decided to spend the evening with Candice. But Jessa was getting smart. She hadn't told the sexy paramedic anything about Elizabeth or Rosemary or why she was really in Winters. She'd only known Candice for a few days. Jess was growing fond of her, sure, but she wasn't about to drag Candice into her shitstorm of a life. Friends with benefits and nothing more. Jessa certainly wasn't about to fall in love with someone so soon. Not after Vanessa. And besides, the only important thing was finding out the truth about what happened to Elizabeth.

The time was creeping toward 5am, and although she had enjoyed little sleep, Jessa was wired. She had arranged to go back to El Granada later that morning to meet Rosemary again, but it was hours away and she was already restless.

Jessa looked at Candice, lying comfortably on her back. Before returning to her hotel, Jessa wanted sex. She slid her hand over Candice's dark breast and down her tummy, kissed Candice's lips while delicately rubbing the girl's nappy pubic hair. Candice stirred awake, flicking her tongue in Jessa's mouth. She then cupped her hand between Jessa's legs and spread a warm tingly sensation all through Jessa's body. They both became intoxicated with lust. It was Jessa's turn to cum hard and she knew it wouldn't take long. Lifting herself up, she straddled Candice, put her legs over the woman's shoulders and perched on her knees, offering herself. The touch of Candie's warm tongue was enough to throttle Jessa into a fit of pleasure and she shuddered in her own orgasm.

*

Killing the filthy whore had appeased Robert's anger and frustration, but the relief was short-lived. Robert was still infected with angst. The psycho who had confronted him at the church—the one who looked so much like Elizabeth, still terrorized his thoughts. He feared she knew something about him and Elizabeth, which made Robert nervous, a feeling he was unused to. He needed to find out more about Jessa Summers. What was she doing in Winters? She must be Elizabeth's sister, but how the fuck was that possible?

Robert couldn't allow the sneaky bitch to cause trouble for him. If the police hadn't scared her off, then Robert may have just found his newest plaything. He wouldn't make the same mistake with Jessa Summers that he had made with Elizabeth.

*

Yesterday's meeting with Rosemary had been emotional for both her and Jessa, but it had only lasted a short time. There were still questions Jessa wanted to ask Rosemary about her sister, but she had to be careful about Rosemary's frailty. Yesterday, Malee had cut the meeting short, taking Rosemary off to bed as she began to cough and grow weak. All Jessa had found out was that Rosemary was very proud of Elizabeth and her art, and that Elizabeth too suffered from depression. Yet Elizabeth had been coping well before the accident, apparently enjoying her life and becoming more confident. At least that was what Elizabeth's husband, Thomas, had said. Thomas was Elizabeth's rock. He had stayed beside her through everything, every high and every low. He had hardly left Elizabeth's side since she was admitted to hospital.

Rosemary also talked about her late husband, Marcus. They moved to California from the United Kingdom a few years after adopting Elizabeth. Rosemary said they had been told about a twin during the adoption process, but the adoption agency claimed Elizabeth's twin had died shortly after the biological mother gave birth. Showing Jessa a photograph of Elizabeth, she nearly fainted. It was like looking at a photo of herself.

It was late in the morning now and Jessa was back in the same room as yesterday, looking through the window at the Pacific Ocean as she waited for Rosemary. The sky was overcast with low, dark clouds—dark like Jessa's mind. She was worried about telling Elizabeth's husband about the affair with Robert Flores. Did he already know? His wife was in a coma. Would the revelation of Elizabeth's unfaithfulness destroy Thomas? And what about Rosemary? She was fragile enough as it was. Jessa didn't want to break the old girl with such devastating news.

"Ah, Jessa." It was Rosemary. Her voice shook Jessa from thought.

Jessa turned from the window and watched Rosemary be carted into the room by a handsome young man. Her facemask hung by an elastic band around her neck.

"Jessa, this is Thomas," Rosemary said. "This is Elizabeth's husband."

Jessa was getting used to the look of shock when people close to Elizabeth met her. Thomas stared at Jessa in silence, making her a little uncomfortable. He was a tall man, slim and muscular with high cheekbones and green eyes. He had short grey hair, receding but neat and trendy. "I'm sorry," he said after a moment of staring. "I was remembering Elizabeth standing in the same spot. She used to stand there for hours staring out at the sea. You're a mirror image of her."

For a second, Jessa thought Thomas was going to start crying in front of her. He might have too, if Rosemary didn't pat him on the hand and crane her head up to give him a reassuring smile. It seemed to calm him. He smiled back at Rosemary and caressed her wrinkled hand. It was obvious they were very close, and both extremely worried about Elizabeth. It made Jessa feel guilty. Jessa wasn't overly upset for Elizabeth. Her twin sister was just a name, a person in a photograph, an image in a dream. Elizabeth was a stranger. Maybe her feelings would change if she could meet her sister in person.

Thomas walked over and gave Jessa a hug. "It's so very nice to meet you."

Memory jolted Jessa, a quick flash of something she couldn't quite capture. She pulled away from Thomas and nearly fell backwards onto the sofa.

"Jessa, what's wrong?" Rosemary asked. Thomas stood awkward in the middle of the room. Jessa looked dazed and didn't say anything. "Darling, what's wrong?"

"Sorry." Jessa gave her head a shake. "It's nothing. I'm fine. Just... this is all very overwhelming."

"For all of us," Rosemary said, smiling.

Thomas helped Rosemary from her wheelchair and into the armchair, and Malee brought a tray of coffee and biscuits.

"I'm sorry your visit was cut short yesterday," Rosemary said as she took Jessa's hand. "It was a little too much for me. I am still shocked, but it is good to see you again, dear. I am so glad you found us."

Thomas pulled up a chair close to Rosemary and sat down. "How *did* you find us?" he asked.

Jessa was looking at her hands, unsure how to proceed. After a moment, she looked at Rosemary and said, "I found you through my dreams. I believe Elizabeth has been communicating with me through my subconscious."

There was an awkward silence. Then Thomas let out a nervous laugh. "Well, that sounds pretty incredible."

"Tell me about the dreams, Jessa," Rosemary said. She seemed genuine enough.

But Thomas snapped at her. "Rosemary, you don't believe her, do you?"

"Thomas." Rosemary gave him a look. "Hear the girl out." Then she pulled her mask over her mouth and nose.

"Sorry," Thomas said to Jessa. "I didn't mean to be rude. It's just that you've turned up out of nowhere. You look exactly like my wife, and I don't know if she's ever going to wake up." He buried his face in his hands, moaning through his fingers. "The doctors tell us Elizabeth is probably braindead. The only thing keeping her alive is the life support machine. I find it hard to believe she is communicating with you through her dreams. It's ludicrous."

"She was pregnant," Jessa said. She had to make an impact before Thomas started calling her crazy.

Thomas jerked and gaped up at Jessa. "How did you know that?" Rosemary slowly pulled her facemask down. "No one knows Elizabeth was pregnant except for Rosemary and I, and the doctors at the hospital."

Rosemary's smile was big and bright with hope. "Elizabeth must have told her," she said. "Elizabeth may be locked in a coma, but she is not braindead, Thomas. She is very much alive, and somehow she's communicating with her twin sister."

CHAPTER 63

Robert had to get away from his house before his wife drove him fucking crazy. She had organised a mid-afternoon wine and cake gathering with their neighbours and everything had to be oh-so fucking perfect. It wasn't like the neighbourly visit had been born of kindness. It was an excuse for his wife to show off their new furnishings. Seeing his wife flaunt his money and tell the neighbours how wonderful her life was made Robert sick.

The Holy Man was due to air live in two days, and Robert needed to revise his sermons. He could easily do it from his home office, but he had to get away from Juliet. Let his wife act like a complete fucking simpleton on her own. Robert would go to his office in Winters. It seemed like these days he could never find peace in his own house, with his own chauvinistic wife. He had come close to squeezing the life out of her many times over the years. One of these days, he just might.

Before going to the church, Robert made his regular coffee stop at Steady Neddy's Coffee House on Main Street. Steady Neddy's coffee was the best in town. As soon as Robert walked into the rustic café, he was relaxed by the delightful smell of roasting coffee. Ned was behind the counter to greet Robert, and a pretty young blonde was busy making drinks. Robert hadn't seen the girl before, but she instantly grabbed his attention. Robert guessed her aged at 19 or 20. She was slim, huge breasts pushing through her tight t-shirt. Her blonde hair was tied into a bun. All he could focus on was her long, delicate neck. He found himself entranced as she fiddled with the gigantic coffee machine, lights and switches like a goddamn cockpit. Robert undressed her with his eyes, allowing himself to get aroused.

"That'll be $7.20 please, Mr. Flores," Ned said, tapping on the cash register. He didn't notice Robert eyeing the young girl.

Robert paid for his cappuccino and salami bagel. Then he nodded at the girl. "New staff, Ned?"

Ned laughed. "Robert, that's my eldest daughter, Kim. She's been travelling around Australia and New Zealand for a year. She only got back a few weeks ago. I managed to convince her to join her old man here at the café to pay off the money I lent her."

Robert had seen Ned at his Thursday evening sermons a few times with his overweight wife, but they weren't regulars. He didn't recall ever seeing Ned bring children to church. Robert would have remembered Kim.

Ned called his daughter over. "Kim, come say hi to our local celebrity, Mr. Flores."

Kim finished wiping a steam pipe with her white cloth, then stepped over beside her dad. She held out her delicate right hand to Robert. "Hi. You're the preacher from TV, right?"

Robert took her hand, letting it linger in his instead of shaking it. "I am. You watch my show?"

Kim blushed. "I've seen a few of your sermons on the internet." Her smile was gorgeous. She had perfect white teeth.

"Well," Robert said, "I hope to see you at my Thursday sermon, and maybe you can bring your old dad along too. I haven't seen him there in a while."

"If he ever lets me out of this place, maybe I will," Kim said, pulling her hand from Robert's soft grip.

Robert left the café with his coffee and bagel and walked to his SUV. Officer Gonzalez was pulling into the space beside him.

"Mr. Flores," Gonzalez said, climbing out of his patrol car, "how are you today?"

"Couldn't be better now that I have this," Robert said, brandishing his coffee.

"Ned sure does make great coffee. Say, had any more problems from the English lady?"

"Nope." Robert shook his head, trying to act like he hadn't even thought about her. "Is she still in town?"

"I believe so, but I think she got the message. She should leave you alone from now on."

"Thanks," Robert said. "Any news on Susie Morgan? It's been almost two weeks, Gonzalez. Her parents are worried sick."

Gonzalez shook his head, looking troubled. "Nothing, I'm afraid. It's like Susie vanished off the face of the Earth. But I'm sure she'll turn up sooner or later."

"You reckon she ran away, huh?"

"That's the opinion around the station," Gonzalez said. Then he lowered his voice. "But you didn't hear it from me. Okay?"

"Wherever she is," Robert said, looking up to the sky, "she's not alone. God is with her now and forever. We will continue to pray for her safe return."

Robert got into his SUV and sipped his coffee, the engine running as he watched through the window of Steady Neddy's Coffee House. He wasn't looking at Gonzalez as he ordered his coffee. He wasn't even looking at Ned. Robert was fixed on the young blonde with large breasts. She was wiping down an empty table.

"What a great day," Robert mused. The police had no clue about Susie Morgan, and Kim had no idea she was being watched by a sadistic serial killer.

CHAPTER 64

Malee had taken Rosemary to the restroom, leaving Jessa alone to chat with Thomas. She sensed he was not convinced by her elucidation. She wondered if he had any idea the baby wasn't his. For the moment, she would keep that information to herself. She wasn't ready to reveal the whole truth just yet.

"So," Jessa said, "what is Elizabeth like?"

"She was—Er, she is a wonderful person. Elizabeth is kind and caring, beautiful, and of course, talented. I love her very much."

Something about Thomas' description of his wife sounded insincere to Jessa. He didn't speak with fondness, and was a touch cold, even apathetic.

"What about you?" he asked.

"What about me?"

"What kind of person are you, Jessa?"

She took a second to consider. "Well, I think I am probably the opposite." She quickly deflected the topic away from herself, asking, "How long have you and Elizabeth been married?"

"A little over three years."

"And how did you meet?"

"A mutual friend introduced us," he said, clearly uncomfortable with being questioned. "She knew we were both single and suggested we would be suitable for each other. She was right. Elizabeth and I were a perfect match."

Rosemary was wheeled back into the room, and Thomas helped Malee get her into the armchair. Rosemary took a few deep breaths from her mask while Malee scampered out of the room.

"I was just telling Jessa how Elizabeth and I first met," Thomas said, resting his hand gently on Rosemary's forearm.

"Ah, yes." She patted Thomas' hand. "Olivia is such a darling, such a good friend to Elizabeth and Thomas. She was their matchmaker. She's always been like a sister to my dear Elizabeth." She looked at Jessa and smiled. "Not to be insensitive to you, dear."

"Not at all," Jessa said.

Rosemary grinned. "So, tell us about your dreams."

*

Although there was no church service on Fridays, the community hall was a hive of activity. An art club, run by volunteers for senior citizens, was underway when Robert arrived. Whenever activities were on in the hall, Robert made a conscious effort to make an appearance. It was part of his job. And besides, he might meet someone who took his fancy. But after thirty minutes of mind-numbing chitchat with a bunch of old cranks, Robert excused himself and walked to the church, around back and into his office.

Sitting in the dull room always seemed different to Robert when the bastille beneath him was void of human life. When a beautiful blonde was held captive and at his mercy, just there beneath his feet, the office was a sanctuary. Its unattractiveness was blanked from his mind. Robert got a thrill every time he walked into the office because he anticipated climbing down the ladder into his secret room and doing ungodly things to whoever he held captive. He obsessed over them tied to the bed down there, replaying in his mind what he had done and what he would do, all the while acting like a God-loving Christian. He had sat behind his desk with an erection bursting through his pants while holding meetings with the town council folk, as a helpless woman was gagged, bound, and whimpering below them. When the room was empty, so was Robert Flores. The office was just a dull unappealing reminder the room below was in need of a new occupant.

He stared at the blank screen of his laptop, trying to focus on making notes for the Sunday sermon, but his thoughts were dominated by three blonde women. He was haunted by Elizabeth Foster, worried about Jessa Summers, and turned on by Ned's daughter, Kim. He kept thinking of all the things he would do to young Kim once he got her into his basement.

*

Malee brought in a platter of sandwiches and an assortment of cakes, placed them on the coffee table and left the room again. Rosemary wanted to know every detail about Jessa's dreams, but Jessa wasn't ready to give it all up yet. She began by explaining how they started, her father's death, her belief that the visions were premonitions. She explained about being a detective in the U.K, about her confusion with Kozlowski, her paranoia that he was plotting to kill her. As she spoke, Thomas merely shook his head and sometimes rolled his eyes. "It's pretty far-fetched," he would say. Jessa got a little sick of Thomas' attitude and took a break to eat a salmon sandwich. She noticed Rosemary looked concerned—and it hit her: Rosemary didn't believe her.

"Are you saying—" Rosemary paused to huff on some oxygen. "That someone wanted to kill Elizabeth?"

Jessa was impressed. Rosemary was sharp for an old lady with one foot in the grave. "Yes," Jessa told her, "I believe Elizabeth's accident was actually an attempted murder."

"This is preposterous," Thomas said. He looked ready to jump out of his chair. "I am sorry, but this is ridiculous. You are suggesting someone intended to kill Elizabeth because you saw it in your dreams? You are insane."

"Thomas, dear," Rosemary said, her breath a bit raspy, "let Jessa finish."

"You aren't falling for this, Rosemary? Don't you think we have been through enough trauma? My wife, your daughter, is lying in a hospital bed. I've lost a child—and now this!" Thomas glowered at Jessa. "This talk of communicating through dreams is ludicrous, even if Elizabeth and Jessa are twin sisters. And to suggest someone wanted to kill her is insane. The police confirmed there was no evidence of that. It was all an accident. This must stop right now."

"As you can imagine," Rosemary said, offering her hand to Thomas, "it's been unbearable for Thomas—for us both. Thomas never knew Elizabeth was pregnant. The doctors said she may not have known herself. It was very early. But she suffered severe injuries, lost a lot of blood, and was very lucky to have survived. The life support machine has been keeping her alive ever since, but we do pray that she wakes soon. And now, Jessa, you have given me hope that one day she will."

Jessa looked at Rosemary, then Thomas. "I know it sounds crazy. Believe me, I've told myself the same thing enough times over the last few weeks. But I'm telling you the truth. How else do you think I ended up here? I never knew I had a twin sister. I never knew a place called Winters even existed. Elizabeth has led me here and I believe she wants me to find out what happened to her.

sister."

Thomas was bewildered, his lips pulled back. Rosemary took some deep breaths with her mask.

"I want to see Elizabeth," Jessa said.

Rosemary nodded. "Of course. I thought you would."

Thomas opened his mouth, but Rosemary cut him off. "And, dear," she said, "I do believe you. I believe every word you have said."

The late afternoon traffic was heavy and slow on Interstate 280, and Jessa was becoming increasingly annoyed. She sneered at the other drivers in their metal cocoons. They all looked as annoyed as she was by the congestion. Her mind was jumbled as always, fragments and information in a chaotic mess. She couldn't wait to finally piece together the vague puzzle in her brain.

Rosemary had told Jessa they would visit Elizabeth tomorrow morning. Jessa was a bit disappointed. She had wanted to go directly from Rosemary's mansion, but Thomas had given her such a look of disapproval that Jessa knew she shouldn't be insistent. She had to try to relax and let Rosemary be the boss.

Everyone in front of Jessa had their blinkers on, merging into the inside lane. She had driven a mile over the last thirty minutes. There must have been an accident up ahead. Fucking American drivers.

Jessa was replaying her conversation with Rosemary and Thomas. Jessa had explained how an image of a water tower, a hotel, and an almond tree had led her to Winters, and how the almond tree painting had led her to the Minna Gallery and Valance. Jessa had described the accident and said she had seen Elizabeth forced off the road by someone, then stuffed back into her own car and propelled off the bank. Rosemary had wept. Thomas had looked completely stunned.

"Who was it?" he had demanded. "Who tried to kill my wife?"

Jessa hadn't mentioned anything about Mr. Robert Flores. Although she was certain the reverend was the culprit, she had no

228

hard evidence. She needed proof, something to link Robert to Elizabeth before she started accusing the son of a bitch and got herself deported. She had told Thomas it was a man who tried to kill Elizabeth; a man without a face.

Jessa followed the snake of traffic, driving torturously slow passed flashing yellow lights and a horde of construction workers digging up the road. She was thinking how to prove Elizabeth's affair before bringing it to Rosemary's and Thomas' attention. She needed evidence first. Everything she wanted to say needed evidence and it was frustrating the shit out of her. She needed to prove Elizabeth had been sleeping with Robert Flores, and that he knew she had been carrying his child—and the son of a bitch had tried to kill her because of it.

CHAPTER 65

The few hours Robert had spent in his office were wholly non-productive. He hadn't written a single meaningful note for Sunday's sermon. Last week's show had boasted the largest viewer ratings ever and the television executives were expecting this week's ratings to be even higher. They explicitly requested more controversy. But he couldn't think of what to say. He couldn't focus. His thoughts were of Kim. Images of Kim swirled in his mind every time he tried to write something down. Her slender body, big voluptuous breasts, innocent young face—Robert wanted her so badly it hurt.

He stared at the document, desperately trying to elaborate on why the world would be a better place without religion. Then he slammed the lid shut in frustration. Enough time had passed. Surely his wife's idiot social gathering was finished by now. It was safe to go home. He would have to endure Juliet rambling on about shit he didn't care about; and Robert would smile and nod and say, "Yes, hon," and then he would sit on the veranda with a glass of wine and lose himself in his own wicked thoughts.

Robert packed his laptop into his leather satchel and walked over to the weathered coat stand beside the window, the window overlooking the church grounds. He put on his jacket while watching an old couple struggle to climb into an SUV waiting outside the community hall. It took the elders an extraordinary amount of effort to get inside the vehicle, and Robert found the whole ordeal quite amusing. The old man bared some resemblance to Albert Einstein. He tried to get inside the massive vehicle three times, once losing his grip on the rail and falling flat on his arse. Only then did the driver, a tubby woman in tight pants and a tight shirt, get out and help him. She looked more annoyed with the doddery old fool than concerned. It wasn't until this elderly freakshow finished up and the SUV pulled away that Robert finally picked up his briefcase and left the office. He hadn't noticed the silver car driving towards the church.

*

Although the hall she passed was full of activity, the church looked closed. Jessa pulled her rental up in front, then sat in the car enjoying the aircon and observed the church's pale façade. She was drained from her visit with Rosemary and Thomas and really wanted to go back to the hotel for a shower and something to eat. She needed to wind down.

But Jessa wouldn't allow herself rest or relaxation. She was getting close to solving the case. Now it was time to get some more information on Robert Flores.

Climbing the wooden steps, a cool breeze brushed Jessa's face. She tried the front doors of the church, but they were closed. She cupped her hands around her face and peered into the front window. All she saw was a gloomy old church with empty pews. So, she walked back down the steps, passed her car, and strolled along the left wall of the church. There were low windows barely off the ground, and Jessa got on her knees in the grass to peer into one. It was more gloom, the main stage area and rows of seats. The place was empty. At the next window, Jessa did the same. She cupped her hands around her face and peered through the glass.

Fucking bingo.

It was the room Jessa had seen in her dreams. There wasn't much light; the place was dim and full of shadows—but sure enough, she saw the old worn desk and the crucifix above it. Then a blast of memory sent Jessa staggering away from the window. It was like something out of a porno. Jessa had the briefest vision of herself bent over the desk, looking dutifully up at the crucifix while she got fucked in the arse.

The vision was too intense. Jessa hunched over and vomited into the grass. Stringy bile dribbled off her lips as she took deep breaths through her nose, holding her knees. The disturbing image was gone but Jessa felt overwhelmingly perturbed. She knew it was her sister's memory—but with the memories always came feelings, too. Intense feelings and what Jessa had felt in that brief vision was sexual pleasure. Elizabeth had been enjoying anal penetration.

231

Wiping her lips, Jessa stood and once more (cautiously this time) looked in through the window. Maybe if she could get inside, she could find something that proved Elizabeth had been here. Maybe Jessa could use it as evidence. But all she could see from the outside was an empty coat stand and a cupboard built into an alcove near the window. Using the palm of her hand, Jessa tried to slide open the sash window, but it was locked-up tight.

She gave up on the window and followed the grass to the rear of the church. She needed to get back into the stuffy vestibule and try and sneak her way into the reverend's office. But as she turned the corner, Jessa came face-to-face with the bastard himself.

*

Robert was speaking to the caretaker, Hank, when Jessa Summers crept around the corner of the church like Nancy fucking Drew.

"Hey," Hank shouted, "what are you doing, miss? You can't be here. The church is closed today." He was giving her a mean look, his old gnarled body tensed as if he was ready for a fight.

Robert didn't know what to do. What the fuck was she doing here? He could tell Hank to escort her off the property. The wily old caretaker had done it plenty of times before. He was strong and mean for his age. And with Hank around, it wasn't as if Robert could grab the blonde bitch by her head and smash it against the side of the church.

"I'm here to see him," Jessa said, staring straight at Robert.

"What do you want with me, Miss Summers?" Robert asked. He sensed that she was scared. In fact, she reeked of fear. Robert could smell it. "I told you before, I don't know you and I'm sure you don't know me."

"I know you don't know me," Jessa said, "but you know my sister. I know what you did to her, you bastard. You tried to kill her."

Now Robert really wanted to strangle the bitch. His face got hot with anger. "I haven't the faintest idea what you're talking about, Miss Summers." He dismissed her with a wave of his hand and walked towards his car. "I have to go. Goodbye now."

"Elizabeth Foster," Jessa said. "She was pregnant with your baby, Mr. Flores. And you tried to murder her to hide the truth."

Robert stopped, stared motionless at his car. For the first time in his life, he felt backed into a corner. He felt like a caged animal. He spun on his heels, about to say something when Hank stepped in.

"Hey," said Hank, "you're that woman from the other day. You shouldn't be here, miss. If you don't leave right now, I'll be calling the police." Then Hank put himself between Robert and Jessa. His wispy grey hair fluttered slightly in the breeze.

"We've had a few weirdos up from the city lately to stalk Mr. Flores," he told Jessa. "One woman even thought Mr. Flores had asked her to marry him. She turned up here in a wedding dress, completely delusional. So, miss, as you can imagine, we don't take too kindly to strangers turning up uninvited. Leave now or I really will call the police." Hank pulled an old flip phone from the front pocket of his grubby denim dungarees and flaunted it. "I mean it now."

Jessa ignored the old fart. "You call yourself the Holy Man? You're a fucking hypocrite. I've seen the disgusting things you did to my sister."

Robert's face was going from red to crimson he was so fucking angry. Jessa turned from him and shouted at Hank, "Did you know that your celebrity preacher was fucking my sister while telling the world adultery is a sin? Did you also know that Mr. Flores fucked my sister up the arse in this very church?"

Hank blinked at her, looking mortified by such a perverted description.

"That's enough," Robert said, his voice like a great clap of thunder. "I will not stand here and listen to your outlandish and vulgar accusations. Hank, please call the police."

The old man gave a nod and started to dial.

"You don't have to do that, Hank," Jessa said, throwing her hands up in surrender. "I'm leaving."

She made her way past Hank, who had lifted his phone to his hairy ear. She stopped and stared Robert in his face. "Mr. Flores, I know you wanted Elizabeth to have an abortion. And I know you

233

tried to kill her because she wouldn't. I'm not leaving this godforsaken country until I get justice for what you did to my sister. Even if it kills me, I will get justice."

Robert had chewed so hard on his tongue he could taste blood. He wished Hank wasn't there so he could drag Jessa Summers down into the cellar and stick his cock up *her* arse. Fucking bitch. All he could do was fume as she walked away. Hank said to him, "The police are on their way, Mr. Flores."

Somehow, Robert managed to keep calm. "Thank you, Hank. Please make sure that woman leaves. And could you please make a note of her license plate number."

"Sure thing, Mr. Flores." Hank went scuttling off after the woman.

Robert stood totally still, his insides fuelled by hatred, his blood toxic soup. Who the fuck was this bitch? He wanted to rip her apart, smash her up good and bury the dumb cunt beneath the church. Because asides from overwhelming anger, Robert felt something else—something altogether loathsome.

Robert felt scared.

CHAPTER 66

The hotel reception was buzzing with excitement when Jessa arrived. Men in designer suits and women in expensive evening dresses chatted and sipped champagne. There was a gold-framed poster on an easel beside the reception desk, congratulating Mr. And Mrs. Whoever on their wedding day. Jessa didn't really give a fuck. She bypassed the crowd and headed to her room.

The door slammed shut behind her and Jessa began to strip off her clothes, throwing them in heaps on the floor. Then she took a long shower. She let the steam fill the room and tried to relax under the hot spray, let her tense muscles ease. She closed her eyes and stood in the shower until wrinkled and lost in her own mind. Of course, she was thinking about her encounter with Robert. She'd certainly gotten under his skin. There was no question that beneath his holy façade was pure evil.

But what about her sister, Elizabeth? From Jessa's vision, she knew her sister was something of a deviant. She liked getting fucked up the arse by the preacher man. And honestly, Jessa was disgusted by it. The image stuck in her head like a bad stain. It made her want to puke again in the shower. She tried to think of the other fragmented messages, memories, visions. Jessa needed proof to convict Robert, the villain in her sister's transmitted dreams. Maybe tomorrow when she would finally get to meet her sister, the connection would be stronger and Jessa could gain more insight into what happened, somehow collecting the evidence needed to bring Robert Flores to justice.

Jessa was pulling her t-shirt on when a knock came at the door. She crept over and looked through the peephole.

"Miss Summers, this is Officer Gonzalez. Open the door." He thumped on the door a few more times.

"Shit," she whispered. Gonzalez and another officer stood in the hallway, both men staring at the peephole. They didn't look like they were on a social call.

Jessa snuck across the room, slipped on her trainers, and grabbed her phone and laptop off the bed. She quietly slid open the glass door and stepped onto the veranda. She heard the officer call out, "We know you're in there, Miss Summers. Now please open the door. Don't make this any harder than it needs to be."

She slid the door shut from the outside and jogged across the garden, passing other hotel rooms until she reached the back of the hotel. The car park was full. Jessa had to scan the sea of cars to find her rental. Then she went calmly across to her car and climbed in, threw her phone and laptop onto the passenger seat and started the ignition. She drove past the young concierge as he scratched his head, and the empty patrol car. She needed to get out of Winters quick and lay low for a few hours. Maybe she'd call Candice or even Rosemary to seek refuge.

*

When the police arrived at the church to take Robert's statement, he remained calm and in control. Robert even told Gonzalez he sympathised with Miss Summers. "Mental health is a serious issue, I know. This woman is clearly in need of psychiatric help." Hank gave an over exaggerated account of the event, saying he had never heard such vulgarity from such a pretty woman. Robert was adamant about his concern for Miss Summers. He told them she was unpredictable and made him nervous. "I don't like to be harassed, you know."

Gonzalez assured Robert they would deal with the situation. He said they were going straight over to the hotel where Jessa was staying. They were going to bring her down to the station. He may not have told Robert the name of the hotel, but Robert was sure he could find which one if needed. There were only two fucking hotels in town. When the Police left, Robert followed them, keeping a safe distance. Gonzalez and his partner passed the discount motel at the edge of town, and Robert eased up and made his own leisurely route to the only other hotel: the Almond Tree Hotel.

Sitting as stealthily as he could in his SUV, Robert watched, wallowing in his own fury. The squad car was empty, the two dumb cops still inside. They'd been in there at least five minutes. How hard was it to drag a stupid blonde bitch out of her room and into the squad car? Hairline cracks started to form on his otherwise calm and collected exterior and he was feeling overly agitated. Why had Elizabeth lied to him about having a sister? The fucking bitch. She could have told anyone about the pregnancy and about their affair. But how did Jessa Summers know he had suggested an abortion? Hadn't he backhanded Elizabeth across the face moments after she refused? It was not like Elizabeth could have called anyone. She had left her phone in the hotel room before running off like a maniac and Robert had kept her cell phone ever since.

Nearly ten minutes now. The police still hadn't come out. Robert was beside himself. He needed the bitch taken care of. But then again, if she eluded the police, perhaps Robert could track her down and take care of her himself. He asked God for guidance.

"Lord," Robert whispered, "you know every decision I must make and every challenge I face. Please forgive me for the times I try to figure this life out on my own. I need you, God. I need the Holy Spirit to give me strength, wisdom, and direction. Amen."

Robert finished his prayer and let out a sigh. And at that very moment, a silver car reversed hard out of a parking spot and kicked up dust as it sped past Robert and away from the hotel. He laughed to himself when he saw the driver, a disgruntled Jessa Summers behind the wheel. "Thank you, God," he said, still chuckling. He started his SUV and drove after her.

Fuck Gonzalez. Robert would handle the bitch himself.

*

Jessa kept checking her rear-view, expecting to see flashing lights behind her, but they never came. There was nothing but empty road. The evening light was fading, the sun sinking behind the mountains. The unfamiliar road stretched to the horizon, flanked by dense trees. Jessa had no idea where she was going. She just had to put some distance between herself and the hotel. The cops would soon be searching for her in Winters.

Headlights glared in the rear-view. "Fuck," Jessa said. She assumed it was the police. "Fuck fuck fuck."

Jessa accelerated hard. She didn't want any trouble with the police. She knew evading them was a bad move. DI Radisson had fed Gonzalez and his department a load of hot shit about her mental instability. They wouldn't believe anything she said about

Robert or Elizabeth. She had to get away from them and solve the damn case on her own. She couldn't miss seeing her sister tomorrow, even if she did end up in jail after.

Jessa's speedometer hit 90mph. The vehicle behind her was coming up fast. Its beams were on full, lights reflecting angrily in Jessa's mirror. But there was no siren. There were no flashing red and blue lights. "Fuck!" Jessa put her foot down. The engine revved and the car lurched but didn't go much faster. The road was a straight line and there were no junctions or turnoffs. She wasn't going to outrun the police in her shitty rental car.

"Fuck!" The vehicle was right on her arse. It was flashing its headlights. "Motherfucker!" Jessa smacked her steering wheel, then let her foot off the throttle. It was no good. She'd never outrun them. She coasted slowly onto the verge and stopped.

"Pull yourself together," Jessa said, teary-eyed. "They already think you're crazy. Don't fucking lose it."

The vehicle stopped behind her, keeping its beams on. The light was blinding inside Jessa's car. There were still no flashing lights. She was trying to think of a quick way out. How could she persuade the police to let her go? Had she even broken any laws? She was vaguely aware of someone coming up to her driver's door—then a forceful yank as someone tried to open her door; lucky it was locked. She saw a big fist hammering madly on her window and she stamped back down on the accelerator. "Fuck this!" she screamed, and took off like a rocket.

*

Robert was sprayed with gravel as the bitch hit the gas and her tyres spun in the dirt.

"You fucking cunt!"

He ran back to his SUV. Jessa Summers was already way up the road, her taillights two little red dots disappearing into the distance. There was less than ten miles before the country road intersected the highway. He had to get to her before that, before there were witnesses. His engine roared as he kicked into gear and got back on the road, his pedal nailed to the floor. He shifted gears and chugged fast up the road, Jessa Summers' taillights coming closer and closer. Some arsehole appeared in the oncoming lane, then passed Robert a second later. Robert was almost on the bitch now. He was a car-length away. He looked in the mirror and waited for the passer-by's taillights to vanish before making his move.

Pressing his foot hard to the floor, Robert nudged Jessa's stupid rental car. She swerved but regained control. He had to act now. He had to ram the fucking bitch off the road. He stomped the gas and pulled up beside her, then smashed hard into her rear end.

*

Jessa had thought her little manoeuvre would give her enough time to get away. She was wrong. They were gaining on her again. The same high beams glared in her mirror. All she wanted was to escape. She hadn't come so far to be arrested now. She had to meet her sister. Jessa had to complete their bond.

The little rental engine screamed, Jessa's foot pressed firmly on the floor. Still, she was no match for her pursuers. The road dipped and a car passed in the other direction, and a moment later Jessa was rear-ended. Her neck snapped. The seatbelt locked and she jolted in her seat. The car wavered, but she managed to get it under control. "You fucker! You fucker!"

That was all she said before she started screaming. It wasn't a cop car. It was a fucking SUV. She caught a glimpse of it as it came up beside her, then barrelled hard into the back door and sent Jessa spinning in a violent circle. She had her hands on the wheel, jerking and trying to correct—but the rental tipped onto two wheels. It bounced back onto the road with a sick crunch and then skidded straight into the trees. Jessa was still screaming when she crashed.

CHAPTER 67

Robert was still pissed. He sat at the kitchen table swirling a glass of red wine. If the incident earlier hadn't been maddening enough, his egotistical wife was pottering around like a nutcase, going on about the neighbours' husbands and the cars they drove, about how successful The Holy Man show was becoming. She hadn't even asked Robert about his day. He knew she didn't care. All Juliet cared about was money and the lavish lifestyle Robert's show was giving her. She had grown accustomed to the wealth.

But she wouldn't shut up! Robert was getting angrier and angrier as she scurried around the kitchen yammering on, fussing with everything. He wanted her to shut the fuck up. He screamed it in his head: *"Shut the fuck up, you stupid bitch! I need to think."* He took a sip of wine and tried to ignore her. It felt like his existence was crumbling around him. He was getting erratic, even unstable. He needed to regain his control after today's daylight attack.

"Robert," she said, "are you listening to me?"

He cringed. Somewhere during the past year, Juliet had acquired a posh, upper-class accent. It was like nails on a chalkboard. He gave her a blank look. She was such an average woman. She was plain, featureless, and bland. Juliet was a housekeeper and a chef. She was a humble disguise for his bad behaviour.

"Robert, I said the Thompsons have invited us for a BBQ next week. He's a gynaecologist. Can you believe it?" She scoffed. "Well, he certainly won't be looking at my lady garden."

"Right," Robert said.

Now she was at the wall calendar. "What day next week?"

He was hardly listening. Robert just wanted to drink his wine in peace and gather his thoughts. Now he wanted to cut his wife's tongue out. "Wednesday," he said gruffly. He was thinking about Jessa Summers. She wasn't a threat anymore. Her car was a hunk of mangled steel twisted around some tree. Still, his little stunt had been careless. Forensic evidence was all over the road. He could only hope the police would label it an accident and not investigate too closely.

Juliet was still yacking. Robert was on the edge of insanity. He needed to do something before he finally ended up murdering his wife. He took a gulp of wine. Now he was imagining Kim and her huge, soft, squishy breasts. He instantly got hard.

Juliet was writing on the wall calendar, still talking. Robert got up and approached her, not saying a word, his massive cock pushing through his pants. He grabbed Juliet by her shoulders and spun her around, then bent her over the kitchen counter and lifted her dress. He kept her pinned against the counter with one hand while he undid his pants. Robert had his wife's face pressed hard against the granite worktop. She had finally shut the fuck up. She knew better than to resist. Resisting only made Robert more violent.

As he plunged himself deep into his wife's stuck-up pussy, he imagined violating young Kim in front of her dad, Ned, right there in the backroom of Steady Neddy's Coffee Shop.

Robert smiled. For the first time in an hour, his wife wasn't making a peep, not even a moan.

CHAPTER 68

I'm waiting for the colours to appear. I'm thinking about how Robert Flores murdered me and our unborn child because I threatened to expose our affair. I still don't truly know who I am. I may never know for sure. For now, I am only Elizabeth.

The ghostly shapes float in and out of the light. They are starting to take on solid forms. They peer at me through the whiteness. They've started calling my name. As their calls become clearer, the tingling sensation becomes more intense. There is only a thin strip of blackness left. I know that soon I will be surrounded by the light. Not long now until I join the ghosts and am forever lost to the whiteness.

I'm feeling anxious and full of dread. Something is terribly wrong. There's a sickening pain in my head as scenes play out in the whiteness like a distorted movie. I see myself in a car hurtling towards a tree. Then I'm being pulled from the smoking wreckage. Now dragged into a room. There's a wooden desk and something hanging on the wall above it. It's the office from the church.

I see myself now strapped to a bed in a windowless room. The blurry outline of Robert Flores towers above me. The scene distorts and refocuses. Robert's looking down at me with his piercing blue eyes, deranged and evil. He's the last thing I see before the white completely surrounds me.

The blackness has dissolved. I'm blinded by bright light. It feels different now, and for a moment I can't understand why. Then I see that my glass walls are gone. My prison has vanished. Is it over? I wonder. Someone calls my name through the blurry whiteness. Shadows appear and gather. There's a featureless grey human holding out their hand to me. I try and move towards them. I want to grab the hand and be guided away. I'm ready to leave this place, but I'm paralysed. I can't even scream.

The whiteness begins to dissolve. There are only seconds left before I'm gone forever. I try desperately to move one more time, but I can't. The light has become a grey hue. The silhouette takes on a more solid form. My name is being called like an echo, getting louder and louder. The silhouette is a woman standing in front of me. I recognise her. It's me. She looks as terrified as I feel. She calls my name, "Elizabeth. Elizabeth, help me," over and over like a crackling radio transmission.

The tingling sensation pulses through my body and my doppelganger's words fade. Everything evanesces into nonexistence.

CHAPTER 69

Jessa was trying to open her eyes, but they were too bruised. She could only see a little through her left one. The right was ballooned and swollen. Her face felt puffy, numbed by some shitty anaesthesia. It was red and black and wet with congealed blood. Her nose was broken, still leaking. She tried to move her legs, only to find them broken. She shrieked in excruciating pain and passed out.

When Jessa came to, her throat felt like it was on fire. "Water," she croaked. Her lips were dry and split open. She was tied to a bed. Through her one good eye, Jessa saw her wrists were tied to the bedpost. She was too weak and broken to struggle. Another wave of unbearable pain sent her drifting into unconsciousness.

Jessa dreamt. It was the dream she so often had after her dad passed. She was sinking through black, murky water, alone and helpless as the undertow drew her down. Her arms and legs flapped hopelessly in her attempt to reach the surface, Jessa's lungs screaming for air. No matter how hard she tried to emerge from the cold, dank water, she was pulled deeper into the blackness. Her lungs were about to give out. Her body screamed for oxygen and her vision faded. Jessa was about to suck the rancid water into her lungs, but through the murkiness came her father's hands to save her. She grabbed desperately for her father. She was almost within reach. But then Jessa was pulled deeper into the abyss.

CHAPTER 70

I'm staring up into the bright light utterly confused. The light didn't take me after all and I'm somewhat disappointed. Maybe I'm in Heaven. Maybe I'm in a confounding purgatory and I'll never leave.

I continue staring into the light, blinking rapidly. It takes me a second to realise the significance of this. I can feel myself blinking! I can feel movement in my fingers! I take a deep breath and feel the expansion of my chest. How is this possible? I focus on the light; it's different. It's not the brilliant white light that besieged me before. It's duller. It makes me feel disoriented and now I'm scared of my surroundings. My head hurts as I look down my body. I'm not naked. I'm lying in a bed with clean linens pulled to my chest. I try to move my arms, but something prevents me. It's a white plaster cover. I have casts from my wrists to my armpits. Glancing over, there is a heart monitor machine. I'm hooked to it.

My god. I'm in a hospital. I'm crying. It feels so good to cry! There's a man looking at me. He's handsome and tall, grey receding hair. I don't recognise him, and he seems confused. Then a nurse comes into the room with a doctor. What are they saying? I almost think this is another vision, but quickly assure myself that it's not. It's too different. This time I'm alive.

*

The phone call from the hospital came early Saturday morning and Rosemary expected the worse. She thought her precious daughter had finally given up and quietly slipped away. Rosemary asked the nurse on the phone to repeat herself three times before she was convinced. The nurse said, "Ma'am, Elizabeth has woken from her coma. You can come see her now." Rosemary broke down and cried tears of joy.

Now the old woman sat in her wheelchair in the hospital room holding her daughter's hand, watching as she slept. If Rosemary didn't know any better, she'd have thought Elizabeth was still in a coma. But Elizabeth had been drifting in and out of sleep all day. The doctors said it was normal.

Thomas walked quietly into the room with a coffee. He looked traumatised staring at his wife. Rosemary offered Thomas her warm bony hand. "Elizabeth is going to be okay, Thomas," Rosemary said. He feigned a smile. Rosemary loved Thomas like she would her own son. He put on a brave face for her, but Rosemary knew he was heartbroken. She thought he must be in shock because of the wonderful news. God had answered Rosemary's prayers and now Elizabeth was free from her coma.

"She's going to be fine," Rosemary said again, looking at Thomas, then down at her sleeping daughter. "She's going to be just fine."

*

Elizabeth, help me! repeats in my mind as I drift in and out of consciousness. An overwhelming dread hangs heavy in the pit of my stomach. I know something terrible has happened. I can see the aurora of colour in my mind's eye, the cries for help getting louder. The colours are much more extraordinary than before. As they get more vivid, the pleas get more desperate. A presence enters my mind, and rather than try to resist, I allow it to possess me. The swirling mass of colour pulsates violently and explodes into an amplitude of brilliant white light.

I'm surrounded by a light grey mist. Everywhere I turn is ashen obscurity. The plea for help floats through the haze from every direction. The presence is strong here and I feel it's leading me somewhere. I let it guide me, walking through the mist until through it looms a white wooden church. The details are faint, but I recognise it instantly. It's Robert's church, completely shrouded by the mist. The front doors are closed. The presence leads me around to the side.

As I approach the rear of the church, the door opens and I walk into the small vestibule, then into Robert's office. The presence is even stronger here. Robert's office is the same as I remember it. The old worn desk, the crucifix on the wall. Nothing is out of the ordinary. I can't understand why it is I've been brought here. Then there's a creak from the cupboard in the corner. I look in time to see the cupboard's door open. I approach, feeling pulled on by the unknown force. Looking into the closet, a trap door springs open, revealing a small dark portal in the floor. I peer down into a dusky cellar. The force is calling me. I climb through the floor space, using the ladder, and into a small concrete room.

The room is nearly vacant. On the other side is a door with a digital locking mechanism. I hear her: "Elizabeth, help me!" She's screaming from the other side of the door. I try to open it, but it's locked. She's screaming louder: "Elizabeth, help me!" I tap a few numbers on the digital keypad but nothing happens. I thump and push on the door but there's no give. I try to call out, only to have my voice deafened by her screams. The presence is trying to pull me through the closed door. Finally, it flies open.

A murky pool of water fills the doorframe. It looks like the room is flooded from floor to ceiling, but the water doesn't spill out of the door. Small bubbles are floating on its surface. I lean in to get a better look and a pair of hands burst through the water. Crooked fingers grab and claw thin air before they are yanked back inside, leaving ripples on the water's surface.

"Elizabeth, help me!"

Without thinking, I plunge my arms through the doorframe, into the murky water and thrash about. I can't feel anything. It's wet and cold. I fear it's too late. The presence drains and the screams for help stop. In the silence, I stretch my arms into the water as deep as they will go, and am shocked when hands grasp hold of mine. I hold them tight. A connection sparks between me and the drowning woman and fragmented images begin to play on the surface of the water. I know instinctively they are the memories of the presence, the person, who guided me here.

With all my strength, I pull my twin sister out of the murky depths.

CHAPTER 71

Robert sat at the breakfast bar turning a mug of cold coffee in his hands, lost in thought. The veil—the precious mask that had been hiding his true personality for so many years—was starting to crack. It was slipping off like so much dead flesh. Even here in his kitchen, Robert felt overpowered by rage. He teetered on the brink of psychosis. Robert knew that if he didn't regain control over his impulses soon, he'd spiral out of control.

"Breakfast, darling?" It wasn't much of a question. Juliet placed a plate of bacon and eggs in front of him. "More coffee?"

Robert glared at her. Even after forcing himself on her last night, Juliet carried on as though nothing had happened, as though being raped by her husband was perfectly normal in her perfect life.

"Would you like more coffee, darling?" She had a well-rehearsed smile on her lips.

I'd like to cut you into tiny fucking pieces, Robert thought. He stood abruptly, scraping the stool across the tiles and making Juliet wince. For a moment, her eyes filled with fear. Robert stared at her with the cold hard gaze of a serial killer.

Before he had anymore thoughts of butchering his wife, Robert walked out of the kitchen.

CHAPTER 72

I wake with a gasp, surprised to see I'm being gawked at by a nurse. Her mouth is moving but I can't hear her speak. I try to lift myself up, but I'm too weak. I can't move. Another face appears. He's the man I saw the first time I woke up. I don't recognise him, but I stare anyway. He looks agitated.

All of a sudden, it's as if someone turns up the volume. My hearing roars to life. The machine beside my bed is beeping, voices are rebounding about the room. The noise for a moment is deafening. There's a frail old woman beside my bed. She's sitting in a wheelchair, crying, cupping one of my hands in hers.

"Elizabeth," she says. "Elizabeth, you're awake."

"Jessa," I whisper, trying again to lift myself up.

"Jessa is on her way," the old woman says.

"No." I shake my head. "You don't understand. Jessa. She's in trouble."

The nurse comes to comfort me, looking disturbed. It's hard to talk and my throat burns horribly. She's saying something and it agitates me. "You need to help her," I say to the old woman. The nurse is talking about hallucinations. "In danger. Robert has my sister."

I stay awake long enough to acknowledge the look on the woman's face. She believes me.

CHAPTER 73

It was mid-morning by the time someone arrived from the dealership with a courtesy car. The vehicle was the same model as his SUV, just red. Robert had called them first thing that morning to book his SUV in for repairs. It needed a new headlamp and side panel.

Robert threw his overnight bag into the backseat of his replacement car and got in the front. Then he was on his way to San Francisco. Robert was due to meet the television executives for an early dinner at the hotel. Tomorrow morning's episode of The Holy Man was anticipated to be the most viewed religious program in US history, and the most controversial to date. Robert was mindful he hadn't prepared anything for tomorrow's sermon. He hoped a few hours in the hotel away from his wife and his shitty little town would ease his mind enough to allow him to focus.

Somehow, his demons were in abeyance during the drive. Robert tried his best to relax. He needed to carry on with his routine, act normal, think rationally. He assured himself there was nothing to worry about. Jessa Summers was being guarded by God, in a place where no one would ever find her. All evidence of the collision and any trace of the English woman would be erased once his SUV was repaired and cleaned. For the time being, Robert's evil within was relatively restrained.

*

The pain was almost unbearable. At least until she tried to move—then her brain would switch off like a tripped fuse and she would be knocked out. Her body was slowly shutting down. Jessa knew death was imminent. She stared at the stark grey ceiling inertly with her one good eye, thinking about all the things she could have done in her life. She regretted not spending more time with her dad, not telling him how much she had loved him. Maybe then he would have told her about the adoption.

She also regretted the way she had treated Vanessa. Jessa's self-absorbed and erratic behaviour had pushed her girlfriend away yet again. She regretted never enjoying music or art, or a simple scenic view. She felt she had squandered her life and a single tear trickled down Jessa's face. She regretted not having the chance to meet her twin sister.

CHAPTER 74

Gonzalez had just returned to the station with a coffee and sandwich from Steady Neddy's. He was about to sit at his desk and eat his lunch with the chief called him into his office.

"Yes, chief?" Gonzalez said, standing in the chief's office with his stomach rumbling.

Chief Stanton was due to retire in three months, but he looked very much like a man who should have retired ten years ago. The heavy lines on his crumpled face marked him as a man who had spent his entire life in the police force—a man who had endured four marriages, suffered three divorces, fathered seven children, and survived two heart attacks. His eyelids were so heavy with folds and wrinkles that at times Gonzalez thought Stanton was asleep at his desk.

"Any news on the Summers woman?" Stanton asked.

"Nothing yet, sir."

"Well, she certainly didn't leave the vehicle on her own. It would have been a miracle if she had the strength to open the door judging by the wreckage."

"We do believe another vehicle was involved, sir," Gonzalez said. "Luckily, that stretch of road isn't a busy one. The crash site wasn't too contaminated by the time we got there. We found two sets of tire marks consistent with a collision, and the boys at forensics believe the trace evidence found at the scene shows two different types of plastic fragments from broken taillights."

"A hit and run?" asked the chief.

"Possibly. But there's no body. We've searched the area and found no trace of her." Gonzalez's stomach rumbled and he paused, sure the old chief had heard it. "She wasn't thrown from the vehicle. The passenger-side door was crushed against a tree trunk. The windshield was badly damaged but still intact. The driver's side-window was blown out, but it's not like she crawled out of it and walked home."

Stanton grumbled, shuffling through the crime scene photos on his desk. "Is it possible someone could have caused the accident and taken the body away? Maybe someone wants to hide the evidence. Perp could have been DUI. Miss Summers might have survived the accident and the perp got scared. Might be he took her away to shut her up."

"It is a possibility, sir. But now we're talking about murder."

No one spoke. The only sound in the room was Gonzalez's rumbling stomach. He couldn't tell if the chief was deep in thought or had nodded off to sleep. His eyes were closed—at least Gonzalez thought they were, and he sat with his head bowed.

Chief Stanton then jerked as if snapping out of a dream. He went on talking like nothing had happened. "I've had a call from a buddy of mine high up in SFPD. He's asked me to check something out for him. The Evangelical church outside of town. Drive over there and take a look."

"What am I looking for?" Gonzalez asked, eyebrows raised.

"It's probably nothing," Stanton said, shifting in his chair. "I mean, it sounds batshit crazy to me. But drive over there. See about a door at the back of the church. There should be an office of some kind. Inside the office may be a storage cupboard, and inside this storage cupboard may be a trap door to a basement."

Gonzalez gave the chief an incredible look, as if to say, *"This is a joke, right?"*

"Just check it out," Stanton said. "You'll probably find nothing, but I owe my buddy a few favours and this is one of them. He wouldn't have called if he thought it was a waste of time."

Gonzalez shrugged. "Okay, chief. But one question. What has this got to do with Jessa Summers?"

"Look," Stanton said, "keep this to yourself, okay? Jessa Summers has a twin sister who's just come out of a coma. The sister experienced a kind of vision or something while in the coma. She described Jessa's accident in some detail. Anyway, she believes Robert Flores caused Miss Summers to crash her car and has her locked up beneath the church."

"The celebrity preacher?"

"Just go and have a look," Stanton said. "Poke around and then report back to me."

Gonzalez had taken his notepad from his breast pocket and was flipping through the pages. "What was the sister's name, sir?"

"Elizabeth Foster."

"Huh," Gonzalez said. He was looking at the name he had scribbled down after his last encounter with Jessa Summers: *Elizabeth Foster*. And he was remembering the conversation with DI Radisson from England. "I'll go there now, sir."

"Oh, and Gonzalez," the chief called before Gonzalez could leave the room, "finish your lunch first. Your stomach sounds like a grizzly bear."

CHAPTER 75

My sister is dying. I can feel her slipping away. I want to reach out and tell her I feel her. I want to assure her that I know where she is and that I'm sending help, but our connection is too weak. I feel nothing but my own pain. I am scared I will lose her before I ever get to know her.

I look at the old woman in the wheelchair, my mother. She gives me a warm smile through her oxygen mask. "Jessa will be fine, my darling," Rosemary tells me. "Help is on the way," she says." But I have seen what Robert's done to her. I've felt her excruciating pain. If help doesn't arrive quickly, Jessa will undoubtedly die.

Although I am awake, I hold no memory of my mother or the man named Thomas, who is supposedly my husband. The doctors have explained to me that amnesia is not uncommon for people newly awoken from comas. My memory could heal in hours or even days. In an extreme circumstance, months or years. The only memories I have are of Robert Flores and my sister, Jessa.

I explained to Rosemary about the accident, how I saw Robert Flores drive my sister off the road and take her to the church. "I've seen it in my mind," I told her. I also revealed that Robert Flores was the one who tried to kill me. Rosemary told me Jessa saw it in her visions, that she knew my crash was no accident. Thomas didn't say a word the entire time, looking at me in a way I couldn't quite read. Disbelief, confusion, anger, relief? Whichever it was, Thomas made me uneasy.

I'm looking at my husband without affection or emotion. He tells me we've been married three years, but all I see is a stranger. He asks how I knew Robert Flores and why he tried to murder me. I lie. I say I don't remember. I'm not ready to reveal I was having an affair with Robert and was pregnant with his baby. At least not until I start regaining my memory and understand why I did the things I did.

I start to feel agitated. A lurking fear crawls through me, not my own, hurting my weak and broken body. "Jessa is dying," I say. "I can feel her presence fading out of me. She needs help."

Rosemary gives me assurances. She tells me everything will be okay, and that the police are on their way. Thomas grows animated and announces he will drive to the church himself if the police don't find anything. I sense no conviction in his words.

Rosemary explained that my late father passed away several years ago. He was an influential businessman of great success in San Francisco. He was well-connected to men of influence. One of those men was the retired chief of police in San Francisco. Rosemary made a call, and he had made a call, and the local sheriffs would be making a visit to the church soon.

"See," she says, "the police are on their way. Get some rest, darling. Everything will be fine."

"They must search the office," I stress. "It's very important they find the trap door."

Rosemary assures me they will search the church, but I'm doubtful since they won't have a warrant. Still, I hope. I hope as I begin to drift off again. I hope Jessa is still alive. I hope the police will find her quickly. My sister's life depends on it.

CHAPTER 76

The sermon was a complete fucking disaster. The show that had been billed as the most controversial to date was the worst performance of Robert's life. He stumbled over his words. There was no structure to his content, not a single note of controversy. Robert knew it was a debacle, and so did the network. So did every fucker who watched it.

Fury burned Robert's insides and malevolence consumed him. He sat in the office trying to compose himself, sipping bourbon from a flask. He thought he was in control, yet he could feel his equanimity being devoured by his monstrous alter ego. The cunt he had tied up in the basement was the cause of his declination. Fucking bitch. He wouldn't be happy or at peace until he knew she was dead. She was too broken to be of any use to him. The quicker she disappeared, the quicker he could restore order and regain control of his personality.

Robert was gathering up his things when someone started knocking on his door. "Mr. Flores. Mr. Flores."

Robert opened the door. A very anxious network employee stood in the hallway. Robert remembered his name was Sam.

"Sorry to disturb you," Sam said, "but we have a bit of a situation."

Robert looked at him with his eyebrows raised, waiting for a further explanation. Screams resonated from down the hall. "What's happening, Sam?" Robert asked.

"Mr. Flores, there is a woman causing a fuss. She said she won't leave the church until she's spoken to you." Sam looked down the hall, more high-pitched screaming echoing into the room. "We've tried to calm her down. We told her you're busy. But she says if you don't speak to her, she'll tell the world about..." Sam hesitated, looking awkward.

"About what, man? Tell me!"

"About the..." Sam hesitated again. "Well, about the sexual relations you had with her."

"She's just a kook," Robert said, snarling at the boy. "Call the police and let them deal with her. I've got to go."

Sam had a cell phone in his hand. "I don't think that's a good idea, Mr. Flores." He forced the phone into Robert's hands. "I took it from her when she shoved it in my face."

Robert looked at the phone and an instant rage curdled his guts and crushed his soul. *Fucking bitch!* he thought. Then he said to Sam, "Bring her in to see me. Has anyone else looked at this picture?"

"I don't think so," Sam said. Then the kid ran off down the hall.

Robert looked back at the phone. The picture on the screen was of him sleeping in a hotel bed. Lying next to him was Patsy, topless and smiling as she took a selfie.

Chapter 77

One big puffy cloud covered the mid-afternoon sun as Gonzalez drove past the community hall and parked outside the church. There were a few vehicles in the parking lot and the hall doors were open. Something must have been going on.

Gonzalez got out of his squad car and wiped sandwich crumbs off his uniform. He debated going to the community hall first to see what was going on, but his curiosity pushed him immediately to the church. Its front doors were closed, so Gonzalez followed the path around the side. He'd never actually been inside the church before. He'd spoken to Robert and Hank in the community hall when he was here last. There was a side door at the end of the church and Gonzalez tried opening it. It was locked. He walked around to the other side and found a window. He peered through it, spying Robert's office. It was sparse and gloomy, but Gonzalez could see the desk and the crucifix on the wall. He could also see the cupboard. Nothing unusual about it, he thought. He was about to try opening the window when someone interrupted him.

"Can I help you, officer?"

It was Hank sauntering towards him. Gonzalez had known Hank for many years and was quite fond of the old man. Hank wasn't an angel. He liked his pot and booze, but his heart was in the right place most of the time.

"Is Mr. Flores here, Hank?" Gonzalez asked, though he knew full well Robert was in the city.

"Nope, he's in the city. It's Sunday. He's doing his show. Or at least he was. I reckon it'll be finished now."

Gonzalez nodded at the community hall. "What's going on over there?"

Hank turned to look, as if Gonzalez could have been talking about anything else. "The congregation's been watching The Holy Man on the big screen. They show it every Sunday, followed by coffee and donuts." Hank frowned at a few people dawdling outside the hall. "There's always the same few that don't want to go home. Every week I tell them I need to clean up and lock the place down, but they still loiter."

Hank scratched his head, looking a bit confused suddenly. "Wait, why are you here, officer?"

"I need you to open up the office for me, Hank. I need to take a look inside."

"Mr. Flores wouldn't like that," Hank said, following behind Gonzalez as he walked back towards the door. "No one's allowed in the office unless Mr. Flores is here himself."

"Come on, Hank, open the door for me. I need to satisfy the chief and tell him I've had a look. That's all. I promise I'll be quick."

Hank shook his head. "Sorry, officer, I ain't opening it without a warrant. Mr. Flores…"

"Hank!" Gonzalez said. "You either open up and let me into that office or I'll go down to your property and sniff about. Maybe I'll check what's underneath that old hay barn of yours." The police suspected old Hank had been growing weed underneath his barn for a while.

Hank was stunned, standing there with his mouth agape.

"Now," Gonzalez said. "Stop being a stubborn old fool and open the damn door."

*

Robert raced along Highway 80 in a fit of rage. "The fucking whore bitch!" he shouted, slamming his hands on the steering wheel. "The fucking bitch!" He couldn't get away from the city fast enough—from the church and that cunt, Patsy. If Robert had spent another minute in his office alone with the blonde slut, he would have ripped her head off.

"How dare she! How fucking dare she!" Robert was shouting and smashing his fists. He looked like a maniac. The dumb little fuck had had the audacity to stand in his office with a smug look on her face and blackmail him. The stupid air stewardess with her over-applied foundation had obviously gotten drunk first. She had stood before Robert so goddamn confident, knowing she had him by the balls. Her demand was $500,000 dollars or else the photo would go viral with the sordid details of their night together. She had demanded it so casually. "It'll make one hell of a story, eh,

260

Mr. Celebrity Preacher Man?" Smiling drunkenly. Stupid bitch. Patsy had said the photo was saved, the copies up there in the cloud. Robert had agreed to the ransom just to get her out of his sight.

Robert accelerated faster down the highway. He had no intention of giving Patsy anything other than a one-way trip to Hell. But he'd have to deal with Patsy a bit later. Right now, Robert was on his way to unleash all his pent-up rage on Jessa Summers.

*

Hank waited nervously in the doorway as Gonzalez scoured Robert's office. It didn't take long. There wasn't much to look at or sift through. The office was drab and smelled musty. It hadn't been renovated since the church was first built. "Not much of an office," Gonzalez said, opening drawers on Robert's desk. There was nothing but a bible and some pens.

"Mr. Flores spends most of his time in the city," Hank said, "now that he's a big shot. He doesn't have much use for this office anymore."

"So, why does the reverend have it locked?" Gonzalez asked. "I mean, there's nothing worth taking in here." He walked across to the cabinet and started fussing with the door.

"Hey," Hank said, "you really shouldn't be doing that!"

Gonzalez ignored him. He was trying to jimmy the cupboard doors open. "What was this room used for before it became an office?"

Hank shrugged. "All sorts of things. It was mostly a storeroom until Mr. Flores started preaching."

The doors on the cupboard were solid. Gonzalez was yanking on the handle but it wouldn't budge.

"Officer, please," Hank said. He was getting desperate. "You really shouldn't be here without a warrant."

"Any idea what's in here, Hank?"

"Nope. I don't come in here without Mr. Flores and I ain't never seen him open the cupboard. Now can we please leave, officer? I need to be cleaning the hall."

"Don't let me stop you, Hank." Gonzalez gave him a look that said he could fuck off at any time. "I'll be on my way in five minutes."

Hank remained in the doorway.

"Five minutes," Gonzalez said. "Give me five minutes and I'll be done. Okay, Hank?"

Reluctantly, Hank left muttering under his breath as he shuffled away. Now Gonzalez was alone. He knew what he was doing pushed the boundaries. He had no right to search the office without a warrant. Although, he had been given consent by Hank to enter the room. Breaking open a locked cupboard, however, could land him in a whole mess of trouble. But there was something not quite right. His police instinct wouldn't let him leave.

It wasn't just the sparse office that bugged Gonzalez, nor that the reverend was so fussy about people entering without him present. It was the sum of all the weird things he had heard over the last few days. Jessa Summers had claimed Robert Flores tried to murder her sister. Then there was the crazy stuff DI Radisson had told him over the phone about Jessa having dreams of someone trying to murder her. And now Elizabeth Foster, Jessa Summers' twin sister, waking from a coma after experiencing dreams of Robert Flores abducting Jessa. It was incredibly coincidental. If nothing else, Gonzalez was too curious not to pull a little harder on the handle. There was a slight crack, but the lock held. He almost walked away. Then he thought of that poor, mentally disturbed girl dying beneath the floorboards beneath his feet, and Gonzalez put some fucking muscle into it. He yanked the handle and the doors cracked open.

*

The traffic on the highway was a nightmare. Robert grimaced at the taillights in front of him, his face contorted in anger and evil. He was still forty-five minutes from Winters, but with the goddamn traffic it was more like an hour and a half. He slammed his palms hard on the steering wheel and screamed, "Fuck!"

His cell phone started to ring. It was Stephen from the television network calling him for the sixth time. "Go fuck yourself, arsehole," Robert shouted. He ripped the phone from its holder and threw it in the back seat.

Patsy's smug face and her stupid voice wouldn't get out of his head: *"It would make one hell of a story, eh, Mr. Celebrity Preacher Man?"*

He let out a beastly roar in hopes of soothing himself. It didn't help. So, he prayed to God to ease his turbulent mind and settle his fury. But it wasn't God who answered Robert. It was the Devil whispering in his ear.

*

Gonzalez pointed his flashlight into the cupboard. It was spacious inside, a row of cardboard boxes stacked neatly at the back. A few suits hung on the rail and on the carpet was a pair of brown shoes. Gonzalez stepped inside and opened a few of the boxes. One was empty. One had a few bath towels inside, and the other had some plastic sheeting. He thumped the walls with the heel of his hand; they all sounded solid. Then he stomped hard on the floor. The first stomp was solid, but as he moved backwards and crashed his foot onto the floor again, there was a hollow thud. He got on his knees and shone the light onto the carpet. About halfway across was a crease. Gonzalez ran his hand along the seam of the carpet and pulled, lifting it easily and folding it back right where the crease was, knocking over Robert's brown shoes. What remained was a trap door with a metal pull ring.

Gonzalez's heart was thumping hard now. He thought the pull ring could be a booby trap. Before touching it, he turned back and looked at the crucifix on the wall. "Protect me, God," he said, crossing his heart. Then he gave a yank. There was no explosion, just a faint *click* as the floor sprung upwards.

"You've got to be fucking kidding me."

Gonzalez lifted the chunk of floor and shone his flashlight into the void below. Then he climbed down the ladder into the basement.

He was combing the room with his flashlight when he spotted the surveillance monitor on the wall. There was an open door to his right, which proved to be a shower room. The other door had a digital lock. It was solid. Gonzalez could tell there was no breaking through it. He hammered on the door with the butt of his flashlight.

"Miss Summers," he called. "Miss Summers, this is the police department. Can you hear me?" He placed his ear against the door and listened—nothing but the beating of his own heart.

"Miss Summers, are you in there?"

Still no response. The room was either empty or Jessa Summers was already dead. Either way, Officer Gonzalez had seen enough. It was time to phone in the cavalry.

*

Robert heard the sirens before he saw the lights. As he cruised past the Putah Creek Café, the emergency response vehicles burst into view in front of him, causing him to smash the brakes. Three patrol cars, a fire truck, and an ambulance sped around the corner onto Grant Avenue and roared east out of town. Robert followed them at a distance. He kept expecting the convoy to turn off and go away, but they kept going. When they turned off Main Street and started down the unnamed road, Robert's heart sank in his chest. They were heading for the church.

"Do not be unnerved, my son," the Devil whispered. *"I am your God now. I will protect you."*

*

Gonzalez was waiting outside the church with Hank for the firemen and paramedics to show up. He could see their flashing red lights way off down the road. He only hoped they weren't too late to rescue Jessa Summers.

The fire truck pulled up and its crew scrambled out, prepping equipment, already geared-up. "What do we have?" the chief asked Gonzalez, walking over and fidgeting with his handlebar moustache.

"I believe a woman has been locked inside a secure room in the basement of the church."

A pair of female paramedics rushed up to Gonzalez and the chief firefighter. The chief was asking, "Do you know if the woman is still alive? Was there any response?"

Gonzalez shook his head. "None. I called out and hammered on the door but there was nothing."

"Right," he said, "show me the way."

264

They marched towards the rear of the church, Gonzalez, the fire chief, and the paramedics. "There's not much room down there," Gonzalez said. And one of the paramedics asked, "Do we know who the woman is?"

"Name's Jessa Summers," Gonzalez said. "She was in a serious accident yesterday. If she is still alive, she's going to be in lousy shape. We'll need you there outside the door."

Candice stopped dead. "Oh my god. Jessa!"

*

Robert's worst fears had been realised. God had finally abandoned him and given up his secret. He could see the emergency vehicles stationed outside the church, their flashing red lights. He saw the fire crew, the police, the paramedics. They were all rushing to the back of the church. And there was Hank, totally bewildered.

It was over.

Robert turned the SUV around and raced off down the road with the Devil riding shotgun, whispering horrible evils in his ear.

*

It was a full forty minutes before the fire department cut through the door. The fucking thing was solid steel. Gonzalez stood back from the opening and the firemen were shouting for the paramedics. Candice was the first responder inside. "Is she there?" Gonzalez shouted. "Please tell me she's alive."

It was a few unbearable moments of silence. Then, a young fireman climbed through the hole in the floor into Robert's office. He looked distraught, the colour drained from his face.

"Is she alive?" Gonzalez asked.

The fireman shook his head and walked out of the room.

CHAPTER 78

The drive from Winters to Robert's home in the suburbs of Sacramento usually took 35-40 minutes. Robert made it home in twenty. He had to get in and out quick. It wouldn't be long before the police were hounding at his door. But Robert didn't have a choice. There was one last thing he needed to do before his maniacal train reached its station.

He burst through the front door and hammered up the stairs two at a time. Juliet was shouting after him, "Robert, is that you? Robert, darling, what are you doing?"

Robert was already in the master bedroom stuffing a duffel bag full of jeans, underwear, some shirts. Then he was pounding back down the stairs with the bag over his shoulder. Juliet stood in the kitchen doorway stunned. "What's the matter, Robert?" she asked.

He barged past, nearly knocking Juliet off her feet. Robert raced down the hall and into his office, his wife screaming after him, "Robert, what's happening?"

Robert was at the safe under his desk. Crouching, he turned the combination. "Fuck." It wouldn't open. His hands trembled. He had to turn the dial slowly, listening to the clicks.

"Robert?" Juliet was in the doorway, staring down at him with her arms crossed. "You're scaring me, Robert. What in God's name is wrong?"

Robert looked over his shoulder, eyes wild. "There is no God, you fucking whore."

She gasped, put her hand to her mouth and took a step backwards. It was almost comical.

Robert had got the safe open and was stuffing bundles of cash into his bag. "As far as I'm concerned, God has abandoned me. Now I'm at the mercy of the Devil."

Robert stood, Juliet shaking in the doorway. Robert's piercing blue eyes were wild. "And so are you!" he said, and he sprang at his wife. She had just enough time to scream before Robert grabbed a fistful of her hair and yanked her head back, pulling her to the floor. He dragged her down the hall like a ragdoll and into the kitchen. She put up one hell of a fight—maybe to compensate for all the years of subservience. She kicked and screamed and scratched, but Robert felt no pain. He slammed the side of her head into the cabinet, grabbed a carving knife from the butcher's block, and in one long-awaited victory, plunged it into his wife's chest.

*

The paramedics had been in the basement for an eternity. Jessa was unconscious and in critical condition. Her pulse was weak, but she was breathing. She had two broken legs, broken ribs, and severe bruising to her face—plus god knew how much internal damage. She needed to be taken to the hospital immediately, but getting her out of the basement and into the ambulance was dangerous. The paramedics were still working to stabilize her. They had to get her out of Robert's murder dungeon without causing even more trauma.

Gonzalez had secured the crime scene as best he could. Only the medical team were permitted in the basement until it was time to move Jessa Summers. The priority was to preserve life and assist the victim. Only then could the scene be sealed off and the CSI teams brought in. The officers above ground had cordoned off the church and its grounds. The chief had been called. Currently, a state-wide APB for Robert Flores was being broadcast across all channels.

*

Robert was speeding down his driveway when he heard the sirens. He didn't bother to brake coming onto the main road, and narrowly missed a collision with a pizza delivery van. Robert's tyres squealed as the SUV fishtailed. Then he was straight, roaring hard down the road. Blue and red lights flashed in his rear-view as he sped through the Sunday afternoon traffic. He had no immediate plan and no direction of travel. Robert was relying on the Devil for safe passage.

"Turn right, my son," the Devil whispered in his ear.

Robert checked the rear-view, saw patrol cars careening around the corner.

"Turn left, my son."

The wailing sirens were getting louder. The squad cars were gaining on him. Robert switched the radio on and turned up the volume, trying to block out the noise of his pursuit. Classical music filled Robert's cabin and he raced through a red light.

"Turn right."

Robert pulled the vehicle right, humming along to the concerto. Blue and red lights appeared ahead of him. Vehicles were pulling off to the side of the road, making a straightaway for Robert and the cops to whizz through. Robert hummed along—"La la la," to the musical arrangement. The cops ahead were forming a barrier. "La la la!" Robert sang louder.

The Devil whispered, *"Veer right."*

Robert yanked the SUV hard to the right, smashing through a safety barrier and a wooden fence, wood splinters ricocheting off his windshield. He bounced through a field, still singing along to the music, cattle looking at him absentmindedly. He swerved left to avoid a row of trees and smashed through another fence and safety barrier, tearing back onto the road and slamming into the side of a police cruiser, causing it to crash into a minivan. Robert had manoeuvred beyond the roadblock and was now accelerating, waving his hand like a conductor in rhythm with the string section. The cops were behind him in hot pursuit.

*

The paramedics had stabilized Jessa, but her condition was still deteriorating. If they didn't get her to a hospital soon, she would certainly die. It was time to move her. Jessa was first sedated, then strapped into a basket stretcher and Gonzalez watched the firemen hoist her from the basement through Robert's vile little hide-e-hole. The fat-arsed paramedic was already waiting in the ambulance with the engine idling. Candice followed Jessa and her stretcher the whole way, out of the basement and through the church, and into the ambulance.

Shortly after Jessa was rushed to the hospital, the senior investigations officer, June Peterson, and a team of crime scene investigators arrived on site. Peterson was in her mid-forties, slightly overweight for her height but kind of attractive if you liked frizzy ginger hair, porcelain white skin, bucked teeth, and a lazy eye. She was standing with Gonzalez in the room where Jessa had been held captive. After seeing the boxes of towels and plastic sheeting, both officers knew Jessa Summers was not Robert's first victim. Certainly, they knew, more girls had been held captive beneath the church.

"But if Miss Summers was not the first," Peterson was saying, "then what does he do with the bodies? I assume he kills his victims when he's finished."

"Well," Gonzalez said, following Peterson out of the room and into Robert's main chamber, "I don't think he brought anyone down here for a vacation."

"Quite!" Peterson said. She was looking up at the trap door in the ceiling. "It's an effort to get a dead body up through there, no matter how strong you are. What's in there?" She pointed at the small hatch on the other side of the room. It was still closed.

"I'm not sure," Gonzalez said.

Peterson walked towards it. "We should take a look, don't you think?"

Gonzalez bent down, used his pen to pry open the door handle. A waft of dank, musty air blasted them in the face as the door swung open. They peered inside and Gonzalez swept his torch across the room, the light casting it's beam over the earthen floor and wooden foundations of the church.

"Sweet Jesus!" Gonzalez was horrified. He was shining his flashlight across mounds of dirt. "Are those graves?"

"Yes," Peterson said, "I would say they are."

After a few moments of stillness, it suddenly dawned on Gonzalez that he may have just found Susie Morgan. Or at least, what remained of the poor girl.

*

Robert raced down Old River Road followed by four police cars. He glanced out of his window and saw a helicopter hovering above the Sacramento river. They were following his high-speed chase. He couldn't make out if it was a police chopper or one from a news network. Either way, he didn't give a shit.

Old River Road was windy. It hugged the Sacramento River. Houses, farms, and fields flashed by as Robert ate up the miles. He had no idea why the Devil had directed him along this route, but he didn't care. He knew he was in safe hands. The road started to climb and soon Robert would be high in the hills with the Sacramento River in the deep ravine below. Miles passed and the road continued to climb, and the river disappeared into the canyon. Robert couldn't outrun the police and he knew it. The chase would soon be over. As the road flattened and then started to descend into the town of Redding, he saw another blockade of flashing lights in the distance. He looked in his rear-view mirror; the police were hot on his arse. The helicopter hovered above the trees, watching him. There was only one way to go.

"Fuck you, Jessa Summers, you cunt!" Robert shouted over the classical music. "Fuck you, Patsy, you greedy whore! And fuck you, Elizabeth Foster. See you all in Hell!"

The orchestra reached crescendo and the Devil whispered into Robert's ear one last time. With a wicked grin and the Devil sitting firm on his shoulders, Robert swerved the SUV across the road and smashed through the final safety barrier. He careened over the edge and plummeted five-hundred-feet into the Sacramento River.

Part 4

Sometimes dreams

are given to you

for a reason

CHAPTER 79

The whole of my memory still eludes me, and even the memories of the dreams I had when in my coma are vague. I grow stronger each day. The plaster casts have been removed and I've learned to walk again. My face is still heavily scarred; it looks like I've been in a fight with Edward Scissorhands. But my other injuries are healing. The doctors said I can go home.

I have no particular feelings about going home. I have no recollection of what home is and no memory of the man who is my husband. At Rosemary's request, Thomas showed me photos of our life together, but I may as well have been looking at images of a stranger.

Other than Rosemary and Thomas, I have had few visitors. Valance, a close friend of the family and flamboyant art gallery owner, visited me a few times and brought me beautiful bouquets of flowers. Olivia, who I'm told is my closest friend, visited me once. She brought me a basket of fruit and was all smiles and hugs, but I didn't recognise her—although she did incite a feeling similar to when you see a stranger and are adamant you have seen them before but just can't place them. My only other visitor was Officer Gonzalez. He came twice to ask me questions about my dreams and Robert Flores. But I couldn't remember much. I told Gonzalez all I knew, that Robert had tried to murder me and my twin sister. Gonzalez told me Robert is suspected of being a serial killer. Thirteen women, apparently. My sister and I are lucky to be alive. When I asked if we were still in danger, Gonzalez assured me that Robert Flores is dead. He drove his car into the Sacramento River. And although they had yet to find the body (only Robert's mangled SUV), Gonzalez assured me that Robert's corpse was likely washed out to sea and would soon wash up on a beach somewhere. He told me not to worry, Robert Flores is dead.

It has been just over four weeks since my sister was brought into the intensive care unit. Her injuries were so severe that she almost died. I was told by the medical team that the first responders saved

Jessa's life. Candice visits her every other day and must be getting fed up with me for thanking her every time I see her.

As soon as I became well enough, I made the short journey down the hall to visit my sister. I've visited her every day since, spending almost every waking second by her side, gently squeezing her hand as I speak to her. I hope she'll squeeze it back. Her condition is still critical. Rosemary assured me Jessa will be receiving the best medical care money can buy. My mother wants me to concentrate on getting myself back to full health.

I haven't felt any strong connection with Jessa since she was pulled from the basement of the church. There are times when I feel a faint tingling throughout my body, and I convince myself it is Jessa trying to communicate with me. I relax my mind in the hope I can feel her, but the sensation always fades. I have spent many hours on the internet researching twin telepathy and reading stories of twins with the ability to feel each other's thoughts and emotions. There is scepticism whether these things are possible, whether twins can hold special psychic bonds with each other, but many believe the phenomenon exists. I am living proof that it's real. The connection between twins can be the most powerful bond possible between two human beings. It was powerful enough to save our lives.

I asked Rosemary to tell me about my childhood and if she knew anything about Jessa's. Rosemary explained that we were adopted when very young by separate families. Rosemary and my adopted father, Marcus, who passed several years ago, lived in England and they moved to the United States a few years after adopting me. They knew very little about my biological parents. They knew only that my mother suffered from severe depression and committed suicide shortly after giving birth. My biological father is unknown. Rosemary and Marcus were told I had a twin, but that my sister had died a few months after being born.

Thomas has now arrived to take me home. I'm reluctant to leave my sister's side, but I will try to return every day. I look at her as she lay motionless in the hospital bed. It feels like looking at a broken image of myself. Her face is bruised and swollen, her thin body shattered. But I know she's a fighter. Jessa is a survivor like me. It's only a matter of time before she wakes from her coma.

She will wake up. I can feel it.

CHAPTER 80

Rosemary wanted Thomas and I to stay with her, but my husband was insistent I stay home. He said being around the house might stimulate my memory. It's been three days and still nothing looks familiar. Some parts of the house feel familiar, but I have no tangible memory.

There have been no visitors. Thomas says it's too early for company. He wants me to rest and get used to the house without distractions. All I've done with my time is think about Jessa. I visited her this morning, but there was no change in her condition. I have, however, been experiencing more frequent and more powerful tingling sensations. I'm sure it means Jessa is closer to waking up. The doctors are not hopeful, but I am. It will happen soon. I can feel it.

My husband has been nervous and on edge ever since I came home. Maybe it's his normal temperament, but it makes me feel anxious. I've caught him watching me with a look of antipathy. It makes me wonder if he knows about my affair with Robert. Other times, it's as though Thomas can't stand to look at me at all. He almost completely ignores me, becoming affectionate only when Rosemary is around. My mother clearly adores him, whereas I have no affection for the man. And yet still I feel disloyal for committing adultery.

Thomas has invited Olivia over tonight for a meal. I'm not really in the mood for company, but Thomas became agitated when I told him that I'd prefer to spend my time alone. He's now in the kitchen preparing food while I make myself somewhat presentable. My hair is slowly growing back, but the deep scars etched into my skull are still visible. Long, jagged scarring also covers my forehead and snakes across my cheeks and nose. It's quite hideous, and perhaps the reason Thomas can't bear to look at me. His once beautiful wife now looks like a disgusting monster. No amount of makeup can conceal my disfigurement, and so I make no effort to conceal it. My hair is not long enough to comb. All I do is put on a pair of jeans and a t-shirt.

I'm making my way down the landing when the doorbell rings. The shrill *ding-dong* jars my memory. It's like an explosion. And it stops me dead at the top of the stairs.

"Elizabeth," Thomas calls.

The memory is gone. It left no impression and I stand at the top of the stairs confused, trying to recapture it. Olivia calls, "Elizabeth, are you okay, honey?"

"Fine," I say, attempting to smile. But my head is fuzzy as I go downstairs and follow Thomas and Olivia into the kitchen. Olivia says, "Oh Thomas, that smells wonderful," and she gently squeezes his arm.

Thomas pours Olivia a glass of white Chardonnay while she takes a seat on a stool at the island. She is elegant, bursting with confidence and stunning in every sense of the word. She's trying hard not to look at my grotesque face, speaking to Thomas, glancing periodically at my scars. And that's when I experience another jolt of memory. It's so powerful that I reel in surprise, take a deep breath and hold the kitchen counter for support. Thomas and Olivia don't appear to notice my sudden anguish. My vision shakes and I fear I will pass out.

"I need fresh air," I say. I stumble across the kitchen and into the utility room.

Thomas calls after me, "Everything okay, Elizabeth?"

"Yes," I say, "I just need some fresh air."

I go outside and huff in the cool, early evening air. I walk down into the garden and another blast of memory shakes me to my core. This time, it leaves a fragmented afterthought in my mind. I suddenly realise that I've been walking around my house blind. I haven't seen what's right in front of me. I turn back to the house and look in through the kitchen window. Thomas has his back to me, talking to Olivia, making her laugh. She's looking at me, then at Thomas, then back at me. She smiles and I remember it—that sneaky fucking smile.

"Oh my god," I say, "I remember. I remember everything!"

CHAPTER 81

I fell in love with Robert Flores the moment I first saw him. It was at the annual art exhibition at the Almond Tree Hotel in Winters. Valance had chosen my painting of the almond tree for the exhibition, and I was there as part of the entourage of artists displaying their work. I had spent months travelling from the city to Winters, painting the most beautiful tree I had ever seen. I was privileged that my painting was one of the chosen few. I stood in front of it smiling at those who stopped to look, feeling uncomfortable in my slim dress and high heels. Thomas never usually allowed me to wear such sensuous clothing, and I was trying to appear relaxed and confident, when on the inside I was a total wreck.

I watched Robert float around the room, going from beautiful woman to beautiful woman and making them laugh. They all gushed over him, clearly uninterested in the art on display. Robert was so handsome and charismatic, yet without being egotistical. He made my heart flutter. I could hardly believe it when he approached me. I was not used to flatteries and his compliments made me blush. I must have looked like an awkward, giggling schoolgirl when I looked into his piercing blue eyes and chuckled.

Our affair started shortly after the day at the gallery. When Robert and I weren't together, I often fell into a terrible pit of depression. Our meetings were few and far between to begin with, and we always had to be extremely discreet about when and where we met. Thomas was frequently away on business, so it was easier for me to escape with Robert. However, he was becoming a big celebrity. People recognised him everywhere we went, and so it became hard to go out together. We booked separate rooms in hotels and I would sneak into Robert's room to spend the night. Sometimes, we would meet in his church office in Winters.

Robert made me feel alive. He gave me a sense of confidence I never had before. And the sex! The sex we had was out of this world. He did things to me I had never experienced before. At first, I was averse to his sordid, carnal perversions. But I soon allowed him to do whatever he wanted to me. I enjoyed every second of it. During our time together, my confidence improved and my mental health stabilized. When I found out I was pregnant with Robert's baby, I made up my mind to leave Thomas.

Robert had told me that he would leave his wife for me, and he wanted nothing more than for us to be together. I believed him with all my heart, but when I saw his reaction and the way he looked at me after I told him about the baby, I realised I had been so fucking naive. I had been stupid and gullible. I had been so desperate for affection that I made Robert my protector, my lifesaver. But he was no saviour. Robert was a hypocritical liar who used me for his own perverted pleasure.

After our fight in the hotel room, I rushed out to my car in complete hysterics. The hotel staff must have thought I was a total maniac as I screamed and cried my way through the halls and out of the lobby. I drove my car recklessly, racing at top speed away from Robert and the hotel. I was planning to go to my mother and tell her everything—my abusive husband, my misery, my affair, my unborn child. I wanted to phone my mother to hear her voice, but I had left my cell in Robert's room. A part of me worried that Robert would chase me down and stop me from telling anyone about the filthy things we had done.

And to my horror, he did. Robert soon came speeding up the road behind me. He was enraged, pointing and waving at me to pull over.

But wait, it wasn't Robert. It was Thomas! He was driving like a lunatic all over the road. I thought he would kill us both. He drove alongside me, shouting, swearing, pointing his finger. Then he tore out in front of me and slammed on his brakes. I had to swerve to avoid him, almost losing control. I came to a halt a few inches from a safety barrier. Thomas climbed out of his SUV. He had a look of pure evil as he stalked towards me. I'd seen the look before when he was punching and biting and raping me. I'd been subjected to so much torture and abuse from my husband, I'd nearly committed suicide countless times. But if there was one thing I could thank Robert for, it was giving me the courage to stand up for myself. As Thomas reached my car, I unbuckled my seatbelt and got out, ready for the fight of my life.

I wanted to take control of the situation, to show Thomas I was no longer scared of him. I'd spent too many years being beaten and abused and told I was worthless. I was about to tell him he no longer frightened me, that I was ready to leave him. But before the words left my mouth, Thomas backhanded me hard across the face. I hit the car and slumped, blood trickling down the side of my head. "You fucking bitch!"

Though I was dazed, I stood and faced Thomas defiantly. "You can beat me all you like, Thomas." There was an anger in my belly I had never felt before, an overpowering anger fuelled by so many hidden bruises and bite marks. "It doesn't make a difference. It's over. I'm leaving you."

Thomas let out a hideous laugh. "You're not leaving me, bitch. You need me."

He tried to grab me, but I shouted in his face, "I'm pregnant, Thomas," and he stopped, momentarily stunned.

I stared into his horrible eyes and said, "I'm pregnant, Thomas. And it's not your baby. I am leaving you. I'm done."

I started getting back into my car, Thomas lingering shocked in the road. My whole body shook, but I felt good. I had stood up to my abusive husband for the first time. He clearly didn't know how to deal with it. I was about to start the car when he jerked my door open and grabbed my hair and yanked me out. He lifted me up and punched me in the gut, then let me fall to my knees and puke and gasp for air. Then he hauled me to the back of my car, popped the trunk and shoved me inside.

The heat in the trunk was stifling. I searched for a latch but couldn't find one. I fumbled along the floor for a weapon, but there was nothing. I had cleaned the car out last weekend. Then the car skidded to a stop and the driver's door opened. Gravel crunched underfoot as Thomas walked around to the trunk. He popped the lid, cool night air washed my face, then Thomas' fist connected with my cheekbone.

I was barely conscious when Thomas pulled me from the trunk and let me crumple onto the ground. There was no fight left in me. Thomas had stolen it. He lifted my deadweight into the driver's seat and clicked in my seatbelt. My vision was blurred. I tried to plea—I wanted to, but I couldn't speak. He was fussing beneath my legs. Moments later and the car was moving, rolling towards the embankment. I stomped on the brake, but Thomas had jammed it somehow. I saw him in the rear-view mirror, standing shadowy beneath the moon as my car lurched over the edge.

CHAPTER 82

The memories are no longer fragmented. They are clear and concise. It wasn't Robert who tried to kill me, it was my husband. All along I thought the reverend had attempted to murder me out of fear I would expose our affair and my pregnancy. My dreams led Jessa to Robert, and now she is in a coma fighting for her life while my creep of a husband laughs and drinks wine with his fucking whore, my so-called friend.

I remember now why I was standing here in the garden with a gun weeks before my crash. I was watching through the window, watching Thomas fuck Olivia in our kitchen. I was intent on killing him that day, and I'm certain I would have it if that bitch hadn't interrupted my plan. I just couldn't tolerate any more abuse. My body had taken enough. I had taken enough! The only way I would be free was to kill either Thomas or myself. But I didn't want to die. I had something to live for. I had Robert.

It makes sense now why I mistook Thomas for Robert in my distorted dreams. Looking at Thomas now, I see he and Robert are both strong. They have the same build and have the same grey, receding hairlines. From behind, Thomas could definitely be mistaken for Robert Flores. And now that I'm watching through the window, I remember Thomas dragging me through the kitchen by my hair, pulling me violently up the stairs. It was just another episode of Thomas' unearned aggression. I remember him throwing me on the bed and punching me in the ribs. I remember Thomas raping me.

Now I'm welling with anger and hatred. Tears stream down my face, run along my scars. I have suffered so much brutality at the hands of Thomas Foster. Him and his whore are staring at me out the window, looking at me like I'm a stupid dog tied up in the yard. But then Thomas' expression changes. He must see the revelation in my face as I step backwards into the bushes. Thomas knows I remember.

I make a dash for the back of the garden, legs in massive pain as I hobble towards the bushes. I find the spot and throw myself to my knees, screeching as my bones feel like they are splintered apart. I begin to dig in the soil with my bare hands. "Where is it?"

I glance back at the house. Thomas and Olivia are walking out of the back door.

"Where the fuck is it?" I'm throwing soil, digging madly.

"Elizabeth?" Thomas shouts. I worry he's already found the gun. "Elizabeth, what are you doing?" They are getting closer.

I start to lose hope, but then I feel plastic beneath the dirt. I cry out, "Yes!" and claw open the bag. My body reels with adrenaline as I pull out the gun.

"Elizabeth," Thomas shouts from across the garden, "what are you doing?"

I'm not thinking. Memories of abuse, torments, horrifying rapes—they flicker in my head and I scream. I spin and see Thomas standing above me with that wicked look in his eyes, like I'm the one who's sick. I point the gun at him and pull the trigger.

There's a flash, a great bang, and Olivia screams. Thomas is lying in the dirt choking on his own blood. He's gurgling, blood bubbling out of his mouth. It makes me vomit. The bullet punctured Thomas' windpipe and exited through the back of his neck. He will soon drown in his own blood.

"Thomas!" Olivia falls to her knees.

I get to my feet, the gun rattling in my hand. I look at my dying husband, blood pooling behind his head, soaking the grass in blotches of red. His eyes are glazed. He's choking. I'm satisfied knowing that Thomas will live long enough to understand he's dying, then be out of my life once and for all.

"What have you done?" Olivia screams. She's looking at Thomas, begging me for help. "Do something. Please help him!"

"No." I limp to Olivia, ignoring the horrible pain in my legs. I aim the gun at her head and smile at her fear. She whimpers, "Please, Elizabeth… please don't."

"Stand up," I order.

"Please, Elizabeth!" She's sobbing pathetically.

"Stand the fuck up!"

Olivia stands. There's a wet stain on her crotch and down the inside of her thigh from where she's pissed herself. I look at her in disgust. "I want answers, Olivia," I scream. "How long have you and Thomas been fucking behind my back?"

"What?"

"How long?" I demand, thrusting the gun in her face.

She doesn't answer, cringing with her eyes shut.

"Damnit, Olivia, if you don't answer me, I swear to god I'll shoot you, bitch."

Olivia blurts, "Before you and Thomas were together."

"What! But you introduced us. You kept coaxing me to meet him. You said we would be perfect together. If you were already fucking, why were you so damn eager to hook us up? You couldn't wait for Thomas and me to get married!"

She blinks through her tears, not saying anything. "Why Olivia! Why did you do it?"

"The money," she says finally, squeezing her eyes shut. "Because of your inheritance."

I gape, feeling like Olivia just ripped out my heart. It makes sense now. I remember the time Olivia was comforting me during another bout of my terrible depression. I was drinking a lot, and at some point, mentioned to her my inheritance. I should have known better. Olivia always had been a fantasiser, talking about winning the lottery, constantly buying herself extravagant gifts she could ill-afford. I told her I was to inherit over six million dollars once my mother passed, and I promised to buy Olivia the sportscar she had always dreamed of. Now that I thought about it, she started talking to me about Thomas, her handsome bachelor friend, only a few days after I told her about my inheritance.

"You planned it from the start," I say to her. "And part of your plan was to kill me. You fucking bitch!"

"No," she cries. "We never wanted you to get hurt. You have to believe me, Elizabeth. Once you received the inheritance, Thomas was going to fraudulently transfer money from your account. Just a couple million, that was it. Then we would use the money to start a new life together." Olivia looks down at Thomas' dead body. I can't tell if she's more distraught over losing Thomas or a few million dollars.

"He still tried to kill me, Olivia," I say, pointing the gun at the centre of her forehead.

"No, Elizabeth." Olivia has her hands up in surrender. "We suspected you were having an affair. Thomas didn't know with who, but he knew you were seeing someone. We started to follow you. We wanted to find out who you were secretly seeing, so we could scare them off. It was only a matter of time before Rosemary…" She sighs. "And well, we didn't have long."

"So," I say, gritting my teeth, "all those times Thomas said he was away on business, he was really with you?"

Olivia doesn't answer, but she doesn't have to. I can read her face. But it still makes no sense. "If I died or if Thomas killed me, there wouldn't have been a fucking inheritance, you stupid cunt. Thomas would have ended up with nothing."

Olivia squirms, and I can tell she knows something I don't. "What is it?" I say, pressing the gun against her temple. "What aren't you telling me?"

"Rosemary amended the will. Your mother loved Thomas like a son, and she changed the will to protect him. She made it so that even if you died, Thomas would inherit her money. She did it because of the suicide attempts, Elizabeth. You were dangerous. But I promise, Thomas never tried to murder you."

"Do you even know what kind of man Thomas was, Olivia? He beat me. He mentally abused me. He raped me. For years I listened to him denounce me and call me worthless, useless, tell me I was nothing without him." I can't stop the tears now, flowing freely from my eyes. "And he tried to murder me, Olivia!"

Olivia looks bewildered and I can't understand why. What does she have to be so shocked about?

"You've got all this wrong, Elizabeth. You're maniacally depressed. You suffer from bipolar disorder and you're a borderline schizophrenic. Thomas never hurt you, Elizabeth. He's never laid a finger on you. You're the one who harms yourself. You attack Thomas in fits of mania. He's the one bruised and scratched. I've seen what you do to him. You're always accusing Thomas of doing horrible things to you, it's all in your head, Elizabeth. All of it."

"Why are you lying?" I ask. "Thomas has been a monster to me our whole marriage. You're a liar." I wave the gun, screaming in her face, "You're a liar!"

"It's true!" she cries. "The night of your accident, Thomas and I followed you to the hotel and waited. We sat there for hours until you came running out. You looked so distressed. You sped off in your car like a maniac. We followed behind you. You were acting drunk, swerving and slowing and speeding. We followed for a few miles and then you just drove off the roadside and down into the ravine."

"No." I shake my head. "You're lying. Thomas forced me off the road and made it look like an accident."

"He fucking didn't," Olivia shrieks. "You tried to kill yourself and failed. Thomas couldn't stand you, but he didn't try to kill you. Your condition was almost impossible to live with. Thomas thought many times about giving up on the whole thing, saying fuck the money and walking away."

"Then why didn't he?" I'm frothing, staring at my dead husband in the grass. "Why didn't he just walk away?"

"Because I made him stay," Olivia says. "I made him stay because of the money. And now it's my fault he's dead."

I look at her with pity. Olivia's no longer elegant or beautiful. Her makeup runs and mucus dribbles off her lip. She's pissed her pants. She's disgusting. I look down at my dead husband. They are both disgusting. I take a deep breath and shove the barrel of the gun against Olivia's forehead. Then I pull the trigger.

EPILOGUE

It was a crisp morning and the sun cast a glow of tangerine over the Dartmoor hills. It was going to be a beautiful day, and Jessa Summers was going to enjoy it. She sat wrapped in a blanket on her balcony, admiring the scenery. She understood now why her dad had bought the house. He used to say he would never get tired of the view, but Jessa always wondered what was so special about it. Only now could she see it. Jessa looked at the world through fresh eyes. The view from the balcony was truly stunning.

Jessa had put her house on the market, and within days had an interested buyer. The offer was below asking price, but she was going to ring the estate agent later and accept it. She no longer wanted to sell her parents home. She had too many fond memories there. Instead, Jessa would sell her house and live in the place her father had loved so much, enjoying the same views he had enjoyed most of his life.

She sipped her coffee, looking out into the distance. Her thoughts drifted to Elizabeth. Jessa hoped she was okay. Her sister was in a secure psychiatric facility awaiting trial for the murders of Thomas Foster and Olivia Barres. Elizabeth had admitted to killing her husband and her friend, but her defence attorneys were building a plea around diminished capacity and Elizabeth's poor mental health. She had suffered from bipolar disorder and schizophrenia her whole life. When asked about Robert Flores, Elizabeth refused to talk about him. She still believed he was innocent of killing all those women. Jessa supposed she understood. After all, she had seen and felt Elizabeth through her dreams and knew her sister had loved Robert. Jessa supposed she still did.

As for Robert, his body had yet to be found, but he was presumed dead. The celebrity reverend was responsible for the deaths of at least fourteen women. Thirteen bodies had been found buried under the church. One of them was the corpse of Susie Morgan, the missing girl from Winters. Juliet Flores had been found dead at their home with a carving knife through her heart.

Why Robert Flores had chosen not to kill Elizabeth would forever be a mystery to Jessa. Maybe he had planned to all along, biding his time until the right opportunity came. Jessa was just thankful Elizabeth was alive. She was thankful they were both alive.

Jessa picked up her mug off the table, wincing at the pain in her side. Jessa's injuries from the crash were still excruciating, but like the scars on her face, they would heal. Jessa was getting stronger each day, both mentally and physically. She had limited use of her left arm and had to walk with a stick, but the physiotherapy was slowly helping. She told herself she'd be back to jogging in no time.

The department had agreed to let Jessa return to work on light duties until she was fully recovered, but Jessa was unsure if she wanted to go back to work. The job was too stressful and the pressure of being a police detective was not good for her mental wellbeing. DI Radisson had been transferred to another police department because of multiple allegations of sexual harassment. So, at least he wouldn't be there if Jessa did decide to return. For now, she would take her life one day at a time and enjoy every second of it.

As of now, Jessa hadn't really given Vanessa much thought. The last Jessa had heard, Vee was working in a grocery store trying to save money to go back travelling.

The sliding glass doors opened, distracting Jessa from her daydream. She looked up and smiled. "Morning, beautiful."

"Morning," Candice said. She bent over and kissed Jessa on the lips. "It's freezing out here. Come back inside and I'll cook us breakfast."

Candice was on vacation visiting Jessa for a week before they both flew back to San Francisco. Jessa was looking forward to spending time with Candice and seeing the Bay Area as a tourist instead of a crazy detective. Jessa had even scheduled time to spend with Rosemary, and there was a particular art gallery she wanted to visit. Jessa also planned to see her sister in the mental facility.

Jessa slowly got up, took her walking stick from Candice, then hobbled inside to the kitchen table. While Candice prepared breakfast and poured Jessa a coffee, Jessa sat back and admired the large oil painting on her wall, the almond tree so lifelike it seemed to grow out of the canvas. Every time Jessa studied the painting, she felt Elizabeth's presence. It was a faint tingle in her body.

Jessa smiled. She knew Elizabeth could feel her too.

*

It was an exceptionally cold night, and Rolex hated working cold nights. It was the type of cold that reached under her clothing, passed through her skin and into her bones. She was actually eager to climb into a stranger's car just to be warm. She'd been standing on the corner for an hour and had already sucked off two guys in the back of their minivan. She couldn't wait for the night to be over.

Rolex recently turned twenty. She'd been working in the dingy alleys of New York City for two years. Her story was like so many other young women disgraced from their American dreams and reduced to being drug-addicted whores, controlled and violated by angry pimps. She'd finished school two years ago and had been looking forward to a year's sabbatical before starting university. Rolex loved animals. She'd wanted to be a veterinarian, but that dream began to slip away soon after she met Connor. Connor was wild and exciting. He was devilishly handsome and a little edgy and Rolex had fallen head over heels for him. Connor introduced her to all sorts of lovely narcotics, and within three months she was a full-blown heroin addict. Instead of studying the anatomy of animals and hanging out with friends, Rolex was sucking cocks and fucking strangers to survive.

Rolex's real name was Page; Page Suarez. She had earned the name Rolex from her pimp, Marty, and it had come with a vicious beating. It was after Rolex sucked off a punter. He didn't have the money to pay her, so the greaseball offered Page his watch as a partial payment. She thought it was worth way more than a shitty back alley blow. Page was too stoned to consider the Rolex watch was fake.

Rolex hoped a punter would turn up soon. She was starting to freeze. Several cars slowed to look at her, but she was too cold to open her jacket and show them her drug-ravaged tits and crumpled stomach. They drove off and looked for something else.

The smack had destroyed Rolex's complexion, but she was still thin and relatively attractive. She wore her blonde hair in pigtails, little red bows on the ends to entice the perverts.

Another car slowed. Rolex opened her coat, revealing her skinny, bone-hard nudity. If she didn't get inside a car soon, she'd freeze to death. She pulled her coat behind her hips, flaunted her long pale legs and hoped the guy would stop. He did. The beat-up car stopped, and Rolex approached, waited while the power window burred and wound down. She leaned in with a smile.

"Hi there, honey. You looking to play?"

"I want the full works," the guy said. "Money's not a problem."

He wore a thick coat with a hood over his head. His face was shrouded.

"Okay, Honey," Rolex said. "But before I get into anyone's car, I like to see their face."

After a slight hesitation, he slowly pulled down his hood, and Rolex let out a gasp. His face was horribly disfigured. Scars covered his brows, his cheeks, his jaw. His head was shaved, and his right eye was partially shut. His nose was bent. Most of his right ear was missing as if gnawed off by a dog.

"I'm sorry," Rolex said. "It's just…"

He smiled, oddly charming despite his deformity. Rolex thought he had a nice mouth. "Don't worry," he said. "I get that a lot. I'll understand if you would rather wait for someone else."

Rolex felt a little sorry for him. "It's fine," she said. She opened the door and climbed in, then introduced herself. "They call me Rolex."

He gave her another smile, feasting on her with his piercing blue eyes. Rolex thought he might have been handsome once. "We're going to have some fun, Rolex," he told her. "You can call me Robert."

Printed in Great Britain
by Amazon